MERCENARY MEASURES

a Brandon Collier novel

BRANDON COLLIER

Edited by: Christine LePorte
Cover art by: Jeremy Paclebar

For more info or inquires, contact bcollierbooks@gmail.com
Or visit www.rainlightpress.com

Other titles by this author include:

Body Traffic
The Silencer: To Kiss and Not Tell
The New Danger
Dirty Blue Aces
The Night Sparkles
Underneath the Palms of Rio
A Panther in Paradise
The Footsteps of Domingo Rhodes

PART 1

BRANDON COLLIER

Long live this novel.

1.

Ten after two in the early morning was when the row of motorcycles made their way down the deserted street in downtown Salvador, Brazil. The lead driver wore a skeleton mask. The other drivers wore purple bandanas over their noses and mouths, and there were two people to each motorcycle. Silver and white buildings lined up each side of the street. The contrast between the dark of the early morning and the bright lights of downtown made the night picturesque. They sped through the streets until they reached their destination, the office building of Bahia Intertek, a financial conglomerate with headquarters in the city. The driver on the first motorcycle gave hand signals to the rest of the drivers as they parked. Soon after, they approached the building with a fragile middle-aged female taken off one of the bikes; she was not dressed like the rest of them. She trembled as she was pushed to the door.

"Do as you were told," the lead driver calmly said to her in Portuguese.

She pulled the card that was attached around her neck and pressed it against the card reader at the side of the door. The door opened, and she was shoved inside. The lead driver made his way in first and pointed to the cameras. Two members of his crew quickly went to the security room to disable them.

The lead driver grabbed the woman and took her to the elevator. He pressed the button, waited patiently for the doors to open while whistling a song, then got inside with her. They made their way to the top floor. The driver, knowing exactly where he was going, made his way to the chief executive officer's office with the woman in front of him.

"Open the door," he said, and she obliged.

The driver began to violently laugh. The woman kept looking at the door for a chance to run. She was about to make her move when he grabbed her and led her past the bar inside the office and to the balcony. He forced her to look below.

"Please," she pleaded. "I'm a mother. I have a family."

The driver took off his mask and revealed his

identity. She recognized him from the news. He was Malestar, the infamous criminal mastermind with long, curly hair, his left eye slightly unopened, and a strange tattoo on his neck. He turned her around and again forced her to look at the street below. The distance to the ground made her panic, and she tried to fight him off.

"Your purpose is complete," Malestar said, and pushed her off the balcony. She landed against the sidewalk below, her body disfigured, and blood pouring from underneath it.

Malestar made his way back to the office. It was spacious, yet bland. In addition to the bar, there was a set of golf clubs in the corner, a leather chair, an expensive desk made from Brazilian wood, photos of the CEO with politicians and celebrities, and a television in the corner. Malestar took a seat at the comfortable chair in front of the desk and laughed some more.

"I'm rich," he said in a pompous voice. "I can do what I want. Let me make some more money while the people suffer."

Malestar stood up and sighed. He opened his jacket, displaying the bomb around his waist. He carefully removed the explosive and placed it on top of the desk. At this time, the rest of his crew was strategically placing more bombs around the building. Malestar left the office and walked down the hallway and to the stairway, where he made his way to the rooftop door. There, two members of his crew with the camera feeds were waiting for him.

A helicopter approached the roof. Malestar waved it down. Below, police cars were making their way to the dead body on the street. He already had a crew near the front entrance with guns in their hands. Malestar climbed inside the helicopter with the remaining crew members as the shootout between the police and his crew was taking place below.

The police had suffered a few casualties, but Malestar's crew was being decimated and they scattered back into the building for cover. The police moved in and shot the remaining members of the crew. They entered the building and began to search the floors. As the helicopter moved away from the building, Malestar looked below with the detonator in his hand.

"The simple joys of life are so underrated," he said, and pressed down on the button.

The building erupted in a ball of fire as an explosion burst through all of the floors and shattered all the windows. The police cars flew in the air. The sound of car sirens was heard along the street, then the sound of more police cars arriving, along with ambulances. The helicopter continued to move away from the scene, the artist of destruction leaving behind his artwork.

*

Mauricio Campos was resting on his boat in his white T-shirt and blue shorts, his eyes closed as the vessel moved through the pristine, azure ocean water outside the bay of Salvador. His girlfriend, Claudia Florez, sat on the edge of the boat in her two-piece yellow bikini, absorbing the sunny weather. Mauricio rested in the shade as his darker complexion didn't need a tan, but Claudia wanted her light brown skin to be a little more bronze. She looked toward the sky with her sunglasses on. This was paradise, and something she had urged Mauricio to do for the longest time. He was a workaholic, and it was nice to have to some rest and relaxation time.

Both Mauricio and Claudia were mercenaries, hired to take out anyone if the price was right. They didn't care if their clients were for or against the law. They didn't consider themselves bounty hunters because they didn't bring people in, and they didn't consider themselves hitmen because criminals weren't their only employers. They were paid to do a job, regardless of their personal conviction or morals, and they did the job well.

Mauricio was by birth an Englishman, born to a Kenyan immigrant father and a Brazilian mother. Before he ended up in Brazil, the family had left London to go back to his father's native country. Since then, Mauricio couldn't fathom the thought of ever going back to

England. He always found himself back in his mother's native country, and that was where he met Claudia. He thought every day how was fortunate he was to have her, as her natural beauty matched her intelligence.

"Mauricio," Claudia said.

"What?" Mauricio responded with his eyes still closed.

"You put any more thought into having children?" she asked in English. Claudia was bilingual, speaking English and Portuguese, but spoke in Mauricio's preferred language around him.

"A good question that deserves an answer, and all answers have questions. But is that necessarily true, if one really thinks about..."

Mauricio's cell phone began to play its electric funk ringtone. "Don't answer that," she said sternly.

"It might be important," Mauricio said, reaching over and grabbing his phone.

"What could be more important than this?" Claudia said, readjusting her body for the sun.

"Hello?" Mauricio said into the phone, and listened for a bit. "Give us a few hours," he said, and ended the call.

"Let me guess, we got a job," Claudia stated.

"The mayor's office."

"We're good guys again. My favorite type of assignment."

"Does it really matter?" Mauricio asked.

"Yeah, I'm willing to take a pay cut," Claudia replied, causing Mauricio to smile.

He was late. Mauricio and Claudia waited patiently in his office in the two chairs in front of his desk. They had changed to business attire, and the office was cool enough to escape the humid day. The sound of the clicking clock was really starting to annoy Mauricio, and he wanted nothing more than to get up and smash it into hundreds of pieces. Moments later, Mayor Vesco Amado walked in, wearing an expensive Italian suit, his salt and pepper hair and black beard perfectly groomed. He had the confidence of a car salesman, which Mauricio thought was needed at his job. Vesco closed the door and took a seat across from them.

"First of all, I would like to say I've heard great things about your performance from a peer of mine that required your service. I understand it is not easy to do what you do. I have an entire police force out there that can't move like you, as they are handcuffed by law and rules. Second of all, I want to say that this job is of the upmost importance, and you won't be the only professional I hire. You will be working with a band of mercenaries, skilled in the very same art of finding people and taking them out. Third of all, I don't have to tell you all of this is strictly unofficial, and confidential. Are we good so far?"

"We're good," Mauricio said, impressed by the mayor's use of English.

"The person we're after is a man that is known by the name of Malestar. He's well-funded from his criminal achievements, has a lot of law enforcement in his pocket, he's intelligent, and he's psychotic. If you find him, I don't want him alive. I just want to know that the job is done. Now, I know your rates, and I'm willing to double them."

"These other mercenaries, are we working with them as a unit or working separately?" Claudia asked.

"What do you suggest?" the mayor asked.

Claudia turned to look at Mauricio, who shook his head no. "I think you've got your answer," Claudia replied.

"At the very least, you two can work out information that is essential to capturing him."

"Let me explain to you something about the mercenary business," Mauricio said. "It's cutthroat. I'm not helping someone else get paid."

"Do as you wish," Vesco said. "I don't care which of you get to him first. Like I said, I just want..."

"The job done," Mauricio stated.

"My assistant will take the details from you that we require, such as your bank information, and what resources you may need. However, there will be no shared information from the police. You will have to work only from the information my assistant will give," Vesco said, getting up from his desk. Mauricio and Claudia stood as well.

Mauricio looked at the framed picture behind Vesco showing him with his wife and daughter. "You have a beautiful family."

"Yes," Vesco said with a smile. "Gives you something to live for."

"It also makes you an easy target," Mauricio replied, and walked out of the office with Claudia.

2.

His favorite room in the mansion he lived in outside the city was the Dance Room. Forty-five minutes east of the city, Malestar killed the owners discreetly and used the home as his headquarters, partly financed by a group he worked with called the Corporation. He made his way to the Dance Room, where five nude women rested on the floor, alive but under the influence of barbiturates. They barely had the energy to look in his direction. Red curtains lined the room and a golden tiger statue was in the corner. In the other corner was a record player that was at least fifty years old with a classical record on queue. Malestar went to the record player to turn it on.

"We need music," he said, and picked up one of the ladies on the ground, a busty young woman who didn't have the ability to move herself.

"Shall we dance?" Malestar asked, and began to swing her around as if they were engaging in a ballroom dance as the music played. "Do you know why I prefer lifeless dolls such as yourself? Because beauty is lost the moment someone speaks. People and their dreams, their wants, their thirst to be someone and do something honorable, is utterly disgusting. They are always all talk and no action. They want the money and good life, but are too afraid to go out and get it. That's why dolls like you are the best. My sister wouldn't let me play with you as a child. So, do you want to know what I did to her?"

Malestar moved the woman's head so she nodded yes. "I carved her like a pig, and I enjoyed every moment of it."

The doorbell to his house rang. He had wired the doorbell system so that it made a buzzing sound throughout the house. Malestar dropped the woman and headed toward the hallway. Before he reached the door, he picked up the mask on the kitchen counter that he wore that made him look like an elderly man. He carefully placed the mask on and proceeded to open the front door.

There was a police officer at the door, a burly middle-aged bald man who wore his shirt just tight enough to show off his muscles. "Mr. Velasco?"

"Yes?" Malestar responded, arching his back forward

and squinting his eyes.

"Your family has been worried about you. Is there a reason why you're not picking up the phone?"

"Oh, I have been out of town for a few days to go fishing. I promise I will return all their calls. I still got to feed my cats too. Do you want to come in for a drink?"

"No, no, no. This is just a routine checkup. Next time you tell someone when you are leaving. You never know when things might...just make sure you tell someone."

"Okay, I will. Thank you, Officer."

The police officer looked at Malestar for a moment, and then walked away. Malestar closed the door and made his way to the living room. There, he went to the large map that covered the wall facing the living room. The map was a detailed one of the city of Salvador, with locations that had been targeted noted with a check mark, and those that hadn't been marked with a red X. He kept the rest of the living room the same, along with most of the house. The furniture was moved to his liking, but he thought of this place as a temporary home. He would stay here until he put the city in shambles. It was what they deserved.

After he had killed his sister, he had gone to court, where the judge had decided to put him in a psych ward until he was of age. He felt like he was perfectly sane, especially compared with other children that drooled on themselves or talked out loud to no one. He resented the city for placing him there. He stayed most of his time in his room, where he began to talk to himself as well. He had big plans for the outside world, the world that thought he was the crazy one. In his mind, they were the ones that were crazy. He was going to make them all suffer as much as he did.

He knew that humans were weak because they refused to embrace their atavistic nature. In the animal kingdom, if an animal was in heat or wanted food, they would just go and get it. They didn't ask for permission, or think about guilt or moral consequences. Why was he wrong because he followed his natural instincts? Since they were too frightened by their petty emotions to do what they really wanted, he was going to make the entire world his prey, taking what he wanted with no apologies.

Malestar stood in front of the map. He studied it for a moment, scouting his next place to strike. He could picture the destruction in his head, the faces of screaming adults and children, and the agony they would feel. A rush of excitement coursed throughout his body, and the feeling invigorated him.

"I will devour you all until my stomach is full, and my delight has gone!" he shouted. "Until then, you will pay for your reservations and judgments, and the cost will be your lives!"

*

Salvador was a city of beauty, located on the peninsula jutting into the Atlantic Ocean in the northeast corner of Brazil. The third largest city in Brazil, it sprawled out eastward for dozens of kilometers. The people here were known to be easygoing and having a relaxed attitude about life. They called themselves *soteropolitanos*, and were looked down upon by those in some other areas of Brazil. However, this wasn't the major issue affecting the city. Social inequity was evident here, with the upper class living in gated communities, and the lower class in slum neighborhoods located in elevated areas. Still, the most beautiful sights were free, and everyone took in their beauty.

Mauricio and Claudia were at such a sight, the Igreja Sao Francisco, perhaps the most beautiful church in the city. Inside, the church was adorned with gold, silver, and other precious stones with ceiling art comparable to the Sistine Chapel. The outside area was painted in white and brown pastel colors. The church was located in Old Town, and Mauricio and Claudia sat at a café nearby, admiring its beauty. The road parallel to them was made of cobblestone. They both enjoyed lemonade with crushed ice on this humid day as a crowd of pedestrians walked by them. The church bells rang, signifying another hour as a flock of birds flew off into the distance.

"You ever think about going back home?" Claudia asked.

"And pass this up? All the beauty I need to see is right in front of me."

"That has to be one of the worst lines I ever heard."

"Yeah, pretend I never said that."

"But I'm serious, don't you ever want to go back to visit?"

"Nah, I'm good," Mauricio said, taking a sip of his beverage.

Claudia's gaze went past Mauricio, and he could see a look of concern on her face. "What is it?"

"There's a group of people across from us, staring at us."

"Let them stare," Mauricio said, taking another sip.

"They look like trouble."

Mauricio sighed and turned around. He saw three people with eyes on him—an Asian man, a tall, voluptuous redheaded woman with freckles, and a tanned man with a goatee who looked like he was a local. They were all dressed in suits. The Asian man in the middle made a gun out of his hand and fired in Mauricio's direction. Mauricio smiled and turned back around.

"Looks like we made some new friends," he said.

"They're coming this way," Claudia stated.

Mauricio patiently waited as the three individuals

made their way over and stood around the table. "Have a seat," Mauricio said, without looking at them.

They sat around the table and the Asian man spoke first. "I'm Ken."

"Sophie," the redheaded woman said.

"Rodrigo," the tanned man said.

"Do you know what we are?" Ken asked Mauricio.

"Of course," he replied. "I know a fellow mercenary when I see one."

"It looks like we're all competing to do the same job," Rodrigo said. "We thought it was best to lay down some ground rules."

"Like get out the line of fire," Sophie said. "If I got him, just accept the loss, and go elsewhere."

Mauricio laughed. "Your confidence will fail you."

"It seems like all of you know who we are," Claudia said. "Why don't you tell us about who you are?"

"Like some meet and greet?" Mauricio asked her. "I don't think civility will work with these people."

"I don't have a problem with it," Ken said. "I think it's good to know your competition. I'm from South Korea. I got into this business by way of my father. He was a businessman. The most-wanted criminals were always found by us. The government didn't care what condition they were in when we found them. After that, we tapped into the global market. He's retired since. I like to think I carry on his tradition."

"My turn," Sophie said. "Sophie, but you can call me Red. I know your first thought must have been that I'm some type of bimbo that can't take care of herself, but in fact, that's what drives me. I was raped at thirteen. They never caught the creep. Since then, I've dedicated my life to finding the world's most notorious criminals and making sure they don't get the benefit of seeing trial."

"One bad mama," Mauricio said.

"Name's Rodrigo," Rodrigo said. "The only thing you need to know about me is that I always get what I'm searching for."

"Oh yeah? How many hits have you done?" Mauricio asked.

"Why should that matter?" Rodrigo asked.

"Oh, it matters," Mauricio replied. "Look, everyone, I appreciate you coming over and introducing yourselves to us, but anything that deals with coordination or sharing information is not going to happen. Personally, I find it insulting that the mayor hired all of us to do the same job. Nevertheless, I'm not one to back away from competition. To the victor goes the spoils." Mauricio lifted his glass for a few seconds, and finished the rest of his drink.

"Can I talk to you in private for a moment?" Ken asked Mauricio.

Mauricio nodded to the street, and the two of them walked past the pedestrians and onto a section on the street that was isolated from traffic. Mauricio could tell that Ken was threatened by his presence in the hunt. He knew the look of fear all too well, and it had nothing to do with the search for a criminal.

"I know who you are, and I'm impressed by your list of hits," Ken said. "But this Malestar is of a different breed. He's someone me or you have never encountered. I think it is to our benefit to work together in some type of capacity. Me and you, we're the best to offer. Everyone else at the table doesn't stand a chance. I just want to know, when it comes down to it, and you need my help, or vice versa, that we have each other's back."

"What makes you think you're so good?" Mauricio asked.

"I found you, didn't I?"

"What's the cut?"

"Twenty percent, both ways. Helping fee," Ken said.

Mauricio grinned. "Know what I think? I think you know I'm the best chance there is of catching him and you want a piece of the pie or this trip to Brazil was a waste of time."

"Perhaps, but remember, you don't have to ask for my help. It's up to you."

Mauricio nodded. "I read you, Ken."

"Good hunting," Ken said, walking away.

Mauricio knew he had to do his homework. He

headed back to the downtown hotel they were staying at as the day was turning into night. While Claudia took a shower, Mauricio placed the map of Salvador on the bed, along with all the information inside a folder that Vesco gave him about Malestar. He marked the map with all of the locations that Malestar had struck with either a bombing or a robbery. Then he went through the papers and photos in the folder.

There were photos of Malestar in sketch drawings, and photos of him as a child. There were details of his past, and Mauricio read how he was locked up in a ward as a youth, and then read the reports of his education inside, which was off the charts in competence. Malestar had rarely had trouble inside the ward, but of all the residents, he was the most concerned with the outside world. After he left the ward, he was off the grid for almost a decade. Theories had it he worked odd jobs, saved money, and planned out his first robbery. Then the robberies came in quick succession. He never got caught, always planned out his exit routes, and stole millions. After that, he built a network of thieves. Once that was accomplished, the bombings began, a hypothesized statement against corporate greed.

Mauricio took a look at the map. The places Malestar robbed and bombed were all within the boundaries of the city. He was definitely making his mark here, and being caught seemed of no concern to him. Mauricio found it strange for a domestic terrorist to do all his attacks in one city, and kept that thought in the back of his mind. He took a closer look at the buildings. They were all financial institutions of some sort, or corporations known for keeping their headquarters in the city. Mauricio picked up the complimentary writing pad and pen on the bedside table, and made a note to remember to look up all the corporations in the city that hadn't been hit and were the most profitable.

Claudia came out of the shower with a white towel wrapped around her body. "Don't stress yourself out with that, baby," she said. "You let me do the background work. All you need to do is pull the trigger."

Mauricio sighed. "I don't think I've faced a criminal like this."

"Stop worrying yourself with that. Tonight, you belong to me."

"Is that right?"

Claudia removed her towel. "Are you going to object?"

No, he wasn't.

3.

Vesco woke up in bed to the sound of a loud thud. He turned to his right and saw his wife still sleeping. Apparently, he was the only that heard the sound. He picked up his gun that rested on his bedside table, his body running on adrenaline. The mayor was a paranoid man, but with a lunatic out there, he felt for once he was justified. He guessed it was somewhere between one and two in the morning. He got out of bed and headed to the hallway, quietly enough not to disturb his teenage daughter the next room over. He made his way downstairs and kept his gun pointed.

Immediately, he heard a clicking sound. It was coming from the kitchen. Vesco was nervous, but knew he had to eliminate any threat to his family. He headed toward the kitchen in a slow pace, not knowing what was inside. Every part of his body trembled with the expectation of danger.

He walked into the kitchen and found a metal box that had a digital screen in front with the words BOOM repeating in quick succession. On top of the box was a stack of cigars tied up to resemble dynamite. Vesco quickly looked around to see if there were any intruders in the room, and then lowered his weapon. He went to the box and knocked over the cigars.

There was a note next to the box. Vesco looked around once more and then picked up the note to read it. The first thought that came to his head was that he would keep it for evidence and have the lab examine it for fingerprints, but on second thought, he knew the author was much too clever to leave any such evidence behind. The words had been typed in English.

The sudden sounds of danger
Always alarms the stranger
Then he will know night and day
That he will always be the prey
I will be coming for you, my dear beloved mayor

Vesco froze in fear, and instantly knew who the letter was from. Why was it written in English and not in Portuguese? Did Malestar know Vesco had secretly hired mercenaries after him and wanted them to read it as well? Was it just a personal riddle for Vesco since he knew English well? Malestar was toying with him now, and someone being in his home was too close for comfort.

Vesco hurried back up the stairs to check on his daughter. She was soundly sleeping with the covers half drawn. Vesco went closer to make sure she was breathing, and she appeared to be fine. Vesco sighed heavily and went back to his bedroom.

There he sat on the bed and watched his wife sleep. She looked peaceful, and was murmuring something in her sleep. Vesco leaned over to listen to her words. Most of what she was saying sounded incoherent.

"You weren't here...already made plans, she was flying....I don't think so."

Vesco smiled, and then felt a rush of guilt. He was never around much because of his work, and perhaps she was talking about his often prolonged absence. He had promised his wife he would step down from his position in a few years and spend more time with his family. But not right now. The city needed him, especially with Malestar on the loose. He didn't care about the accolades he or the police department would receive for finding the criminal, as evidenced by his hiring of mercenaries. He just wanted the general public to be safe. He knew there would always be crime with a large population of the city in poverty, and there was no amount of legislation or awareness programs to change that fact.

His wife began to murmur some more. Vesco leaned over and kissed on her cheek. She smelled sweet, and a smile came across her face. Nineteen years of marriage between the two of them and she still was in love with him like the first time she fell in love. She was just as beautiful to Vesco. She had stayed by his side when he was an underpaid officer, and years later, when he spent most of his time behind his office desk. She had sacrificed many of her own dreams to raise a daughter and to be the steady rock by his side. He didn't know how he would live if he ever lost her. He just wanted to know that his wife and daughter would be okay if something should happen to him. That was part of the reason he worked so hard. However, if Malestar was going after his family, then that was something else altogether. He had to protect them by any means, and his own life was secondary.

Vesco thought about the note and wondered if he should tell anyone about it. He could show it to the mercenaries, but should he show it to all of them, or one or two? Were they working in coordination? He figured it was best not to give one the advantage. Besides, the note didn't provide any clues. It was just a reminder to Vesco that he could be touched at any time. Vesco had a security system in his house and that didn't matter. His family and him could be targeted and killed at any given moment.

The problem Vesco struggled with the most was what type of criminal was Malestar? Was he a psychotic killer out for some type of revenge, and did people just get killed in the process of his robberies and bombings? Was he after the institutions or the people? Vesco had guessed he was after both, and he knew at some point Malestar would personally come after him.

*

Claudia was still asleep, but Mauricio woke up early for the continental breakfast. He took a shower, got dressed, and headed downstairs for the dining room next to the lobby. The hotel itself was nothing fancy, nice enough to not be disappointed, and bad enough to not draw attention. Mauricio had to admit that the green carpeting was hideous, but that didn't interfere with his getting a good night's rest.

He walked in and made a quick glance of the room. It was a habit in his profession to always gauge his surroundings. In the corner, he saw Sophie, or Red as it were, sitting by herself, eating a piece of toast.

"You got to be kidding me," Mauricio said.

He went over to her table, and she looked up to give a warm smile. "Great minds think alike," she said.

"You following me?" Mauricio asked as he took a

seat.

"I want to be just as discreet as you are, if not more. With you, he can see you coming. However, with me he wouldn't even suspect my presence."

"Humbleness is not a strong trait in our profession."

"Obviously," Red replied.

"So, Red, how many people have you found?"

"I don't put a number to such things, just know I do my job very well. I learned a lot when I was back in Kansas City and donated most of my youth to this program I ran, which helped the local police find wanted criminals and alerted the neighborhood of repeat offenders. After that, I thought about joining the police force, and making a difference that way. But then I saw all of the corruption that was taking place and thought that wasn't for me. And let's face it, if I pulled you over for something, would you take me seriously?"

"Of course," Mauricio replied. "You would have a badge."

"A badge doesn't cover these," Red said, pointing at her cleavage. "A blessing and a curse. I want to be taken seriously and respected for my skill. So I began freelance work, and alerted the police where they could find the criminals."

"I'm sure you were appreciated."

"Not at all, because they would find them dead, not alive. Isn't it nice you can always fall back on self-defense? Anyway, people seem to think that rotting in a jail cell is the most powerful punishment. I disagree. I don't think some people should live to see another day. I'm assuming you agree too. Isn't that reason you're doing this?"

Mauricio looked away. "I rather not talk about that."

"All of us have scars, Mauricio. Which one has the worst one is all subjective."

Mauricio turned back to her. "I'm a throwback. I believe in an eye for an eye, tooth for a tooth. You can call it cowboy justice, I call it karma. You get what you deserve, and I'm just the enforcer of the rule. The legal system is a failure. Sure, it works sometimes, but I see innocent people go to jail and criminals run free like it's going out of style, often supported by the people that should be locking them up. I'm just doing my job."

"You and I both know there's more to it than that."

"What would you have me say? That I have some longing need for vengeance, and that I'm fulfilling it by chasing down the most notorious men and women?"

"That would be a start," Red said.

"This conversation is over," Mauricio said, and went to get some orange juice out of the dispensing machine. He grabbed a plastic cup and began to fill up.

Red went over and stood next to him. "I hope this doesn't hurt our ability to work together."

Mauricio grinned. "What is with you chums? Why do you insist on working with me?"

"Just think about it this way, Mauricio. You didn't know any of us before yesterday, yet we all know who you are. We want to learn from you, and some of us even want to be you. Let us learn from you."

"Sorry, red mama, I work alone with me and my lady."

"You say that now," Red said, and returned back to her table.

Mauricio finished off two pieces of toast, a muffin, and some orange juice at a table by himself before returning to his hotel room. He thought about telling Claudia about Red, but knew that would be no benefit to him. As he walked back to his room, Mauricio walked by a family that had a little girl between the two parents, holding both of their hands. They carried her as she swung happily between them. This made Mauricio think about Claudia's wishes for a family, and how he was holding her back.

Why was he hesitant to tell her yes? He tried to tell himself he didn't know the reason, but his intelligence knew better. He feared what type of father he would be. His father was regarded as a saint in the community, but at home he was a different person, a real person that became angry and saddened. Sometimes his anger would lead to outrage. Mauricio wanted to be different, and he told himself he would be when he had children of his own, but right now he was too afraid to have them. His past had scarred him, and he didn't want to look at his old wounds.

He didn't know how long he was going to be able to pretend or hide his innermost feelings and thoughts. At some point, he was going to have to address them, and he was not looking forward to that day. He had come to Brazil to get away from his past, to reconnect with his mother's side of the family, and pretend his other side never happened. But there was no denying his roots because they were a part of him. Also, he would have to tell Claudia what he was feeling and either reject what she wanted or decide that having children was something he wanted as well. Now was not the time.

When he arrived back at the room, he saw Claudia dressed and looking over the information in the folder regarding Malestar. Their bags were still on the bed as Claudia thought it was a good idea to always be ready to leave. She always used to say that you never knew when danger would strike.

"Early start, eh?" Mauricio asked.

"All of this seems minimal. I'm sure the police department has more information than this. Why are they withholding?"

"I have no idea."

"I'm going to request more files," Claudia said. "What I want you to do is go here." Claudia handed him a piece of paper.

"What's this?"

"It's the place where he was kept before he came of age."

"Sounds like a waste of time," Mauricio said.

"Well, what separates us from the police is our ability to track down our prey with the smell of who they are. Find out who he is, and it will give you a better sense of who we are trying to find."

She was right. In order to catch a criminal, you had to think like one. A lot of detectives had problems tapping into the dark areas of their psyche, the area where morals were thrown out and selfish behavior was dominant. This was a familiar place to Mauricio, and he actually enjoyed diving in this way. There was something nostalgic and comforting being in that mindset.

"Claudia." Claudia continued to look at the paper in front of her. "Claudia," Mauricio repeated.

"What?" she asked, turning her attention to him.

"Be careful."

"Of course. Now go out there and get our man."

"Okay, boss," Mauricio said, and headed out the door.

4.

The Community Psychosocial Center had long hallways and nurses pushing carts amongst the sounds of screaming and laughter. This was a place that would drive someone crazy if they weren't crazy already. The square lights above the hallway seemed to continue into infinity. Mauricio had called ahead of time to make an appointment with the doctor that had monitored Malestar for quite some time here. He agreed to meet Mauricio at his office. Mauricio got the directions from the first desk clerk, but found himself in a hurry to get there.

A man that talked to himself walked by him in the hallway, wearing a white gown that was split in the back, followed by a woman that drooled on herself and looked off into the distance as if she was in another location.

Mauricio felt sorry for these people, and wondered if any of them ever were normal. He knew in a place like this that the pills came at a constant pace, and that if people constantly told you there was something wrong with you, eventually you would believe it. He knew if he followed through with the thoughts he had as a child that he would be locked in here too. There was a thin line between sane and insane, and those that were on the borderline could easily play the part of someone on the opposite side of where they were actually on.

Dr. Humberto Cuevas was a bald man with glasses who wore a navy blue lab coat that went almost to his knees. His office was standard, with his accomplishments on the wall and a computer at his desk. Dr. Cuevas presented Mauricio with a seat and then sat down behind the desk. He crossed his hands in front of him and waited for Mauricio to speak first.

Mauricio found it odd that the doctor didn't close the door. The discussion of former patients was obviously not frowned upon. He also figured someone or some people from the police station had already come here with their questions. Mauricio figured the doctor didn't mind visitors from other professions as it deemed himself an important person.

"What is the most important thing I should know about Malestar that the public does not know?"

Dr. Cuevas leaned forward. "That is a loaded

question," he said in English, and his accent was strong. "What is it that you do again, my friend?"

"I'm a consultant to the police. They fear that if the police find him they will fire first and ask questions later. They want me to save him from a wrath of bullets and bring him back to a place like this so that maybe he can be fixed."

Dr. Cuevas leaned back. Mauricio didn't know if the doctor believed his lie, but he seemed satisfied with his answer. "Malestar is a complicated individual just like anyone else that is free to walk about society. Is he mad? In the sense that he doesn't conform to laws and what people conceive as good morals. He is not acting out of evil, but he is inflicting pain because he believes that is what society deserves. He is not trying to punish you, he's trying to awaken you."

"He has a strange way of doing it," Mauricio said.

"As a child, he suffered from borderline personality disorder, characterized by impulsive behavior, unstable interpersonal relationships, feelings of abandonment, an unstable sense of self. It was then he began to dissociate from others and devalued anyone that wasn't like him. The behavior is often classified as a black-or-white thinking style. You were either with him or you weren't with him. Suicide sometimes occurs in this state, but Malestar showed no signs of such action. However, it was my personal opinion that his diagnosis at an early age would carry over unto his adult life. But there's a board that overlooks these things and has the final say."

Well, there it is, Mauricio thought. The doctor wanted credit for being in the right, and wanted to tell anyone willing to listen that he knew what he was talking about. Most of these doctors that examined others all day should be treated for their narcissist personalities.

"What is the lesson he's trying to teach us?" Mauricio asked.

"That we should give in to our inner ambitions. We all have human instincts such as the need to eat, kill, and reproduce. What separates us is our minds and realizing that many of these actions are not beneficial to society as a whole. Plus, it makes protecting your family more difficult. We have values, morals, and empathy for each other. In my opinion, he wants the city's attention by draining the monetary flow. I see the news. The police are hesitant in requesting assistance from the federal government. They don't want to give in to his need for an audience. Until he gets what he wants, the violence will not stop."

Mauricio nodded. "He's always going to be one step ahead of us, isn't he?"

"Only until he wants to get caught."

Mauricio stood up. "I thank you for your time."

"I applaud you."

"What for?"

"Most people want to kill a monster. You want to bring it back to its cage and examine it. There's no fix, but just some understanding of what it is."

It was strange to hear the doctor tell him that there was nothing he could do, but maybe there was a realization that there was no helping Malestar. Mauricio walked out of the office not feeling any more confident than he did coming in. However, understanding Malestar just a bit more may prove valuable in the long run.

*

Claudia stormed into Vesco's office and closed the door behind her. The mayor knew she was coming and sat back at his desk with a reserved manner. He dealt with irate people all the time as a politician, and not giving enough information to the public was an anger he was familiar with. This should be child's play. Vesco listened to her rant while thinking about what he was going to counter with.

"This is unacceptable," she said. "You hire us secretly to do something without giving us all the information needed to do so. What is this? Tell us what the police know."

"If you knew what they know, do you really think you would be further on with the investigation than they are?"

"Yes," Claudia replied.

"And why is that?"

"Because you shouldn't trust law enforcement. The very people that are supposed to protect and serve could be under the payroll of the man that they are trying to find."

Vesco hadn't considered that. Did he trust his local police force? That was debatable. Maybe it was time to give the information that he kept hidden. He looked over at the wall at the pictures of his family, and then turned back around. He reached into his pocket, took out his key ring, and used one of the smaller keys to open up a drawer at his desk. He took out the folder that was inside and stood up to hand it to her.

"He wrote a manifesto. Don't let it warp your mind. I still want him killed. You can read it here if you wish."

Vesco left the office and closed the door. Claudia opened the folder to see a stack of paper that was printed in Portuguese. Claudia estimated that there was over a hundred pages. She looked at the first page and began reading.

I am not who you think I am.

The public may know me as Malestar, a horrible man that robs and kills for the sake of doing so.

But this is not true. I am a simple man, and I only want to open the eyes of the public. There is no type of law enforcement that will stop me from doing so.

What do I want you to see? I want you to see that you're not as free as you think you are. The powers that be still control you. They tell you how you feel, how you should behave, what to eat, what to see, what you can do, and how to live. How is this freedom? As humans and animals on this Earth, we should be able to do what we please without someone telling us otherwise. Who are they to tell us how to behave? It is time for a new revolution, one that is led by someone that does not let another man tell him what is normal and what is not. I am free, and I will do what I need so that you will see how you can be free as well.

Some people may need to suffer and perish along the way. This is necessary for any real change. It will take time to get past the sacrifice, but once that is done, you will see that I am right. I am going to do what I want to do, and you should do the same.

Now, regarding the way I killed my sibling...

Claudia put the stack of paper on the ground and took out her cell phone. She dialed for Mauricio, and moments later he answered the phone. She was glad to hear his voice as a panic was building up inside of her.

"Where are you?" she asked.

"At the bank," Mauricio said, standing in line. "Just following through on a payment we're supposed to receive."

"Malestar wants to teach us to view the world like him."

"I know," Mauricio replied. "I've got to make sure no one gets that lesson."

*

Ken had read about places like these before coming here, but the slums looked much worse than the words he read. He had read about Lower City, and the slums with a high concentration of Afro-Brazilians in the neighborhood of Liberdade. However, he wasn't afraid as he sat in a parked car across from an abandoned building covered in graffiti with Rodrigo sitting next to him. They had invited Red to come along as well, but she said she had other things to do. Ken's guess was that she was going to find an edge to get on the other mercenaries in their search for Malestar. Ken had thought about doing the same, but he figured Rodrigo's contact would prove far more valuable.

The streets were full of bags, needles, trash, and homeless people walking about, with colorful buildings on either side of the street that had stripped paint and graffiti. Ken could smell the scent of fish, and thought there was a fish market somewhere close by. The window was rolled down all the way inside the rental car and Ken could still feel his skin warming from the scorching sun. He was never going to get used to this heat. He glanced over at Rodrigo, who seemed perfectly fine while waiting.

"Are you sure he's a good lead?" Ken asked.

"Yes, I'm sure. Just relax. It will work out."

Ken frowned. "You scare me."

"Why is that?"

"You seem too calm for a job like this."

"It's about balance. I know when to turn it off and on," Rodrigo said.

"I prefer to always have it on. You never know when danger might strike."

Rodrigo shook his head and laughed to himself. "What?" Ken asked.

"You have forgotten where you are. This place is laid back, and prides itself on that fact. You need to learn how to relax. Not doing so is not good for your body."

"So now you are a doctor?"

"Whatever. If you fall over, it would just be less competition," Rodrigo said.

"If I fall over dead, I will come back and haunt you for the rest of your life."

"Of course, you would miss me so much." Rodrigo

looked past Ken and saw the teenage boy with the purple bandana around his neck walking past the abandoned building. The boy stopped to get a bag of something from a man standing there, and looked around him. He saw the rental across from the street with Ken and Rodrigo inside. He froze for a moment, and then he made a run for it.

Rodrigo got out of the car as Ken started the engine to drive down the street. Rodrigo gave chase to the kid as he turned down the alley. He ran as fast as he could, looking back to see how far Rodrigo was behind. At the end of the alley was another street. Rodrigo and his longer legs were gaining ground. The kid ran through the busy street while cars braked to avoid hitting him. Rodrigo followed behind. Ken made a quick U-turn on the street he was on and made a quick right turn.

The kid threw the trashcans to the side of him, placing them in the path of Rodrigo. He continued to run down the sidewalk and glanced back behind him. Rodrigo was now only a few feet behind him. He reached out and grabbed the kid by the collar, and jerked him toward him. That move led to an elbow in the stomach. Rodrigo's grip loosened, and the kid turned down another alley.

The kid sprinted down the alley only to see Ken pull the car next to the alley to block the entrance. Ken got out of the car as the teenager stopped and turned around to go in the opposite direction. Rodrigo blocked his path to go that way. Ken and Rodrigo casually walked their way toward him.

"What do you want from me?" the kid asked in Portuguese.

"You know who I am," Rodrigo replied as they stood next to him. "I used to pay you all the time for those on the wanted list."

"That was years ago. I'm done being a snitch."

"What's he saying?" Ken asked in English.

"That he needs a little motivation," Rodrigo replied in English, and then went back to Portuguese. "If you don't tell us what we want, I will go after your family. You do know what I do to my targets once I find them?"

"Yeah," the kid replied.

"I promise you that same fate will be with your family if you don't start talking."

The kid shook his head, thought about it for a moment, and sighed. "What do you want to know?"

"What do you know about the terrorist called Malestar?"

The kid laughed. "You have no chance against him. He will teach you all the right way to live."

"By killing innocent women and children? Because that's what he's doing. He doesn't care about you."

"But you're wrong," the kid said. "He's going to help us all. You will see. It's people like you that will suffer."

"What's he talking about?" Ken asked.

"You're delusional," Rodrigo said to the kid. "We will find him, and kill him."

"It's too late," the kid replied. "The pain has just begun."

5.

Mauricio waited patiently in line at the bank, but was getting annoyed at how slowly the line was moving. Three people ahead of him was a man who kept complaining that the amount he had inside his account was wrong. He knew things moved a bit slower in this part of Brazil, but this was ridiculous.

Malestar and his crew landed on the roof of the bank after parachuting from the plane. From the rooftop, they were in close range to the ledges of other rooftops in the area. The crew removed their parachutes, took out their weapons from their bags, and began placing on their purple bandanas. Malestar made his way to the rooftop door as his crew followed behind. He turned and nodded to them, and they entered the building.

The security guard inside the bank received the text message on his cell phone to lock the doors. He casually made his way to the front doors and locked them when no one was looking. He walked back to his standing post as Mauricio turned his head to see him. The guard forced a smile, and Mauricio turned back around.

Malestar and his crew approached the back door leading into the bank. He knew ahead of time that the door would be locked. One of the crew members strolled to the front of the group with the bombing equipment in his hand. He placed the bomb carefully against the door, and the rest of the crew stepped back. He did as well, and they waited a few seconds until an explosion forced the door open.

The customers in the bank heard the explosion, and began to look around to see what was going on. As they did so, Malestar and his crew hurried down the hallway of the bank and into the main room, where they began to wave their guns and make demands. Malestar, standing amongst them, nodded to the security guard. The security guard walked over to the manager and took out his gun.

"Everybody to the ground!" one of the crew members shouted, and Mauricio knew enough Portuguese to know to hit the ground. The customers were nervous, but did as they were told. Mauricio had a gun against his back hip but didn't reach for it. He looked up as the security guard hit the manager on top of the head with his gun and forced him to the back. He turned his head the other way to see the group of bandits in purple bandanas surround the group of customers and point guns at them while they were on the ground.

"Ladies and gentlemen," Malestar stated out loud. "I am your friendly bank robber, and I promise you this will just be a short inconvenience. Please don't let this experience make you change banks, as the savings rate in this place is actually not that bad. If you do what we say, no one will get hurt. If you want to play hero..."

Malestar walked past Mauricio. "Then you will surely face death."

One of the tellers, a middle-aged man who tried to hide his nervousness, cautiously moved down the counter to get closer to the button underneath near the edge. Malestar took notice. He raised his weapon quickly and shot him in the forehead. Some of the customers screamed in fear. Mauricio moved his hand closer to his gun.

"Some people have a hard time listening, or they want to be a martyr. I can appreciate that. However, you have to be smart enough to execute what you want," Malestar said, and checked his watch.

Mauricio scanned the room. He counted five men including the leader, all armed and patrolling the customers on the ground. That meant six with the security guard in the back. The odds of surviving a shootout were slim. Mauricio looked back at the leader. He figured he was looking at the infamous Malestar, as the purple bandanas were a signature of his crew, per the information in the folder.

"Do all of you want money as much as I do?" Malestar asked out loud. "You work so hard in your daily lives just to get so little, while it takes me less than thirty minutes to get enough for a lifetime. How is this fair? It's fair because I choose to do what I want, while you all are nothing more than pathetic sheep. The sheep will never have a fulfilling life."

There was the sound of two gunshots. The security guard came from the back of the bank with two full bags in his hands.

"Please, collect our reward from our friend," Malestar said to one of the crew members.

The reward was collected, and the security guard was shot in the temple by the crew member. "Farewell, sheep," Malestar said, and took out a smoke bomb from his hip. He dropped the bomb to the ground. A sudden burst of smoke filled the room, and Malestar and his crew made their way back to the way they came in.

Mauricio got up quickly, and faintly saw the sight of them leaving through the smoke. He took out his gun and followed them in the direction they left. Malestar and his crew ran for the hallway door and headed up the stairs.

Mauricio followed close behind. The trailing crew member saw Mauricio and fired once in his direction. The bullet missed, and Mauricio fired back. His bullet landed in the man's back, and he dropped to the ground. Mauricio stepped over him and continued up the stairs.

Malestar reached the rooftop door and swung it open. His crew members followed him out, and the last one closed the rooftop door. Malestar headed toward the ledge when a crew member shouted in his direction. "Jorge didn't come up!"

Malestar turned around. "You want to sit around and wait for him? Come on!"

"We just can't leave him behind!"

The rooftop door swung open again. Mauricio fired his weapon and the two men near the door were sprayed with bullets from his gun. Both were shot in the chest and fell upon the roof. There was only crew member left, the one carrying the bags of money, and he jumped the ledge to the next rooftop over with Malestar. Mauricio ran toward them and then jumped the ledge as well.

Malestar jumped upon another roof that was ten feet below, and then made his way down. A helicopter started toward him, and Malestar waved it down. Malestar's last crew member made his jump with Mauricio right behind him, and Mauricio landed on top of him as he hit the ground.

The helicopter began to touch down as Mauricio and the crew member engaged in a fight. Both men got to their feet, and the crew member swung first, a wild punch that missed Mauricio's face. Mauricio ducked down, using the opportunity to strike the man in the chest. The man grabbed hold of his neck and shoved him toward the ground. Mauricio wrapped his legs around his back and blocked the man's punches for his position on top.

"Finally, a citizen with some fight in him!" Malestar shouted as the helicopter landed. He grabbed the bags of money and hopped onboard.

Mauricio continued to block the man's punches and managed to get his legs around the man's neck. Mauricio squeezed his legs as hard as he could and the man's face began to turn red. Mauricio then connected with a right punch that drew blood. The man tried to punch his way out, but Mauricio continued to absorb the blows. The man quickly lost his circulation, and he became stiff and still.

Mauricio pushed him off and stood up. The helicopter had already taken off and was moving away from the rooftop. Malestar waved goodbye. Mauricio was not used to not getting his prey. An anger built up inside of him, and he went back to the man lying on the ground. An idea came to his mind. He grabbed the man by the collar and picked him up. It was time to move before the police arrived.

*

Red always enjoyed presents. This one was wrapped in purple and red. She removed the bandana from his face and saw that his face was covered in blood. Behind her were the rest of the mercenaries that Mauricio had called in, and Mauricio as well. They stood behind Red in the deserted football field in the slums with more dirt patches than grass.

"Consider this a housewarming gift," Mauricio said to Ken and Rodrigo.

Red hovered over the beat-up man. "Hello," she said, when his eyelids opened and he gazed upon her.

"*Puta estúpida!*"

Red punched him across the jaw, and the man spit the blood out his mouth.

"She can pack a punch," Mauricio said.

"I'm starting to like her," Rodrigo said.

"Why the sudden change to help us?" Ken asked Mauricio.

"I'm helping all of us," Mauricio replied. "Stop asking questions or it won't happen again."

"Rodrigo, can you come here?" Red asked.

Rodrigo walked over to her. "I need you to translate for me," she said. "Tell him if he doesn't start answering my questions, he's going to get the most pain he ever felt."

Rodrigo translated what she said to him. The man tried to spit upward. Red responded with another blow to the face.

"I feel sorry for the man that ends up with her," Ken said to Mauricio. "She's all woman, but she's scarred. Too dangerous for me. In fact, any relationship in this business is. I'm surprised you're able to keep one."

"Trust me, it's not easy," Mauricio replied.

"What's the secret?"

"Being with someone that will fight with you."

"I had a wife once," Ken said as more blows were delivered to the man on the ground. "Ten years younger, and she was a beast in bed."

"You don't have to continue," Mauricio said.

"She used to rock my world. We had this kittycat game we used to play, and I did my best to make her purr. Anyway, I proposed to her after two months of knowing her. Thought I could be the guy to come home, be a domesticated animal, and do my husbandly duties. But I couldn't. I was always traveling. It lasted a year. She got a lawyer and tried to rob me for everything I got."

"So now you are broke and constantly working hard, right?"

"No, I killed her," Ken said calmly.

"You're joking, right?" Mauricio didn't have time to get a response as Red called them over. As they arrived, they saw the man not moving and a pool of blood surrounding his head.

"He wouldn't say where Malestar is, but he did tell us where we could find the captain of his crew," Red said. "He said he's pretty high up in a group called the Corporation."

"So he finally opened up?" Mauricio asked.

"In a way. He basically gave up that information because it's a death trap. The captain will be at some slum party they are having tonight. I expect you will see nothing but purple bandanas, fast women, and lots of alcohol."

"Sounds like my type of party," Ken said.

"You think we should go?" Rodrigo asked.

"Whatever it takes to get us closer," Mauricio replied. "Everyone have weapons?"

Ken, Red, and Rodrigo took out guns from their hips. "All right," Mauricio said. "Let's have some fun."

*

When Vesco came back to his office building, his assistant told him he had an urgent message awaiting him in his email. Vesco quickly entered his office and closed the door. He sat at his desk, opened up his laptop, and turned it on.

Soon after, an image of Malestar appeared on-screen. Vesco's natural instinct was to turn off the computer, but Malestar waved his finger across the screen. "I can see you," Malestar said. "Look up."

Vesco did so, and noticed a miniature camera attached to the ceiling. He froze in his seat. Malestar smiled, sitting at his desk that was in a room inside the mansion. Around him was nothing but white walls.

"Now that I have your attention, I would like to request some information from you. If you don't cooperate, I will go after your family, and we both know how easily I can do that, don't we?"

"Carry on," Vesco said.

"Now, who did you send to find and kill me? And before you start to lie, may I remind you that I have an ear to the streets."

"I hired a few mercenaries," Vesco said.

"Mercenaries? Interesting. I admire your insolence. You figured a police department which I partly control would be no match for me. Who are these mercenaries?"

"Does it matter? Please, don't threaten my family. I will call them off."

"No!" Malestar shouted, and slammed his fist on the desk. "What fun is a game if you have no one to play with? I look forward to a challenge. Who is the best amongst them?"

"Mauricio Campos. He will find you, and put this

madness to an end."

"Madness?" Malestar repeated, pressing his face close to the screen. "You haven't seen the start of it."

Malestar ended the feed and gave a loud shot in anger. He roughly rubbed his face. Then he left the room to head to the Dance Room.

There, he lay with the nude women lying on the floor. They covered his body as he looked at the ceiling. He rested his hands against his stomach.

'Mauricio," Malestar said. "Your fate is now in my hands."

6.

Claudia watched Mauricio put bullets in his gun as he sat on the hotel bed. His demeanor was calm and collected, and there was an attraction to her that danger could be so cool. They both had dressed to go out, and he was looking sharp in his gray dress shirt and black slacks. That was as underdressed as he was going to get. She opted for something simple, a turquoise spaghetti-strap top with white shorts. She looked around the room and wished she had a larger space to rest at.

"When do you think we are going to get a place of our own?" Claudia asked.

"That was random," Mauricio replied.

"Inquiring minds want to know."

"Look, all this talk about a future…"

"You don't want one with me?" Claudia asked.

Mauricio stood up and held her hands. "Yes, I do,

but you have to let it flow."

There was knocking against the door. Claudia went to answer, opening the door to see Red standing there in a red top and jeans, and Ken and Rodrigo behind her, Ken in an East Asian red print loose shirt with white slacks, and Rodrigo in a yellow shirt and jeans. Mauricio joined Claudia at the door.

"You ready?" Red asked.

"Of course," Mauricio replied.

"Bullets, beer, and broads," Ken said. "I don't know if a party can get any better than that."

"Very professional," Claudia sarcastically stated.

"Let's get going," Mauricio replied.

As they pulled up to the slums in Alagados, the night grew dark, and Mauricio could sense that danger was in the air. At first, the streets were poorly lit, but closer to the party they could hear the sound of funk and samba fusion music. Poorly constructed stilt houses were made of boarded wood held in place with nails, with the ocean adjacent to the homes. Trash covered the ground, and the houses were barely above water with wooden walkways separating homes. The party was at the far end of the street. They could see people of all ages standing outside, half-clothed, smoking and drinking.

"We should park here," Mauricio said.

Rodrigo parked the car on the far end of the street, and everyone got out of the vehicle. "Stick to the plan," Mauricio said. "And we all might get out of here alive."

They approached the entrance of the building where a group of bodyguards were guarding the entrance, guns around their shoulders held by strap bands. The majority of them were shirtless. A few people standing outside gave the group looks as they walked closer to the entrance.

Rodrigo went to the front of his companions. He said a few words to the guards, and then gave one of them a handshake that left with money in the guard's hand. Rodrigo motioned for everyone else to follow inside, and they did so.

Inside, the building was dark with purple lights flashing and music blaring. It was crowded, and people were dancing near the center of the room. Wooden benches were in the corner where men were playing some type of card game. Mauricio looked around the room and found an open bench in the corner. He headed that way, and the other mercenaries did as well. They took a seat.

"You sure you know who he is?" Mauricio asked Red.

"Based on what he told me, yeah," Red replied.

"Find him then," he said. "Ken..."

"Yes, I know. I will be watching her," Ken said as he got up from the bench as Red made her way through the crowd.

"I'm going to find out as much as I can," Claudia said, and got up to leave. Mauricio stood up, but Claudia placed a hand on his back. "I'll be fine."

Red walked over to the curly-haired man that was standing in the corner talking to a couple of men. Their trademark purple bandanas were hanging from their hips. The curly-haired captain wore a shirt and had a gold medal against the right pocket of his black jacket. Red walked with seduction in her step, and the captain immediately became aware of her. The two men he was talking to took notice as well. Ken watched from a distance, his hand near the gun on his hip. She stood before them, confident, and with the charm that had lured so many men into a fate they didn't desire.

Red went up to the captain, touched his cheek, and then walked past the main room of the building and toward a hallway. The men watched her walked away. The captain shared a laugh with them, and then followed her to the hallway. Ken discreetly followed behind.

Meanwhile, Claudia made her way through the party, and felt comfortable moving amongst the crowd. She had been at parties like this before, growing up in Fortaleza before coming here as an adult. She had spent her youth going to parties like these with her friends, looking at boys, sometimes dancing, sometimes drinking. She lied to her mother about where she was, and she lost her virginity to a boy she had met in a place like this. And like her as a youth, the people here were enamored by the older people that attended, the people that had the money, and the respect of the streets.

Claudia made her way to a group of girls standing around a table full of beer bottles. She had at least ten years on them, but age wasn't a major factor in a social setting such as this one. Claudia picked up a beer and stood next to them.

"I like your skirt," she said to one of the girls. Claudia tried her best to talk in the local dialect, hoping they couldn't tell the difference.

"Thank you," the girl replied. "We were just talking about ways to make money. You're pretty. Who are you shacked with?"

"This is new territory to me," Claudia replied. "You have any suggestions?"

The girls giggled at one another. "We know just the man for you," one of the girls said.

Ken watched as the captain pressed up against Red and held on to her hips. Ken kept his cover behind the corner of the hallway. Red was playing the part well. He had never seen her in action, and the captain was oblivious to the danger in front of him.

"What's your name?" Red asked.

"Caetano," the captain said.

"You speak English?"

"Not enough," Caetano said, and began to press up on Red more as he tried to remove her top.

"Stop!" she shouted, and kneed him in the stomach. Ken rushed over. Red followed the knee with a right hook to the face. Ken grabbed Caetano and shoved him against the wall.

"You're coming with us," he said.

"That way," Red said, pointing at the back door, and then she made her way to the opposite side of the hallway to return to the party.

Red met up with Rodrigo and Mauricio. "Time to go," she said, and began to head for the front entrance. Mauricio and Rodrigo stood up, and Mauricio nodded to Claudia that it was time to leave. Before they all could do so, the two men that were talking to the captain earlier stood in front of the mercenaries.

"Where is Caetano?" one of them asked.

"Don't understand you," Mauricio said.

"He's asking..." Rodrigo started.

"Doesn't matter what he's asking. Tell them to get out of our way."

Rodrigo translated what Mauricio had to say. The two men laughed, and then began their attack. One went toward Mauricio, the other at Rodrigo and Red.

Mauricio stood his ground as the man charged at

Mauricio. Mauricio struck him in the face, and he immediately fell down. The other man that went at Rodrigo and Red was receiving punches from both of them. He stood there and took the punishment. A crowd started to form around them. Mauricio joined in on striking the man, and blood began to pour out of his mouth.

People ran out of the party to go get other members of the crew. "Let's go!" Mauricio shouted, and they headed outside. Claudia exited the building and ran right behind them.

They ran back to the car, where Ken was holding Caetano upright against the back door. "There's not enough space," Red said. "Put him in the trunk."

Ken dragged the man to the trunk as Rodrigo popped it open. Ken placed him inside and struck Caetano's face with his right fist. He became unconscious, and Ken closed the trunk.

Caetano woke up to his face being smacked repetitively by Rodrigo. Mauricio was standing beside him. Another few seconds passed, and he realized he was on the edge of a balcony. Rodrigo shoved him further back, and Caetano screamed in fear.

"My friend here wants to torture you," Rodrigo said. "But I suggested throwing you off a balcony to give you a quicker death. Consider it a gift from your fellow countryman. Now, where is he? Where is Malestar?"

"I don't know!"

Mauricio nodded, as he expected this as a first response. He had his tools ready. He picked up a blue plastic bag and a bucket of water. He placed the bag over Caetano's head as Rodrigo held him down. Caetano began to panic, and his inhaling caused the bag to press in toward his face. Then Mauricio poured the water on top of the bag.

Caetano tried his best to get out of Rodrigo's hold, but was unsuccessful. Mauricio waited a bit longer to remove the bag from his head. "You want to start talking now?" he asked in English.

There was no need for a translation. Caetano began to sing like a canary. "He's outside the city, in this big house somewhere. Every time we visit he covers our eyes so I don't know the way to get there."

"And what is his next plan?" Rodrigo asked.

"I don't know. He's taking out everyone that does business with the mayor. Every corporation involved has dirty hands. All he does is give us orders and I supply the manpower. All I know is that he sometimes stays in an abandoned warehouse on Avenida Jose Joaquim Seabra. That's all I know!"

"Well, not anymore," Rodrigo said, and lifted him up. Then he dragged him back into his hotel room and shoved him onto the bed. Mauricio took the gun from out his back pocket.

"Please! Please!" Caetano pleaded with his hands out in front of him. "I have a family!"

"Hold him down," Mauricio said, and Rodrigo pressed Caetano against the bed, and grabbed a pillow. He forced the pillow over Caetano's face while using his body weight to keep him down.

"No right, no wrong," Mauricio said, placing the silencer on the gun. "It's just a job."

Mauricio fired once into the pillow, and Caetano lay still. Rodrigo took out a pack of cigarettes from his pocket and offered one to Mauricio, who declined. Rodrigo took one out, sitting on the bed next to Caetano's dead body. He got the lighter out of his pocket and lit the cigarette.

"Never easy, eh?" Rodrigo asked.

"It's not so bad," Mauricio said, leaning against the counter next to the television.

Rodrigo took in a long smoke, and exhaled. "You know Malestar's crew are going to come after us."

"I welcome the challenge. Of course, I don't think I'll be staying in the city long after this. Just get my money, and go."

"Our money."

"Sure," Mauricio replied with a smile. "You former military too?"

"Yeah, got out. How did you know?"

"I have a knack for such things."

"Have you ever thought about doing another line of work?" Rodrigo asked.

"Not very often."

"I have. I had a partner when I first got into this business. He was a friend of mine from my childhood. Vesco used to hire us all the time for petty criminals that he had business with, and then wanted to take them out. Vesco is not as clean as you think, so these attacks don't surprise me. Anyway, we went on this routine job to stop this Guatemalan bookie named Hector that was making bets for the mayor and a number of other high-ranking officials. Hector was at a bar, sitting down by himself like he was expecting our arrival. My partner and I came walking in, and I thought it was an easy job. Only two other customers inside, and the bartender who was too old to fight. Easy money, we thought."

Rodrigo took another long inhale, and a slow exhale. "But this Hector guy had this place as a trap. We approach him, and the bartender comes out the counter with a shotgun in his hand, and the two customers are pointing guns at us. I almost urinated on myself. What's a man to do in that situation? I panicked. My partner took out his gun. I began to run out of there. My partner didn't even have the chance to fire. They shot him down, filled his body with bullets. You must think I'm a coward for that?"

"No, you did what you had to do to stay alive," Mauricio said. "At the end of the day, what we do is just a job. We're not trying to create a legacy."

"That's easy for you to say. You're the man everyone looks up to."

"I still make rational decisions. I'm not out there trying to be a hero. If that's what you're in this for, you're going to get yourself killed."

"Would you respect me then?" Rodrigo asked.

In a way, Mauricio felt sorry for the man. Rodrigo had considered Mauricio a mentor of some sort, and the least he could do was show some empathy toward him. He was a child, looking for his father's approval. He knew the feeling, although he left that feeling a long time ago.

"I will respect if you stay alive and help me find Malestar. Come on, let's tell Claudia what we found out."

7.

Rodrigo drove as Mauricio sat beside him in the early morning. The majority of the trip back to Mauricio's hotel was quiet. They had placed Caetano's body in the trunk, and dumped it in the local landfill. Mauricio looked at Rodrigo and saw a scared young man who tried his best to look and act the part. He was like Rodrigo when he was younger, eager to make a name for himself, and to prove to his employee that he was more than capable. Now that Rodrigo was hired without his partner, who Mauricio guessed did much of the shooting, that task was immensely harder. Mauricio told himself that he wasn't going to get involved with personal matters, especially with his competition, but another part of him decided that he should help.

"You have a family, Rodrigo?" Mauricio asked.

"I have a mother that lives in the city. My father left us when I was three. No siblings."

"Any girlfriends?"

"No," Rodrigo said. "I'm married to my work."

"That's a sad statement," Mauricio replied.

"You don't become the best at what you do by wasting your time with nonsensical things such as feelings and love."

"This line of work has made you cold. Even you said you thought of doing something else."

"Yeah, forget that."

Mauricio smiled. "No, tell me what else you were thinking about doing."

Rodrigo looked at Mauricio for a moment, and then focused his attention back on the road. "I was going to paint."

"A painter? That is something I never pegged you for. I could be sitting next to the modern-day Picasso."

"Make fun all you want, but painting helps me relax. In a weird way, this line of work is like art, too. But stop giving me a hard time. How come you don't talk about yourself that much?"

"There's nothing to talk about, really," Mauricio replied. "I was raised by two immigrants in a foreign land that had their own ideal of what respect should be. Work hard, build relationships, and do honest work and people will respect you."

"What's wrong with that?"

"The fact it isn't the truth. What people respect is power, and being in fear. Those two things are the catalyst to make people view you how you want. Slaving away at a factory is no way to live. Painting, for that matter too. They may admire your craft, but they won't respect you when it comes to controlling their behavior."

"And what if you don't live for respect?" Rodrigo asked.

"Then you're in the wrong business, my friend."

Rodrigo drove down the street near Mauricio's hotel, and noticed an unmarked white van pull up and park next to the hotel a little further down the street. Five men came out of the van, and Rodrigo could see the purple bandanas hanging out of their pockets and the bulge of guns underneath their jackets. Rodrigo drove past as they walked toward the hotel.

"We have a problem," Rodrigo said. Mauricio looked out the window to see the hotel down the street.

"What's that?"

"The hotel is surrounded by Malestar's men."

"That seems more like a challenge. Turn back around."

"I got a better idea," Rodrigo said, and turned the corner to head to the back parking lot. "You have your key card for the back door entrance?"

"Sure do."

"Let's ambush them." Rodrigo sped down the back parking lot and parked the car near the back door entryway. They quickly got out of the car, and Mauricio used his key card to open the door. They ran down the hall and passed the elevators, opting for the stairway. They ran up the stairs with Mauricio leading the way. They withdrew their guns from their hips, and kept them pointed.

They made their way down the hallway and found it to be empty. Mauricio glanced in the direction of the elevator, then they hurried to the hotel room, where Mauricio used his key card to open the door. The rest of the mercenaries were inside, crowding around the television. The news was showing footage of a reporter at the sight of the bank robbery. Mauricio and Rodrigo entered the room.

"Claudia, get our bags! We all got to get out of here! They're on to us!" Mauricio shouted.

Claudia picked up their suitcases from the bed. Everyone else began to take out their weapons. Mauricio peeked his head outside the door to see the light above the elevators light up and the sound signifying the doors were opening. Claudia stood next to Mauricio.

"Don't be afraid," Mauricio said. "Go toward the back door with Rodrigo. He has his car there."

Claudia nodded, and left the room with Rodrigo

right behind her. They sprinted to the stairway as the elevator doors began to open. Mauricio stepped outside the room with Red and Ken. They stood in the hallway with their guns drawn toward the elevator, with Red having one in each hand.

Three of the men came out, and the mercenaries fired away. Before they had the chance to take out their guns, they were riddled with bullets. They fell, and blood exploded from their bodies. Ken made his way toward the stairway, and Mauricio and Red began to back their way toward the door as well. They stepped through the door as the other two men came out of the elevator. One was a scruffy one, unshaven and tall, and the other a rounder man with longer hair. Mauricio fired a few cover shots in their direction as they fired back.

Mauricio descended the stairs with Red and Ken in front of him. The men in the elevator were only seconds behind and would soon reach the stairway door. Red made it first out the back door as Rodrigo was pulling the car around. They got into the car with Claudia in the passenger side and Rodrigo driving. Mauricio stood with his gun pointed at the door.

"Mauricio!" Claudia shouted.

"Go!" Mauricio shouted back.

Rodrigo drove the car away. The back door opened, and Mauricio fired his remaining bullets in their direction. He kept pressing the trigger, and then realized he was out of ammunition. The two men came out the door. They stood with their guns drawn and with smiles across their faces. Mauricio had only one option now, and that was to run.

Mauricio ran down the parking lot and across to the front of the building. He crossed traffic on the street, holding out his hands for cars to stop. The two men gave chase. Mauricio turned the corner and bolted down a street with hanging advertisements on the sides of the building and heavy pedestrian traffic. The two men that gave chase pushed through the crowd. Mauricio made his way inside a compact convenient store and ran toward the back. Customers watched as he did so. There, he waited in the stockroom.

The two men entered the store. The customers looked the other way, fearing to be a part of a crime or even a witness to one. The clerk behind the front counter tried to do the same, but caught the glance of the man with the beard.

"You tell us where he went, or we will kill you," he said to the clerk. The clerk nodded toward the back.

Inside the stockroom behind the freezers, Mauricio waited behind the door. He knew his chances of survival were minimal at this point, and he would have to rely on his fighting instincts, and try to stay calm. The last part was the hardest part. His heart was racing, and felt it would jump out of his chest. He could hear footsteps coming in his direction. The door swung open, and Mauricio was ready to attack.

He charged at the lean, bearded man and knocked him against the shelf of beer bottles and cans, causing some to break open against the floor. Mauricio followed up with multiple strikes to the face using his forearm. The heavier-set man came from behind Mauricio, pulled him off of the bearded man, and threw him to the ground. Mauricio got back up and charged at him. He was met with an elbow in the back and was thrown once more, this time into a set of shelves in the corner, knocking over bottles that landed on top of him. The leaner man was beginning to recover.

"The big man puts up a good fight," Mauricio stated. "That's quite all right. Even big men can be taken down."

Mauricio charged at him again, and this time the round man reached into his back hip and took out his Taser. He turned it on and shoved it against Mauricio's back, causing his body to convulse from the jolt of electricity. The leaner man came over and used his Taser as well. An intense pain went over Mauricio's body, and then he lay still on the ground.

*

He had returned to his recurring dream. He was twenty years younger then. There he was, walking down the street to his parents' home in Kenya when he saw the smoke rise in the air in its direction. He began to run as fast as he could. A rising panic was inside of him. His body ached with fear. By the time he reached his home, he saw the smoke clearly coming from the house, and the roof and sides still burning.

Mauricio rushed inside. Smoke filled the air, and he tried to cover his mouth with his arm. The visibility inside was low. He coughed loudly as he searched inside the living room. In the corner was where he found both of his parents, unmoving, and leaning against the wall as if they were sleeping peacefully.

At first, he couldn't move. The fear had frozen him. Mauricio was not a man that usually was fearful of anything, whether it was bullets or death-facing situations. But this gave him pause. Sorrow filled his heart, and he began to cry as he finally made his way toward them. Both of them were filled with deep cuts into their chest and face. He held his mother in his arms and cried.

"We should have never come back here," he said. "We should have never come back here."

It would be a while longer before the sorrow would briefly go away. Then he thought of the reason why. Mauricio got up and headed to the master bedroom. The room was ransacked, and clothes were thrown all over the place. Mauricio knew what they were looking for. He went to the drawers; the bottom drawer was already opened. The wooden box inside was open too.

The diamond that had been passed down through generations was gone. His great-grandfather had taken it from the mines of Sierra Leone, and brought it back to Kenya with him. It was Mauricio's father who had run his mouth about it with his friends, his new friends he made when he returned home. Mauricio knew they couldn't be trusted. He had warned his father, but he didn't listen. These were the consequences, and Mauricio wished he was wrong.

Mauricio sat on the bed. He didn't care about the smoke, or the house burning down. He wanted revenge. Then the smoke was filling the room to the point he was violently coughing. For a moment, he thought about staying here and going down with the flames. He could be with his family for eternity. His father wanted to go home, and he should join them.

But then he thought otherwise. He had warned his father. And there needed to be someone to carry out vengeance. All of those years of his father working hard to earn respect, and this was the end result. Respect was earned, it was taken. Why hadn't he just listened to his son? Mauricio coughed again, and he knew his lungs could not take much more. He ran out of the room and back into the living room.

He kneeled beside his parents. He picked up his mother and carried her out the house. He placed her on the sidewalk, and came back for his father as he heard the sounds of fire trucks arriving. He picked up his father, his own body weak and struggling to carry the weight of the older man. He placed him on the ground and closed his eyelids. He kneeled beside both parents until the ambulances and fire trucks came.

Mauricio closed his eyes tight, and wished it all away. This day, this life, the death he saw in front of him. Maybe all of this was some disturbing dream, and he would wake up back in London, and his mother would tell him he was having a nightmare. His father would come into his room and tell him he had second thoughts about going back to Kenya, and his feelings of being homesick had gone away. Perhaps they would go to his mother's country of Brazil instead. She was a long way from home, and she had been away for far too long. Her only wish was to return some day, and Mauricio could see Brazil for himself.

But when he opened his eyes, he was still in Kenya, and his parents were lying still on the ground next to him. He was living the nightmare. Flashes of his childhood appeared, the time he spent with his parents, the time he spent in the military, and everything in between that led up to now. He knew this moment would be the worst moment in his life, and there was no turning back.

8.

He felt the sensation of cool water against his face. He opened his eyes to realize he was handcuffed to a pole that extended to the ceiling, and his feet were tied around the pole and the tips of his shoes were touching the ground. The room he was in was large and full of machinery and cargo vehicles that were used to transport materials across the floor. In the corner of the room was a small radio. Mauricio guessed he was inside the abandoned warehouse that Malestar had sometimes used. Mauricio assumed by the darkness in the room that it was sometime during the night. Flashes of light came through the windows in the corner that most likely came from traffic on the street. In front of him was Malestar, looking at Mauricio as if he was studying him.

"Do you know who Lasar Segall is?" Malestar asked with a bucket of water and a tool kit next to him.

Mauricio shook his head no.

"He was a terrific painter and sculptor whose work was derived from expressionism, modernism, and impressionism. You see, I study art, and I find it all to be so fascinating. Lasar was well liked in Brazil, but back in Europe they found his work to be degenerate, and cast him as someone who showed the negativity of human existence. But there is pain, in life, so was he wrong to show it? People want to live in this bubble of hope and eternal life, when the truth is staring them right in the face. Human suffering is a part of life. It's like breathing. Why are we quick to pretend it doesn't exist? Am I a madman for showing people what's right in front of them?"

Malestar moved closer to Mauricio and held his face up with his right hand. "I want to help you. I want you to see and feel what I feel inside."

Malestar went over to his set of tools and began to sort them out. He found a hand knife, and went slowly over the grip with his hands. He closed his eyes, and he could picture the amount of pain he was going to enforce. He then made his way back to Mauricio, who grimaced at the sight of the knife.

"This is an instrument of pain, and I play it like a

pianist plays the piano. The music it makes can only be heard by the few that appreciate the tone and richness of destruction that it brings. Not everyone has the ear for this sort of thing. Shall we make a composition? Let's call it, Mauricio's Lament."

"You're sick! You mark my words, you will get caught, and when you do..."

"What? Are they going to gut me like a fish? I look forward to that day. I'm not afraid of pain. I'm not a coward like you."

"Then cut yourself!" Mauricio shouted.

Malestar laughed. "You would like that, wouldn't you? I found it to be more entertaining when it's done on others. Then they will feel the pain that I feel inside."

"Look! Let's talk about this! We can work something out!"

"Trust me, I'm an expert. If I wasn't, well, one wrong place and you would die almost instantly. And that's no fun."

Malestar jabbed him in the side of the stomach with the knife. Mauricio shouted in pain, which brought a smile to Malestar's face. Blood came out the wound, and Malestar waved his hands in the air.

"We need music!" Malestar shouted, and went over to the radio to turn it on. Immediately, samba music started playing.

Malestar began to move his hips as if he was dancing

with someone. Mauricio shouted in pain, trying his best not to let Malestar hear him suffer, but the pain was too excruciating. He placed his head down, and tried harder to absorb the throbbing intensity.

"Oh, we have a warrior!" Malestar yelled. "Don't think I haven't seen this before. You're trying to show me you're not hurt, and you're tough enough to take the pain. What does that prove, by the way? This isn't a test. You might as well succumb to the most powerful and liberating feeling there is in the world. Once you have pain, no one can take it away from you. No one!"

Malestar cut him again, this time on the other side of his stomach. Mauricio shouted in pain once more. Malestar began to dance again.

"If you even think about stopping me, you must first experience the pain. I'm going to make you a better bounty hunter, whether you like it or not. I need a challenge, Mauricio. I need someone that is going to come at me with the best they got. If you want to be that man, then you need to be on my level."

Malestar stopped dancing, and stood in front of Mauricio. "Embrace it, Mauricio. Embrace it! Tell me, what do you feel? Do you want to give up? Is that what you want to do?"

Blood began to drain toward the ground. Malestar rubbed his hands against the wounds on Mauricio's body, and tasted the blood. He licked his hands clean.

"Now tell me, how do you feel?" he asked.

"I'm....I'm going...to kill you."

Malestar began to laugh. Then he held unto Mauricio's face. "That's what I want to hear. You're learning," he said as he began to walk away. "I will be back later to dress your wounds, only so that I can cut you some more."

And with that, Malestar exited the door, and left the room.

Mauricio was silent, watching blood leak out of his body and fall into the pool already on the ground below. He could feel the life draining out of him. He had always thought that he would feel hope in a situation like this. He did not. What he felt was pain, and wanting revenge, and that feeling was keeping him alive.

*

They figured this was as good a place as any to meet again. Early in the morning Claudia, Red, Ken, and Rodrigo stood on the football field to discuss the absence of Mauricio, and their next plan of attack. Claudia was the most concerned about Mauricio's disappearance, and with good reason. The fact he didn't return to the hotel surely meant he was in trouble. It wasn't like him to not contact her after he left her side.

"You think they got to him?" Red asked the group.

"Or he's lying somewhere in the ocean," Ken stated.

"Watch your words around the missus," Rodrigo said.

"We have to find him," Claudia said. "I need to know if he's okay."

"Would he do the same for us?" Ken asked.

"We're a group now," Red said. "And I think we can kill two birds with one stone. We go after Malestar, and we hit him hard. Rodrigo says he knows where he is."

"I know where he could be," Rodrigo said. "It's nothing definite, but it's worth trying."

"I agree," Claudia said.

"I don't," Ken replied.

"If you don't want to help, that's on you," Claudia said. "But just remember, Mauricio won't forget this."

"That's if he's alive," Ken said.

Claudia slapped him across his face. Ken looked at her for a moment, and was about to strike her back when Red grabbed his arm. Rodrigo kept his hand near his gun as he was unsure what would happen next. Ken continued to stare at her, and then loosened up his arm. Red let go of her grip.

"Fight your own battles," Ken said, and began to walk away.

"Ken!" Rodrigo shouted after him. Ken didn't look

back.

"Are we losing you too?" Red asked Rodrigo.

"The man has a lot of wisdom I could use," Rodrigo said. "So I'm willing to fight."

Ken took retreat in the hills of a city with a morning jog to clear his head. He thought about his ex-wife, and his entire life leading up to this moment. From an early age, he decided on being a rebel. His parents wanted him to run his father's company, and walk in his shadow and become a businessman. His father and he had shared the same traits of getting what they wanted, but the prospect of sitting in an office all day had turned him off from the corporate world. He needed to participate in the fight, not just talk about it. He remembered in detail the day he took off his tie, quit, and walked out the office. That was the day he was liberated, and he found a profession where he could do what he wanted and get paid for it.

Yes, there were bad days in this business, but those were often disregarded when the money came rolling in. He had stared death in the face numerous times, but always managed to find a way out. He was coming closer to facing his inevitable fate, and he knew it. Was he afraid to stare in its face? No, he was fearless. He had trained himself to be that way. So why didn't he go along with the rest of the mercenaries?

There was no reason to deny the truth to himself.

Mauricio was a threat, and he didn't want to help save a threat. Yes, he had told him earlier that it was better to be a team, but here was a chance to have the best competition out of the picture, assuming he was even still alive. Now he could get Malestar for himself. This business was a cruel one, and now he could have the ultimate prize all by himself. All he had to do was let the other mercenaries get killed along the way. The plan could work out perfectly.

So why was he feeling some type of guilt? There was only one other person that could make him feel that way, and that was his ex-wife. He would come home from days or even weeks on the road, and she would give him that face that he hated to see. She didn't have to say a word. It was always that face that gave him a guilt trip, and he would lower his head and head to the bedroom. It was not to go to sleep, of course. No, that would have been lovely. It was to gather his pillows and blankets that he wanted for the night, and bring them down to sleep on the sofa.

That was how he was treated, a stranger in his own house. It had been years since he lived those days, yet the anger never went away. He despised her for the way she made him feel. He felt she had manipulated him to have feelings for her, something he never really felt for anyone else. He knew feelings could get you killed in this business, and having a family was a weakness. The best thing to do was to be a cold-hearted assassin, and disregard all natural emotion.

Maybe others could have done that, but for him, it would be impossible. He may have been a psychopath in some sense of the word, but there was a part of him that had compassion. However, he wanted to turn that side of him off. Mauricio would have done the same thing. Wasn't he that way when he first met him?

Ken stopped running at the top of the hill, and took a moment to catch his breath. When he did, he looked up to catch a view of the city, a spectacular panorama of the downtown buildings and the nearby ocean. The average tourist might have appreciated the view, but to Ken, another city was nothing more than another paycheck. There was no time fall in love with a city because once again, that required emotion. When most people found beauty, he had to see the darkness. And looking at the city once more, he saw plenty of it.

*

On the way to Malestar's secret warehouse, Claudia looked out the window as Rodrigo drove next to her, with Red in the back seat. Claudia had grown accustomed to Mauricio being in difficult situations, but he always reported back. She had liked to think it was because he wanted to hear her voice, but it was more so to comfort her and to let her know that he was okay. She couldn't imagine a life without Mauricio, but knew the possibility of him not coming back was increasing by the day.

That was why she was persistent on him retiring, and together, starting a family. She had enjoyed this line of work at first, and Mauricio had called her a mercenary, but really all she did was most of the tracking and coordination. It wasn't like that work was easy, but Mauricio was the killer, and the one that dealt with the person they were looking for in a personal manner. The amount of bloodshed sometimes in play was too much for her, and she knew it was wearing on Mauricio. She was hoping that feeling would lead to an early retirement.

She wondered what kind of father he would be. He didn't talk much about his own father, and she knew the tragedy that took away his parents. She could tell he was afraid, but she didn't know what was more fearsome—the prospect of their children knowing what their father did to provide for them, or the fact he wouldn't be around to raise them and they would experience the same sorrow that he did. It was ironic to Claudia that a man so fearless when it came to facing death every day was afraid of children. That's why it was imperative that he retire soon, with enough money so that he would never have to work in this profession again.

Claudia looked out the window and noticed the

streets were starting to fill with pedestrians. A feeling of anger came across her. Here they were, walking around as if everything was normal, not knowing the danger she and her boyfriend were going through to keep them all safe. They might have been offering their services for monetary value, but still, they were catching criminals and being the jury and the verdict. And what did they get in return? It was a chance to see an early grave, and nothing more. At least men of the law were awarded medals and thanked. She and Mauricio and others like them were the unknown heroes that did what the law could not do. She could lose the only man she truly loved, and the people walking about couldn't have cared less.

There was a moment where she felt like she shouldn't help them ever again. But the city needed people like her, like Mauricio. He had saved many without them knowing it, and now she could return the favor and save him for once.

9.

Rodrigo parked across the street, and when the mercenaries walked over to the warehouse, they found a metal gate across the front of the entrance. Rodrigo and Red stood in front and thought of ways to bypass the gate while Claudia headed toward the alley on the side of the building. Sunny weather was beginning to arrive, brightening the alleyway with direct sunlight. It was there she saw the back door inside the warehouse, a worn blue door that was locked.

"Over here!" she shouted. Red and Rodrigo made their way over to her.

"It's locked," Claudia stated.

"Not for long," Red said, and began to kick at the door. Each time she did, the door loosened until the lock broke. "See, problem solved," she said, and took out her gun. The other mercenaries did as well as they entered the warehouse.

Red entered first and kept her gun pointed. The open door brought in sunlight to see into the large room that was filled with machinery. Then she noticed Mauricio toward the corner of the room. She ran over to him, and then Claudia saw him as well.

"Mauricio!" she shouted.

Mauricio had his head down, and appeared to be dead. Red checked his pulse and found him to be still breathing. She noticed the pool of blood on the ground and that he was tied up.

"Rodrigo, get the car!" she shouted.

Claudia began to cry, touching Mauricio's face and pulling it next to her own. "I just can't lose you. I can't..."

Rodrigo drove the group to emergency care at the nearest hospital. Claudia and Red sat in the waiting room. Red twitched her leg nervously, and Claudia kept her head in her lap. Red struggled to find the right words to say to comfort her, and felt a bit of guilt for trying to use her charm against the man Claudia loved.

"I'm sure he's okay," she finally said.

"You don't know that," Claudia replied.

"This business is rough," Red stated.

"Don't you think I know that?"

"I'm just saying..."

"I know what you're saying," Claudia said, looking up at Red. "You're saying that it has always been a possibility it would turn out like this. You don't think I knew that? I just believed in Mauricio. He's the best there is—well, at least that's what everyone keeps telling me. You know, every day I tell myself that he's special, he can beat the odds. But I know what the reality is. And if I don't get him out of this business soon, I will lose him. I know it."

Red sat down next to her. "I've always been jealous of people that knew how to have emotions such as love in this business. In order to keep it, though, you're going to have to stay strong through the tough times. You have to stay strong."

Red rubbed Claudia's back, and felt compassion for her sadness. She knew the all-too-familiar feeling of loss and awaiting the outcome of someone's prognosis in a hospital. She hated hospitals—the smell of them, the quietness of the hallways on some floors, and all the waiting. The waiting was torture. She didn't want to be here any longer than she had to, but for Claudia and Mauricio she would. Strangely with them, it felt like she was part of a family, however dysfunctional the people in it were. She didn't know how long it would last, but she enjoyed this feeling of an alliance. It was a healthy break from the solitary life of a mercenary.

*

Ken decided to do something useful and look for information that could lead to the capture of Malestar. He knew this was dangerous on his own with someone that had the clout of the man he was chasing, but he didn't join this business to go somewhere and hide. He headed for the slums with no plan in mind other than to seek something that would be a link to Malestar. He knew the slums were the key. There was a criminal underworld here, and all the rumors and dealings that dealt with crime against the city and police were heard here. Ken loved being in the mix of the danger, and today was no different.

Ken saw a group of teenagers hanging out near a corner store and approached them. They were curious as to what a man of his ethnicity was doing in the slums of Salvador. The scrawny one kept his hand near his gun. Ken remained calm as he stood next to him.

"You don't want to do that," Ken said.

"Who is this guy?" the kid asked his other friends in Portuguese.

"Any of you speak English?"

The young man tried to take out his gun, but Ken saw it coming. He grabbed the kid's hand and twisted his arm back while the other two tried to attack. Ken gave them swift kicks to the stomach. They fell back and Ken broke the arm of the kid holding the gun. The boy dropped the gun and screamed in pain. The other two teenagers got off the ground and ran down the street until they reached a shanty that looked like it was going to fall apart at any moment. Ken followed them there and was winded by the time he reached the home.

Ken took the gun from his back hip and entered through the open door. In the living room was a young woman breastfeeding her kid. She didn't seem surprised by Ken's appearance. A small television was playing in the corner. The volume was high and was the only sound Ken could hear in the home. Clothes and beer bottles decorated the floor. Ken made his way to the hallway area with his hand firmly on his gun.

He heard talking coming from the last bedroom on the right. Ken walked slowly toward the room. The conversation stopped. He paused behind the corner of the room and took a deep breath. Then he made his way inside with a quick turn of his body.

The gun was immediately knocked out of his hands by one of the teenagers. Before he had to chance to fight him, he caught the glance of Malestar in front of him, standing with a smile on his face. The two teenagers that had run away from him quickly pushed him against the wall. Malestar took out a stun gun from his coat and charged at Ken, placing the weapon against his stomach. Ken's body went into shock and everything went to black.

*

Red was sitting poolside at her hotel, taking in the sunny morning and trying to relax. It had been a stressful week, and she was still awaiting news from Claudia. She had only brought one bikini with her on the trip and it was the red two-piece that hardly covered anything. Normally, she liked the attention she got from wearing it, but today she just wanted to be left alone. She had noticed a few men looking in her direction. She sighed, leaned back, and closed her eyes, trying to disappear in the warmth of the day.

"Taking time off already?"

Red looked up to see Mauricio there with Claudia's arm around him to help support him. Immediately, Red got up to give him a hug. Mauricio gave her a pat on the back but Red embraced him warmly, and a little too long for Claudia's comfort.

"So glad to see you on your feet," Red said.

"Good to be back," Mauricio replied. "What have I missed?"

"Rodrigo is looking for Ken, and he's nowhere to be found."

"Well, he's a big boy. He's allowed to work on his own."

"Some of us don't see it that way," Red replied.

"And we're glad you don't," Claudia said, and led Mauricio to one of the available poolside seats. Red sat down beside them.

"Just give me some time to recover and I will join you all in the hunt," Mauricio said.

"Take your time," Red replied. "So, care to tell us what happened with Malestar?"

"Nothing to tell, really. He talked his propaganda and carved me up."

"He could have killed you," Claudia stated.

"He wanted me alive to make me suffer," Mauricio replied. "The man is beyond cruel. He honestly believes that what he does makes perfect sense. There's no amount of rehabilitation that's going to change him."

"Well, we're going to find him and we're going to make him suffer," Red said. "Right now, what you need to do is relax. Salvador is a beautiful place. When you're ready, that's when we'll strike."

Red got up and headed toward the pool. Mauricio watched her jump into the water and swim to the other side of the pool. He then turned to Claudia, who seemed concerned.

"What?"

"She's not to be trusted," Claudia said. "Don't get me wrong, I like her, but that doesn't mean I have to trust her."

"Fair enough," Mauricio replied.

"Maybe we should just give up on this job."

"Claudia..."

"Look how close you came to death. I can't afford to lose you. Maybe you don't value your life, but I do. Am I the only one that wants something to life other than this? Is that all you want to do? We spend so much time running across the world chasing people when we can actually make a difference by raising a child and teaching the right way. If I'm the only one that thinks that way, let me know now."

"Are you seriously going to bother me with this right now?"

Claudia shook her head, got up, and left. Mauricio rubbed his head and closed his eyes. He didn't want to think about having a family right now. The only thing he wanted to do in the near future was to get revenge against Malestar. The man had toyed with him, and was using him as his own experiment. The man needed to stop, and there was no way he was turning him in now. Usually, if given an option to take them dead or alive, Mauricio would take him alive if he could. But there was no secret, the mayor and every law-abiding citizen in this city wanted him dead.

Mauricio opened his eyes to see Red stepping out of the pool and squeezing her hair as she approached him. He had to admit that he found her attractive. But he knew women like her, and everything about her spelled trouble.

"Problem with the missus?" she asked.

Mauricio grinned. "You know, despite what you think, Claudia is a good woman that has always been there for me."

"I don't doubt it," Red said. "I can tell she really loves you. The question is, do you love her back?"

"I believe I do," Mauricio replied.

Red dried off with the towel from the chair next to Mauricio, and sat down next to him. "It's not fair, is it?"

"What are you talking about?"

"The moment you think you found what you want is that exact moment you want it, but you really want something else as well. Life is not fair that way. I say, go after everything you want."

"And tell me, what do I want?" Mauricio asked.

"Only you can answer that question," Red replied. "I just know that if I want something, I just go and get it."

Red looked at him in that seductive way, and Mauricio knew exactly what she meant by that. What was her angle? Have him fall deeply in lust for her so that way she could control him, and perhaps give up the money? Her eyes were on the prize, and nothing more. He had seen this playbook before, and he wasn't going to fall for it.

"So what if something like what happened to me, happens to you someday, Red? Who are you going to call? The life of getting what you want, and not caring for others, is a long and sad one."

"Says you. I can look after myself."

"Yeah, that's what I used to say," Mauricio stated. "To answer your question, I do know what I want. I want someone that's going to be loyal to me. Someone that I can count on. Someone that doesn't play mind games. That's the type of woman I want. In fact, I think I'm going to take the woman I love out somewhere special just for the sake of it. Relationships take work, and yes, it's easy just to look the other way. But for me, it's just not worth it. Now, if you excuse me," Mauricio said, standing up and holding on to the bandages around his waist, "I have a date to plan." He walked off, and Red leaned back in her chair.

She shook her head, not wanting to think of the possibility that he was right. He was a fool to have emotions in this business. That made him weak. Or did it? She didn't want to think about it anymore. That would bring up the sadness she would sometimes feel when she went back home alone to an empty house. She didn't know if she wanted children or a family, but the prospect of having someone care for her would be welcomed. She was unlucky in life when it came to men, and she was tired of trying to find the perfect one, if that even existed. The fact was that she was jealous of what they had, as much as she didn't want to admit it.

A skinny young man with his rib cage visible on his skin walked over to Red. He said something in Portuguese that she didn't understand. She didn't bother looking at him.

"Get lost," she said, and leaned back on the chair.

The young man left, and Red closed her eyes. She needed to take her mind off the thought of being alone the rest of her life, and the job here as well. The problem was, when she was not thinking about one, she was thinking about the other. Too often to fill that void, she would use her sexual appeal to get what she temporarily wanted. She was too afraid to show her true self, and to be rejected for who she was. And she dared not share her past unless she wanted to play the victim.

So what else could she do to preoccupy her mind? She thought of the answer. She would go downtown and see what types of shopping districts were within the city. Red wasn't someone that would consider herself rich, but she had enough money to do a little bit of splurging.

Finally, something that would take her mind off the two men she wanted, each in a different way.

10.

Mauricio chose the upscale seafood restaurant based on the reviews he read online. The restaurant was tucked away in the Cabula neighborhood of the city with high-rise buildings seen in the distance and plenty of tree-covered areas far from the center of the city. Inside, the atmosphere was rustic and the proprietor was friendly with the customers. The restaurant was fairly crowded, but the staff was still quite attentive. Mauricio couldn't stop looking at Claudia, who looked stunning this evening. She wore a white summer dress with her hair up, and the diamond earrings he bought her last year. She had always been naturally beautiful, but with makeup, Mauricio wanted to skip dinner and have her.

They started off with an appetizer, the *casquinha de siri*—a dish made out of crab—and then ordered the *casquinha* with octopus and shrimp. Their drinks were natural fruit juices taken out of the restaurant's garden. The food was delicious, and Mauricio was trying to convince Claudia that the food back in London was just as delicious. His convincing did not work. Mauricio had a couple of dark Pilsner beers, the typical kind in Brazil, and was feeling better than he ever had the last couple of days. Claudia thought about something that was off topic.

"You mind telling me what Red is doing at our hotel?" Claudia asked.

"Long story."

"A story I want to hear, but you're right, now is not the time. Tonight, it's about us," Claudia replied. "I remember we had nights like this all the time before our work took over. Our job seemed to be more carefree then."

"Do you remember that job we did in Prague with finding the man with the long scar down his face, and we couldn't speak the language, so we kept doing this." Mauricio made a line down his face with his hand.

Claudia laughed. "Some of those people thought we were looking for a man that always cried."

"He was bloody hard to find too. We searched almost every nightclub in the city. There's a serious underworld in that city too. There's plenty of corruption to go around that makes everyone a suspect, and no one willing to help. We even went to his mother's flat, and she gave us the runaround. It was a nice touch getting that translator to go with us. I don't think those people saw anyone like us before."

"I didn't like his mother at all. She was a mean old woman. I've met mothers like her before, but she was in complete denial. She was shocked and kept insisting her son was a good man with a decent heart. Tell that to all the men he killed. We did the world a favor."

"No, we did his competition a favor. Don't forget who hired us," Mauricio said.

"Either way, I think we did some good."

Mauricio took a sip of his beer. "Do you wonder sometimes if we're any better than the people we're chasing? I mean, we're killing people too. I know I believe that whole it's an eye for an eye thing, but aren't we supposed to be better than them?"

"What did that man do to you?" Claudia asked. "We are better than them because they made a choice to do something bad, and we're here to make sure they pay for it. It's not like we're going out there and intentionally killing people. It may be a payday, but we are making sure these monsters never see another day. This man named Malestar has half the city scared to death to step out of the house. Do I have to remind you he bombed countless people and threw a woman off a building? And now you think you're just like him?"

Mauricio grinned. "Okay, I was wrong. I don't know what I'm saying. I just know that when I looked at him, into his eyes, I saw that he was genuine in what he felt. I think he just wants me to see his world, and somehow I will understand it."

"Can we talk about something else?" Claudia asked, leaning back in her chair.

"Of course. Let's talk end game, and what I mean by that is, after this job."

"Really?"

"Sure. Where would you like to move to?"

"Somewhere warm. Somewhere that I can speak Portuguese and is along the coast. Knowing the city would be a plus."

"Please tell me you are not talking about this city," Mauricio said.

"Isn't that the reason we came here?"

"We came here to get acclimated with Brazil. Besides, with this whole ordeal…"

"Okay, what about Fortaleza, or Rio?" Claudia asked.

"Rio sounds like fun," Mauricio said, taking another sip of his beer.

"Sounds like a place that you want to do some extra work."

"I'm offended by such an accusation."

"No, we need a sleepy fishing town where we can spend our days on the boat, and our evenings watching the sun set along the shore. Some place where the people are friendly, and not nosy enough to get into your business. Then we can spend days snorkeling or fishing, and eating the best seafood this side of Brazil. Now that would be paradise," Claudia stated.

"Aren't you going to miss it?"

"Miss what?"

"You know exactly what I'm talking about," Mauricio replied. "The action and the chase. We're predators by nature. What are we supposed to do with our free time?"

"I can think of a few things," Claudia said.

Mauricio leaned against the table. "Doesn't sound like retirement will be a bad thing after all."

His cell phone began to play its ringtone for a text message. Mauricio reached into his pocket and looked at who was sending him the message. "Who is it?" Claudia asked.

"It's Sophie."

"Who?"

"Red." Mauricio clicked on the message. "It says that Rodrigo got a strange call and was told that if he wanted to find his friend Ken, that he would be at this address."

"We should go."

Mauricio raised his arm to signal the waiter to come over. "I hope I'm wrong about this."

"About what?"

"It's Malestar. I think he's toying with us."

The sky had darkened by the time Mauricio and Claudia arrived at the address. The location was a dead-end street in the slums, and Mauricio parked his car a block away just to be safe. He had Claudia stay behind him and he held his gun firmly in his hand as he made his way down the street. The lighting was poor in this area and he felt like eyes were watching him. There were shanties on each side of the street, and he could hear the faint sounds of music being played.

Someone was coming down the adjacent alley. Mauricio stopped walking, and Claudia did as well. He waited for the footsteps to get closer until he could see two figures emerging from the alley. He waited. He could make out the figures as they walked down the street and Mauricio gave a breath of relief when he realized it was Red and Rodrigo.

"Someone playing games with you, Rodrigo?" Mauricio asked as walked over to them.

"The address was here," Rodrigo said. He pointed off in front of them. "Can't really see ahead."

"Watch the roofs," Mauricio said as he made his way down the street with his gun pointed. As he moved, he noticed a body hanging from the window of a building. The body had a rope around the neck. A closer look revealed that it was Ken.

Immediately, Mauricio knew there was no point to check if he was alive or not. He began to drag the body down by pulling down the rope. The other mercenaries came to his side. They rested Ken's body on the ground, and the mercenaries had different reactions to the sight of him dead. Claudia and Red felt a bit of sadness, Rodrigo took it as a sign that he was next and was somewhat nervous, and Mauricio became angry. This was a message from Malestar. The crazed man had kept him alive, but killed Ken. This was all a game to him, and his playing with his prey.

"Does anyone know if he had someone to call, like a loved one, or a friend?" Mauricio asked.

"The only person he talked about was his ex-wife," Rodrigo said.

"We should call it in," Claudia said.

Mauricio took a look around and noticed a scrawny teenager standing on the other side of the street. Although Mauricio didn't know it, it was the same man Ken had chased down earlier, with his appearance mostly unseen by the dark. Mauricio didn't have a good look at him, but he would have sworn he saw the kid smiling. The other mercenaries took notice as well and they all pointed their guns at him.

The scrawny teenager had no choice but to stay in place. Mauricio calmly approached him, and stood not more than a few feet away from him. "You find something funny?" Mauricio asked.

The kid didn't respond, but kept his smile intact. "Can I get a translator?" Mauricio shouted, and Rodrigo went to where Mauricio was standing.

"Ask him what he is doing here," Mauricio said to Rodrigo. Rodrigo asked the question to the kid in Portuguese.

The kid replied in Portuguese. "To see the sadness in your eyes when you say your friend dead."

"You work for Malestar, right? Where is he?" Rodrigo asked him.

"The flock of birds that do not return to their master shall perish at his hands."

"Where is he?" Rodrigo asked more demandingly.

"Do you wish to join us?" the kid asked.

Rodrigo pointed his gun at the teenager's face, to Mauricio's surprise. "I don't have time for your games. You're going to tell me where he is!"

"Easy," Mauricio said, not knowing what he was saying, but noticing the increased tension.

"Why are you standing up for him?" Rodrigo asked Mauricio.

"I'm not. He's just a kid."

"Well, this kid is working with Malestar and he's not telling me what I want to know."

"How is killing him going to help? Are you in this business to track down a criminal or to kill people along the way?"

"You saw what they did to Ken!"

"That was Malestar, not him," Mauricio replied. "We will find him."

Rodrigo was itching to pull that trigger. He had never experienced fear like this before, a fear that he was defenseless in his fate. He should be the danger when chasing the criminal, not the criminal becoming a danger to him. He had spent all his life in Brazil and he had seen countless teenagers like this one throw their lives away on behalf of some drug kingpin, a narcissist crime boss, or to chase a lifestyle. Shooting this kid wouldn't solve the problem because the slums kept producing their children to want more, and to take what they wanted by any means.

Rodrigo put the gun down. "You tell your boss that we will spill his blood on the streets for all to see," Rodrigo said to the kid. Deep down, he was afraid of Malestar, but he hope he came off as fearless.

The scrawny kid took off and ran down the street, disappearing into the darkness. Red and Claudia sprinted over to Mauricio and Rodrigo. Rodrigo turned to face them and noticed that all eyes were on him.

"What? We have a job to do," he said.

"Not killing kids," Red stated.

"You don't know those kids like I do," Rodrigo replied. "They think they are men, and they act like men. They want to carry guns and rob people, then they should face the consequences."

"Is it me, or does he sound like a madman?" Red asked.

"I don't have to explain myself to you. You're nothing more than sexed-up windup doll that looks pretty and tries to be tough."

"I'm not the one peeing in my pants at the mention of Malestar," Red replied.

"Now, you listen here, you redheaded...."

Rodrigo's words were stopped by the explosion that came from Ken's body, and a large eruption of fire burst into the air. The explosion startled them and they jolted away from the fire. Ken's body parts were burned and tossed into the air, landing on the ground in front of them.

The mercenaries looked at each other, not knowing how to react or what to say. Rodrigo was the most visibly shaken in the group. His body was slightly trembling, and he felt like he was in the moment he was in when he lost his friend Hector. For a moment, he almost panicked, but was able to keep his composure.

"You all right, Rodrigo?" Mauricio asked.

"Yeah," Rodrigo replied.

The fact was, he wasn't. He needed his medication. After his partner Hector had died, he began experiencing constant headaches with dizzy spells and his body slightly trembling. He went to the doctor, and they told him it was because of a panic attack. He took fluoxetine for a while, and then he felt like he didn't need it anymore. Nothing could have been further from the truth at this moment.

"I'm going to the car," Rodrigo said, and made his way back.

"What's with him?" Red asked.

"His friend just got blown to pieces," Mauricio said. "Not exactly a day in the park."

"Well, he's going to have to get that together if he wants to be in this business," Red replied.

Mauricio sighed. "I'm going to have a talk with Vesco. I'm not liking this one bit."

At the car, Rodrigo climbed in the driver's side and slammed the door closed. He leaned back in his chair, angry at himself for not being able to control himself better. How would the others judge him as a mercenary if he couldn't contain his emotions and physical reactions?

He felt like he had embarrassed himself out there in more ways than one.

He could have killed a kid just a moment ago. What was he thinking? He came into this business to catch the bad guys, or at the very least to go after the targets he was hired to take out. He was losing his sanity with each passing moment. He had to get this under control if he wanted any part of the pay to capture Malestar. Once he had the money, he would reevaluate what he wanted to do. Until then, he was going to have to find a way to manage.

Rodrigo reached into the glove compartment and looked around for his medication. He could see his arm trembling. He found the pills in the right corner, and quickly took out the bottle to open it. He took out twice the recommended dose and quickly swallowed the pills. Everything was going to be all right, he told himself. He looked ahead and could see Red coming toward the car. She got into the passenger's seat and looked over at Rodrigo.

"You let me know if I can do anything to help," she said.

Rodrigo looked her up and down. "Except that," Red said, and closed the door.

11.

Vesco, dressed in his typical business attire, waited on the rooftop of the downtown building, looking off into the city he had vowed to help protect and look after. The city was just beginning to awaken and the streets were starting to fill. With his *acarajé*—essentially a deep-fried "bread" made from mashed beans from which the skins have been removed—rice, and jerked beef in hand, he thought about the discovery of Ken's body the night before. His plan was working well. These mercenaries just might be the distraction needed for Malestar not to concentrate on the rest of the city. In the meantime, he could use them to try to catch the fabled criminal. It was a win-win in his mind.

Vesco loosened his tie and finished his food. He looked out into the city and tried to think what got him into politics in the first place. At one point, he did want to make a difference, but now he was just fighting to keep something he didn't have passion for. What was it all for? Respect? Dignity? He wasn't a quitter, and he wasn't going to start now. He knew it was going to be a tough job to clean up the city and balance the budget. The people had high expectations, and he did as well. Vesco wanted Salvador to be the shining star not only of the state of Bahia, but for all of Brazil. He wanted to be the mayor that was personable and open to the public, but the hiring of the mercenaries made that impossible.

After all, it was the city that was paying for their services. But this wasn't the first time he used the city's money. He had a partnering team that helped him with personal enemies and drug dealers. But one of them died, and this job with Malestar was too much for the one left over. He needed an experienced person that wouldn't stop until he finished the job. Someone that would finish the job on the principle of determination and will, not just because of monetary reasons. So that's who he hired. Then he hired other mercenaries as backup insurance. Someone was bound to get close to him, and he was fortunate Malestar didn't mind the challenge. Otherwise, he and his family would be dead.

He thought about his wife and child, and truly believed he was doing all he could to protect them. He was doing the best he could with a psychotic killer out there. Vesco still had faith in doing honest work to protect the city from the filth of criminals trying to steal and kill from hardworking families just trying to get by. The people below deserved the best when it came to their protection, and he supplied the city just that.

That man came through the rooftop door and stood behind Vesco. "I hope you're happy with yourself."

Vesco turned around to see Mauricio walking toward him. "In general, I am. Now, what's so urgent that you had to meet me?"

"I don't like the way you work, Vesco, not at all. This whole ordeal with hiring all these mercenaries doesn't sit right with me. The one that lives gets the money? Is that how it works? You've been playing us from the beginning." Mauricio stopped in front of him.

"From now on, this is my job only," Mauricio stated.

"I can't let you do that," Vesco replied.

Mauricio grinned. "The man says he can't let me do that." Mauricio grabbed Vesco by the collar and pushed him toward the edge of the building. He leaned Vesco's body over the edge so he could get a clear view of the street below. Vesco saw the moving cars and the distance, and a rush of fear went through his body.

"I don't care for people that play games," Mauricio said. "Do we have an understanding?"

"You don't understand!" Vesco shouted. "I can't! Malestar knows about you. He knows about all of you. If you stand any chance against him, then I'm going to need you all."

"We're all disposable to you!" Mauricio shouted. "All you care about is yourself and your precious reputation."

"No! He's going to kill my family. I hired you because you are the best. I won't make it without you!"

Mauricio pulled him back up. Vesco adjusted his suit and tried his best to return to a state of calm. His hands were shaking; for a moment he'd thought he would be dropped.

"Use that scare tactic a lot?" he asked.

"It works," Mauricio replied. "How does he know about us, Vesco?"

"How do you think? I told him. I had to. He threatened my family. I'm not letting that maniac anywhere near my family or risking the chance of him terrorizing this city. I refuse for this city to end up like Manaus."

"What happened there?"

"A few years back, the city of Manaus had a serial killer on its hands whose signature was this machete he used on his victims, mostly prostitutes walking the streets. At first, no one seemed to care for reasons I don't have to explain to you. But then other people were being killed, mothers that stayed at home, and children walking home from school. There was no pattern for the police to follow. He was killing anyone, at any time. The faith in the police department lessened. No one believed in the law anymore. And worst of all..."

"The mayor did not get reelected?"

"The killer was never caught. The killing stopped out of the blue, but the repercussions of his killing spree are still left in the city. People are still afraid to go out at night. People are still skeptical of the police. The trust in the city is ruined."

Vesco looked away for a moment, and then back at Mauricio. "You may think I'm an evil man, Mauricio, but I'm doing what's best for this city." Vesco started to walk to the rooftop door.

"You act like you're some type of angel sent to rescue the city," Mauricio said. "I bet there is blood on your hands just like everyone else. You know what I think? I think you're just as corrupt as the police officers in your force and then some. You're a selfish man, Vesco. You're doing this to protect yourself first, and your family second."

Vesco walked back toward Mauricio. "Do you think you're better than me? Remember what you do. I hired you to kill because that's what you do. Why do you care what my reasons are? You should only be concerned about your paycheck. Isn't that why you contacted me? So you could have all the money for yourself?"

"I came here so more of us won't be killed," Mauricio replied.

"So you care more about your fellow mercenaries than the citizens of this city?"

"This isn't my city."

"Innocent people are being killed!" Vesco shouted.

"Don't blame that on me. That's because of the ineptness of your police department. You might not think much of us, but we have a code, and that is you go after your target and no one else. If people stand in your way, you take them down, but that doesn't include other people in our profession. I bet you're enjoying this too, having us compete with each other and kill each other if need be. But it's not going to work like that. Your money doesn't mean that much to me. I'm done."

"Well, now, wait a minute..."

"Now you can go," Mauricio replied.

Vesco wanted to say something else, but instead he stomped toward the door. He opened the door, and turned around to face Mauricio. "I had you judged wrong."

"How's that?"

"I knew the money wasn't all that important, but I thought you would finish the job because it's the right thing to do and innocent people are counting on you."

"There are other people you can hire," Mauricio replied.

"I wanted the best." Vesco left the rooftop, and Mauricio stood there, wondering if he made the right decision.

*

Claudia was on her laptop in the hotel room looking up information on serial killers in Brazil, both to get a better understanding of what they were up against, and because of sheer curiosity. There were four she found to be the most intriguing. There were others, such as the Park Killer, and another serial killer that was in Sao Paulo, but she found four to be the most appalling. Malestar was similar to and different from all of them.

The first one was Edson Isidoro Guimarães, a nursing assistant that confessed to five murders, four of which he was convicted. However, he was suspected of committing over a hundred murders. His victims were chosen patients who were in extreme pain and whose conditions were irreversible. He was caught by a hospital porter seeing him fill a syringe with potassium chloride and injecting it into a comatose patient who immediately died. He was paid sixty dollars for each death by a local funeral home so the funeral home could make money off of the deceased's relatives. The theory was that he did it for money at first, but then spiraled out of control and began to enjoy what he did. He was convicted and sentenced to seventy-six years in prison.

The second one was Anísio Ferreira de Sousa, a doctor who ran a satanic ring that killed boys in the city of Altamira, Brazil. The reason for choosing boys was never understood. He was convicted of the murders of three boys and the attempted murder of two others. However, the unsolved murders of nineteen boys were linked to him.

The third one, and the most disturbing one to Claudia, was Abraão José Bueno, another man that worked in the nursing profession. While working in a children's ward in Rio de Janeiro, he began injecting babies and older children with overdoses of sedatives, causing them to stop breathing. The victims he chose had irreversible diseases such as AIDS and leukemia. He would then call medical staff to resuscitate them. In the course of one month up to fifteen children were thought to have been targeted, all between the ages of one and ten. The reason he did this sent a chill through Claudia's body. It was thought that Bueno committed his crimes so that he could be the first to notice a problem with a patient, thereby earning the respect and admiration of his co-workers. He was sentenced to a hundred and ten years of imprisonment for the murders of four children.

The last serial killer, and the one that most resembled Malestar, was Pedro Rodrigues Filho, better known as Little Peter. He was born on a farm in Santa Rita do Sapucaí, south of Minas Gerais, with an injured skull, the result of beatings his father had bestowed upon his mother's womb during a fight. Pedro said his first urge to kill happened at the age of thirteen. During a fight with an older cousin, he pushed the boy into a sugar cane press. The boy almost died. Pedro took great joy out of that scenario. At the age of fourteen, he murdered the vice mayor of Alfenas, Minas Gerais, because he fired his father, a school guard, at the time accused of stealing the school kitchen's food. Then he murdered another guard, supposedly the real thief. The precedent for his disdain of authority had been set.

Soon after, he killed his own father at a local prison, after his father butchered his mother with a machete. As part of his revenge, Pedro cut out his father's heart and ate a piece of it. Pedro was caught and sent to prison. Once there, he killed at least forty-seven inmates. Pedro claimed the total was over a hundred. He was sentenced to over four hundred years in prison. However, after thirty-four years, he was released. Claudia was astounded that he was able to be set free, but then again, she understood how the prison system in Brazil worked. After prison, he went to the city of Fortaleza in Ceará. He was arrested once again inside his home, where he worked as a housekeeper. This time the charge was for causing a riot and false imprisonment. To this day, some consider Little Peter the most notorious serial killer.

But Malestar was soon going to surpass him. She didn't quite understand his motivation, but she refused to believe he was killing and robbing for the sake of doing so. He was making a point, but what was it? Then again, it would be a waste of time trying to figure out a psychotic person. He was going to make a name for himself, regardless of the reason he was killing, and the police were helpless to stop him. Claudia knew there would be more bloodshed, and it wasn't going to stop anytime soon unless they could find him.

She closed the laptop and sighed. She had to admit to herself as much as she wanted Mauricio to walk away from this job and the criminal-hunting business, she wanted this man to be stopped. She figured she would feel a fair amount of guilt if they walked away now. With this being her home country, she felt responsible in some way, especially if she had the ability to help save innocent lives. That was part of the reason she liked this job, the fact she was doing something good. Was she being selfish by wanting to get away from it all, especially when there was a terrorizing psychopath wandering around?

There was one thing that stuck out in her mind about Malestar and what happened with Mauricio. He had kept him alive. Why? It seemed like he took great pleasure in killing people, and Mauricio would have been another victim. Was there a feeling of mutual respect or did Malestar see something in Mauricio that was similar to him? Whatever the reason, she was glad he didn't finish what he started, but still, it begged the question of the reason behind the madness. There had to be one. If she could somehow figure that out, as little as the chance may be, then maybe they could put a stop to the madness. She didn't know if Malestar would kill him if given the chance a second time, but the fact he kept Mauricio alive made her somewhat more comfortable about them staying on the chase.

Ultimately, it was Mauricio's call. His life was the one that would be on the line in a face-to-face situation. She decided right then and there to stop pressing him about leaving and go along with whatever he decided.

Claudia's cell phone began to vibrate. She picked it up on the bed and answered the call. "Hello?"

"I think I want out," Mauricio said, still standing on the roof of the downtown building.

Claudia couldn't have been happier, but she tried to hide the emotion in her voice. "If that's what you want to do."

"I'll say me and you escape all of this."

"Where?"

"Wherever you want to go," Mauricio replied.

"You won't get an argument from me," Claudia replied.

Mauricio smiled. "Love ya, babe."

"I love you too." Claudia ended the call, feeling joyous, and leaned back against the bed. She was in state of bliss, but then it was subdued. A new feeling of guilt set in, and she tried her best to suppress the emotion.

12.

One of the most popular landmarks in Salvador de Bahia, Brazil, is the Lacerda Elevator. The elevator leads up the mountain into a large corridor with plenty of windows for a panoramic visual of the picturesque harbor with the boats coming to shore and the nearby high-rise buildings. Inside the station where the corridor is located there is a small shop where some of the best ice cream in the city is served. It was there that Malestar, with a cap over his head and wearing a fake moustache, enjoyed a vanilla ice cream while looking off into the city.

A large and robust clean-shaven man who wore a navy blue business suit and was named Carlito stood next to him with a folder in hand. "The Corporation is very pleased with your work so far," he said.

He handed Malestar the folder. "Your next job is a company we've been meaning to hit for a very long time. Our cut will be the same, of course. You should find all the details you need to know as usual. Keep Vesco alive. He may be a nuisance, but he's our nuisance. We think we can bring him back."

"I'm getting very tired of your plans," Malestar said.

"Then I suggest you remember who let you go when you were found in Sao Paolo. We hired you not to ask questions but to make us all rich. Now, why ruin a good thing?"

Malestar turned to face him. "While you are sitting in your fancy offices with your fancy suits, there are kids running in the streets with their loyal purple, risking their lives every day so you can have money in your fat pockets. Does that seem right to you?"

"Why do you care?"

Malestar got in Carlito's face. "You tell the Corporation that Malestar doesn't want to play by the rules any longer. I make the rules from here on out. I strike when I want to strike, any place and any time. I dare you to stand in my way."

"The others are not going to like this," Carlito said.

"Why don't they try to stop me? This constant bossing around is really becoming a nuisance. Give me your hand."

"What?"

"Give me your hand," Malestar said with more demand. Carlito reluctantly offered his hand, and Malestar held it in his own right hand.

He closed his eyes and took a deep breath. "I can feel your energy. I can see your life flash before my eyes. I see a fat boy wandering around the school yard looking for friends, trying desperately to fit in. No one wants to talk to him. So he decides he will show them up one day, and get rich and get the respect he so desperately craves. Even though he is fairly successful, people in his field still do not give him the respect he deserves, and women resist him like the plague. And he doesn't realize it's the fact he reeks of desperation and a wretched existence."

Malestar took another deep breath. "I can just smell it on you."

Carlito quickly released his hand. "I'm not going to stand here and get belittled by a psychopath about being desperate. Everything you do is pathetic."

"Ah, to the contrary, my friend. I am in total control now. And please don't pretend that you are not like me. From now on, I'm doing things my way."

After his talk with Carlito, Malestar headed back to the slums in Alagados, entering the same building that the mercenaries had entered for the party they attended. This time, it was during the day, and most of the teenagers that worked for the Corporation were inside as Malestar stood on stage. The teenagers sat on the benches and listened attentively.

Malestar looked around the room and noticed that Fernanda, the over-six-foot Chilean woman that he had lured over with money, was standing amongst them. Fernanda was an expert assassin in her country, and her looks were just as deadly. She stood out amongst the teenage boys with her exposed midriff, black high-heeled boots, and bright red lipstick. The teenage boys knew better than to fawn over her because that most likely meant their last breath on earth. Malestar kept a mental note to himself to have a private meeting with her later. Until then, he looked around the room and waved his arms in the air.

"The time has come for us to take what belongs to us. The city will be ours. All this time, they've been trying to tell you how to feel, how to live, but this time we are going to decide for ourselves. There is infinite opportunity waiting for us out there. The police can't stop us, and the people of the city can't as well. That means that absolute freedom is yours for the taking. We are not going to let them dictate how we live anymore. This city is ours! Everyone else just doesn't know it yet."

There was a great amount of applause in the room. Fernanda stood without clapping, looking seductively at Malestar. She knew what she was doing, and Malestar was lying to himself, refusing to admit he liked it. He waited for the applause to die down before he spoke again.

"Now, we cannot waver and be afraid of what could happen to some of us. There is a price to pray for freedom and we should be willing to make the sacrifice. We are all brothers, and the memory of those fallen will only make us stronger. The time for us to rise is now. We will take over this city!"

Fernanda nodded to the hallway and took off in that direction.

"Be ready when the time comes. I will be looking for a new captain soon." Malestar got off the stage and headed toward the back hallway. He walked past the restrooms and headed toward the back room, which served as an office space.

Fernanda sat on top of the desk, facing the door with her panties fully exposed. Malestar could tell her by her face that she was under the influence of some type of drug. Who was he to tell what type of condition an assassin should be in? All he knew was that she was good for the job.

"You ever ask yourself why the good mayor never asked for you in their hunt for me?" Malestar asked in Spanish, closing the door.

"Why's that?"

"Because in the mind of the mayor and the people that he hired, there is a difference between an assassin and a mercenary. Do you know what that difference is?" Malestar asked as he walked up to her.

"I'm sure you are going to tell me," Fernanda replied.

"Motive. An assassin such as yourself may not do a job just for monetary reasons. You would do it for fun if you could, and you also would do it because you know my cause is worthy. You know the taking back of the city is a necessity. Also, hitmen, or hitwomen, in your case, are usually loyal to a side or cause and on retainer. As for a mercenary, they are hired to do a job, without any sort of patriotism for a cause, and kill only when necessary. They go back and forth as they please. He needed someone that would be loyal to the money. As for you, you are loyal to the cause."

"What makes you think I'm like you?" Fernanda asked.

"Oh, I know my own kind. In fact, there is a man in the mayor's pocket that is after me that is just like me too. He just doesn't know it yet."

Malestar began to run his fingers down her leg. Fernanda sat there, daring him to go further. "My living and breathing alter ego is out there. His name is Mauricio Campos. I want you to find him, and make sure he experiences pain. If you feel like killing others in the process, so be it."

"This sounds like something you'd very much like to do yourself."

"Yes, but I'm preoccupied for the time being. You will be better served to take my place."

"You do know my asking price," Fernanda said.

"Yes, and I am willing to pay."

Fernanda placed her hand against Malestar's chest and ran her fingers down. "You do know you're playing with fire, right?"

"You must think I'm a fool for trying to do what is against the wishes of the Corporation. But there is a new king now, and I am claiming my throne."

"Well, it looks like I have a job to do," Fernanda said, getting down from the desk. Malestar grabbed her arm.

"No excuses. Get me what I want," he said.

"I will die trying," Fernanda said, and left the room.

She headed back to her car, a beat-up maroon sedan, and opened the trunk. Inside was a wide selection of weapons, from axes to guns. She took out two guns and placed them on the gun holder that she also used as her suspenders. She closed the trunk and climbed into the car, taking out a pack of cigarettes that was in the glove compartment. Fernanda took out a cigarette, lit it with the lighter inside the compartment, and took a long smoke. It was a habit of hers to be calm and smoke before she made a kill.

She had heard of Mauricio Campos. The mercenary had made quite the name for himself. Even in Chile, she had heard of his reputation as a man that always got his target. Of course, only those that hunted men and women knew about him. They said he always found his target, and one time, spent three days in the Sahara to track his man and bring him back dead. This was not a man to take lightly. However, Fernanda was confident enough in her skills to think that she had a chance.

There were many ruthless men out there, and from what she knew of Mauricio, he was a mild-mannered, logical individual. He didn't go out of his way to be cruel. Maybe she could find a way to seduce him rather than outright attack him. Seduction was always the best tool to get close to men. If that didn't work, then she would just go about her business the old-fashioned way. Every man had a weak spot, and she only had to find what his was. When she worked in Chile, she was often hired to lure men into bed using her sexual nature and to have them in compromising positions, often naked and slobbering on her neck. That was when she would kill them, and it would be all so easy. Sometimes men thought with the wrong head.

Fernanda closed the door, started the engine, and pulled away from her parking space. This was the part of the job she loved the most—the hunt for her target. There was no other feeling like it, and that made the danger of being killed in the process worth the risk.

Soon after Fernanda left, Carlito entered the office. Malestar was sitting behind the desk, checking his cell phone for messages. Carlito took a seat and waited for him to finish. Malestar took his time, and seemed not to be paying any attention to the man sitting down in front of him. Carlito cleared his throat.

"What do you want?" Malestar asked, without looking up.

"You're making a mistake."

"You came all this way to tell me that?"

"The Corporation has been around for years. It's not going to fold down because of one man. That said, I understand your need to try to take over, but the world does not work like that. I am willing to go back to them and tell them that you need our manpower to make more attacks on the city. I'll do my best to convince them."

Malestar turned his head to look at Carlito. "If you haven't noticed, I already have your precious manpower under my control. They belong to me now. I suggest you sit back and enjoy the show."

Carlito sighed. "We hired someone like you, once. A man intent on destroying the world and killing everything innocent to teach everyone a lesson. A complete maniac, in my opinion. Didn't like authority too well, but did so in order to get what he really wanted, and have the access and money to truly fulfill whatever sick desire that was in his head, as long as it was in accordance with what the Corporation wanted. Everything was perfect until he decided he wanted more. He wanted the control. I don't have to tell you that the Corporation wasn't pleased. They sent the best men after him, and he ended up in a box, cut into enough pieces where they couldn't tell the head from the feet. I'm sure you don't want to share the same fate."

Malestar nodded, and got up to sit on top of the desk in front of Carlito. "Since you like telling stories, let me tell you a story. I have killed a lot of people in my life, but as a youth, I was timid about taking out someone with importance or of the law. After all, their death meant a powerful organization would soon come after me and seek retaliation. But I didn't care. I wanted their blood. So I chose my first victim, a police officer who had connections with some very important people. I started by cutting off his limbs, and kept him alive as long as I could. I enjoy the look of pain on their faces. To me, that makes people real, and it shows me that they are really alive. Sometimes I sing the song my sister used to sing. That song used to drive me crazy! Death comes for us all, and we don't appreciate how soon it can come until it hits. If anything, I'm making people appreciate life more.

To my surprise, law enforcement looked the other way. You want to know why they did that?"

"I suppose they feared you in some way."

"Oh no, nothing like that. They risked their lives every day. That's the nature of their jobs. What kept them in line is that they were afraid of what I would do to their families. Little boys, girls, it didn't matter. I will kill them all and send you their tongues after they screamed. For instance, I know you have a little boy…"

Carlito stood up. "The Corporation will not tolerate the works of a madman on his own!"

Malestar quickly grabbed Carlito by the throat until his face became red. He began to recall his sister's song, and the music played in his head. Carlito could only manage to stare at Malestar's face, and the one eyelid that drooped in front of him.

Malestar began to sing. "There his Master comes, what it does what he says, then the boss comes, saying what it does. Oh! There the angry one comes!"

Carlito was losing air quickly. Malestar began to laugh. Right when he knew Carlito was on the verge of death, he released his hands and Carlito gasped for air and held onto his neck. Malestar laughed harder now.

"Now wasn't that fun! You see, we could have so much fun together! All you have to do is know your role. The Corporation is mine now. If you want to stay alive, it's in your best interest to remember that. From now on, I'm your boss. I want you to address me as so. Do it!"

"Patrão." Carlito, still gasping, could barely get the word out.

"Good, good," Malestar said, running his fingers through Carlito's hair. "See, only in death do you appreciate it. Now you value your life more than ever. I don't at all, but it's good that you do."

Malestar made his way back behind the desk and took a seat. "Now, is there anything else I can help you with?"

Carlito got up, still making gasping noises as he left the room. Malestar couldn't help but grin. He knew this day would come. He had always wanted to give in to his urges, and his desire to take over the city, but his intelligence told him he had to wait for the perfect time, until he had control over the pawns of the Corporation. He knew once he did that, the power belonged to him. Now he was going to attack the city in any way he wanted, and they would discover the pain that they tried to run away from.

13.

Recife/Guararapes-Gilberto Freyre International Airport was a modern airport which was customer friendly, clean, and close to the city. Mauricio and Claudia stood on one of the winding elevators that went down, on their way to the southern line of the MetroRec subway system that led downtown. Claudia held Mauricio's hand, even though he wasn't the biggest fan of affection in public places. Both of their free hands were carrying their luggage. They made their way to the train, and Claudia noticed Mauricio kept looking around. She squeezed her hand against his tighter, and he flashed a smile. He knew that meant to relax.

They waited at the platform for the train to arrive. The station was clean, with maroon floors and silver ceilings, and advertisements that lined up the back walls. A guard in a black cap and white dress shirt walked amongst the crowd. It was fairly crowded on the platform, and Mauricio and Claudia had to move their way through the throng to get to the front of those waiting.

There was a reason Claudia had chosen the city of Recife to visit. That she had family there was the most important. An uncle lived in the city, and just seeing some sort of family would make her feel more at ease. Another reason was the city itself. Recife was the largest metropolitan area in the northeast region of Brazil, with beautiful beaches and lots of rich culture. Claudia was also excited about going to the Shopping Center Recife, a megamall in the city with plenty of opportunities to spend their hard-earned money.

Growing up in a poor neighborhood in Fortaleza, Claudia had always fantasized about the nicer things in life, and wished to have the clothes and jewelry of the older girls walking the streets. She knew what they were, escorts for the drug dealers in the area. Still, it was human nature to want they had, even though she knew the way they obtained it was not for her. She used to date boys that wanted the finer lifestyle and had dreams to do so, no matter how misguided. By the time she had reached college, though, those thoughts were fading away and she wanted to talk only to people with substance.

She realized a long time ago that poverty in this country wasn't going away anytime soon, and probably never would. She felt guilty sometimes when she bought nice things while other people were suffering and struggling to survive, especially since she had firsthand experience of poverty herself. Then she realized that she shouldn't feel guilty about her success, but always find a way to give back. The poor had it twice as hard and she wanted to give a helping hand when she could. She felt like it was her responsibility in a way, and there was a sense of urgency deep down in her to give back to the community.

However, Claudia couldn't help but to feel a sense of relief at this moment. She had gotten Mauricio away from his job, and even though she had done that before, she hoped this time it was permanently. This time she felt like he was sincere about what he said, and he meant it. They could start a new life and try to escape the constant violence that was around them.

The train doors opened, and Mauricio and Claudia entered. They found empty seating in the right corner and took a seat. Mauricio couldn't resist looking at all the passengers hurriedly coming aboard. There was a wide range of people, from elderly couples to grandchildren. One man who looked like a transient entered alongside a woman that was almost as tall as the homeless man, perhaps taller with heels. Mauricio sat back in his seat and tried to relax.

He had spent most of his life doing this type of work, and it scared him to try to do something else. He had money put away so that they would be good for a while, but he couldn't spend time at home doing nothing all day. What could his skill set be used for? Perhaps he could do some contract work where he wasn't the one hunting. Maybe he was going to look for missing dogs all day. Mauricio sighed, knowing most of the action and danger was going to be gone from his life.

The tall woman that had boarded the train had sat three seats in front of him and now was looking back at him. He could see that she had eyes of seduction. Did she not see that he was sitting right next to his girlfriend? She was an attractive woman, with short hair and smoky eyes, but something about her signified that she was dangerous. She had the aura of pure confidence as she bit her bottom lip. She was going out of her way to be noticed, and Mauricio now felt like he was a target to be played.

Claudia placed her head on Mauricio's shoulder. The train began to move and the lady turned her head back around to face the front. Mauricio was at ease and thought about how much he liked trains. He still had the memories from his youth and that filled his head with joyous nostalgia.

As a child, Mauricio remembered being with his parents on a train somewhere in Africa, and looking out the window to see the scenery. He saw a herd of elephants in the distance. Mauricio remembered asking his father how the elephants communicated. His father told him it was through infrasound, and then explained the process. Apparently, it involved a low-frequency sound that is less than twenty Hertz, and for humans to perceive such a sound, the sound pressure must be unusually high. The sound could be carried through the ground and felt by the feet of other herds. Also, humans' eardrums could be hurt if such a sound was released even if the humans didn't actually hear the sound. Mauricio did not understand this until he was much older.

That was when he experienced his first explosion and could feel his ears ringing long after the explosion. The sound used by some animals was being experienced by a human. Mauricio didn't think there was that much of a difference between the human race and animals when it came to instincts. Every living creature on this earth had needs and desires they wanted to be fulfilled. However, there was no moral compass in the animal kingdom. For years, that was the way he approached his job. There was no right or wrong, but only a need for survival.

However, there was a reason humans did not hear the infrasound. There was a clear separation between living creatures as much as there was a link. We were supposed to be thinkers, capable of seeing the big picture, and doing what was right for the entire animal kingdom as a whole. It was our responsibility. If we wanted to survive, we had to be better animals, better people.

And so on a train in Africa he was given a lesson. Mankind was both instinctive and intellectual. Those that did not contribute to the betterment of mankind were branded as crazy or outcasts. But Mauricio didn't find them any crazier than the lion that went after its prey. They had the thirst to kill and take what they wanted. That didn't make them wrong because they chose a different value system, but rather partakers in the origin of life. Mauricio had always entertained the thought of all of them living on reserved land that was designed for anarchy, where they could kill and steal from each other as they pleased. You didn't want to be a part of society, fine, but don't ask for its protection either.

The train was slowing down as it approached the next stop, Tancredo Neves, named after a popular, former politician. Some of the passengers rose to get off the train, and Mauricio noticed the woman did not get up, but turned her head to see if he was still there. Mauricio stared directly at her, and she forced a smile. Mauricio knew at that moment that this was beyond innocent flirting.

Mauricio turned her head to whisper into Claudia's ear. "We're getting off at the next stop," he said.

"We're there already?"

"No, but we have trouble. You go first, and take the luggage."

"Okay." Claudia knew better than to look around.

The passengers unloaded and more passengers came on. The doors closed, and soon after, the train began to move again. The tall woman never took her gaze off of Mauricio. The smile had faded away. Claudia leaned up off of Mauricio's shoulder and casually reached for the luggage next to their feet. The woman took notice and got out of her seat to approach them.

"Stay calm," Mauricio stated. "Wait for me at the hotel."

Fernanda made her way over to Mauricio, and then leaned over his seat. "Excuse me, I couldn't help but notice you looking at me," she said.

"That's because you were looking at me."

"Do I know you from somewhere?" she asked.

"He's taken," Claudia replied.

"That's a shame. You look like a man that knows what he wants, and I saw you looking at me. You can have what you want, you know."

"I'll pass," Mauricio replied.

"I can tell when a man has desire in his eyes," Fernanda stated. "A man can only be with one woman for so long. They get an itch that needs to be scratched. Otherwise, they would go mad. You must be a sad man, and I bet she's always nagging about something. I promise you, if you came with me tonight, you could have your way with me. I like to be handcuffed against the bed. I can please you in ways you can't imagine."

Mauricio looked her over. He had to admit that she was well built, with tight jeans with slits to show skin, and black boots with rhinestones on the straps. She smelled of sweet jasmine, and she bent over so he could get a good glimpse of her cleavage. Claudia was about to get up to attack her, but Mauricio placed a hand in front of her.

"Back off," Claudia demanded.

"She's cute, I'll give you that, but put her back on the leash before she gets bit."

"He doesn't want you," Claudia stated.

"Well, let's let the man decide."

"No, thank you," Mauricio replied.

This didn't happen too often, and Fernanda did not appreciate rejection, especially from a man she found somewhat handsome. She stood up straight. "Well, you're coming with me whether you like it or not."

Mauricio laughed, and stood up himself. The train began to slow down again for the next stop. Fernanda figured it was time to make her move now. She reached for her guns as Mauricio pushed her against her shoulders. She fell down, and Mauricio turned to Claudia.

"Go, now!" he shouted.

The doors to the train opened. Claudia ran out. Fernanda reached for her gun on the right side, and Mauricio kicked the gun out of her hand. Passengers began to see what was going on and quickly left the cart or the train itself. Fernanda grabbed Mauricio's leg and forced him to the ground.

Relying on her ground training that her former boyfriend taught her, she wrapped her legs around his neck and began to squeeze. Then she tried to take hold of his left arm. Mauricio held her off, and felt his circulation cutting off. He used the remaining strength he had and rose to his feet with Fernanda on his back. She tried to squeeze harder as Mauricio swung his body around. He was losing air quickly. He collapsed against the glass window of the train and Fernanda went crashing out the window, landing on the platform with Mauricio on top of her.

The train doors began to close. A crowd started to gather around. Mauricio and Fernanda were both immobilized in their pain. Fernanda got out from under Mauricio and was about to attack him again when a guard arrived on the scene.

"What's going on here?" he asked.

Fernanda turned around to strike him. The guard grabbed her arm in the process. She kneed him in the groin. He bent over, and Fernanda took out the baton from his belt. She bashed him in the face with it, knocking out a few of his teeth, and he fell to the ground. She kicked him a few times in the stomach to reinforce her power over him. Then she realized she was indulging in the moment. Fernanda turned around to find Mauricio gone.

Mauricio sprinted onto the street as Fernanda went after him. There was a crowd of people outside the train stop and she lost him for a moment. Fernanda fired one shot in the air, and the crowd immediately dispersed. Mauricio ran across the street onto incoming traffic and almost got hit by a compact white car that braked hard. Mauricio went to the driver's side and banged against the window. The driver put the car in park, stepped out, and shouted at Mauricio in Portuguese. Mauricio pushed him aside and got into the car. The man began to argue some more.

Fernanda aimed her weapon in that direction and began firing. A bullet landed between the man's eyes, and he fell back. People began to scream and run. Mauricio put the car in reverse and backed away from the street, crashing into other cars along the way. Fernanda fired her gun once more, and the bullet landed against the front window, shattering the glasses, the bullet flying inches from Mauricio's head.

Fernanda cursed out loud and ran toward the motorcycle that had stopped during the commotion. She pressed her gun against the driver's head, and he swiftly abandoned the bike. Fernanda got on the bike, placed her gun in her holster, and turned it around to follow the car Mauricio had driven off in.

She accelerated down the street and swerved through traffic to catch up to the car. Mauricio looked through the rearview mirror to see Fernanda approaching. He sped and weaved through the traffic ahead of him, but Fernanda managed to move through traffic more efficiently. She caught up to his car and pulled up to the driver's side. She withdrew her weapon and aimed it toward the car. Mauricio sped up as she fired. The bullet missed, and Mauricio turned the corner.

Fernanda made her way onto the other lane, which was incoming traffic, to catch up. She got in between the two lanes of cars coming in her direction, amidst plenty of honking horns, and then crossed the center divider to make her way right behind Mauricio's car. She fired again and shattered his back window. Mauricio kept his head low and increased his speed, tapping the bumper of the car in front of him, which made the car move out the way. Mauricio continued to weave through traffic, and Fernanda followed. He made his way to a bridge over the Capibaribe River.

By now the police had picked up on the speeding. A row of police cars had their sirens on and traffic began to disperse in their presence. The police cars made their way behind Fernanda on her motorcycle. Fernanda fired her remaining bullets in their direction. The police cars began to maneuver to the side of her to surround her motorcycle as Mauricio passed other cars and got off the bridge. Fernanda didn't have any other option. She slowed to a stop and the police parked their cars and pointed their weapons at her. She kept her hands in the air as they shouted demands.

Mauricio pulled over to the side of the road and abandoned the car. He jogged down the street, looking back to make sure no one was following him. He was angry at himself for being careless and not realizing that he was marked. He knew then and there that as long as Malestar was alive he wasn't going to have a true vacation.

14.

The detectives swarmed around her in the isolated room inside the police department that they used for interrogating purposes. Fernanda found their attempt to get information out of her somewhat entertaining. She followed them with her eyes as they moved around the room. There were three of them, two medium built, one heavyset. They were all of middle age and smelled of musk. They would rotate with their questions.

"What are you doing in this city?"

"Who do you work for?"

"What did you want with the man driving?"

Fernanda asked for a cigarette. One of the detectives reached out, placed one in her mouth, and lit it for her.

She took a long drag before she began to speak in Spanish.

"I've been to a lot of countries in South America, and some of the finest cities, and met lots of people along the way."

She took another smoke. "But you guys have to be the most idiotic men I have ever met."

"You show us respect," the man said, taking the cigarette away from her mouth.

'I wasn't done with that," Fernanda stated.

"Too bad."

Fernanda stabbed him in the foot with the heel of her shoe, and the man shouted in pain. She then followed that with an uppercut to his chin and he was out cold. The other two men began to attack. They swung wildly, and she blocked most of their swings, with one striking her on the side of the face. She grabbed a hold of the man that struck her by the arm, and pulled it back the other way. He shouted in pain. The other detective tried to swing at her, and she took hold of his neck, and quickly turned the side of his face to crack his neck. He fell, and Fernanda approached the only man standing, the one with the broken arm.

He backed into a corner. "Please, don't."

Fernanda ran her fingers down his chest, and then grabbed his crotch. She squeezed as hard as she could.

The man fell to his knees. Fernanda took the keys from his pocket and left the room.

She made her way through the police department discreetly, passing only an officer and offering him a smile. Then she headed to the parking, lot where she pressed the button on the keychain to find out which car belonged to the detective. The alarm sound came from a black, beat up sedan in the corner of the lot. She smiled, and headed in that direction.

*

Mauricio arrived at the hotel room to find Claudia pacing inside. She immediately gave him a hug as he walked through the door. Mauricio closed the door and she wouldn't let go of her grip around his waist.

"I was worried about you," she said.

"I thought you knew me better than that," Mauricio replied, and Claudia gave him a slow, sensual kiss.

Mauricio picked her up and she wrapped her legs around his waist. Mauricio carried her and placed her against the hotel wall, where Claudia began to unbutton his shirt. Mauricio pulled down her jean shorts. She carried her weight backward and Mauricio backpedaled and fell on the bed. They began to remove each other's clothes piece by piece. Claudia moaned as Mauricio explored her body with his tongue. She closed her eyes and held on to the bed cover. As Mauricio ravished her body, she could feel his body pulsating as it touched up against her. She wanted him inside of her now.

Moments later, he was. Claudia let out a moan she was sure the neighbor in the next room could hear, but she didn't care. Mauricio picked up the pace in his grinding and she felt like she was in heaven. She closed her eyes and enjoyed the warmth that filled her body.

Mauricio lay shirtless on the bed with a nude Claudia by his side touching his chest with a smile on her face. She wished all of life could be in this serene moment. In her entire lifetime, she had never felt the passion like she did with the man lying next to her. She had doubt she ever would, too.

When Mauricio first approached her, she was younger, naïve, and had a clear distinction of what was right and what was wrong. Now the lines were blurred. Mauricio told her what he did for a living, and at first she was appalled at his profession. How could he kill people for a living? Didn't he have a conscience? Yes, the government often played judge and executioner but that didn't give him the right to do so as well. She thought he was a wicked man and she should get him out her life as fast as he could.

She continued her work as a waitress at the restaurant that Mauricio visited every morning. She would ignore him at first, but he always sat at the stools in front and ordered the same meal—a double espresso, a *queijo de coalho* (grilled cheese), and some fresh fruit. He would smile at her, and she would walk away, trying to get other waitresses to bring him his meal. They teased her and told her to do it herself. Reluctantly she would, and he would make small talk with her. She didn't want to be rude so she engaged in conversation with him.

He didn't say much at first. He talked about how much he loved the Brazilian culture, and that this was his mother's native country, and what were some of the best places to go in the city. Claudia found him to be likeable, but not sociable. She was the same way, and with each passing day that he came in, she became more attracted to him.

Then she got to know him as a person as he continued to pursue her. She found him to be charming, nice, and well cultured. He knew a lot about current events, and he was always straightforward with her. She liked that. There was never a dull moment with him and he never pretended to be something he wasn't. Little by little, she began to open up as well, and after the first time they made love, she was hooked.

Now he was her lover, friend, and her confidant. He had flaws like anyone else, but she loved the man and that's all that mattered to her. Lying next to him felt like time had frozen. She looked at Mauricio and he seemed worried.

"What's wrong?" she asked.

"We can't have a future unless we erase our past."

"So what happened with that woman?"

"The police took her down, but that's not the point. Someone is on to us. Either Malestar, or Vesco, the deal he made with us."

"I'm not scared."

Mauricio turned to face her. "Oh yeah, and why's that?"

"I know you'll think of something."

"No pressure," Mauricio replied. "It seems the predator has become the prey. I'm not willing to be on the run the rest of my life. We have to fight this head on. I'm going to draw them out and see what they know."

"And I take it you just want me to sit here and wonder if you'll ever come back to me again. I wanted to see my uncle."

"You said it yourself that you weren't scared," Mauricio said, and kissed her on her forehead.

"If it has to be done, then it has to be done. I want a future, love."

"Then I'll just do what I do best," Mauricio replied.

Claudia gave him a kiss, got up, and headed to the bathroom. He loved to see her walk away, and watched her backside as she left. Moments later, Mauricio could hear the shower water running. He got up, got dressed, and reached into the desk drawer near the bed to take out a pad and pen. He wrote a note to Claudia that he would be back soon. Then he left the room and headed toward the lobby.

On second thought, he went back inside and entered the restaurant inside the hotel. He walked past the double doors to the kitchen, where the cooks quickly shot him confused looks. Mauricio ignored them, looked around, found a cutting knife, placed it in his pocket, and proceeded out. He dared someone to try to stop him from leaving.

He began to wonder how he had been found. Did they put some type of tracking device on him? Mauricio checked his phone. He was sure it was giving off a signal that Malestar had placed inside. He was about to open the phone when he paused. On second thought, he wanted to be found.

Mauricio made his way back to the lobby and out the front doors. Aurora Street was crowded as small businesses lined the streets and heavy traffic was on the road, including many buses that were filled with passengers. Mauricio looked amongst the waves of people moving about. Any one of them could be after him. He didn't like being on the other side of the equation. He knew all the tricks of blending in a crowd and hunting down his prey. In fact, his opinion was that he had mastered the trade. Now that he was on the other side, he realized the chilling feeling that someone was always watching him, and using the best opportunity to kill him.

Stay in a public setting, he thought to himself. He knew some contract killers that preferred public places to make their kills, as it often led to commotion that made it easier to escape in the crowd. On the other hand, it made things messier, especially if you missed. Then if you did flee, there was opportunity for witnesses to place you at the crime scene. In his opinion, it wasn't worth the risk unless it was properly planned ahead of time. On-the-spot assassination just wasn't smart. Now the trick was to bring out the assassin in his view, as the best option for them was to be to follow him until he was vulnerable.

The woman on the train had been stopped by the police, but Mauricio didn't count her out. Were there more like her after him? He now figured it was Malestar that sent her here. Now it was assassins against assassins. Mauricio respected the danger he was facing because he was one himself. The semantics of labels didn't matter to him. They all killed people, got paid for it, and were experts at making it clean.

Mauricio walked further down the street until he came across a small clothing store on the corner. He went inside and pretended to browse the aisle of jeans as he kept glancing at the entrance to the store. Pedestrians continued to walk down the street and walk by the glass window in front. A store clerk, a young woman with curly hair and hazel skin, approached him.

"*Você precisa de ajuda?*" she asked.

Mauricio dismissed her with a wave of his hand. The woman was blocking his view. She walked away, and Mauricio looked out into the street again. Everyone seemed to have their eyes forward or they were moving about in a normal fashion. Mauricio was beginning to think this exercise was futile. He was about to head back outside when he spotted her.

The same woman from the train was across the street and walking in his direction. It had to be the phone. Mauricio took out his cell phone and removed the chip that was in the back compartment as she approached the store. He placed the chip inside a pair of jeans as Fernanda entered the store. She looked professional in a suit jacket, slacks, and high heels. He understood most assassins took their jobs very seriously and considered themselves professionals, often dressing like one as well. He did the same when he was out looking for targets, unless the situation called for blending in with the environment.

She saw him right away as he stood in the back. She scanned the store as any good assassin would, to determine how clean of a hit she had. Mauricio could see on her face she thought there were too many customers inside. Fernanda casually made her way over with a smile on her face.

Mauricio could feel his adrenaline rising. Was it from her physical appearance or the fact she was dangerous? Either way, he had to keep his guard up if he wanted to survive. The second he started thinking with the wrong head, the second he was dead. Fernanda flashed that seductive smile he guessed had worked on plenty of men.

"We meet again," she said in English.

"I couldn't pass up a chance to get to know you better," Mauricio replied.

"So you wish to dance? We both know what I'm here for, and we both know that you are just as skilled at what you do. So let's stop pretending. How about you be a gentleman and let the woman go first?"

Mauricio grinned. "I know a lady like you."

"Oh yeah?"

"Deadly looks, nice body, uses it to throw someone's game off, and then rips his heart out at the right opportunity. It actually has been happening for years. You just kill people when you are done."

"A girl has to make a living."

"I bet you ripped the heads of your dolls when you were younger."

"You're wrong. I played with toy guns. I wanted to be like my father, who was good with a weapon. Never got his expertise in long-range shooting, but that didn't matter, because I like it close and personal."

"I bet you do," Mauricio replied. "Tell me, do you even enjoy sex or is all of this some sick, twisted game for you?"

"I enjoy it like any other woman. Even more, I would say. However, I get an even better feeling from killing people. It's such a thrill. I'm sure you feel the same way."

"I'm nothing like you," Mauricio replied.

"I bet you said the same thing to Malestar when he cut you up. You're just denying it. You know you like it the same way I do. The rush you get from the life being taken away from them is irreplaceable. You wouldn't do this job if you felt otherwise. Now you tell me, why do you keep denying who you truly are?"

"Why don't you just use your gun to stimulate yourself and get off that way?"

Fernanda smiled. "I like you. It's going to be a shame to kill you. How about I'll make you a deal? I'll give you one night with me, and then you let me have my way."

"You crave me, don't you?"

"You're giving yourself too much credit. I could have any man I want, although there's something about you that entices me. I think it's the fact that beneath the surface you're nicer than most men in this profession. You won't believe how hard it is to get a date when you tell people you're a professional killer."

"That can be a deal breaker," Mauricio replied.

"One night with you could be spectacular, but I regret to inform you that by the end of the night, I still have a job to do."

"You're not going to kill me," Mauricio replied.

"And why is that?"

"Because if I know Malestar, he wants me alive. The sick bastard wants to see me in pain."

Fernanda got closer to Mauricio as if she was going to kiss him. Then she turned her head to whisper into his ear. She still had that addicting perfume on, but now he could smell a hint of sweat.

"You're smart, but not smart enough," she said. "You're right. He does want to see you in pain. Do you know we tracked you to the hotel you are staying in?"

"Claudia," Mauricio said.

Fernanda grabbed his arm before he had a chance to run. "I already sent locals to finish the job. Now, if you come with me..."

Mauricio stabbed in her the abdomen with the knife he had hidden in his hand that he got from the hotel kitchen. Fernanda's face showed surprise as she held on to her wound. She collapsed to the ground and Mauricio ran out of the store.

He began to run back toward the hotel as fast as he could. The thought of Claudia in danger terrified and angered him at the same time. He couldn't lose Claudia, the only person that mattered to him.

After she got out of the shower, Claudia got dressed and placed on some makeup for the rest of the day. It was late in the afternoon now and she realized she hadn't really eaten anything all day. She thought about ordering room service but never liked paying for overpriced food. Perhaps she could wait until Mauricio came back. She had read the note that he left, but it didn't specify when he would return. She decided she would wait and opened up the balcony window to get some fresh air.

*

Back at the store, Fernanda was losing a lot of blood. The manager called for an ambulance as she lay on the ground, still holding the stab wound and blood pouring out at a furious rate. She used the remaining strength she had to stay alive. She told herself she couldn't go out like this. Yes, he was a worthy man to be killed by, but not by a stab wound. She was going to get revenge, even if it killed her.

Fernanda tried to stand up, but ended up falling back to the ground, slipping on her own blood. Customers in the store pleaded with her to stay where she was. Then they noticed the two guns on her suspenders underneath her suit jacket. They backed away immediately. Fernanda began to drag herself toward the door as the ambulances raced down the street.

*

Claudia stepped on the balcony, and from the third floor she could see the busy street below. This city was a lot different than Salvador, always busy, with people anxious to get to their next destination. She could hear cars honking as pedestrians crossed the street without waiting for traffic lights to signal the cars to stop. She turned her head to see a man running down the street.

Wait, wasn't that Mauricio? There was knocking against the hotel door. That *was* Mauricio down there.

Instantly, Claudia knew she was in danger. She quickly put all the items she had left out inside the suitcases and brought them to the balcony. Mauricio had now spotted her. Claudia tossed the suitcases over as Mauricio collected them.

"Get out of there!" Mauricio shouted.

Claudia gauged that the jump was too high for her not to get injured. The door to the hotel room burst open. Two men stood at the doorway with guns drawn, and their infrared beams placed across Claudia's face. She dared not move.

"Claudia!" Mauricio shouted from below. "Claudia!"

15.

Mauricio dropped the luggage and headed inside the hotel. He jetted across the lobby and toward the staircase. A few curious heads turned his way as he did so. He didn't care. All he wanted was a chance to save the love of his life.

"Now, let's talk about this," Claudia said, placing her hands in front of her as the two men stood before her with their guns drawn. One of the men searched the bathroom to make sure no one else was in the room. When he was convinced there wasn't, he made his way back to the other gunman.

"You don't want to do this," Claudia said. "I'm more valuable alive. I can lead you to where he is. Just put the guns down."

Mauricio continued to run up the stairs, his heart racing, and his thoughts going all over the place. He didn't want to think the worst. He was almost there, and finally found himself on the hallway floor.

"Please," Claudia said, tears now falling from her eyes. "Just put the guns down."

Mauricio was now running down the hallway but stopped in his tracks when he heard the sound of gunshots. He knew what transpired. He ran faster toward the room, and he wasn't thinking about how he would defend himself. He didn't care. He had to help Claudia in any way he could.

Two men in suits came out of his hotel room, putting their guns away. They saw Mauricio, smiled, and casually walked away. They knew there was nothing he could do. Mauricio dashed inside the room and immediately looked for her. She was nowhere to be found. He made his way to the balcony and looked down. Below was Claudia, her body disfigured and lying in a pool of blood.

Mauricio fell to his knees. The moment was surreal at first, but then the image of her body sunk into his thoughts. He felt his entire world come crashing down. He didn't want to see tomorrow, another minute, another second. He wanted to lay with her and wanted those bullets for him. He didn't want to live, and he bowed his head in sadness and grief.

*

The whistling kettle signified that the tea was ready. Ramon, dressed in his wooly vest and slacks, made his way to the kitchen inside his tiny apartment while taking a break from writing. At one point in his career, he was an accomplished writer sought by every newspaper in town, but now he was struggling to find work. He lived alone with his two cats, and spent most of his time inside his apartment. He was a private man, with no ambition for sharing his life with anyone else.

He reached into the cupboard to get a cup when he heard the doorbell ring. Ramon went to the door and looked through the peephole. A man he had never seen before stood outside. Ramon didn't know if he should open the door or not. There were two types of people he would never open the door for—criminals and cops. The man looked neither, but Ramon had to be sure.

"Who are you and why are you here?" Ramon asked in Portuguese.

"I don't speak Portuguese."

Ramon recognized the English language, and was fluent in it from his studies at school. What was an American doing at his door? It had been years since he had befriended one, and not enough for them to come to his house.

"I'm here because of Claudia."

Ramon opened the door to see Mauricio standing in the doorway. "Come in," he said.

Mauricio walked inside the small apartment and waited for Ramon in the entryway. Ramon closed the door and turned to face Mauricio. "I haven't heard from my niece in years. How is she doing?"

"She's dead," Mauricio replied.

Ramon was stunned by his reply. "Let's sit," he said, and led the way to the sofa in the living room. They both sat. Then Ramon remembered he had tea on the stove.

"Would you like some tea?" he asked as he rose and made his way toward the kitchen.

"No," Mauricio said, trying to hold back his emotions. The sadness had returned, and just mentioning Claudia was enough to draw tears.

Ramon poured himself a cup of tea, and when he returned, he could see tears forming in Mauricio's eyes. "You loved her," he said as he sat down.

"Yes," Mauricio replied. "Very much so."

"I haven't talked to her in so long. From what I remember of her, she was such a smart young woman who treated people kindly. She had a rough upbringing, you know. She was trying her best to make it in this world like everyone else. May she rest in peace."

"It's all my fault," Mauricio said, tears coming down his eyes. He hadn't cried in years, and each tear opened its way to more sadness. "I put her in danger's way. I tried to save her. But I should have never left her alone in the first place. She would still be here if it wasn't for me. I should have never been in her life. I loved her. I loved her so much."

"Sometimes things happen for a reason, son. I'm sure she loved the time she spent with you."

"I'm sorry for this," Mauricio said, standing up and wiping his tears. Now he felt anger rush through his body. "But the people that killed her will pay. I will get vengeance. I want them all dead, each and every one of them. They will suffer by my hands!"

Ramon leaned back in his chair, and stayed calm. "Have a seat, son." Mauricio saw down and saw that his hands were shaking.

"I've seen this happen before. I am saddened by the news as well, but you cannot let anger cloud your mind. Once you enter the world of darkness, it is hard to control and escape it. My advice is that you let it go. Anger will not bring her back."

"The people that did this, they will not stop hurting me unless I fight back. I have to do something."

Ramon thought about what he said for a moment, and then went to the armoire across from the sofa. He opened it up and took out a small wooden box. From inside it he took out a key and handed it to Mauricio.

"Take this. It's a key to a small villa I have on the island on Itamaracá. It used to be a great place for writing for me, but not lately. Stay there until you figure out what you want to do. You are not ready for the world right now."

"Thank you," Mauricio replied.

Ramon took a seat again. "I don't need your name because it doesn't matter. I don't want to ask what your profession is, but my guess is that it deals with something on the criminal side. Now, if there are people after you like you say there are, I would like for you to never come here again, unless you are returning the key. No offense."

"None taken."

"Her father wanted her as far away from that criminal lifestyle as possible, even though he was a part of it himself. Did she speak much of him?"

"Not much at all," Mauricio replied.

"He treated her like a princess. However, he kept her humble and couldn't afford much. He wasn't making much in the stealing ring he was a part of. You see, my parents had two sons, and only one got intelligence. The other had looks. Me and her father never got along much. I moved away at the first chance I could get and became a middling writer. He continued the side jobs he did, and eventually got caught. He ended up in prison with a lengthy term. Didn't get to live out his sentence as he was stabbed on the inside."

"She just told me that he was out of her life."

"Sometimes it's better to think of people in that way. The best thing he ever did was stay away."

Mauricio nodded in agreement. "Well, just to let you know, there's no will, and nothing to give to you or to anyone else. They will probably send whatever was on her to you. She wasn't a woman that got attached to materialistic wealth. She left me only with memories."

"No one can take those away from you. That's all I have from the past. I wasn't close to my family, but I will tell you this. There will be a time where you will fall in love again. You might not believe me, but it can very well happen. And when you do, don't let it go, or it will be the biggest regret you ever made."

"Something to think about, I suppose. Well, I wasted enough of your time," Mauricio said, standing up.

"Not a waste. This is not joyful news, but it's something I should know."

"You're a very wise man. If it's any consolation, she was excited about seeing you again. Part of the reason we came here was to see the only family she said had a good head on their shoulders. We thought this would be the place that we would start a new life together."

"When a chapter ends, a new one begins," Ramon said.

"That's what they say," Mauricio said as he headed toward the door. He opened the door, and Ramon stood up to go to the hallway and see him out.

Mauricio left the apartment, and Ramon closed and locked the door behind him. He stood at the door for a moment, and then headed toward the bedroom. He went to the closet and looked through the top closet shelves in the corner. After a while of searching, he found what he was looking for—a photo album that he hadn't gone through in years.

He had told Mauricio all the answers that he thought would cure his sadness, but the truth was that there was no cure. The sadness would always be buried somewhere deep down in the soul. There was a lot of sorrow in him as well, but he knew how to hide it and control it well.

Leafing through the photo album, he found a few pictures of Claudia when she was a little girl, sitting on her father's lap. Ramon remembered those moments, and tears came to his eyes as well. That was the girl he remembered, innocent, and a father that was young but swore to protect her. That was a past he sometimes wished he could go back to. But then he remembered the constant run-ins with the police, the fights his brother had with his girlfriend, and the poverty that was all around him.

But the past was just that—the past. He regretted not getting the chance to really get to know Claudia, and now the opportunity was gone. Ramon closed the photo album and put it away. The memory was still there, and that's all he would have left of her.

The night had brought a drizzle of rain to fall down on the city. Mauricio had called for a taxi to pick him up, and got into the back seat. The driver asked him something in Portuguese, and Mauricio handed him a handful of money and told him to drive. The driver seemed to understand. He drove around the city and Mauricio stared aimlessly out the window. Then he would think of Claudia, and reach into his wallet to take out the picture of her. A rush of his memories with her came at him, and he didn't know if he wanted to even remember right now. The sadness was too much to bear. Mauricio put the picture away and stared once again out the window. The rain was starting to pick up.

Without Claudia, Mauricio had no direction in his life. He finally was at peace for himself for leaving the only business he was good at. Now what was he supposed to do? What was the end game now? He had saved up plenty of money so that one day he could buy a place somewhere or live on the boat he had and just go up and down the coast of Brazil. He was planning for a life of happiness. Now it was all taken from him in an instant, and he had to cope with the fact there was no way to bring her back.

He was done crying. The rain was now the representation of the tears that he had before this moment. He was ready to become numb, to shut down from the outside world. Ever since the incident with his parents, he had been low on feelings, especially those that connected with other humans. Claudia had opened him up to love, and caring for someone else. She was easy to talk to, and didn't judge him for what he did. He didn't think he would ever have that again. Sure, there were the Reds and Fernandas of the world, but they were empty vessels. They used sex to fill the void that was inside of them, and they were numb inside as well, having lost their feelings for companionship and love a long time ago. That's what made them good at their jobs. Mauricio should have been the same way, but he didn't regret falling in love with Claudia.

He wished he would have told her more often. She should have known how much he cared for her. He could have done more, could have said more. Then again, it was never enough. He would have to cope with that, someway, somehow. Until then, he would have to settle with the memories.

"Stop here," Mauricio said, and the taxi pulled up to the curb.

Mauricio got out of the car and left the back door open. He stood out in the rain and let the water fall down on him. In a strange way, he felt like he was being cleansed. He stood there as his clothes got soaked and wanted to feel like everything was going to be okay. He wanted to wake up tomorrow morning and realize all of this was just a dream. But it wasn't going to happen. He had to get soaked in the reality and in his own pain.

The driver said something in Portuguese. Mauricio got back inside the taxi and closed the door. Somehow he felt like he was closer to Malestar than ever before and understood the pain and anger that he felt. The very thought frightened him to the core. He couldn't be a part of civilization like this. He had to get away before he became a monster, but he feared it was too late.

"Drive," he said, and the taxi pulled away from the curb.

*

Vesco came home in a good mood. He had a great day after finally coming up with a plan to balance the budget, and the majority of his colleagues agreeing on the principle of the plan. He opened the front door and then closed and locked it. After that, he pressed the combination code to the new security system he had installed. Ever since he got that letter from Malestar, he was on edge and scared for his family's safety. This new security system made him feel better. He hummed a tune as he made his way to the living room.

There, he found his wife and his daughter, both tied to chairs and gagged at their mouths. Vesco froze in fear. The living room was dark, but he could see a figure emerging from the darkness. When the figure came into view, he recognized it instantly.

"Hello, Mayor," Malestar said.

"What is the meaning of this?"

"The city is mine now. You should have a seat as well."

Vesco could feel the room spinning. His feet were giving out on him. Then he fainted and fell to the ground.

16.

The island of Itamaracá was situated on the Atlantic Ocean, and a popular place for fishing and tourism. The island was about thirty-eight kilometers to the north of Recife. The topography consisted of small coastal rivers, mangrove and coconut trees, and some of the most pristine beaches in Brazil. Ramon's place was at Sossego Beach, a quiet beach with gentle winds and water. The villa was up on the hill overlooking the beach, and its privacy provided the perfect retreat for Mauricio.

The villa itself was clean with minimal furniture inside. There was a bedroom with a desk, a chest of drawers, and a bed and lamp, and a living room with two chairs, and a sofa in the corner. Turquoise curtains covered the balcony that overlooked the ocean. The kitchen was small, yet efficient, with everything he needed to use if he was to cook. There was only one thing Mauricio wanted to stock the mini refrigerator with, and that was alcohol.

He spent his first few nights drunk off of rum and wine. He stumbled around the villa and the premise, and barely ate anything. He lost weight. He carried a bottle of alcohol wherever he went but it wasn't enough to take away the sadness. He began to grow a beard.

He hardly left the villa. When he did, it was often to the beach that was nearby. He would take a walk on the sand and look at all the tourists with their appearance of living perfect lives, and always being so happy all the time. He wished they would experience the same pain he was feeling, to understand what life was really about. Then he remembered what Malestar told him, and realized he was becoming him. He shouldn't be jealous of their happiness. He should aspire to have same thing. But he wasn't in the mood.

He found a young couple in love running toward the water and holding hands. The sight of them made him sick to his stomach. The woman left her purse in the sand. Mauricio went to it and rummaged through her bag. He found the usual stuff a woman keeps, along with a bottle of depressants. He took the bottle and walked away.

There wasn't that much more action further along the beach. There was a couple of families lying down or running around, but nothing that sparked his interest. He only wished he had the island to himself. He thought society was nothing more than a failed experiment. He thought it was only as good as the people willing to make it work. A lot of people didn't even try, yet were reaping the benefits. Mauricio thought he was better off on his own, with no place to call home, no place where he owed them his civic duty or where they taxed his money. From now on, he was going to be the loner he was born to be before Claudia came along, and embrace who he was. He promised himself this, knowing he could change his mind at any moment.

He went back to the villa, opened up a bottle of wine, and headed to the bathroom. He drank directly from the bottle. Then he placed two pills in his mouth and washed them down with more wine. He looked at himself in the mirror. He was a worn man, and the life was out of his eyes. The rest of the world couldn't see him like this.

Mauricio stayed in and began to watch local television. Many of the shows were in the soap opera mold, with overdramatic characters and plots such as sisters in love with the same guy who is actually their stepbrother from their parents' secret marriage. Mauricio didn't understand the majority of what they were saying, but he was slowly beginning to pick up on the language. Claudia had tried to get him to understand more and taught him some words, but hearing conversations and constant dialogue was helping him associate the words. He had always wanted to be well-rounded when it came to language.

As a youth he was taught English and never learned his father's native language. His mother's native tongue was Portuguese, but she rarely said anything in the language since she had been with his father. He spent most of his life in Europe and Africa, and could speak some French and Italian. But over there, English was more understood, in his opinion. He wanted to learn something else, to go out and explore other lands. He was his father's son in that regard.

They had both fallen in love with Brazilian women. There was something that had drawn them in. Perhaps it was their carefree nature, their loyalty, and their appreciation of family. Then again, that argument could be made for any region or country across the world. All Mauricio knew was that he had fallen in love with Claudia, and he didn't have to dissect the reasons behind it. He just knew what he had was real and it wasn't going away anytime soon.

There he went thinking about Claudia again. If he kept thinking about her constantly, it would kill him inside. But then again, he didn't want to stop. He just wanted to feel good again. He needed more wine.

The pills were starting to get to him with the combination of wine, but he wanted more. He was seeing double and triple of everything in the room. He stumbled his way to the kitchen and took out another bottle of wine. He found the bottle opener on the counter and pressed it downward, but ended up getting air instead of the cork of the bottle. He laughed out loud. He tried a second attempt, lunging forward, and ended up slipping on the kitchen tile, slamming his chin against the kitchen counter. He fell backward and collapsed on the kitchen floor.

He was sure he would be in intense pain later, but he began to laugh it off. Why worry about the later? He was living in the now, and his head was sky high, and his body had alcohol flowing through the bloodstream. He closed his eyes and thought of a present alternative universe, one where Claudia was still with him and his parents were still alive. He could see the images vividly in his head.

They were all on a boat sitting down, laughing and enjoying each other's company. There was no land to be seen in the distance, and nothing but azure ocean water surrounding them. He could almost feel as if he was there. He raised his arm into the air as if he was reaching for Claudia on the boat. She came over and sat on his lap.

His father had said something. "What?" Mauricio asked.

"Stop blaming yourself," he said. "It accomplishes nothing."

He looked at his mother and she agreed. Then Claudia held him tight around his waist. She gave him a kiss as if she was saying goodbye.

Mauricio opened his eyes, still on the kitchen floor, and began to cry. He reached for the wine on the counter and was nowhere close to reaching it. He could feel some pain in his back. The fact he was crying and feeling real physical pain made him dive deeper into an abyss of sorrow. He cried until the alcohol took over, and he fell asleep.

One afternoon he decided to leave the villa and take a walk along the beach. He kept the bottle of rum in his hand and staggered as he walked. He watched the waves come in and the sun setting against the ocean. He took a seat on the sand and took a long drink. He was calm, and numb with sorrow. His mind flashed images of his past—times he spent with Claudia and the incident with his parents. He knew he couldn't allow himself to love again. This was what happened when he cared for people. They would leave his life and he would be left to soak the pain. He had enough of it, and it was bad for business.

Mauricio leaned back on the sand. The alcohol was starting to take control. He listened to the waves come in and was soothed by the sound. His body was warm and the air around him was cool. Mauricio closed his eyes and tried not to think of anything.

He returned to the villa to sleep, and didn't wake up until the next afternoon. He woke up with a hangover, his head throbbing and his stomach queasy. He thought he would step outside for some sunlight. He covered his squinted eyes as he had to adjust to the light coming in. His slippers hit something below as he stepped out. Mauricio looked down to see a package outside the door.

He picked it up and brought it inside with him. The address at the top showed that it was from Ramon. He quickly opened the package by ripping off the paper and opening the box inside to find out its contents. When he did, he found items that were on Claudia they day she was shot—lipstick, some of her clothing, and her cell phone. Mauricio picked up her cell phone as there were a few missed calls and a voicemail. He recognized the number. They came from Red and were made two days ago.

He thought about listening to the voicemail to see what she wanted. No, he was not going to go back. He wasn't ready. He owed it to Claudia to be in remorse and in pain. But then again, Claudia would have wanted him to get vengeance, and to do what he did best. He was conflicted. In the end, he pressed the button for voicemail and listened for the message against his ear.

"Hey, this is Red. I know we've had our differences, but I could really use your help and Mauricio's as well. The rumor is that Malestar is planning something big, and we could use your help to stop him. We have all the weapons you need over here. It's not even about the money anymore, but if you like, Rodrigo and I will gladly share the pot with you two. I just know we can't do this alone."

The message ended. Mauricio tossed the phone aside. A plethora of thoughts filled his mind. What was Malestar up to? Was Red really that desperate? He could go back to Salvador and get his vengeance. Wasn't that what he really wanted? No, he told himself. He wasn't right, and he didn't want to think right now. Mauricio rushed to the bedroom and closed the door.

He rested until his body couldn't take it anymore and the night had arrived. He had to eat something. There was no food in the refrigerator so that meant he had to step out. He put on the best clothes he had left, and made his way to the restaurant that wasn't too far from where he was staying.

It was a place that specialized in seafood, and music in the style of *ciranda* was playing, from a well-known singer by the name of Lia de Itamaracá. The place was fancy enough to warrant the medium-high prices, with tropical art pieces on the wall and bamboo chairs.

Mauricio waited for seating, and the hostess looked at him strangely, as did some of the customers. She found him a small table in the corner and gave him a menu. More looks continued to come his way. They acted like they never saw someone eating alone before. Then he realized he hadn't shaved since he came here. He figured he probably looked like a homeless man dressed up for a fancy dinner.

Mauricio browsed through the menu and realized it didn't matter what he ordered. He just wanted something to put down so that he would stop feeling so queasy. He motioned the waiter over and placed his hand next to one of the words listed under the entrées. The waiter approved his selection and walked away.

The social setting he was in forced his mind to start thinking quickly again. He scanned the room for threats, and didn't find anything or anyone to be concerned about. Then he reached into his pocket and took out Claudia's cell phone. He placed it on the table and thought about calling Red back. He could help. She was right. It wasn't about the money anymore. It was about payback for taking a life for someone he loved. He couldn't help but have this feeling for revenge. Then he remembered what Claudia's uncle had told him about anger. He put the cell phone back in his pocket and waited for his meal.

He thumped his fingers against the table and stared back at the people that were looking at him. His patience for others had worn thin. Claudia's death had not returned him to the normal state of numbness he had before, but had made him a bitter and irritated man. He could tell that their eyes were always judging, always creating stories in their head over the appearance of someone else. They were clueless. If any of them had a price on their head, he would gladly blow their brains out and send them to his employer in a box. He looked at them as if he would kill them all, and they turned their heads away in fear.

The anger was continuing to rise. He couldn't be here. Mauricio stormed out of the restaurant and returned to his villa. He slammed the door closed and headed toward his bedroom. The hunger he had earlier was gone. He sat on the bed and stared at the door. His face was still filled with anger, and he found his body slightly trembling. He wanted revenge in the worst way.

17.

Fifteen minutes after three in the morning, hundreds of motorcycles sped through the street and lit up the dark sky. The sound of their motors and mufflers echoed throughout the early morning. Most of the drivers had purple bandanas tied around some part of their body. Some shouted out loud. They knew that this was just the beginning of the takeover of the city.

The motorcycles headed downtown and approached the skyscrapers that made up the skyline. A large white semi turned the corner of the street and began following them. The motorcycles stopped in front of the downtown police station, and the truck did as well. Malestar got out of the truck wearing a pearl white suit with the first few buttons of his light blue dress shirt underneath, unbuttoned. His hair was combed back with gel. He made his way in front of the motorcycles with a bullhorn in his hand. The members of the motorcycle posse got off their bikes and pointed their guns at the building.

Malestar stood in front of the building and spoke into the bullhorn. "The great protectors of this city—come out and play!"

Malestar went to the truck and opened the back doors. Two men were already there and Malestar helped them unload a cannon and wheel it to the front of the building. The doors to the police station opened, but the police officers were hesitant in coming out.

"Don't be shy!" Malestar shouted.

Malestar turned to face his crew and placed his hands in the air as if he was the maestro that was conducting a symphony. He moved his arms and the crew began to load their ammo and take off the safety of their guns. Malestar made his way to the side and raised his arms up high. When he put them down, everyone began to fire.

The bullets pierced through the building, shattering the glass windows in front and placing bullet holes all over the building. The cannon placed holes in the walls of the building. Malestar placed his hands in the air once more, and the shooting stopped. He then placed his right arm forward.

The crew members charged at the building, shouting in unison as they did so. Malestar calmly walked toward the entrance as everyone else ran, and handed the bullhorn to a man on his crew. The crew members rushed inside and were met with gunfire by police officers. People were shot on both sides. Desks and walls were shot, and paperwork was floating in the air. The police officers retreated toward the back of the building and locked themselves in storage, where a security code was needed to get in. Malestar walked amongst the fallen police officers to find one that was still alive.

He found one with a bloody chest and his arm reaching toward the ceiling. Malestar kneeled down beside him. He rubbed the man's head as if he was a sick child.

"I know you are in a lot of pain, but I can make it go away. Just tell me what the pass code is to get through the door."

The man started to whisper something. Malestar leaned over and pressed his ear against the man's mouth to him. Instead of words, he got spit on his face.

Malestar calmly wiped the spit off. He took a knife from his pocket and placed a hand over the man's mouth. Then he began to stab him repetitively in the stomach as the man gave muffled shouts. Malestar's face showed the concentration involved in his murderous rage. Blood splashed upon his face and clothes and he continued stabbing even after the man was dead. The rest of the gunfire had stopped and the crew members stood still to watch him. Malestar stopped his stabbing, and bowed his head. He was still. The crew members looked at each other, wondering what was to come next out of Malestar's unpredictable behavior.

Malestar stood up and looked amongst his crew. He thought about bringing the cannon inside, but there wasn't enough time. He knew it wouldn't be long before more police were on their way to rescue their fellow officers.

"Everybody leave!" he shouted.

The crew members rushed out of the building. Malestar made his way to the locked door and took out the explosives he had placed inside his suit jacket. He placed them against the door and then calmly walked outside the building.

The rest of his crew had already climbed back on their bikes. A helicopter was coming toward the building and Malestar could hear the sound of police sirens coming closer. "Let's go!" he shouted.

The motorcycles started to take off. The cannon was placed back inside the back of the truck. Malestar headed to the front of the truck and got into the driver's side. On the passenger seat were his cell phone and the remote to the explosives. The police cars were coming down the street as the motorcycles sped past them. Some of the police cars drove off after them. Malestar rubbed his hands together in excitement. He pressed the button on the remote and the police building exploded, a burst of fire coming from within. Malestar laughed heartily. Then he put the truck in drive and went toward the row of police cars.

Malestar pressed down on the accelerator as he approached them. The police cars seemed like they were up to the challenge in the game of chicken. Malestar was not backing down. His face was full of exhilaration. The police cars only had seconds to drive away before getting hit. The first few did, but some of them didn't manage to move in time. The truck ran into them and they were crushed and pushed to the side.

The police cars that moved out the way managed to turn around and follow him. The back door to the truck opened. One of the crew members was inside and got behind the cannon. He began to fire at will against the police cars behind the truck. The windows of the police cars shattered, and the bodies of the cars were damaged, causing the police cars to stop on the road. Malestar let out a shout in the front seat.

"The city is mine!"

The helicopter came back around and was now following the truck. Malestar could hear over their speaker the demands they were giving him to stop. He looked up through his window to get a view, and began to laugh.

"You want to play. Let's play!"

Malestar had a helicopter of his own. He picked up his cell phone and dialed the last number he entered.

"Need a pickup," he said.

He drove further down the road and saw his own helicopter approaching. The police helicopter started to come down toward the truck but Malestar's own helicopter was beginning to fire a machine gun at the police helicopter. The police helicopter backed away as quickly as it could. Malestar stopped the truck and got out. He waved his helicopter down. Then he went toward the back of the truck, where the crew member was getting out.

"You take this truck and you go right back at them!"

"They will kill me!" the young teenager said.

"This is about a message, not about your life! Do as you are told!"

Malestar patted him on the back as his helicopter approached. He jogged to it and climbed inside as the teenager reluctantly got into the truck with the engine still running. He pressed his hand on reverse, and fear crept through his body. He knew instantly that this would be his last day on earth. However, he would make Malestar proud, and that gave him motivation to continue on with the mission. Malestar's helicopter rose up from the street and into the night sky as more police cars were on their way.

"Let them hear our message!" Malestar shouted below.

*

She could feel sunlight coming from the hotel window even though the curtains were mostly covering its radiance. Red leaned up in bed in her tank top and panties, and rubbed her eyes. She got up, turned on the television, and went to use the bathroom.

The channel she had left it on was the news, and they were reporting on the shooting at the police station and the gunfire that followed. When Red came back into the room, she sat on the bed and watched. Since she didn't understand the language, she focused on the imagery. There were images of the bodies of the police officers spread across the station's floor with blood everywhere— on the walls, on the ground, covering the bodies. Red had seen a lot of death in her line of work, but even for her the scene was gruesome. She wanted to turn away, but she couldn't help but to watch. There was footage of the building and it was completely destroyed. There were no survivors. Then they showed the damage done on the road from the car crashes. This whole event was clearly a message to law enforcement throughout the city.

Instantly, she assumed that this was the work of Malestar. She realized this job was too big for her. With all the jobs that she had worked on in the past, the criminal was always running from the law, not putting his work on display for the world to see. Malestar did not fear being caught, and he was challenging not only the mercenaries to come after him, but anyone that had the authority to do so. A panic swept through her and she pulled her suitcases from underneath her bed. Then she went to the closet to begin packing.

There was knocking against her front door. Red looked through the peephole. Rodrigo. She opened the door to let him in.

Rodrigo noticed the suitcase right away. "Going somewhere?"

"Have you seen the news? I knew this was coming. This maniac has taken over the city, and I hate to say it, but as good as we both think we are, we're no match for this guy. I say we get out while we're still breathing."

"I can't just walk away like that. This is my home," Rodrigo replied.

"Suit yourself," Red said, returning to her suitcases.

"I thought you were this super,-tough woman that wasn't afraid of anything."

"Oh, no, honey. I have my limits. I do what I can. If I think I can manipulate my way into finding a target or get them on my own, then I'll do it. But I'm not chasing down some psychopath. I'm just not cut out for it."

"This is why people like him get away with stuff."

Red put her clothes down for a moment. "Hey, it is not my job to protect the city. The people have a police department to do that for them. You would come with me if you had any brains."

"I was hired to do a job," Rodrigo replied.

"Then do it, cowboy," Red said.

"He's right."

Red and Rodrigo turned to look at the doorway. Mauricio was standing there, clean shaven and wearing a brand new black suit. They were both surprised to see him stepped inside and closed the door.

"Where's Claudia?" Rodrigo asked.

"She's dead," Mauricio replied.

Rodrigo and Red looked at each other, speechless. "Save your condolences for later. We have a maniac to catch. Red, can you get me a gun?"

"Of course," she said, reaching into the drawers near the television and taking out two handguns. She kept one for herself and handed one to Mauricio. Mauricio inspected the weapon for a moment, and then placed it in his back hip.

"Red, put on some clothes," Mauricio said.

"I wasn't exactly expecting visitors," she replied, and went to get a pair of jeans from the closet. Rodrigo watched as Red slipped a pair of jeans on and placed a pair of running shoes on her feet. "Ready," she finally said.

"Let's go," Mauricio said, and left the room.

Rodrigo turned to look at Red. "You of little faith."

"This is so exciting!" she said, and they headed out the door.

Fifteen minutes later, Rodrigo parked curbside in front of Vesco's home. "Wait here," Mauricio told Rodrigo from the passenger side. "Red, you come with me."

Mauricio got out of the car, and Red did so as well, but not before sticking out her tongue at Rodrigo for getting to go with Mauricio. They were nothing more than children, Mauricio thought. The two made their way to the front door, where Mauricio pushed the button for the doorbell.

"He's probably not home," Red said.

"It's the weekend. I called his office and he has the day off. There is no way a city official works more than he has to."

Rodrigo watched them from the car. He kept his eye on Red, and wondered if she was the type of woman that could truly fall for someone else. She was a woman that was nice to look at, but he definitely didn't want someone like that in his personal life. She would be in control of him, and he would be helpless in his desire for her. He watched the body language between Red and Mauricio, and he could see that she was attracted to him. Women like that always wanted men they couldn't have. Rodrigo shook his head and looked around the street to see if anyone was watching them.

Moments later, the door opened. Vesco stood in the doorway wearing a robe, unshaven, and it looked like he hadn't gotten much sleep. Mauricio didn't wait to be asked in. Red followed him inside and closed the door.

"You look terrible," Mauricio said.

"Thank you for noticing," Vesco responded. "Would you like some coffee?"

"That would be nice," Mauricio replied.

"I'll take some too. Thank you," Red said.

"Why are you dressed?" Vesco asked.

"Because I'm a professional."

"That you are. It's one of the reasons I hired you. Most people in your profession would quit right about now. There is much to tell you," Vesco said as he headed toward the kitchen.

"I'm still asking myself why I don't just put a bullet in between your eyes right now," Mauricio stated in a tone loud enough that Vesco could hear.

"Now why would you want to do something like that? Keep in mind, I'm the one that's paying you," Vesco said from the kitchen.

"It's not about the money anymore."

"I feel the same way," Vesco stated.

"And why is that?"

Vesco came out and stood at the entrance of the kitchen. "Because Malestar has my family hostage."

18.

After Vesco prepared the coffee, the three of them sat in the living room. Mauricio was amazed how calm Vesco was, considering his family was at the mercy of a psychopath. However, being emotional right now was not going to help them in any way. Maybe he knew being rational was the best approach. Vesco was a mindful man, but a terrible maker of coffee. One sip and Mauricio could figure that out.

"I think it's time to tell you about the Corporation," Vesco said. "I didn't want to introduce my guilt into this manhunt I hired you for, but you might as well know the entire story. Years ago, I was part of this group, a collection of lawmakers, police officers, judges, and businessmen and women. The bottom line was profit, and using criminals to our advantage. We got drug czars to give us a cut in order for them to run their business on the street, and when they didn't comply or wanted out, I hired mercenaries to get rid of them. Rodrigo and a partner used to do this work for me, unbeknownst to them. They never asked questions, or shouldn't have. I met with the Corporation on a weekly basis, in secret locations or through web meetings. They were like-minded people that had one goal in mind."

Vesco took a sip of his coffee, and Mauricio wondered how he managed to swallow it. He noticed Red didn't touch hers after the first sip either. Vesco continued talking.

"We ran our operation like a business, with profit sharing, appointments made, minutes of meetings, a budget for overhead, and cutting our losses whenever we could. It was a very profitable business. We shook down criminals and made them work for us. The police department is mostly dirty too, and the few that aren't bought are targets. Then they came across Malestar. They thought he was such an engaging and intelligent criminal, they helped him avoid jail, and funded his operation to hit all the big businesses and banks of the city and the competition of our business people. I thought it was a dangerous game they were playing.

"The plan worked at first, but Malestar had other plans. He wanted to terrorize the city and take control of it. Obviously, that would be a conflict of interest to what my job entails. So I got out of the Corporation. I hired you to take out Malestar, and used all my resources to gather as many hired help as I could. Needless to say, the Corporation and Malestar weren't too happy with my decision. So here I am, with my family awaiting their fate, and the city in peril. I'm afraid it's too late. I've lost it all, and I deserve everything that comes my way."

"You're just going to give up on your family like that?" Red asked.

"I don't have much of a choice. The only people that can help me are you two. If you were to help me, I would first find Carlito Santos. He's the figurehead of the Corporation and runs a software business downtown called CTV Santos."

Mauricio sighed. "The last thing I want to do is to help you, but I will for personal reasons. I want you to double the pay, and pay all of us."

"I can't afford..."

"Find a way," Mauricio said, and stood up.

"Honestly, I don't think I have to. I hired the best but I don't think anyone can stop him."

"Thanks for your faith in me," Mauricio replied. Red stood up as well, and they headed toward the front door. Vesco followed them.

Red turned around. "What I don't get is why he kept you alive."

"He wants me to suffer. He wants us all to suffer."

Mauricio and Red headed back to the car and got in. Rodrigo started the engine. Red tapped Mauricio's shoulder and he turned around on the passenger side.

"About Claudia…"

"Don't speak of her until we finish our job," Mauricio replied.

"Where are we going?" Rodrigo asked.

"Downtown," Mauricio replied.

The downtown streets were crowded as usual as Rodrigo drove down Torquato Bahia Street, where grey buildings lined the streets and motorcycles and cars were parked alongside the buildings. A street vendor was pedaling a bike with a cart of fruits in front of him. The day was a humid one, and most people were wearing shorts and T-shirts. Pedestrians crossed the street without regard to the moving cars. Rodrigo drove around but couldn't find a parking space.

"Might take a while to find something," he stated.

"Don't worry about it," Mauricio said "Just park over there and drop me off. I'll call when I'm ready."

Mauricio took out his phone. "Oh, I've been meaning to tell you. This is a prepaid phone I picked up. Only call when needed." Mauricio dialed Rodrigo's ringtone and his new number showed up on Rodrigo's phone. "Give it to Red as well," Mauricio said.

"Paranoid, are we?" Rodrigo asked.

Rodrigo dropped Mauricio off, and Mauricio made his way inside the building. Inside, a long hallway led to a pair of elevators in the lobby, and a security post behind it. There was a list of businesses next to the elevator, but Mauricio didn't know which one was affiliated with Carlito. Then he remembered his conversation with Vesco about a company called CTV Santos. Mauricio looked at the list. Fourth floor. He pressed the button on the elevator and waited, feeling like he was being watched by the security guards near their post across from the elevators. He turned around and found out that he was right. One man in particular was looking at him. Mauricio stared back at him, and the young man looked away. The elevators doors opened, and Mauricio got inside.

As he waited, he tried not to lose focus. When he did, he found himself thinking about Claudia. Instead, he thought about how he was going to get his revenge. In order to take down Malestar, he figured he better start thinking like him. Malestar wanted him to understand the pain, and with Claudia gone, he was starting to know what it felt like. But that was where the similarities ended. Mauricio didn't want the whole world to suffer; he only wanted one man to suffer. Society wasn't the problem. It was a few people in society that were the problem.

He didn't know if he was making things better or was part of the problem himself. There was guilt inside of him, and he didn't know if it was because of his own moral compass, or the one society had placed on him. But that guilt soon went away. He was back to his old self now, and he was starting to care less what people thought of his actions. It seemed like everyone else was living their lives the way they wanted and not what was best for everyone as a community, and he was going to do the same.

Mauricio began to wonder why the police force was helpless against Malestar. Could it be true what Vesco said? Were most of them bought to look the other way? Malestar was made possible because of the corruption in the city. That and the Corporation created a monster and now they had no control over their experiment. They didn't understand that evil could not be bottled and controlled. Evil wanted to do what it was born to do—to destruct everything in its path.

The elevator doors opened and Mauricio stepped out into a floor that was as empty as it was quiet. There was a hallway with doors to four suites, and a stairway door to the side of the elevator doors. Mauricio silently walked to the left corner where Carlito's business name was on a placard near the door. He opened the door and found himself in a small room with a few chairs, a desk for an assistant, a large window in the back, and an office to the right. Mauricio turned his head to see the assistant, an older woman with thick glasses and curly hair. She asked him something in Portuguese, and Mauricio could only make out a few words.

"English," he said.

The lady continued to speak Portuguese. Mauricio saw through an opaque window of the closed office door that there was someone moving about inside. He made his way to the way to the office as the assistant stood up and spoke louder.

Mauricio opened the door to see Carlito standing there in his business suit, talking to someone on his cell phone. Mauricio took out his gun. The assistant came to the door and froze when she saw the gun. Carlito ended the call.

"Its okay, Ana, just get back to work," Carlito said. Ana left and Mauricio closed the door.

"Please, have a seat," Carlito said, walking behind his desk and sitting down.

Mauricio took a look around the office. There were framed degrees on the wall, pictures of Carlito and other business people, a window on the back wall, and one with a plaque from the mayor. Mauricio grinned at that one. There were a few pictures of Carlito on vacation in what appeared to be the Amazon, with a few pictures of him and a large snake. A mini bar was set up on one corner. A set of golf clubs rested in the opposite corner. Carlito noticed Mauricio's gaze.

"Do you play?"

"Not really. Busy killing people, and all," Mauricio replied.

Carlito grinned. "Vesco sent you over here?"

"Maybe."

"I should have had him killed."

"Pay me enough money and I might do it for you."

Carlito grinned again. "I love the fact there's no loyalty in your business. Just like in my world, everything is cut-throat. Of course, it would be easier for me to have someone kill the both of you for a lesser price. I'm sure someone of your stature has a high asking price."

"And the chances are, I kill whoever you send after me, and then come after you," Mauricio replied.

"Yes, you are quite right."

Mauricio finally took a seat across from Carlito. "No family?" he asked.

"Never was my thing," Carlito replied. "I see it as a weakness. Some may say I'm a psychopath that made his way through life by stepping on others and my insouciance for others is despicable, but I just call that part of the process of being successful. It takes a special person to know what they want and won't stop until they do. Emotions get in the way of progress."

"The last time I checked, greed was an emotion."

"Quick with the draw, I see. Look at you, programmed to be the weak individual that you are. That's how society controls you. Why can't you see that? They make a set of rules that you decide to follow, but in the meantime, they are making all the money in the world from you while you helplessly follow instructions. I refuse to be played, and I'm not the only one."

"The Corporation," Mauricio replied.

"Yes, I see you are well informed. Did you come here to try to stop us? Well, it's too late. Do you know how powerful our organization is? This city practically belongs to us, and if it falls apart, it's because we allow it to. We're unassailable."

"But you aren't, and neither is Vesco. Your greed made a madman that you can't control. You will be punished just like anyone else."

"Believe me, I tried to stop the will of Malestar, but he's like us in a way. He just doesn't mind being seen doing his dirty work. I, personally, do not wish to go to jail and like to live a fulfilling life with my riches. I take calculated risks and do not want any sort of fame. Malestar wants it all. He's not afraid of you, me, the law, or death. His plan is to destroy the fabric of the city."

"You're responsible for this," Mauricio said. "And you're just going to sit here in your office and pretend everything is fine? Do you understand what's going to happen to you?"

"Yes, I will get rich. There is much profit to be made from destruction. I gave this some thought. If we let Malestar have some fun, and then promise law officials we'll bring him in for a price, then they will negotiate. Whether we can or not remains to be seen."

"That is not how this is going to work. We're stopping this now. I want you to bring me to him."

Carlito laughed. "You can't be serious. You wouldn't stand a chance."

"You let me worry about that."

Carlito sighed. "You're taking this personal."

"You're going to give me what I want," Mauricio said.

"Is that right?"

"You're not naïve enough to not know what I do. My whole profession is based on stealth and extermination. Would I take you out now? Of course not. I will wait when you are most vulnerable, whether that's you on the toilet, walking down the street, or taking out your trash. The good news for me is no one would even ask questions or wonder where you are. You have no wife, no family, no one you care for or care for you. You're one of the easiest targets I would come across. Do you really want to be looking over your back for the rest of your life?"

"I can see what I can do," Carlito said.

"You do that now."

"Right now?"

"Did I stutter?" Mauricio asked.

Carlito picked up his cell phone from his desk and dialed a number. He stared at Mauricio and Mauricio met his glare. Carlito flashed a smile.

"Security," he said into the phone.

Mauricio quickly stood up. "You made a big mistake."

"Are you going to shoot me now?"

Mauricio wanted to, but now wasn't the time. He quickly made his way out of the office, and out of the suite. He walked to the staircase entry that was outside the door. He ran down the steps and saw that two security guards were on their way running upward. Mauricio withdrew his weapon and pointed his gun at them. The security men froze.

"Move out of my way!" Mauricio said, and the security guards stood straight against the wall. Mauricio walked past them and ran down the rest of the stairs.

He made his way outside where Rodrigo had the car parked out front. Mauricio got into the passenger side and Rodrigo drove off. "How did it go?" Rodrigo asked.

"Nowhere," Mauricio replied. "Drive."

As Rodrigo drove off, Carlito watched from his office window. He picked up his cell phone once again, dialed, and waited for the other line to pick up. When they did, he went straight to the point.

"We have a problem," he said. "But something tells me you're going to enjoy this one."

19.

Malestar danced around his home wearing a black top hat on his head and a white mask around his face with his jaw, nose tip, and the area around his eyes covered in black paint. His teeth were drawn in on the mask and circular designs covered the forehead portion of it. He wore a black suit with a scarlet bowtie, colorful beads around his neck, and black boots. He danced with the drugged women in his room, but this time they were somewhat clothed, as they wore their panties and bra. He would dance with one of them, then drop her and pick up another woman on the way. He tossed his hat to the side and danced some more. This was a joyous occasion. The city was slowly becoming his. Then he remembered he had to check on his new friends.

Malestar headed to the other room down the hallway, still humming the melody to the song that had been playing. The room he entered was bare of furniture. There were two people inside the room, Vesco's wife and daughter, tied up against each other with a rope around their waists as they sat with their backs pressed. Their ankles were tied as well. Both were still wearing their sleeping attire and barely able to keep their eyes open. Malestar had injected them with something to help them relax and not want to fight back. A large, silver bowl of water was in front of them with water spilled on the floor. Above them, a small window was covered by a black curtain that was taped against it. Malestar closed the door and looked inside the bowl next to them.

"You are probably wondering about my mask. Well, this is the mask of pain. Get it?" Malestar gave a deep, dark laugh.

"You can't tell me you two aren't thirsty," he said. "Drink!"

He lifted the bowl and dumped the remaining water on top of them. They were too strung out to be terrified or angry. Malestar bent down and grabbed the back of the daughter's hair and pressed her forehead against his face. He didn't lust over her body and her figure, but the control he would have over her. He thought about having his way with her, and then tying her up again. Her body was still forming and he could teach her a lesson or two. Then again, it was never a good idea to mess with the bargaining chips. Then the money to the police wouldn't matter as much and they would be forced to not look the other way. No, there were too many women at his disposal to mess with someone not matured.

"You're very beautiful, you know that?" he asked to her. "You take after your mother. I know somewhere deep down, you are very frightened right now, and I want to tell you that it's okay to be scared. You should be scared of me. I can feel your innocence. You are a lost child. You need to experience pain, real pain."

Malestar's cell phone played its ringtone in his pocket. He quickly answered the phone. "What?" he asked in Portuguese.

Outside the home, police cars lined the street and a group of police officers already stood near the door with their guns drawn. Behind the police cars was the captain with a cell phone in his hand. The police were waiting until the captain gave them a go-ahead sign. He wanted to address Malestar personally, and get all the credit for his capture. As part of the precinct outside the city limits of Salvador, he wasn't part of the Corporation's payroll. He was going to make a difference and his reward would be his fame.

"We have you surrounded," the captain said on the phone. "Come out with your hands up, and we'll see what we can do about not shooting you on sight."

"Captain Morales," Malestar said, still staring at Vesco's daughter. "You're a little late to the party."

"Party is over," the captain said. "If you have any armed men in there, tell them to come out with their hands up. Otherwise, they will all be killed. I promise you that. You have no other moves here. Just come out and face your fate."

"Oh, but you are wrong," Malestar said, and made his way back to the Dance Room. He turned off the music that was playing as the drugged women were slouched against the back wall.

"Camila Morales, isn't that your daughter's name?" Malestar asked. "Gabriela Gómez, Carolina Pérez, Thais Galleti, Juliana Villa. All of these are names of the daughters of high-ranking officials, and guess what, I'm looking right at them."

The captain's confidence drained from his face. He didn't know what to say. He looked at the home and all he could think of was his daughter that he hadn't heard from in a long time. A group of teenagers dressed mostly in purple came from the side of the home with their guns drawn.

"I'll take your silence for compliance. Now you realized who is in control. Tell your men to put their guns down and walk away before they get killed."

The captain didn't want to oblige, but he was fearful for his daughter's safety. He told his men to stand down, and they began to lower their weapons and make their way back to their cars. The captain looked up at the second floor, wondering what condition his daughter was in.

"I need proof of life," he said.

"You won't get it," Malestar said. "Just know I'm taking real good care of your daughter. And if you tried to pull this stunt again, I have this place rigged with explosives. You can say goodbye to them all."

"If you touch her..."

"You will what? You will what?" Malestar asked in a shout as left the room and made his way to the front door. "You don't understand the severity of the situation. I can do what I wish. In fact, I want you to beg for me not to touch her. Do it now!"

The captain was almost at tears. "Please...."

"That's more like it. Now, come to the door." Malestar unlocked the front door and opened it wide enough to see the police parked in front and his street soldiers pointing their guns at them.

"Come to the door right now or your daughter will suffer!" Malestar shouted.

The captain made his way to the door, where Malestar opened it wide. The captain, taken aback by the mask that Malestar was wearing, almost jumped back in fear. Malestar stood in front of him and turned his head sideways as if he was examining him.

"Great pain will come your way, and I'm the man to deliver it," he said. Then he pushed the captain away from him and closed the door.

Captain Morales turned around and looked at the scene around him. He knew he had lost respect from the officers. Still, his family was the most important thing in life, and this was a small sacrifice. He would contact the police of Salvador and count on someone being courageous enough to step forward. He didn't understand how money could triumph loyalty so easily, but he was starting to find out that the police officers of the city thought differently. He needed to go into the city to find help, and he knew just the man to find.

*

Corruption in Brazil was nothing new. Some would say it was just a cultural acceptance in some professions. Others would say it was because of the increased regulation of foreign trade and investments, and the multiple levels of government agencies involved. There was plenty of blame to go around and not many had bothered to find a solution. Whether or not the problem could be solved was another issue altogether.

The Brazilian criminal justice system appeared to lock up people on social standing, rather than merit. Being able to have resources and high-priced lawyers made a tremendous impact on time served, if any at all. Half of the population in prison was still awaiting a trial. Plus, there was something called open and closed regimes. An open regime meant that the convict did not have to stay day and night. Only recently had politicians and rich business people had their high-priced lawyers take advantage of this part of the law.

Corruption was also rampant in the business field. Now with Brazil gaining economic growth and becoming the major player of trade in South America, companies were competing globally and business-minded people were always looking for ways to cut costs and increase profits.

However, the majority of the corruption came at a local level with law enforcement and politicians. In fact, a certain level of corruption was expected and thought of as normal. Government intervention in the economy had been shown to create numerous opportunities for corruption. Regulations required enforcement, and those chosen to enforce may face others who wished to circumvent such regulations, especially in emerging economies. This also led to corruption. In general, everyone was accustomed to getting a piece, and the local police here were no different.

In some police stations, it was bad practice not to take bribes. You were looked down upon amongst your peers. In order to fit in and to make enough money for their families, it was common practice to take the dirty money than to be left out.

There was too much money to not try to take. The system wasn't going to change anytime soon either. The players changed faces, but the action remained the same, and this was the precise reason Carlito had gotten a group of officers from the police department to go after the band of mercenaries. Squad cars left the police stations across the city looking for them as the real culprit that was destroying the city was relaxing at home.

Carlito had made the gamble to let Malestar free, for now. He had debated what to do about Vesco. He had grown quite fond of him over the time he had spent with him at meetings and at the golf course. Carlito respected Vesco's need to protect his family, but not his need to protect the city. The inhabitants weren't making him money. It was the Corporation that had done that for him. It was the ultimate betrayal. Perhaps it was time to put an end to him as well.

*

Red was sitting on her bed in a cross-legged fashion while cleaning her guns and watching a comedy movie on her portable DVD player on the bed. She laughed at her favorite scene in the movie. It had been a long time since she had felt relaxed. With the citizens of the city in panic, and a crazed lunatic having his way, she still felt an inner peace right now. Perhaps it was the presence of Mauricio. He had returned and he was simply the best. He had reinvigorated her passion in head hunting, and she still hoped he would mentor her along the way.

With Claudia gone, she felt guilty for her play on Mauricio. It wasn't a respectable move, even though she had done it multiple times in the past. She always was one that wanted something she couldn't have. The thrill of the chase was part of the fun. Now, it was different. She felt sorry for the man and was attracted to him, but she didn't think she could flirt like she did before. The thrill was gone, and she was ghastly afraid that he would see her for the real her.

That was risky. Letting anyone close was. It was best just to travel around the world and never get close to anyone, and get paid for what she did best—manipulate and conquer. The world was too cruel to see the real her, and if they did, the possibility of rejection was too much to overcome. She hated thinking about her own insecurities all the time. She tried to think of something else. Did that contact in Europe ever fix that problem he had? Maybe she could go over there for a year or so. There was a lot of rich culture there as there was here, but maybe more people would understand English.

There were two knocks at the door. Red knew who it was. She looked through the peephole to confirm, and there he was. She opened the door and Rodrigo walked in. "You're ready?"

"Aren't we a bit early?" Red asked, and took a seat on her bed to return to her guns. "I haven't even got dressed yet."

"Good, I've been meaning to talk to you about something," Rodrigo stated.

"Rodrigo, I'm not sleeping with you."

"It's not that," Rodrigo said, leaning against the wall. Although he wasn't pleased that she verbally said he had no chance.

"It's about Mauricio. Maybe it's not the best time to be following him in his revenge mission. He's had a loss, and his head isn't right. Do you think we should sit this one out?"

Red looked up from her gun cleaning. "You're in the wrong business, sweetie."

"Don't act like you never get afraid."

"That's part of the rush," Red replied. "You said it yourself you want him to mentor you."

"I don't know, Red. Sometimes it's hard to get inside his head."

"Well, this dinner is a good thing. It will be a chance to gain some knowledge from the wise one."

Rodrigo grinned. "Why are you in this business anyway? As hot as you are, you should be on some rich guy's arm traveling around the world."

"You really don't get laid much, do you?" Red asked. "The reason I don't do that is because I'm not that type of woman."

"What are you talking about? You flirt to get whatever you want."

"Not in the way you're thinking of. I'm just doing my job. I know what some men's weakness is and I use it to my advantage. It doesn't work all the time."

"But you hope it works on Mauricio?" Rodrigo asked.

Red placed her guns on the bed. "Can you wait for me outside?"

Rodrigo placed his hands out in front of him as he backed toward the door. "I can put in a good word in for you."

Red tossed a pillow that landed against Rodrigo's face. "Or not," he said, and he left the room.

The implication that she would try to seduce Mauricio at this time was insulting and absurd. Yes, she knew how to get what she wanted, but she also had a heart and understood compassion. Besides, it wasn't like

Mauricio liked women like her anyway. Claudia was beautiful, inside and out, and Red only had one of the two. Maybe one day her inner beauty would come out, but if she wanted to survive this business, it was her in her best interests to keep that part of her to herself.

20.

Mauricio stared at the bottle in front of him. He sat on his bed in his rundown motel room and he could hear police sirens rushing down the adjacent street. The motel was cheap, but Mauricio wanted it this way. He didn't feel like living lavishly or decent anytime soon. The walls were stained, the room smelled like cheap cologne, and there were cigarette burns on the carpet. He looked at the whiskey in front of him and wondered if he was becoming an alcoholic. The very thought made him laugh.

He took another long drink. The burn soothed his throat and his mind. He didn't feel like going out to eat, but the other mercenaries had insisted. Perhaps it was best for him. He needed to keep his mind off the death of the only woman he had ever truly fallen in love with. He was a man that believed karma was real, and her death was the consequence of all the people he had killed.

A flash of all the kills went through his mind. He could hear their shouts and pleas in his head. He envisioned all the bodies being filled with bullets, and all the bloodshed that soon followed. He had learned to become numb to it all. But he never forgot his first one. That one always made him feel guilty.

His name was Benito. He was on assignment in Madrid, Spain. It was spring, and he remembered the weather being perfect for his liking. The temperature was warm, but not warm enough to cause a sweat. Mauricio followed his instructions and tracked the man for two weeks. By then he knew his habits—the route to go home, the restaurant he frequented, and the hotel he went to with his girlfriend when he told his wife he was working late. For a politician that got paid well, he did very little work. He noticed right way he was a man that did not like to be alone and enjoyed the company of others. The only time he was vulnerable was when he was with his girlfriend. The kill would have to be messy.

For a small fee, Mauricio had hired a prostitute to distract the front desk clerk away from his desk. As she flirted with him in the hallway, Mauricio took the spare key for the room Benito was in and made his way back outside. The hotel only had two floors, and the room he was looking for was on the second floor. The canary yellow building was nothing special to look out, but it did its job, which was to house married men for a few hours with their mistresses, and prostitutes to do their job with clients.

Mauricio made his way to the door and opened it up. Benito was on the bed, with his girlfriend on top of him. They both turned their heads as he walked in. The woman screamed and jumped to the side of the bed. Mauricio pointed his gun at Benito. He still remembered the frightened look on his face, when he realized his life was coming to an end. Benito placed a hand out in front of him as if that was going to stop the bullet. Mauricio fired once, and the bullet landed between his eyes. He fell against his pillow with his eyes till open.

The woman screamed and ran to the bathroom, locking the door. Mauricio kicked it open. She pleaded for her life. Mauricio bent over, grabbed her by the back of her head, and placed a gun to her forehead as she leaned against the back wall. Tears were coming down her cheeks. She closed her eyes and wept.

"*Lo siento. Lo siento*," she said.

Mauricio removed the gun from her forehead. She opened her eyes to see Mauricio nod toward the bathroom door. She got up and ran out as fast as she could. Mauricio returned to the dead body on the bed. He looked at Benito's face once more, and the image was etched into his mind.

He had enough of these bad memories. Mauricio took another drink and stood up to leave. He also had enough of this feeling sorry for himself. He had to move on, whether he liked it or not.

*

One of Rodrigo's favorite restaurants was a colonial house, called a *sobrado*, located in the Pelourinho section of the city. Outside, the restaurant looked like the standard colonial buildings of the area, but inside was where the restaurant had its advantage. The three mercenaries sat at a courtyard further into the restaurant with tables painted in pearl white, pink, and light blue. Plants were everywhere and vines wrapped around a tree branch lined the open ceiling. A brick fireplace was on the side of the table with an assortment of plants hanging nearby. There was a park bench in the center of the courtyard and a brick-paved pathway that led back inside the restaurant.

Rodrigo insisted everyone try the *moqueca*, which is fish and shrimp made with coconut milk and a lot of spices. They received their meals and began to dive in. Rodrigo was right, the food was delicious. Mauricio wanted to save room for dessert, but he was full. Instead, he ordered a round of drinks for everyone at the table. As they finished eating, Rodrigo looked like he wanted to say something to Mauricio but he was too afraid to say it.

"What is it?" Mauricio asked.

'I just thought maybe you could give us some tips of the trade. Something that will help us survive this profession. Red and I—"

"No, this is just you," Red said.

"Well, I've noticed you keep things inside. I just wish you'd share some of that knowledge you gained throughout the years on to us. That's all I ask."

Mauricio looked at Red, and then back at Rodrigo. "I didn't know I was teaching a class."

"Just humor him," Red said.

"First lesson. Don't get killed," Mauricio said.

"Okay, forget it."

"All right, all right," Mauricio replied with a smile. "You want to know what it takes to make it in this business. Well, first, you need intelligence. I see that both of you have that, and know how to play the situation to your advantage. Then you need perseverance. I shouldn't have to tell you how hard it is sometimes to track down your target. Sometimes it's a long assignment and you need plenty of patience. Also, don't take jobs that are above your level of expertise or tolerance level of danger. In this business, we mostly work alone, so you are only as strong as what you can do. Don't ever try to take on too much. And finally, and probably the hardest thing to do, is to think like the person you're tracking. Once you master that, the world opens up and the hunt becomes a simple sport."

"What about having no emotions?" Rodrigo asked.

Mauricio's smile faded away. He stared at his cup of beer and seemed to get lost in his thoughts. Red looked at Rodrigo and wondered what Mauricio was thinking.

"From a professional standpoint that makes sense," Mauricio said, still looking at his cup. He then looked back at Rodrigo. "Especially when it comes to your targets. You can't feel any sympathy for them. The person that hires you is going to say they are the worst people in the world. It doesn't matter if you believe them or not. They could donate everything they have to charity, and adopt a village, but none of that matters. What matters is that you have a job to do. You do your job, and get paid. No questions asked."

"So, we're no different than the targets we're chasing. Ruthless, and without regard to what other people feel," Rodrigo said.

Mauricio flashed a grin. "There was this man in Mombasa that drove around a tuk-tuk, which you would know as an auto rickshaw, and he used to transport people up and down the city wherever they wanted to go. He was good at conversing, a very personable person. I mean, he could go on for hours. He had a wife and a son waiting for him when his night shift was done and he returned in the morning, and he would tell them all about his adventures of the night. Apparently, one night he was waved down by one of the city's most violent criminals. The man could have refused him a ride, which would have been a noble gesture, but this man, well-liked by almost everyone, decided to give the criminal a ride, not judging him on his deeds. He had a job to do. Needless to say, the man was scared for his life during the entire ride. The criminal could have shot him at any moment's notice and robbed him of the money he needed to feed his family. But he pressed on, following the criminal's instruction on what streets to run. Finally, the man from Mombasa was confused, as the criminal's instruction was to stop in front of the police station. However, he did what he was told and the man turned himself in."

Red and Rodrigo looked at each other in astonishment. "I tell you this because the universe has a way of correcting itself," Mauricio said. "Always has, always will. Without good, there is no evil, and vice versa. Fate will be the judge, and you will do your job."

Mauricio picked up his cup and Rodrigo picked up his as well. "I'd like to propose a toast," Mauricio said. Red raised her cup. "May good fortune come our way and we prosper until we decide to retire."

"I'll toast to that," Red said, and everyone tapped their cups together. They followed that with a long drink.

"What kind of beer is this?" Red said, almost choking to keep it down.

Mauricio and Rodrigo laughed. "The best Brazil has to offer," Rodrigo said. "You can't tell me American beer is any better."

"Yes, I can. This stuff is way too bitter."

"At least it has taste," Mauricio said.

"Thank you," Rodrigo replied. "Good taste is not recognized by many."

"Explains your clothing," Red said, and they all laughed.

"You know, when all of this over," Red said, "I'm inviting all of you back home where I'll show you how a good time is really done."

"Is that a proposal?" Rodrigo asked.

"You wish," Red replied.

There was commotion coming from within the restaurant. Mauricio stood up and positioned himself to the side of the wall leading back to the restaurant. He stuck his head through to see what was going on. Two police officers were walking among the guests and asking questions, showing a picture of two men and a woman. There was a loud murmur going amongst the customers. Mauricio immediately waved over Red and Rodrigo.

They went to him and stood behind him. "We have to make a run for the side door," he said.

The officers had their backs turned as they approached tables to show them the pictures. Mauricio figured there were spies all over the city, and someone had spotted them come in. The reason the police officers were looking for them was still debatable in his mind. It could be for any amount of reasons, from previous shootouts to Vesco or Carlito turning them in. Then again, Vesco needed their help. However, it was no time to think about such things.

Mauricio made a run for the door. Rodrigo and Red followed, and as they did, one of the police officers looked up to see them sprinting away. He shouted to his partner, and they withdrew their weapons. They followed the mercenaries to the side door and out to the street.

Mauricio had made his way further down the street as Rodrigo and Red struggled to follow behind. Rodrigo decided to make a break toward his car. The police were right behind them.

"Pare!" one of them shouted.

Rodrigo and Red froze in their tracks. Rodrigo placed his hands in the air. The officers stood behind them with their guns pointed.

"Vire lentamente!"

Rodrigo turned to Red. "What do you want to do?"

"There's no way I'm going to jail in Brazil. We have a job to do, right?"

The police officers started to walk slowly toward them. The restaurant customers looked on. The police officers came closer and Rodrigo and Red looked at each other, knowing what they needed to do.

One of the officers put a gun to Red's back, and she quickly turned around to strike the man in the face with her arm. The other officer turned to shoot her. Rodrigo grabbed his arm before he had the chance to fire. Red kicked her police officer in the stomach and took his weapon from him. Rodrigo struck his police officer in the face with an elbow and the gun dropped to the ground. Then Rodrigo took his stun gun from his side.

"Don't even think about it!" Red shouted, pointing the gun at the police officer.

The police officers began to back away. "We can't let them leave," Rodrigo said.

"What do you want me to do?"

"Keep your gun pointed," Rodrigo said, and walked toward them. The police officers stopped in their walk. Rodrigo went up to them, and one by one, he placed the stun gun against their chest. They both fell to the ground with their bodies convulsing.

Red went over to their bodies. She looked to her side. People from the restaurant were watching, some taking video with their cell phones. "Whatever you want to do, we better do it fast."

"Help me move the bodies," Rodrigo said.

They dragged the bodies back to the police car, and Rodrigo took the car keys from one of them. They got into the police car, and Red got into the passenger side. She turned to face Rodrigo.

"Are you sure about this?" she asked.

"There's only one way to find out," he said, starting the engine.

*

Mauricio continued to run down the street. He turned down an alleyway, and a beat-up silver compact car followed him inside. Mauricio sped up his pace. The car sped up as well, and Mauricio took the gun out of his back hip. The car pulled up next to him and the passenger side door opened. Mauricio was ready to shoot, but he wanted to get a good look at the driver. There was a man inside the car with a tan shirt and black pants. Mauricio didn't make him for a cop or a member of the Corporation. He thought about shooting him, but the car suddenly stopped.

Mauricio continued to run until the man got out of the car and shouted," I need you."

Mauricio turned around to face him. "What for?"

"To stop Malestar," Captain Morales said.

21.

Captain Morales was an interesting man. He had been raised in a very small village three hours west of the city, and learned to speak English from a priest that was volunteering his services in the town. His favorite pastime was cock fighting, and he once had a pet parakeet he took to school. He had a rough childhood, and his family was always poor. However, his parents had raised him to always do the right thing, and in turn, he taught his daughter the very same values. There were plenty more stories, but Mauricio tuned most of them out. The man liked to talk about himself as he drove through the streets of Brazil with Mauricio sitting next to him.

Finally, he returned to the topic of why he picked him up. "He has my daughter," Morales said.

"Seems to be going around," Mauricio replied.

"I know you can't go to the police because they're on payroll. They're going to look away to anything he does. Your best bet is to lay low, and figure out when he strikes again. I will help in any way I can. We might not be successful, but we are going to try. The city is missing people like us."

"You have me all wrong," Mauricio said. "My reasons are not for saving this city."

"I can see a good heart when I see one."

Mauricio was about to say something else, but he decided to let it go. "And how are we supposed to know when he strikes?"

"Good point. I got a better idea. We get him where he lives."

"Wait, you know where he stays?" Mauricio asked.

"Sure do. We can stop by your hotel and get your things. You'll be staying with me from now on. We have much work to do. We have to be careful because I think there are trackers out there following me. I can't be sure, but I don't think I was followed. Now, where are you staying?"

Mauricio told him the address, then said, "Tell me why the bribery money never tempted you. And don't give that lame reason it was your parents. Money is money. You could have done a lot to help your family."

"Is money all that matters to you?" Morales asked.

"It's a means to get what you want."

"It can be, yes, but having plenty of it doesn't mean your life is better. People use it, and try to obtain it to hide their insecurities. They're not happy with the simple things of life. A new boat or a new car is not going to make you live longer, and brings a false happiness. I don't need money to feel rich. You live your life chasing money, at the end when you get it, you realize you lost the point of it all."

"And what is the point of it all?" Mauricio asked.

"To live every moment like it's your last, and love the people that love you."

Mauricio smiled. "You're the sensitive type, aren't you? I bet you cry yourself to sleep."

"Everyone cries," Morales said. "Are you immune to doing so?"

Mauricio's smile went away. "I can't say I am."

"I used to be like you when I first got into police work. I had this notion that I was bigger and meaner than everyone around me. No one could stop me. When it came to marksmanship and endurance, I shined every time. I mean, I was the best. I had a lot of heart and intelligence to go with it. I walked in the police station thinking I was going to be feared by everyone in the street. I felt invincible."

"I'm aware I'm a mortal being," Mauricio replied.

"Just hear me out. Then I saw all of the dead bodies, and blood, and children. Some of the sickest things that shouldn't be seen by anyone. They kept telling me I would go numb, and it will go away, and at first it did. But then all of it got the best of me. I cried for the families, the parents that lost their children, the children that lost their parents. I became compassionate for my fellow men and women, not a robot. I realized this business will make you inhuman if you let it. I know contract killers like you are taught to not feel, but you're doing yourself a disservice."

"And you can tell all of this by just meeting me?"

"I used to be a detective. It's what I do," Morales replied.

"Oh yeah? What else can you detect?"

"Some hostility."

"Is it that obvious?" Mauricio asked.

Morales laughed. "I did my research. You have quite the reputation. In some circles, you are regarded as a killer of all bad men. There are criminals that fear you, and criminals that want to hire you. Tell me, how do you decide on a client?"

"I wasn't the one doing the selecting. But I'm on my own now, and I got a new strategy."

"What's that?"

"I want to know more than just the minimal. I want to know the reason behind the target."

Morales scrunched his face. "I don't know many criminals that are willing to give out that information."

"I don't know many people that can track the way I can."

"You got too much confidence," Morales said. "That's not a good thing."

Morales made a turn and drove up a street that didn't have much traffic on the road. Mauricio figured this was a quicker way to get to his hotel. He didn't know if he could trust the guy just yet, but he had no other choice.

"Let's lighten the mood," Morales said. "Tell me something funny."

"What do you call a cop that doesn't take bribes?"

"Don't know."

"A corpse," Mauricio replied. Mauricio laughed, and Morales followed with a loud laugh.

His laughter was cut short. As he crossed the intersection, a white truck slammed into the car via the driver's side, and sent the car spiraling across the street. Mauricio held on to the top of the car as it spun in circles until it crashed into a light pole and spun around it. With the car stopped, Mauricio turned to face Morales. He wasn't moving, and his face was covered in blood. Mauricio checked his pulse. There was no heart rate. He was dead from the impact.

Mauricio reached over and took the man's wallet and keys and placed them in his pocket. He then quickly got out the car. As he did so, bullets pierced the windows and the side of the car. Mauricio took out his gun, glancing through the window to find the source of the firing. He was surprised at what he saw, and for a moment he thought his mind was playing a trick on him. There she was, the assassin Fernanda, with a gun in hand, wearing a black top, leather skirt, and black boots, and determined to kill.

She stopped shooting and flashed a smile. "Mauricio, did you miss me?" she shouted in his direction.

There was no point pretending he wasn't there. "I'm not your enemy!" Mauricio shouted back.

"I'm disappointed. I thought you knew how it is. This isn't about enemies. It's about finishing a job."

She was right. This was nothing personal. He only regretted not killing her when he had the chance.

"Come on, let's talk about this," Mauricio said. "I'll take you back to the hotel, and we'll have some tea, hash it all out." Mauricio looked underneath the car and saw that he had a direct shot of Fernanda's boots.

"As good as that sounds, I'm going to have to pass."

"I'm a good listener." Mauricio pointed his gun at her foot.

"Still killing you," Fernanda replied.

"Can't say I didn't try." Mauricio pressed the trigger and the bullet landed in Fernanda's foot.

She screamed in pain and tried to hobble away. Mauricio stood up and shot her in the side of the neck as she moved. She dropped her gun and held onto her wound.

Mauricio made his way over to her. She fell to her knees, and Mauricio kicked her gun away. He pointed his gun toward her head.

"Do it," she said, blood pouring out her neck at a furious pace.

"I don't have to," Mauricio replied, and soon after, Fernanda fell forward with her face hitting the concrete.

Mauricio reached into his pocket and took out the wallet of Morales. He found a few bills of money, pictures of his family, and a driver's license. He looked at the driver's license, and then down at Fernanda. He was sure she was dead this time.

*

The wife of Morales opened her eyes from her sleep because she thought she heard a noise. The room was dark, and she turned to her side to listen for a sound. It was quiet. Perhaps she had imagined it. She went back to sleep, thinking about her weekend trip to Salvador.

Downstairs, Mauricio crept to the office room and turned on the light. There was a desk in the corner, a desktop computer, and an oak bookshelf in another corner that had a glass covering half of the front area. Mauricio turned on the computer and headed toward the bookshelf. It was locked. Mauricio reached into his pocket and took out Morales' keys. He looked for the smallest one and placed it in the keyhole. The bookshelf unlocked.

The top shelves were full of books, ranging from self-help books to fiction novels, mostly of the police procedural kind. On the bottom shelf of the bookshelf were weapons, ranging from rifles to handguns. Mauricio picked up one of the rifles and aimed it ahead of him. It was a nice weapon, with a good grip and made well. Morales had taste. He put the rifle back and picked up a few of the handguns. He placed them on the computer desk and sat down in front of the computer screen.

The desktop came on screen. The wallpaper was a picture of Morales with his wife and daughter. Mauricio went to the main drive and into the Documents folder. There were spreadsheets dealing with taxes and household expenses and repairs, and a half-written novel by Morales dealing with a detective story. He searched elsewhere. He found a folder titled Cases and opened it. There, he found documents of cases that were assigned numbers and letters, some of them solved, some of them unsolved. One of the unsolved cases was titled 1685Mal, and Mauricio clicked on the folder. A document came on screen, and a picture of Malestar did as well. Then there were reports of crimes in Salvador. Mauricio couldn't read much of what was written. He clicked on the icon on the bottom right, and connected to the Internet. Once there, he opened up an online translator and placed the words there.

Then he began to read what was being said. The stories of crime fit the description of Malestar, and Morales was trying to build the link. He was doing extracurricular work outside his own jurisdiction. Was this pleasure or concern? From all the evidence gathered, it didn't take a rocket scientist to figure out the crimes were being made by Malestar. However, the police department was looking the other way. Was Morales making a case against their negligence? Did he even know about the Corporation?

Seeing the folder of Malestar was of little help to him. Mauricio clicked out and went to the Pictures folder on the main drive. There were plenty of pictures labeled by holidays and dates. Mauricio went to the most recent date and clicked the folder. He looked for a picture of the daughter alone, and he found one. She was smiling toward the camera, wearing her school uniform and showing her braces. Mauricio couldn't print out the picture for fear of making too much noise. He kept a mental picture of the girl in case he came across her.

He was determined to help the captain if he could. From what he knew of him, he was a good man that didn't understand he had to march with the system. Anybody that wasn't with them was against them. However, Morales was almost protected in this small town. If only he hadn't decided to stick his head into the business of Malestar. His daughter was taken, but there was nothing he could do. He was just one man, taking on a system. So was Mauricio. The difference was Mauricio had nothing to live for. He was going to get Malestar or he was going to die trying.

Mauricio turned off the computer, turned off the light, and left Morales' wallet on the desk. He then grabbed the two handguns and headed out the front door. When he opened the door, he heard movement from upstairs.

"*Amor, é que você?*" the wife asked from the upstairs hallway.

Mauricio stopped before leaving as a moment of sadness hit him. It could be any time, in a few hours, or tomorrow morning, but she was going to get a call about her husband's death. He wished he could tell her that her husband died trying to protect his family and to find his daughter, but there were no words to replace life and he knew that personally. Thoughts of Claudia came back into his mind. Mauricio softly closed the door and stepped outside.

He entered the driver's side of Fernanda's white truck, which was parked out front. As he reached over to turn on the engine he could see his arm trembling. He placed his arm down and leaned back in his chair. This was harder than he thought. He thought on this vengeful mission that he would feel better and some of the sadness would go away, but now it was just a constant reminder of the pain. Somehow he was going to have to find a way to deal with it. But right now, he couldn't afford to delve into his memories.

He took a deep breath and started the engine. He could see the living room lights of the home turn on. He drove off, not knowing where he was going to go, but some place where his thoughts were elsewhere and he could rest.

22.

Vesco's wife and daughter were still tied up, and were still as fearful as ever, but were afraid to scream, afraid to make any type of sound. They knew a madman had taken them and it mostly had something to do with Vesco. They hated him for that, but loved him more than ever at the same time. The only comfort they had was that they were still alive, and that meant they were being used as bargaining chips at some point. That was their hope. The other conclusion was that they were being used for the madman's personal enjoyment.

The door swung open and Malestar walked in with a silver plate of shredded beef. "Your master has arrived with a gift."

Malestar placed the food down in front of them. Together, the two females bent their heads down and ate away at the food on the plate. It wasn't their preferred meal, but at this point anything somewhat edible would have sufficed.

"Ladies, I have good and bad news for you. The good news is that your knight in shining armor is alive and well, and I will not touch him. I think he is doing a fabulous job as mayor. No harm shall come his way as long as I have you two in my possession. If the police do what's best for them then you don't have to worry about him. Now for the bad news. You are both my slaves. I will do with you as I wish. Fortunately for you, I have something very big to plan, something the city of Salvador will talk about for hundreds of years! But to do this, I have to leave the country for a bit. So, in my absence, I want you two to decide which woman I would have first in bed. Trust me, I tried to resist you two, but my other bodily parts think different. But let's keep it a secret between us. Now, will it be the vivacious daughter in normal circumstances or the compassionate mother? You decide."

Malestar left the room, and closed the door. Then he opened it again. "Isn't life beautiful?" he asked, and closed the door, this time with a maddening, echoing laugh.

*

Mauricio woke up in his seat with the sun rising, and a direct view of the Atlantic Ocean waves coming in. He had parked the truck in the parking lot of the beach entrance, and now a few surfers were making their way to the beach. He wiped his eyes and leaned forward. He looked at the ocean for a moment, and experienced a moment of calm, something he hadn't had in a long time.

He remembered his first time seeing the ocean in Mombasa. He was a child and he went with his mother. They had to catch a bus to get there and he remembered the day was scorching hot. His mother held his hand as they made their way to the beach, and she watched as he played in the sand. Then he went toward the water.

He was scared, and just put his feet in at first since he didn't know how to swim. Then he took a step further in, and another step, and suddenly he went under, head first, and the water rushed over him. His mother looked up and saw that her son was gone. She got up and called his name. She panicked and shouted his name louder, running down the beach.

Mauricio felt all the weight of the world when he was underwater. He was drowning and struggling to stay afloat the water that was holding him down. But he wasn't going to quit. He put his arms in front of him, made his way to the surface, and stuck his head above the water.

He heard his mother screaming, but he tuned out her voice. He looked around him. He was surrounded by water. He turned his back against the beach and looked ahead. The water seemed to go on forever. He floated in the water and took in the tranquility.

At that moment, he felt the same calm he was experiencing now. Life continued to go on, and all the problems of the world would not change that. He would have to stop some time and just enjoy the beauty that was around him.

The memory soon faded away. Then he had a thought of curiosity. He got out of the car and headed to the back trunk. He looked inside and saw a red blanket covering something underneath. The outline it made was in the shape of an adult male. Mauricio looked around to see if anyone was paying attention. There wasn't. Mauricio removed the sheet from the body.

A man he recognized was tied up by his hands and feet, and his mouth stuffed with a rag. Mauricio removed the rag and helped the man forward. He then began to work on the rope.

"Thank you," Vesco said.

"What are you doing here?"

"The gigantic woman took me from my office. She said she was going to hide me away somewhere. Malestar is just trying to torture me to death."

"I know the feeling," Mauricio said.

"After she tied me up, I heard her on the phone. Malestar is going to Granada to make a deal for weapons. He's planning something big and the Corporation is still behind him. I could make a few calls and find out who he is most likely holding a meeting with. I could also get you to Spain. Please, just help me find my wife and daughter."

"That means I would have to trust you," Mauricio said.

"Of course you can."

"You're a former member of the Corporation, or at least you say you are. How do I know you're not still working for them and this is a ploy to get me away from the city?"

"Did you not see me tied up just a minute ago? They have my wife and daughter!"

"Calm down," Mauricio said, looking around to see if anyone heard them. I'm going to have a few friends here to keep an eye on you."

"They're not your friends, Mauricio. They're your competition."

"Then I will be closest to the prize."

Vesco let out a laugh. "Well played."

"What I don't get is why the police department and all of law enforcement in the city are willing to look away at the planning of such an authoritative attack."

"Then you have to ask yourself who benefits the most from chaos and panic. The Corporation keeps them happy."

"Disgusting," Mauricio replied.

"It's a sick world we live in, my friend."

"You are definitely not my friend. Come on, let's take you home."

"Are you crazy? I can't go back there! Anywhere but there."

"Anywhere?"

Vesco knew he was going to regret saying those words as Mauricio grabbed his arm.

The three black Rottweilers were barking ferociously with saliva dripping from their mouths. They were chained to the opposite side of the fence of where Vesco was chained, in the backyard of Rodrigo's childhood home. Vesco huddled as close to the fence as he could. A dog bowl was in the center of the worn grass riddled with dirt patches. The sun was visible and high, bringing with it plenty of heat to the city.

"Get me out of here! Do you know I am? I am the mayor of this city! I will not tolerate such cruelty!"

Red went over to put something in his mouth to keep him quiet. Mauricio stood next to Rodrigo at the entrance to the backyard. They both had a soda bottle in hand as they watched Vesco squirm.

"I appreciate this," Mauricio said.

"This is temporary. My mother is out of town visiting family. It feels strange treating the mayor in this manner. He's also my former boss."

"I would have thought you said it felt good."

"That too," Rodrigo replied. They shared a smile.

"How do you know where to go?" Rodrigo asked.

"On the way over here, he made a few calls. Some terrorist group is taking refuge there. They do black-market dealings all the time. Don't understand why they didn't fly down and have Malestar come to them, but I'm hoping I will find out. Then again, some people only like conducting business a certain way."

"You sure you don't want us to come along?"

"No, I need you to watch him. I don't trust him yet."

"I was hoping for some on-the-job training."

"I'm not too sure you're meant for this job," Mauricio replied.

"How can you say that? Did you know I used to track down people for Vesco all the time?"

"Yeah, I know. How many kills did you make?"

Rodrigo looked away. Mauricio patted him on his back. "I got a plane to catch."

Mauricio walked away. Red walked over to Rodrigo. She seemed to enjoy having someone under her control.

"Upset you couldn't go with him?" she asked.

"Not at all," Rodrigo said, looking away. "I'm going to help him whether he likes it or not. His making a big mistake not using my help."

"Ah," Red said with a laugh. "Sometimes you are just too cute." She grabbed his jaw and moved his face back and forth.

"Stop it," he said, and pushed her hand away.

"What's your problem?"

"You don't take what we do seriously sometimes," Rodrigo replied. "You do understand all of us could be taken out at any moment? We have the mayor of the city chained up against the fence like a dog. What if someone finds him? I'm putting my family at risk. The police of the city are on the hunt for blood, and a psychopath is turning this city upside down. Does that mean anything to you?"

Red took a step closer to Rodrigo. "What matters to me is that I get what is coming to me, whether it is good or bad. I'm not going to live life anymore being afraid about what's out there. Danger strikes at any time. If you want to start shaking in your boots like a little schoolgirl, then so be it. Just remember, being weak in the mind makes you weak in the street."

Red started to walk away but Rodrigo grabbed her arm. "Let me go," she said without even looking at him.

He made a quick conclusion that he didn't want to see her angry. He released his grip. "You're telling me you never have doubts about all of this?"

Red turned her head to face him. "I live for this."

She walked away. Rodrigo turned back around and focused his attention back to the mayor. Vesco was trying to say something to him. There was a part of Rodrigo that wanted to go over, untie him, and just walk away entirely. But he couldn't. He was in too deep now. This was what he was going to be, whether he liked it or not.

*

Breakfast was splendid as usual. The men in suits and the women in business attire that sat down inside the downtown restaurant were some of the most influential and powerful people in the city. They laughed, told stories, and ate well. These were the group of people that capitalized on the struggle of the common man, and benefited greatly from their work. Carlito was amongst them, his stomach full and his wallet filled with corporate credit cards. The restaurant itself was simple, yet elegant, with marble tables and grey walls, and a kitchen that specialized in local cuisine. The aura of arrogance from the table of the well-to-do that was in the room drew looks from the waiters in the restaurant, but they all wanted to serve them because that meant large tips. They were disgusted by them but glad they were there, and were used to their kind. The waiters had to combine most of the tables in the restaurant so they all could sit together. There were hardly any other customers inside.

Carlito tapped his glass with his fork, and the room became quiet. "Everyone, if I may have your attention. I want to congratulate us all for being steadfast in the face of recent events, as although the course may change, the goal remains the same. We have seen great adversity in the building of our business, but now is just the beginning of a promising future. Of course, I can't speak on specifics..."

This line drew laughter. "I think we all are aware that we lost a peer of ours. Someone we all thought would be there with us as we march to a stronger future. It's always disappointing to have someone that helped found a vision of what you could be walk away from it all. But you know what? We don't need him. He is no longer with us, therefore he is against us. Now, will you all join me to—"

The doors of the restaurant burst open, and a group of teenagers in purple jackets came rushing in with guns in their hands. The people at the table froze with fear.

"What is the meaning of this?" Carlito asked.

The teenagers made their way to the table and pointed their guns at the people sitting down. The waiters rushed to the back of the restaurant. One of the teenagers struck Carlito in the back of the head with a gun, causing blood to leak out the top of his head, and his attacker dragged him away from the table. When he put up a fight, others helped carry him away.

"Do you know I am? Do you know what I could do to you and your families?" Carlito shouted.

"We need your jet," one of the teenagers said.

Carlito was carried to the exit. The rest of the businesspeople sitting down looked at each other, and tried not to move. The teenagers at the table raised their weapons and opened fire. Bullets filled up the men and women of the table, and dishes and silverware were moved back and forth across the table. They continued to shoot until they were convinced all of them were dead.

Smoke and blood decorated their bodies. They sat still. The teenagers raised their guns in the air as they headed toward the exit. Their job was complete, and their leader would be proud. They raised their guns in unison and shouted that the city was going back to the people.

23.

Snow came down on this dark night, on the ski slopes of the Sierra Nevada mountain range, outside the province of Granada, Spain. A popular destination for skiing, the slopes were populated at day and quiet at night. The wind had picked up as the Iberian ibexes along the mountain range searched for warmth from the snow. Part of the mountain range was included in the Sierra Nevada National Park, which incorporated the villages and municipalities in the area.

One such village called Trevélez was where a row of trucks carrying cargo came from the west to enter the city. The mountain ranges were seen in the distance and the city's Welcome sign had a bike chained against its pole. The city as well could be seen, built on the sloping hills that led to panoramic views of the mountain range.

The city itself was a quiet one, known for its terrace housing, air-cured hams, and their most wealthy and powerful resident, Diego Leon.

The trucks rumbled into town and parked at the estate of Diego, a large home with plenty of gates and security around the premises. The winding road that led up the hill and to a large white building was barely covered in snow. The rest of the village was quiet and the movement of trucks could be heard outside the house.

Diego stood in his living room in his silver dress shirt and black slacks, staring out the window at the snowy weather outside. Diego was middle-aged, his hair short cropped, and he was clean shaven. He had a cigar in hand, and took another smoke. Life was good. His right hand-man Vega came over and stood next to him. Vega was taller, had long hair, and was skinnier than his boss.

"The shipment has arrived," Vega said.

"Excellent," Diego replied. "Call the buyer."

*

The tapas bar was in the center of the city of Granada, Spain, and was still quite full in this early morning. Free tapas were served with the purchase of drinks. The building had been built sometime in the early twentieth century and hadn't been repainted since. The tables, bar, and floor were all made out of multicolored wood. There was a pair of couples at one table, a man eating alone at another with his head down and wearing a black beanie and gloves, and finally a table full of college students at a table near the bar. They were the loudest in volume. The mood inside was quite content until the doors of the bar opened.

"Drinks on me!" Malestar shouted in Spanish as he made his way in with a group of his hired crew from Brazil, Carlito amongst them. Carlito was pushed by Malestar's hired help into a table in the center. Malestar took a seat at the table, wearing his pearl white suit, and yelled for a waiter. The college students cheered at the gesture of free drinks. Malestar's men took a seat and forced Carlito to take a seat across from Malestar. The waiter approached and Malestar ordered drinks for everyone on the table, and told the waiter to give drinks to anyone else in the bar that wanted one on his tab. Carlito sat across from him, and had never wanted to kill someone so bad his entire life. Of course, he knew that he wouldn't survive another minute in his attempt.

"Come on, Carlito," Malestar said, switching to Portuguese. "This is a celebration. We're about to make a deal of a lifetime. You are about to get rich off your wildest dreams."

"Why did you bring me here?" Carlito asked.

"Is that any way to talk to the man responsible for making your fortune? Enjoy yourself and drink! We are both getting what we want. You need to learn how to relax."

"You of all people..."

Malestar snapped his fingers and one member of Malestar's crew punched Carlito in the stomach. "Watch your tone," Malestar said as Carlito held his stomach.

"This is ridiculous! We're on the same side. I'm letting you do what you want," Carlito said.

"Letting me? You have no say in what I do. The next time you insist you do, I will cut off your fingers and serve them to your dogs. Now drink!"

Carlito picked up the shot of liquor in front of him, drank what was inside, and slammed the shot glass in front of him on the table. Malestar did the same and gave a loud laugh. Other members of his crew finished their drinks as well.

"Give us more!" Malestar shouted.

The table of college students raised their shot glasses they had just ordered, and pointed them to Malestar. "*Salud!*" they shouted.

Malestar stood up and made his way to the table. A few beer pitchers were on the table, along with half-filled cups. "I presume all of you are students," he said in Spanish.

"That's correct," said the scrawny one with an empty seat next to him. "Thank you for the drinks. Would you like to have a seat?"

"Don't mind if I do," Malestar said, taking a seat. "I bet what you are learning mostly is how to get women and get drunk."

"Can you blame us?" a bearded young man asked from the other end of the table. The men at the table laughed and some picked up their glass of beer to take a drink.

"Can't say I do. This is the prime of your lives. This is when the freedom of making choices can shape the person you will become. The formative years, as many would say. However, most of what you learn does not come from a classroom."

"Truer words cannot be said!" stated the bearded young man. "Books don't teach you how to party!" The young men shared a laugh again.

"How do you guys feel about the law?" Malestar asked.

The young men went quiet. "It's okay, I suppose," the scrawny man finally said.

"Okay? Okay?" Malestar slammed his hand against the table. "Can't you see what they're doing to you? The law only exists to keep you from revolting and to keep them rich. Since the beginning of time it has always been this way. They are taking your struggle and using it to buy big homes, nice cars, and fancy trips to remote islands with your hard-earned money. They get satisfaction from watching you suffer. Are you going to allow them to continue on?"

"Are you a terrorist or something?" one of them in the middle asked.

All the young men laughed but Malestar did not. "Carlito!" he shouted.

Carlito was shoved in Malestar's direction. He straightened up his suit jacket and made his way to the table with the young men and Malestar. Carlito stood next to Malestar.

"Tell these young men what you do," Malestar stated.

"I'm a businessman," Carlito replied.

"Tell them the truth."

Carlito sighed. "I steal money off the backs of the youth's crime in the city and from the man who you are fortunate enough to speak with."

"See, that wasn't hard," Malestar said. "A man in a nice suit, presumably with lots of money, presents himself to you as nothing more than a petty crook. Is this the kind of society you want to live in? Where the people that make the rules benefit and laugh at your expense? You all are nothing more than brainwashed sheep waiting for your slaughter. The comparison actually offends the animals. You are useless other than the consuming goods you buy for the rich to get richer."

Malestar pointed to Carlito. "Look at this man! Do you think he cares about any of you? Can't you see that society is a disease? This man will lie, and cheat, and kill until he gets what he wants! He foams at the mouth like a wild dog whenever a new baby arrives in this world and they train him to believe in some greater good and we're all in this together propaganda. But I'm here to tell you the truth. The truth is even though you have matured into your primes as physical human beings, mentally you have the intelligence of a bag of rocks. All of your mothers should have had abortions. You are nothing more than stupid puppets that happily pull your own strings, believing in a dream that is never going to come to life."

There was silence in the room as all customers inside were now listening to his words. The young men were stunned and their mouths left open. Then there was the sound of clapping coming from the back of the bar. The man in the black hat and black gloves lifted his face and Malestar felt like he had lost command in the room.

Mauricio stopped clapping, stood up, and picked up his chair. Everyone in the bar fixed their eyes on him. He made his way to the table. Malestar's crew kept their guns pointed at Mauricio, surprised by his brashness as he took sat on the opposite side of Malestar.

Mauricio stayed calm. He looked for a moment at Malestar, who had leaned back in his chair and was curious as to Mauricio's next action. Mauricio looked around at the young men and began speaking.

"Do any of you speak English?" he asked.

"I do," the bearded young man said.

"This is a man that preaches for anarchy." The bearded man began to translate as Mauricio spoke. "He dismisses society like it's a bad thing and laws are put in place just to benefit the wealthy. This is not true. Yes, there are people out there like this man standing whose only purpose is to get rich off of you and participate in the corruption that plagues this world. But just think about how life would be on your own. No government to protect you from your neighbor that wants to steal, to kill, to rape your wife. We are all stronger in greater numbers with all of us contributing. Psychopaths like the one sitting before you are not any better than the corrupted minds of the world. They only want to twist your mind to get what they truly want. All of us together can demand what we want and we will always have the power to do so. The people as a whole decide what type of rule we want over us."

"Even you don't believe what you're saying. You're not seriously suggesting democracy is real," Malestar said.

"That's what I'm saying. Unpopular power only yields for so long before the people revolt."

"You seem to forget how weak the people are. Case in point, the power belongs to those with the guns. And as you can see," Malestar said, motioning toward his crew behind him, "you are powerless when it really matters."

Mauricio flashed a grin. "Unlike you, I'm not afraid of those in power."

"And why is that?"

"Because they're a ticking bomb waiting to explode," Mauricio replied.

Before his arrival at the bar, Mauricio had kept himself hidden at the airport hangar of the private airport outside the city. He had used the airport to fly in himself using a jet at Vesco's expense. He also carried with him as much firepower as he needed for the trip. Vesco's contact had told him of the major supplier in the area and which private airports were closest to the city. Mauricio had arrived in Spain ahead of time as Carlito's jet was delayed with a few phone calls from Vesco's contacts. Mauricio was dressed in janitorial clothing as the two cars that were escorting Malestar to the city had arrived. He cleverly bugged them both. Then the jet arrived. He watched from the hangar as Malestar and his crew got off the jet. Then he overheard the conversation Malestar had in the car about coming to the bar after a brief stay at his hotel.

Mauricio rushed in his rental car to the bar as the night grew dark. He strategically placed explosives around the perimeter of the building. He then walked inside and awaited their arrival. He chose the table the furthest away from the bar in an area that wasn't well lit. The remote was in his pocket, safely covered with a plastic top.

Mauricio smiled again. Malestar's mind was trying to figure out the reason Mauricio was so confident. Mauricio reached into his pocket and took out the remote for all to see. The students at the table were taken aback. Mauricio and Malestar kept their eyes locked on each other.

"Nice touch," Malestar said.

"I like to think so," Mauricio replied.

"You enjoy life too much. You're not just going to blow us all up."

"Remember, you and the Corporation took away my reason for living. I'm just here to finish the job."

"Don't be ridiculous. You won't get paid."

"This isn't about money! This is about you taking everything I cherished away from me! You will suffer!"

"So be it!" Malestar shouted. He stood up and placed his arms to his sides. "I always wanted to go out with a bang! End the pain! Do it! Just remember, you're giving me the easy way out."

"I thought about that, and I do wish you to suffer greatly," Mauricio said.

"Your move then. Tick, tick, tick..."

"I want you to bleed." Mauricio raised his other arm to draw his gun and shot Malestar in the shoulder, and he shouted in pain.

Malestar's crew raised their weapons to fire at Mauricio but he showed them the remote as a reminder. Malestar began to laugh. Mauricio stood up and made his way toward the door, keeping his gun pointed at Malestar. He then shot him in the other shoulder, and Malestar dropped to his knees.

"Shoot him! Shoot him or he will kill us all!" Malestar shouted.

Mauricio started to back away toward the door as Malestar's crew kept their guns pointed at him. They were conflicted in what to do. The one furthest from Mauricio decided he had to put his fate in his own hands. As Mauricio moved his way out the door, he fired once into Mauricio's arm, causing him to drop the remote.

Mauricio ran out the door as more firepower came seconds later. The glass to the entrance shattered and Mauricio ran to his rental car. There was just too much firepower to compete with. He started the engine and held his arm for a moment to stop the bleeding. He realized the bullet entry wasn't that deep. Mauricio gave a sigh of relief and smiled. He was glad he could make Malestar feel real pain, a stepping stone to his vengeance ploy.

Inside the bar, Malestar frantically waved his arms around. "Stop!" he shouted, his arms covered in blood. He went over to pick up the remote. He looked at it for a moment, and then at everyone inside the bar.

"You want to do something right, you got to do it yourself," he said as he rushed out the broken door with the remote in hand.

Everyone else took notice and began to run out as well. They didn't make it out in time. Malestar opened the top and pressed the button. The building exploded and a rush of fire came out the entrance as Malestar jumped to the ground. Parts of the building came falling around him. Malestar was in intense pain from the jump to the ground and the bullets in the shoulder, but he still managed to have a smile on his face. It felt good.

24.

Mauricio sped to Trevélez, and as he went up in altitude, the snow started to come down more. He had placed the directions in his phone, which had an application that showed his destination. He was on his way to see Diego, and he had no idea what he was going to say once he arrived there. He only knew he would try his best to convince him not to do business with Malestar. The city of Salvador and the welfare of its citizens were at stake here.

His heart was racing, and he realized that he had almost committed suicide. It would have been for the greater good, and his vengeance would have been completed, but something within the moment made him change his mind. Perhaps it was the fact that Claudia would have wanted him to live, or the fact that he would be giving Malestar an easy way out. The man needed to suffer. That was part of the reason he didn't believe in capital punishment. People needed to pay for their sins and cruel acts, and taking them out of this world wouldn't make them see their ways.

Then again, Malestar was too lost to ever admit any wrongdoing. He thrived on the weak and on gaining power, and any truth of how destructive he was would be met with how he was doing a great service to the community as a whole because he was letting them be free in some sick way. He had programmed his mind to make him believe he was actually doing good deeds. The world needed to get rid of people like him, but there was always someone else to take his place. Once again, good and evil needed each other.

Mauricio checked his speed as the road got steeper. The snow made visibility somewhat of an issue and he began to slow down. He could barely see the mountains to the side of him and the steep drop of the roadside to the valley below. He wasn't a man afraid of heights, but the distance below was intimidating in this weather. As he drove, he checked his phone to see how close he was. It was a delicate task to keep his eyes on the road and look at the phone. At one point, he quickly straightened the car as he swerved. He put the phone away and drove on.

Finally, he approached the village and could see the homes against the side of the mountain. Plenty of trees outlined the city. There was a large building in the background. Mauricio sped up again, anxious to put an end to Malestar's reign. He held onto his bloody left arm and tried not to think about the throbbing pain.

Diego's right-hand man, Vega, came into the room with a white towel in hand as Diego was doing laps in his indoor pool. Diego found the exercising relaxing, and it helped him stay alert. A large window adjacent to the pool showed the snow coming down outside. A series of small light fixtures surrounded the pool to keep the area lit. Around the pool, the floors were heated. The home had taken him many years to customize but it was well worth the wait.

Diego stepped out of the pool and Vega dried him off. "We have a guest," Vega said.

"Ah, the buyer has arrived."

"No, it's somebody else."

"Well, what does he want?" Diego asked.

"We don't know yet. He's speaking English. He keeps saying, 'No deal. No deal.' Should we just shoot him down?"

"No, no. Let's not waste bullets for things we do not know. Let's see what he wants."

Diego picked up a robe from a nearby wall hook and placed it on himself. "We really have to start making meetings during the day. I can't stay up like I used to."

"You should try Vitamin B," Vega replied.

"I don't like the pills," Diego said as they made their way to the living room.

"There's always those energy drinks."

"How disgusting. The first time I tried one of those, I nearly vomited right then and there. There's got to be something else."

Diego and Vega made their way to the living room, where Mauricio was sitting down on the elongated, white leather sofa. A few nondescript paintings hung on the wall above him. Three bodyguards stood nearby with guns to their sides. Mauricio stood up at Diego's presence.

"Didn't mean to intrude but this is an urgent matter," he said.

"No English," Diego replied.

"You can't make the deal with Malestar."

"Malestar?" Diego asked. He noticed Mauricio was holding on to his arm, and saw the blood all over his sleeve. "He's a mess, and he could bring us problems," he said to Vega. "Shoot him."

The bodyguards pointed their weapons at Mauricio, who stuck his hand out. "Wait! Um, *quieren dinero,* for uh..." Mauricio made a gun with his hand. "Bang, bang."

Diego and Vega looked at each other, both perplexed. "Is this a joke?" Diego asked Vega.

"Maybe he's homeless."

"Does he look like he's from around here? You are as stupid as you look," Diego replied.

"No deal. No deal," Mauricio said, waving his hands out in front of him.

"It's the same thing he was doing before," Vega said.

Diego sighed. "Put him in a room, and get a translator in the morning to see what he wants."

"You heard him," Vega said to the guards.

The guards put their guns down and went over to drag Mauricio away. "Get someone for his arm," Diego shouted as they carried him away.

"You're making a big mistake!" Mauricio shouted.

'I really have got to start learning a new language," Diego said.

"You should try that Rosetta thing," Vega replied.

"Does it work?" Diego said as they walked away from the living room.

"From what I hear."

*

He was losing blood but Malestar continued to walk. He walked down the deserted street with his shoulders slumped and blood covering both of his arms where it had run down from his shoulders. He was feeling nauseous and lightheaded. His vision was in and out of focus and he could feel his brain starting to shut down. He heard the sirens of the ambulances rushing down the street as they rushed to the scene of the explosion. He could see lights approaching as he staggered up the street like a drunk man. Were the lights from a car or a building? Everything was hazy.

He made his way toward the light and passed through a set of doors. He had entered a bar. Malestar collapsed on the ground in front of the crowd. The music stopped. People began to gather around his body and someone called an ambulance. The police were notified as well.

When the ambulance arrived, Malestar was put on a stretcher and placed in the back of the ambulance. The police came to the scene, and had been previously given a tip that Malestar was in town. They followed the ambulance back to the hospital and were ready to question him at the first opportunity.

*

Mauricio woke up with his arm bandaged and saw that he was inside a large room with a desk, a walk-in closet, a large wall-sized mirror, a wall-mounted big-screen television, and he was lying on a king-sized bed. It took a moment for Mauricio to realize why he was here. Then he remembered that he had come to Diego's home. The move seemed to be salient when he made the decision to come here, but now it seemed, at the very least, a risky one.

He opened the door and noticed a large bodyguard with curly hair and a gun strapped around his shoulder standing outside his door. He quickly closed the door. Then he stood in the room and began to think.

Was it even possible to stop the meeting? Were they going to kill him afterwards? Panic started to set in, an uncharacteristic feeling to him. Mauricio felt his hip and realized his gun was gone.

The door opened and Diego came in, this time with a plain-looking woman, probably in her early twenties, with her hair in a bun and wearing black-rimmed glasses. She didn't wear much makeup and her body poise was professional and without emotion.

"I have five questions to ask you," Diego said, and the translator immediately began translating. "If any of the answers give me displeasure, you will receive a bullet to the head. Shall we begin?"

Mauricio had no other choice. "Yes," he said, and the translator repeated his words in Spanish. She continued to translate the entire conversation with pauses between responses as Mauricio and Diego listened.

"Who are you?" Diego asked.

"My name is Mauricio. I'm a mercenary for hire," Mauricio replied after the translation.

"Mercenary? What a strange term. Why not hitman?"

"Is that question number two?" Mauricio asked.

Diego grinned. "What do you want?"

"To stop the deal with Malestar. What he's doing with your weapons will destroy the city of Salvador, Brazil. This may not concern you, but it affects many. Many lives will be lost and it will be on your hands. It would be a mistake."

"I will decide that. Who do you work for?"

"Is that really important?"

"I ask the questions here," Diego replied, halfway through the translation as he knew it was question. "I usually don't have a temper, but when I do, I sometimes make very brash decisions. You don't want to see that side of me. I have tortured many in my line of work. It's not something I'm proud of, but something that is necessary from time to time. Trust me when I say you don't want that to be you. Now, who do you work for?"

"He's a politician. You wouldn't know him, but his name is Mayor Vesco Amado. He hired me to clean up his city."

Diego was amused. "Oh, you have traveled so far and gone to great lengths just for one man. I admire your dedication. This is what I want from my men, someone that doesn't quit until the job is done. You set a great example."

"Thank you," Mauricio said.

"It's too bad I have to kill you. I'm sorry to say that I need this deal. Business hasn't been that great lately and the government is always on the search for illegal guns. Europe, in general, is very strict on gun ownership. I had to resort to living in this desolate town just to escape their grasp. So, I give my apologies to the citizens of Salvador. Now, how do you want to die?"

"That's the thing. I'm not ready for that yet."

"I'm not giving you a choice."

"It's not your choice to make," Mauricio replied.

"Oh, but it is," Diego stated. "Guards!"

At that moment, the sound of a helicopter was heard coming toward the home, and then the sound was directly overhead. "Secure the building!" Diego shouted to his guards.

Everyone rushed out the room and went into the living room. Then the windows of the home shattered and bullets came flying in. Mauricio ducked behind the sofa for cover, pulled the translator with him. Vega went with Diego to the kitchen area. Diego's men tried to fire back at the helicopter, but were filled with bullets and fell to the floor.

The shooting stopped. Diego turned to Vega. "Get me a hostage."

There was a voice from a speaker demanding everyone to put their hands up and to stand in front of the windows. The translator was the first to stand up and raise her arms. She began to walk toward the windows, but Vega ran to her and placed a gun to her head.

"Go away or I will shoot her!" Vega demanded in Spanish.

Mauricio crawled away from the sofa and headed toward the hallway. As he made his way there he heard the sound of an automatic machine gun. He ran into the bathroom and found that there was no window. He then tried the bedroom across the hall. There was one inside there. He opened it, climbed out, and scaled down a wall and onto a dirt hill in the back of the house. He jumped over a fence and entered the backyard of a home that was below Diego's home. Then he ran to the side of the house and onto the street.

The neighborhood was poorly lit in the dark night. He could still hear and see the helicopter as it shined its bright light toward the house and around the perimeter. Mauricio continued to run until he reached the Bajo neighborhood, which was the lower part of the city. He was almost out of breath by the time he reached the neighborhood. There was no one on the street and the area was quiet here. Mauricio found his car where he left it, parked on the side of the street.

Mauricio got in the driver's side and closed the door. He took a moment to catch his breath. The job was done, even if it wasn't the one he wanted. The deal had been off whether Diego was alive or not. He wondered how the police came upon the property so quickly but decided to think about that later.

There was still one job left to do, and that was to take out Malestar. Malestar had sliced him up, and he shot him down. The revenge on that aspect had been settled. But he wanted to be the one to personally put an end to that monster. He would have to track him down once more to make that happen.

Mauricio checked the glove compartment between the seats; his cell phone and wallet was still there. Then he felt something cold on the back of his head. Instantly, he knew that there was gun on him. Mauricio froze and tried to stay calm. He closed his eyes, waited a few seconds, and realized he was still alive. There had to be a reason.

"Who are you?" Mauricio asked.

"I'm the one responsible for what just happened back there. You're welcome."

The voice was one that he recognized with a Portuguese accent. "Can I start the car?" Mauricio asked.

The gun was taken off his head. "I insist."

25.

Word got out of Malestar's stay in the ambulance and his consequent arrest. The news traveled back to Brazil, and the remaining members of the Corporation were undecided what to do next. They feared there was no way they could ever help him again, especially after the shooting of many of the upper Corporation members inside a restaurant. Malestar was power hungry and he couldn't be controlled. They decided to go into hiding, and would only meet privately for financial matters. For once, they decided to be legit businesspeople.

Many police officers of Brazil were upset by the news. A lot of them had depended on the money that Malestar was providing to feed their families and pay for their children's education. The government kept them underpaid, making it almost a necessity to carry out corruptive acts. The officers that were clean were glad to see him arrested. The citizens were even more so. The psychopath had done damage for far too long without anyone stopping him, or even trying to stop him. They felt the city had returned to normal, even though crime didn't go away completely. Still, citizens could feel comfortable in the normal sense of danger. Malestar was unpredictable, whereas the streets of the slums had an understanding that if you dealt with crime and lived within the boundaries of it, payback would soon find its way against you.

Malestar's home outside the city had been raided, the men protecting the home were shot down, and the drugged women inside were rescued. Members of Malestar's crew had heard about this and decided to disseminate until his return. The women were reconnected with their families while cameras were rolling, and it was a memorable moment for many that had watched. Some of the women had parents that were deceased, making the story even more heartbreaking.

Vesco had been released from Rodrigo's backyard and he was on a television tour for every major channel that his publicist could find. He wore his lucky silver suit, and appeared more charming and charismatic than he ever could be in person. He gave radio interviews as well. Vesco angled himself well so that he could get some claim into Malestar's arrest. He even hinted that he was responsible for the Spanish authorities capturing him. His most memorable interview came on a morning talk show when he was interviewed by a host that was a pageant queen a few years back. She wasn't the savviest of hosts, but the viewers kept watching for other reasons.

Vesco sat in his seat, looking confident as always with his hands folded in front of him. The interviewer sat across from him, wearing a bright, blue suit with her legs crossed toward him. "What do you take away from all the attention being placed on this one man that terrorized the city for so long?" she asked.

"First of all, I would like to give my condolences to all of the families that lost family members during his crime spree. It was such a tragic nightmare for many of our city's outstanding citizens. My heart goes out to each and every one of them. I can only imagine the pain they are going through. The attention is good because it shows the compassion this city has when tragedy strikes."

"And what of the police department? Many say they were inept to stop him, and others question how this madman was funded to do so much damage. Do you have any insight on that?"

Vesco stared at her for a moment, but never lost his cool. "We will launch a full-scale internal investigation on such matters. Every stone will be turned to see how this could have happened. We will find answers, and I assure you we will try our best to make sure this doesn't happen again."

"What about the rumors that there is widespread corruption that is responsible for the rampant crime throughout the city?" she asked.

"Nothing can be further from the truth. The police department is one of the cleanest of all the states in Brazil. These rumors don't have merit. We have fine men and women in this city committed to the safety of all of our citizens. And I have a message to all criminals out there that think they have a chance to do harm."

Vesco turned to face the camera. "No one, I repeat, no one is above the law."

*

Malestar sat patiently with both of his shoulders bandaged inside the interrogation room of the police station. He stared directly at the door with a glare that would frighten many. He stayed calm, but his mind was full of plots to get revenge. He tried to figure out what went wrong.

Someone back home had turned him in. He thought he had the entire police department under his control. Who would dare halt his plans? Perhaps it was the mercenary himself, Mauricio Campos. Malestar closed his eyes for a moment and thought of the sweet, horrific pain he would inflict on him if they met again. Mauricio was right about one thing. It was always better punishment to make a man suffer and not just take his life. Mauricio was starting to understand and was embracing the darkness that was inside of him. This was the key to growth in Malestar's mind. Then it was acting outside the restraints of society. Only then could an individual truly grasp their inner instinct.

Everyone in this world was just so pathetic. Why couldn't they see the world the way he saw it? He had read somewhere that roughly from one to five percent of the world's population were psychopaths. They were described as being unrealistic, promiscuous, impulsive, irresponsible, abnormal, and having a knack for criminal versatility. Some of this was true. However, he didn't think he was abnormal in any sense. He was the one that was free. As far as he was concerned, he was ahead of the curve. There were times in history where the masses held beliefs that, while in the majority, were wrong scientifically and morally. What did a group's opinion have to do with the absolute right or wrong? It was all subjective, interpreted in any that those in power would benefit. In his mind, no one should decide how another man should live. That should be the only rule the entire world should follow.

What if he had not done this crime here or even become the person that he was? What if he grew up just as pathetic as everyone else in society and was nothing more than a mindless sheep? He could picture his sister all grown up, beautiful and outgoing. She had always liked to sing so maybe she would have been a singer. She would be with a band, with a group of guys that wanted to have sex with her and be touring somewhere in Sao Paolo. She would come back home a few times a year and talk about her trips, and he and his father would listen as if they were interested. In reality, no one would care about her wretched music or who she was. As far as Malestar was concerned, he did her a favor.

She would have definitely been the star of the family. Her natural beauty alone would have led to this. Still, his father would have treated her badly if she was still alive. The man just wasn't capable of embracing anyone that loved him.

And what kind of relationship would he have with his father? There was no denying who he was. Malestar had inherited his non-altruistic ways. Could they be cohesive and sit around the dining room table and discuss politics and literature? He would be kidding himself if he thought that was possible. What he became some would call fate. The writing was on the wall. If you got all the ingredients to make a cake, and then placed it in the oven to bake, you don't expect something else. This was ordained. This was destiny.

Malestar opened his eyes and continued to stare straight ahead. He could imagine the two detectives through the rectangle-shaped one way window at the side of the door. One was older, bald, and had the gut of a pig. The other was about ten years younger, but had enough wrinkles and stress on his face to show that he had seen and been through a lot. These were probably the best detectives the department had. They were probably discussing their strategy in questioning. Malestar stared at the window and could picture them both covered in blood and looking at each other in confusion. Then blood would gush out their eyes and they would collapse to the ground. They would scream for their mothers. The very thought put a smile on Malestar's face.

The door opened and the detectives walked in, closing the door behind them. His imagination wasn't far off. The bald man went toward the desk as the other detective stood against the wall. "I'm Detective Armas," the bald man said, "and that is Detective Solis. We contacted the authorities in Brazil and they're on their way. We reached out to a lawyer for you, but I understand you relinquish that right."

Armas sighed and took a seat across from Malestar. The man seemed like he hardly got any sleep. Malestar could tell he didn't like this part of the job.

"Your matters with Brazil do not concern us. However, what happened at the bar and the subsequent event at Diego Luna's house do. I'm almost certain there's a connection. At this point, we can't even identify the bodies. There was a remote trigger found outside the bar. I presume it was you that caused the explosion. My first question is simple. Why?"

"Have you ever been in love, Detective?"

"I ask the questions here."

"I've gone out of my way to not have a lawyer and I'm willing to answer all of your burning questions if you answer mine. Answer the question!"

Armas looked back at Solis, who shrugged, and then turned his attention back to Malestar. "What makes you think I'm not married?"

"No wedding ring, the disgust of life on your face, and your overall repulsive hygiene."

Armas gave a hard swallow. "I'm married to my job."

"But you're not in love with it. In fact, I think you despise it. You have to come to work and see countless people abuse the system you hold precious and make a mockery of it. You get used to this, and realize that the very system you hold dear is nothing more than a joke. Then you question what the point of it all is. Am I really making any difference at all? You want to kill yourself but you are too much of a coward to pull the trigger. You know your life is meaningless, but you continue to show up to work every day, if for nothing more than to see your friend here in some tight pants."

"You're out of line!" Armas shouted, pointing his finger at Malestar. "It's your turn to start answering my questions!"

Malestar leaned back in his chair with a smile. "Yes, I pressed the trigger. Those were mostly my people inside the bar. You're asking me the reason I did it as if I had some grand motive behind it. The reason is simple. I did it because I enjoy it."

Armas could see the excitement in Malestar's eyes as he relived the moment that explosion occurred. Malestar looked at Solis, who seemed disturbed by Malestar's response. Solis was not capable of dealing with a criminal of his kind.

"Besides, my crew wasn't doing their job. I should have gone with a more experienced one."

"And what are you doing here in Granada?"

"My turn. This question is for the gentleman in the corner. Have you ever killed someone?"

Solis confidently strolled over with a smug look on his face. "A matter of fact, I have."

"Look at you, big man, all confident in his stride. Tell me, was the person facing you or had their back turned?"

The smugness went away from Solis' face. "The point is, I took down a criminal."

"The point is, you are a coward. But I forgive you. You want to know why? Because you were fortunate enough to get the feel of taking life. How rich! Didn't you feel more alive than ever?"

"Next question," Armas said, and Malestar slowly turned his head to face him. "What is your business in Granada?"

"I am here to start the beginning of the end."

"And what does that mean?" Armas asked.

"You ever go to the zoo and watch a caged tiger? Its entire life it's bombarded with a life that is against everything its natural instinct wants it to do. Humans interact with it, and feed it, and try their best to domesticate a beast. But as they say in love, you can't control what the heart wants. It wants to kill, it wants to hunt, it wants to relish in its spoils. The human mind prevents this. I want people to be free in the same manner. People like you corrupt minds." Malestar pointed to his head. "There's so much imagination and desire that hasn't even been tapped because society restricts you and makes you feel guilty about any choice they deem immoral. Who are they to judge you? They're human just like me. That doesn't make them better than me."

"You are sick," Solis said.

"Because I speak the truth? You know as well as I do the entire system is built for control and power. You're just expendable pawns in the grand scheme of things."

"Pawns that could put a gun to your head and take you out," Solis said.

"Easy there," Armas said, putting a hand out in front of him.

Malestar laughed. "Don't you want my back to be turned first? Tell me, did that make you feel like a man? Did it compensate for all the physical parts that you are lacking?"

Solis tried to charge at him but Armas held him back. Malestar stood up and stared down at Solis. Solis' face was red with anger, and Malestar was not backing down.

"You better hope I don't get out of here," Malestar said. "Because if I do, not only am I going after you, I'm going after your family and raping all the women I can find. Then I will cut them, and slice them like the trash that they are. You will suffer, I promise you that."

"I'm going to kill you!" Solis shouted, and Armas grabbed him by the waist and carried him out the room.

Malestar sat back down with a smile on his face. He ran his fingers through his hair and calmed himself down.

He reminded himself that there was just too much money to be made for someone not to help him. He could do all the work and they wouldn't even have to get their hands dirty. It was only a matter of time.

Malestar looked directly at the door again, waiting for the next time it would open.

PART 2

26.

Mauricio began the drive back to Granada. He looked a few times in his rearview mirror to see the person behind him in the car, and then returned his attention to the road. As he made his way down the mountain, the snow had stopped. It was now early morning and the sky had turned into electric blue. The heat in the car was turned on, and Mauricio kept the radio on a news program at a comfortable audible level. Words were not spoken, and Mauricio preferred it that way.

The drive back gave him some time to think, and he once again entertained the idea of leaving this job behind. The confrontation he had Malestar terrified him, but excited him as well. He knew at any moment he could have been taken out, and it didn't matter. That type of rush he experienced would be hard to replace. A life in retirement could save his life though. He had been dancing with death for far too long. He could just sail away, and never shoot another gun or deal with someone else's problem. There had to be more to life than him just killing people and getting paid for it. He should just leave it all behind and be content on surviving throughout the years.

But he wanted more. As long as Malestar was alive and well, he was going to create destruction and cause pain. Mauricio didn't feel like he had a moral obligation to stop him but an obligation to continue for the loss of a loved one. He didn't know how he was going to proceed next. The first thing he needed to do was to find out where Malestar was, and from there, target the next time to strike. Yesterday proved that Malestar was only a man that was capable of being defeated.

If anything, he was sure Malestar was going to up the ante. Malestar was like him, a man with pride who continued on for principle. If he had the chance again, he was going to go after Mauricio, and Mauricio looked forward to it.

"You're a good tracker," Mauricio said.

"I try to be," Rodrigo said from the back seat.

"Can you put the gun away? You're making me nervous."

"Sure," Rodrigo said, and put the gun on the seat. "I want you to admit you needed me out there."

"What did you do with Vesco?"

"We let him go," Rodrigo said. "He's the mayor, and he has a city to run. Don't tell me you're upset by that."

"You did well," Mauricio said with a smile.

"I knew I was meant for this profession."

"No one is made for what we do," Mauricio said. "We make a choice to do it, and become efficient at it."

"And how did you learn?"

"The military had a lot to do with it. I suppose I was like anyone else when it came to taking another human life. It's not natural for a human to enjoy it. And to this day, I can't say I do. It's just a necessity in this business. The military forced me to do it, and after a bit, it just became second nature. I was a marksman, and I built my reputation from there. Just be patient. We all have to start somewhere."

"I think I'm in getting closer to your league now," Rodrigo replied as he texted someone on his cell phone.

"I don't know if I would be proud of that. Where are we headed to anyway?"

"Your hotel. We are staying with you."

"We?" Mauricio asked, looking through the rearview mirror. He could see a smile come across Rodrigo's face.

Mauricio had chosen this hotel in the Realejo neighborhood of Granada because of the friendliness toward foreigners and the staff's ability to speak English. As he pulled up to the canary yellow hotel, he could see Red standing outside in the parking lot with two suitcases to the side of her. Mauricio parked the car nearby where she was standing. She ran up to the car.

"My two favorite people are still alive!" she stated.

She hugged them both as they got out of the car. Then they all stood near the side entrance while the early morning sky continued to change to light. "I've been waiting here for a while," Red said. "Do you know how dangerous it is for a woman at night?"

"Something tells me you can fend for yourself," Mauricio said.

"So where's the room?" Rodrigo asked.

"You guys can afford one yourself."

"Booked up," Red said. "And we want to stay close to you since we love you so much."

"Can't believe you said that with a straight face," Mauricio said.

"I'm like a zombie right now. I can sleep anywhere," Rodrigo stated as he picked up the luggage.

Mauricio took out his key card from his pocket and opened the side door. "I hope that's true."

They head toward Mauricio's room that was in the corner of the hotel on the first floor, next to the ice machine and elevators. Inside, the room was nothing special, just a queen-sized bed, a small television in front, and a table to the side with two chairs. Salvador Dali replica paintings were on the walls. The room was cozy and traditional, far from the luxurious rooms that were standard for tourists. Red went straight to the bathroom as Rodrigo headed toward one of the chairs.

Mauricio sat on the bed across from him. "You know, you guys are starting to change my mind about something."

"What's that?" Rodrigo asked.

"There is strength in numbers."

"Even the wise man can still learn," Rodrigo said, and closed his eyes. Mauricio smiled, and knew that he was right.

Not long after Mauricio closed his eyes, he began to dream. He was walking down the streets of Salvador, with everything around him on fire. People were running down the street, some on fire, others running to stay away from its path. The fire swept across the street and caught a bunch of teenagers trying to run away. Mauricio continued to walk and saw that the police department was on fire. One of the officers ran out screaming, his body covered in fire, and he collapsed on the ground and burned to death.

Mauricio started to tremble, and he remembered how his parents were killed in the same manner. He didn't want to look anymore but his eyes forced him to see, and his feet kept walking. A horizontal line of fire was on both sides of him. The pupils of his eyes saw nothing but fire, destruction, and people in pain, fear, and death. His feet kept moving forward. He could hear a deep, sinister laugh that echoed throughout the city. Mauricio began to sweat, and there was a large blaze on of fire suddenly in front of him. He squinted his eyes to try to see through it.

He was pushed through the fire by unseen hands, and on the other side was Malestar, standing there and laughing. Then his eyes met Mauricio's eyes. Mauricio realized he was staring at the face of evil.

"I want to thank you for helping me," Malestar said.

"I'm not trying to help you," Mauricio replied.

"But you are. Doesn't it feel good?"

"But this is not what I want. It's not what I want!"

Mauricio opened his eyes and realized he was still in his hotel room. In front of him, lying directly next to him, was Red with her arm around his waist. She seemed to be sleeping peacefully. She looked like an innocent woman up close, and Mauricio could see the freckles that were usually covered up with makeup. She was naturally beautiful, and she must have been having nice dreams as a smile was on her face.

Then he heard the sound of snoring in his ear. He turned his head and saw Rodrigo with his mouth open and snoring loudly. Rodrigo tried to put an arm around his waist as well, but Mauricio removed his hand. Mauricio shook his head and turned his head forward, thinking that now he regretted that strength in numbers comment.

*

Vesco sat at the dining room table with his wife and daughter. He had a newspaper in hand and was reading the piece about him and how he vowed to protect the city. The story brought a smile to his face. He was receiving a fair share of positive coverage lately, and he knew it would benefit him politically. That old adage that said all publicity was good publicity was simply not true, especially in his profession. The people wanted their politicians to be scandal free, appearing to be uncorrupted, and always talking about a willingness to help, solve problems, and work with others. They didn't want to know the truth. He figured that most people knew that the majority of politicians were crooked. They just didn't want it be shoved in their faces. He likened it to a trophy wife marrying a football star, knowing that adultery was bound to happen. She just didn't want to know about it or see it directly.

He looked at his wife and daughter and realized how fortunate he was to have them both sitting across from him. He knew he would have done anything just to see the both of them again, and in his mind, all of the decisions he made in the past to make more money had been with them in mind. Now, his family hardly made eye contact with him and ate their breakfast quietly. They hadn't been the same since they were rescued. Vesco wanted to say something but struggled to find the right words.

He looked at them and saw that they had both lost weight. They had bruises on their waists and ankles. Barely a word was spoken between the two of them since they came back. What did that maniac do to them? He had spoken with the paramedics at the scene, and then with the doctor after the examinations, who said there was no forced entry and they were fine from a physical standpoint, just a bit malnourished. He didn't know what he would have done if he had found out otherwise.

He knew Malestar was in custody of the Spaniards and that Brazilians authorities were on their way to retrieve him. That in itself was not too encouraging.

There were plenty of men with dirty hands that were bringing him back to be extradited. What if Malestar bought his way out, or made promises of future revenue like he did with the Corporation? Malestar was certain to come after him and his family once again. Vesco would have to be prepared this time, and ensure their safety. A gun at his residence and a security alarm wouldn't suffice. Malestar had had no problem breaking in and threatening him. Vesco's family needed around-the-clock protection if they were going to stay in the city. No, staying here would be too dangerous. They would have to leave.

Vesco closed the newspaper and placed it on the wooden table. "How would you two like it if we decided to take a trip down south? We could go to Rio or Sao Paolo, and you two can go shopping until your feet get tired. Now, doesn't that sound like fun? We could take a trip to the museum or theme park. Let's have some family time together."

The two women ignored him and continued eating. "Did you two hear me?" Vesco asked.

They continued ignore him. Vesco stood up and slammed the palm of his hand against the table. "You will respect me in my house! After all I did for you to bring you back here, and all those nights worrying about you, and you can't say anything to me? You should be thanking me! Without me, you would have been dead!"

"Without you, we wouldn't have been kidnapped in the first place!" yelled back his daughter, who stood up and left the room.

Vesco turned to his wife. "Surely you know I can't control what a madman does."

His wife looked at him for a moment, and then walked away as well. Vesco stood there, trying not to feel guilt and logically trying to find a way where he wasn't at fault. But he couldn't. He sat back down as a defeated man that had lost a connection with the people he loved the most.

His eyes began to tear with sadness. He hated feeling this way. He was an accomplished man and not an unstable boy. He was better than this. Ever since he was young, when there was a problem, he was quick to find a solution. However, he didn't know if he could ever repair the damage that he had done. He had failed, and he had to accept that. He could only try to gain back their trust in that he could protect his family.

Vesco wiped his eyes and turned his focus on the newspaper on the table. On the front page was a picture of Malestar, followed by the story of his arrest. It was at that moment Vesco realized that the criminal that was apprehended in a foreign country was more exciting than what he said. Malestar was the true star of the city. Whether or not people agreed with what he did, the citizens were fascinated by his every move. This was supposed to be his city, his spotlight. Anger came across him. Vesco was going to steal the spotlight back. He grabbed his car keys on the table and headed for the front door.

Then a thought crossed his mind. What if Malestar's crew in the slums came after his family? He had to act quickly. Maybe he would wait until they cooled down and ask them again. He would convince them that there was an immediate danger and that they needed to leave. They would understand.

If they didn't, then they would all be targets. He could just try to wait it out and get a feel for what Malestar's crew was up to. But if Malestar made it back and gave the hit, he and his family were surely dead.

There was only one other option. He didn't want to think of it but the thought came to him. He could try to start up the Corporation again. He could make more money than ever before. He would do it to protect his family. Vesco didn't want to have to make that choice. He left the house to begin his mission to take back the city.

27.

The three mercenaries woke up late and missed the continental breakfast that was served down the hallway. Red was the last to wake up. She sat up in bed to see Mauricio and Rodrigo already dressing. She took in the moment, watching two handsome men getting dressed—one wise and embattled, the other naïve and eager. She ran her fingers through her hair and sighed.

"So what are we doing today, fellas?" she asked.

"We?" Mauricio asked.

"Quit the act. You know we're a team now," Red replied.

"Do what you want," Mauricio stated.

"Charming as usual," Red said.

"I'm going to do some shopping if you want to come with me," Rodrigo said. "I could use a new suit. To stay professional, you have to look professional."

"I'm going to have to pass. Mauricio, what are you doing?"

"Taking a walk, and then handling some business."

"You could use company," Red said.

"I never said that."

"You didn't have to," Red said, getting out of bed and heading to the bathroom.

Rodrigo was the first to leave. He headed toward the shopping district downtown and walked the many narrow streets, observing people and absorbing the culture. This place had a lot of similarities to back home. He found lots of culture, people that enjoyed the warmer weather, and boutiques and cafes that lined the streets. He found the suit warehouse location using his phone and walked inside.

Traditional Spanish music was playing inside the store and a short man with measuring tape around his shoulders stood behind the counter, observing a tailored suit that he was preparing. He didn't seem to pay any attention to the potential customer that walked inside the store. Rodrigo made his way to the racks of suits on display. He looked at the prices and noticed they were above the mean asking price. However, the stitching was fine as well as the material.

Rodrigo found a blazer he liked, took off the suit jacket he was wearing, and tried on the new blazer in front of the mirror. The man behind the counter finally began to take notice. Right away, he noticed the gun in Rodrigo's hip. Rodrigo moved around to see himself in the mirror and caught the shop owner's gaze. He turned around to face him.

"I'm just here to buy a suit," Rodrigo said in Portuguese. The man seemed to dismiss his words and headed toward the telephone.

Rodrigo rushed over to the counter and prevented the man from finishing his call. "I'm here to buy," Rodrigo said, showing his wallet to the man and the bills inside. "No problem."

The man nodded, and took his hand away from the phone. "You want to buy?" he asked in Spanish.

"Sí," Rodrigo replied.

The man seemed confused for a moment, and then walked around the counter. "Come," he said. "I will make you look like a real gangster."

Rodrigo was about to correct him, but then thought what was the use. "I need to look professional," he said.

"I have just the suit for you."

Rodrigo smiled. He was going to be the next Mauricio Campos. He was going to look the part, and he was going to play the part. A real hitman needed style and class, and could blend in anywhere. Then he would be charming and could get any woman he wanted. He would collect bodies during the day and party during the night. There was no time for sleep. He would have to take that part out of the equation.

When he had a partner, Rodrigo was content on just getting through the day and surviving. Even to this day, the fear of being shot and not returning home was real. Any day could be his last. Still, he wanted the glory of being well respected and feared. That was the side he had always dreamed about. The downside was terrifying, and he tried to block those thoughts from his mind. Someone in this business had to be good at compartmentalizing thoughts. Otherwise, the fear would take grasp of your mind and never pull back. He didn't want to be a nutcase and he had heard stories of such cases.

One of the thoughts he tried to block was the one of his partner, and the day he got shot. As much as he tried to block it out, the memory of that day occasionally crept to his thoughts. However, before it had a chance to manifest itself, Rodrigo would think of something else. Right now, he thought about how Red would see him now with a new suit and the swagger to win her over.

Red had told him he was infatuated with the image of being a hitman. He disagreed. He chose this life because he could make the image in his head real. This wasn't a fantasy. He could be the man one day, the leader of the new generation of hitmen throughout the world. He was going to stop taking jobs that required them to come back alive. He was going to be the king of this field. All he had to do was learn from the best, and take his knowledge with him.

"You like this?" the man asked, showing him a black Italian suit.

"That will do," Rodrigo said.

An hour later, Mauricio and Red had made it to their destination and walked along the Carrera del Darro, a street alongside the Darro River where close by there were quaint shops and bars within the pathway. From here, there was a great view of Alhambra, a scenic part of the city. Colorful buildings in light pastel colors provided the backdrop to the street, and shrubs and grass surrounded the river below. The weather was warm and embracing, the type of weather Mauricio loved the most.

"It's a beautiful city," Red said. "This part of the world is one of my favorite places to work in. So much culture, so much beauty. When I was a little girl, I had lavish dreams of going to Paris and Madrid, and being swept off my feet by a ravishing gentleman that would give up his life for me."

"I can't picture you doing that."

"I'm still a woman, you know, and I was a girl once. I used to believe in fairy tales just like any other girl."

"Why don't you go by your real name, Sophie?" Mauricio asked.

"I'd rather not talk about it."

"Oh, we're talking about it. You insisted on coming with me in a time I designated to think, so I will burden you with my questions. As long as I've known you, you've been fearless, and now you are afraid of a question?"

Red sighed, and stopped to look over the bridge and across the river. Mauricio stood next to her. Red was hesitant to answer the question, but needed to do so for herself more than anyone else.

"My mother loved that name. When I was in her womb, she came to the conclusion that it would be my name. She didn't have to run it by anyone because my father left us five months into the pregnancy. He couldn't stand being in Kansas City anymore, and even more, he couldn't stand being around my mom. They fought like cats and dogs. Anyway, as soon as I was born and started walking, that's all I heard. 'Sophie, you're such a beautiful girl.' 'Sophie, you're going to make your mother proud one day.' I felt like the name was something she always imagined me to be, not who I was. And then after what happened to me..."

Red took a moment to gather her emotions, but struggled to do so. "Can you believe she had the nerve to be mad at me? She said it was my fault since I was too physically mature for my age, and my clothing was too revealing. She went through my closet and threw out everything she could get her hands on. She kept saying, 'I'm so disappointed in you, Sophie. You know what the neighbors are saying about me, Sophie. It's your fault they think I'm a bad mother.' I tuned her out. I didn't want to speak to her, and I wanted to run away. I still don't understand why she blamed me. But I stayed, and the first chance I got, I left home, got my own place, and joined the police academy. The years I was Sophie were the worst days of my life."

Red wiped the tears from her face and turned to face Mauricio. "So I'm Red now. I'm dangerous, I'm fearless, and I'm in control of what happens to me."

"I believe you," Mauricio replied.

Red looked away, and for a moment, neither spoke.

"So what type of business do you have to handle?" she asked.

"I didn't get much sleep last night because you two couldn't keep your hands off of me." The comment made Red flash a smile. "I saw the news and they showed pictures of Malestar. He's alive and they have him in custody. I had to turn on the subtitles to figure out what was going on. The Brazilian government flew in last night to come get him. He's being transferred in a few hours."

"So what are you planning to do?"

"Say hello," Mauricio said with a smile.

"Please don't tell me you are trying to take him out."

"If he goes back, he has the chance to unleash havoc again. He knows too many people and there are too many dirty hands. This is my chance to put an end to it all."

"It's too dangerous. There will be police everywhere, and that's not including the people on the street and the millions of people watching on television. I know you are good, but no one is that good."

"Lots of people have done their job in those conditions."

"What type of sniper rifle are you using?" Red asked.

"Who said I was using one? I'm going to make this personal."

"Are you crazy?"

Mauricio laughed. "Maybe I am."

"You're letting him get to you. You know as well as I do that you have to make the right calculated decision."

Mauricio nodded. "You may be right, but if I have the chance to do it, I will. His blood needs to come from my hands. Come on, we should get going."

*

Malestar waited outside the doors of the police station with two Brazilian officials behind him, one holding one of his arms while his hands were handcuffed behind his back. Behind them was a group of police officers from the precinct, Malestar's local lawyer, and an official from Interpol. Malestar absorbed all of the attention that he was receiving. He could hear the crowds outside, obviously upset about the explosion at the bar and him being in the city. Malestar took a deep breath and could feel the pulse of the crowd.

The calm before the storm was always the best part. Malestar played "Andante" by Johann Bach in his head, one of his favorite symphonies from the eighteenth century. He closed his eyes and listened to the music in his head. There was shouting behind him. It was time to move. Malestar opened his eyes as the doors were opened from the outside.

As soon as he walked out, photos were taken of him and cameras kept their focus on him. There was a crowd formed outside and they immediately began to shout profanity in his direction. Malestar smiled, loving every moment of it. He was escorted by a group of police officers that were waiting outside and was led toward the white van that was parked on the street curb. Members of the media came toward him but were pushed out of the way. Malestar looked amongst the crowd to see the many faces that were abhorred by his actions. And then he saw him, and stopped in his walk.

Mauricio stood next to Red amongst the crowd as everyone around them was shouting. They stared each other down. Mauricio thought about running toward him, making his way past the guards in front of him and shooting him once in the chest. Then he would see the light go out of his eyes. He pictured what would happen next. The police would rush toward him and pin him to the ground. He would be arrested immediately. He would be cheered by the crowd. However, he would definitely go to jail afterwards, something that wasn't on his top-ten list of things to do before he left this earth. Prison was a rotting place, and he much preferred being killed on the field than to rot away in a cell.

Malestar was not backing down. He kept his glare on Mauricio. Mauricio felt the urge to make his attack now.

"Don't do it," Red said.

If he was going to strike then he would have to do it now. The cameras were on Malestar and the world would be watching if he did it. A part of him didn't care. Another crowd of reporters came toward Malestar, and once again, they were shoved away. The moment to strike was fading away.

"You want to be able to walk away," Red said, being the voice of reason. "Now is not the time."

When was the right time? No such time existed. Perhaps prison would be worth it, or he could be shot down by police by firing at them. Mauricio reached for his gun inside his hip. He was going to do this for Claudia.

His window of opportunity went away. Malestar was shoved from behind to keep walking. He began to move forward again, still staring at Mauricio. Both men wanted each other killed. Now just wasn't the right time.

Malestar climbed into the van accompanied by the two officials from Brazil. The doors closed, and the van began to move. Malestar leaned back in his seat, and remained calm. The two people that shared the ride kept their focus on him.

"Is there something you want to say to me?" Malestar asked in Portuguese.

"You will pay for your crimes," one of them, a man named Jorge, said. Malestar took a look at the two men. They were almost identical. Both were middle-aged, had non-prominent features, and had tanned skin. However, they looked familiar.

"Have we met?" Malestar asked.

"A lifetime ago," the one to the right said. "At a time when the rules were different."

"And what are the rules now?"

"We're in charge," the one to the left said. "Like I said, you will pay for your crimes. Your cut will be severely diminished, as well as your power. You try to overthrow us like you did the others, and you will quickly see your way into a jail cell, and that's if you're lucky."

Malestar smiled and rubbed his hands. "So, what is my first assignment?"

28.

Mauricio stormed back inside the hotel room with Red right behind him. He was angry at himself for not killing Malestar when he had the opportunity, even though the circumstances were not ideal. Rodrigo, wearing his new suit, had been staring at himself in the bathroom mirror. Mauricio gathered his luggage near his bed and began packing, picking up his stuff on the corner and in the bathroom.

"What's going on?" Rodrigo asked.

"We're going back to Brazil. We have unfinished business," Mauricio said.

"But we just got here," Rodrigo said. "I thought maybe we could take some time off and enjoy the local scene."

"You do that," Mauricio said, walking around the room. "Me, I'm on the first flight out of here. I contacted Vesco and he has the arrangements already set in place."

"Did I miss something?" Rodrigo asked.

"Don't ask," Red replied. "Are you in or out?"

"Of course I'm in," Rodrigo replied. "What do you think of my new suit?"

"I'm not concerned with it," Red said.

"You should be. I paid a lot of money for it."

"Malestar is going back to Brazil," Red said. "We've got to leave immediately. We have a taxi waiting outside to take us out the city. Hurry up and pack."

Minutes later, they exited the hotel room and made their way to the lobby and out the doors. The taxi cab had its engine running. They loaded their luggage and the taxi took off. Red sat in the front seat with the driver.

She wished they had more time to stay in the city. Europe to her was the perfect getaway, a place that was far enough to get away from her past, and close enough to all the modern amenities that she was used to. She would get lost here, and feel like a completely different person than who she really was.

It was here that she had become Red, and this place felt more like home than anywhere else. She had had an employer in London that paid her handsomely for his list of criminals, and she enjoyed the work. She had gone down the list one by one, until it was down to her last target.

The last one took the longest, and was by far the most dangerous. He was an infamous ecstasy pusher, and her employer wanted her to eliminate the competition. It was a far cry from the jobs she had taken back in the United States, but whether it was protecting the community or helping other criminals, that still meant another criminal off the street.

She went from club to club in search of his whereabouts. She had a few people on payroll that consistently gave her information on the latest news involving the activities of the drug dealers in the city, but even they didn't have much information. News got around that she was looking for him. Now she was a target as well, and that was never a good thing when you were on the hunt. There were a few times when she was almost caught by the drug dealer's men, and even exchanged gunfire once, but she managed to escape. She thought about leaving the job behind, but that's not who she was. She was going to finish the job, get paid, and find more business. That was the way it had always been.

She got lucky. She found him in one of the dance clubs she had frequented, and as she walked along the balcony next to the upstairs bar, she caught him sitting in the VIP section of the club. The dance floor was to the side of him and gave way for a clean shot. People were dancing and conversing all around the club and blue strobe lights constantly flashed across the dance floor. The music was blaring, and the bass was so loud it made ears muffled. Her target was laughing with an escort that often posed as a girl just dancing by herself in the club. She enticed her prey by kissing his neck as he rubbed her back. Red stood from the balcony, debating with herself on what she would do.

Public hits were always messy. She would be recognized, would have to escape quickly, and probably could not work in the same city for a very long time without the assistance of someone in law enforcement. Then other people could end up hurt. She was not in the business of hurting others, and really wanted the opposite. She wanted normal people to be protected. And the last thing was the possibility of being shot back. The target had two bodyguards near him, and they were both carrying guns. She had to do this hit with skill.

She decided to do it. She took out her gun, shot him in the head, and the crowd dispersed. His bodyguards returned fire. Red made her way to the emergency exit, and to her car that was parked nearby. She hadn't returned to that neighborhood since.

Her employer paid her, and she realized her time in Europe was going to be short lived. She had been renting an apartment in the north end of the city, and had her belongings placed in storage. She could have stayed around and waited for more work, but then she got the call from Vesco. She had been recommended by her employer. Then came the trip to Brazil. She had come a long way from Kansas City, and thought about going back to visit, but she didn't know if she could handle the trip.

But those were thoughts for another time. Right now, her concentration should be on going back to Brazil and finding Malestar. She didn't know long it would take, and what she would do after he was found, but she did know that being around these other two mercenaries gave her a sense of family. A feeling she had long missed.

The taxi was five minutes away from the private airport when a compact red car came closing in from behind. Mauricio looked out the back window and didn't recognize the driver or the passenger in the front seat. He turned around and saw the taxi driver's eyes look through the rearview mirror.

"Just keep driving," Mauricio said.

The car behind followed at a steady pace. The cab driver continued to look through the rearview mirror and Mauricio could tell that his nervousness was increasing. Mauricio looked out the back window again and figured that he could take both men out with the help of the other mercenaries in the car. He reached for his gun.

"It looks like we got trouble," he said. "Everyone, stay ready."

The other mercenaries reached for their weapons. Then the police sirens of the car behind came from the dashboard.

"You got to be kidding me," Mauricio said. "Driver, pull over."

The taxi pulled over and left the engine running. The mercenaries kept their hands near the guns as the red car parked behind him, and the passenger stepped out. He slowly made his way toward the car and then knocked twice on the glass on Rodrigo's side. Rodrigo lowered his window.

"The name is Detective Solis, and that is my partner Detective Armas in the car. We would like for you to get your luggage and come with us."

"Sorry, we got plans," Mauricio said, amused by the detective's accent. He hadn't heard a Spaniard trying to speak English in a British way since he lived in England, and the tourists would often visit.

"Your plans can wait. Unless you would like to be in this country for a very long time."

Red looked at Mauricio for any indication to make a move. She was ready to shoot this man and the man in the car if need be. She had never killed anyone from law enforcement, but a threat was a threat. She figured

Mauricio felt the same way. So it surprised her when he sighed and took his hand away from his hip.

"Do you know who we are?" Mauricio asked.

"We do."

"Then why didn't you bring the cavalry?"

"We would like to make this friendly if that's all right with you."

"I figured as much. Rodrigo, pay the driver."

On the banks of River Darro in Granada was Alhambra, which means *red castle*. Named after its reddish walls, this remarkable landmark was Nasrid architecture whereas every piece of the structure was exquisitely carved, from the pillars to the arches. It was often flooded with tourists, but some areas were not open to the public. One such area was an extensive hall with golden pillars that seemed to reach toward the sky and had a white, polished floor below. There was an open space outside of the hall where a circular fountain was on display surrounded by guarding animal statues. Mauricio stood in the hall with his hands in his pocket with Red and Rodrigo beside him. Across from them were the two detectives, Solis holding a folder.

Mauricio looked down the hall and then back at the two detectives. "Is there a reason you chose this place?" he asked.

"A lot of meetings are held here," Armas said. "It's the sort of place where the badge and the street can talk. Quiet enough to conduct business, close enough to the public without anyone being in harm's way. People like it like that."

"What do you want?" Mauricio asked.

"The same thing you do. Peace, happiness, money," Solis said.

"Let's go," Mauricio stated.

"Wait," Armas said. "I assume you know Malestar is being transported to Brazil."

"I'm aware of that," Mauricio replied.

"We don't exactly like when criminals come into our country, do a crime, and get to walk away. Doesn't sit right with me. We want to make sure justice is served, no matter where it is."

"Well, good luck with that," Mauricio said.

"Witnesses put you at the scene of the attack at Diego Luna's house and around the city. You're wanted for questioning and any police personnel are supposed to bring you in. At the private airport I'm assuming you were going to, there's at least thirty armed men waiting for you."

"It's like a new inmate in a Turkish prison," Solis said.

"How's that?" Rodrigo asked.

"You're fucked," Solis replied. "You can await your fate at the airport if you like."

"I'm guessing you're here to provide an alternative," Mauricio said.

Armas smiled. "We can help each other out. If you help me, I'll see to it that you arrive back in Brazil without the nuisance of the police force ready to arrest you."

"And what do you want?"

"We have a job for you. A hit on a criminal that has been quite elusive, and we want him off the street, dead or alive. Your choice. You do that for us, we help you get Malestar. We won't get in your way."

"And how can we trust you?" Mauricio asked.

"Do you have any other choice?" Armas asked.

"We could kill the both of you right now, and then take our chances the airport," Mauricio said.

"I stand corrected," Armas replied.

"Who is the target?"

"Diego Luna," Armas stated.

"I'm confused..." Rodrigo started to say.

"Someone tipped us off that he was there at the shootout at Trevélez where his right-hand man was and a translator was used as hostage. They were both shot down in the crossfire. Diego was nowhere to be found during a sweep of the house. He must have escaped."

"What did I get myself into?" Mauricio said to himself.

"Isn't this what you do?" Armas asked. "This should be child's play for you." Armas turned to Solis. "Give them the report."

Solis handed the folder to Red. "You should find everything you need to know about the target, or at least, everything we know about him." Solis gave Red a flirting smile that was met with a menacing glare.

"What is the timeline on this?" Rodrigo asked. "We have to get back before Malestar strikes again."

"I wouldn't worry about him for a while," Armas said. "A lot of the police force back in Salvador are being investigated and they are trying to clean up the city of corruption. Besides, he's under arrest."

"You're clueless," Red said.

"Perhaps, but even if he did plan something, it would have to be meticulously planned as the world is watching now," Armas said. "Worry about our assignment first. Else, spend time in prison."

Mauricio shook his head and looked at the other mercenaries. "What do you two think?"

"I think I'm anxious to put a bullet in both of them," Red said. "That said, I say we do the job."

"I could sharpen my skills for the big finish," Rodrigo said. "This one is mine."

"There you have it," Armas said, and handed over his contact card to Mauricio. "Your luggage will stay with us until the job is done. You call me with important progress or when the job is done. Remember, if you don't follow through, you won't be able to leave the city. The law is all over this one. I'm sure you know how to follow through on a covert operation. Who knows, maybe one day you will need my help. Until we meet again."

Armas and Solis started to walk away. "No difference," Mauricio said.

Armas turned to stop. "What was that?"

"I've been in this business a long time, and in every country I visit, the law is always the same. A bunch of self-interested, narcissistic people that think they can change the world."

"You take the jobs. What does that say about you?"

Armas and Solis walked away. Mauricio turned to Rodrigo and Red. "You fellas don't have to do this. I got myself in this situation, and I'm the one they're after."

"I wouldn't mind sitting this one out, but take Rodrigo with you," Red said. "He's eager to please."

"I'm eager to start being respected around here, starting with you," Rodrigo said.

"Settle down," Mauricio stated. "Red, could you find out what's going on in Brazil for the time being. Also, find out what you can about the two detectives."

"I can do that," she replied.

The sound of conversation from tourists was heard, and then the sound of laughter. A tour was being taken nearby.

"We better work on those stealth skills now," Red said.

"This way," Rodrigo said, and they quickly made their way down the hall.

Armas and Solis opened their car doors and got inside. Solis turned to Armas. "We are going to be heroes!"

"Relax, one thing at a time. He has to follow through."

"Oh, he will follow through. He has no other choice," Solis said with a smile. Armas shook his head. Solis waited for Armas to start the engine.

"What is it?"

"Something about what he said. We should be good enough to do the job ourselves."

Solis sighed. "The law only allows us to do so much. We've been wanting this criminal for years. Don't let him get to your head."

"I'm hoping he brings him back alive."

"And why is that?" Solis asked.

"Prison time will make him pay for his crimes," Armas replied.

"And if he's dead?"

"We're heroes either way," Armas said, and started the car.

29.

The day had turned into night, and the night had turned into day. Rodrigo and Red each got their own hotel room not too far from Mauricio's hotel. Rodrigo had tried to convince Red to share a room to save costs, but she didn't like the idea at all. All of the mercenaries bought new clothes since their luggage was held hostage and retreated back to their respective hotels. Rodrigo found himself bored, waiting in his room until later today when Mauricio would call to start their tracking. Mauricio was the one with the folder on Diego, and Rodrigo felt slighted that he wouldn't have handed it over. Mauricio may have been a superior tracker, but Rodrigo was the one that was up and coming. Mauricio had the benefit of having Claudia doing most of the tracking. He was a one-man show now too, after the death of his partner.

Rodrigo quickly blocked the thought. He went to the mini bar inside the room and started drinking the 1.7-ounce mini bottles of whiskey. He fell back on his bed and poured another bottle down his throat. He wasn't going to get drunk on these, but it was better than nothing. He rubbed his goatee and thought about shaving it for tomorrow. Then the thought of Ken arrived in his mind.

He couldn't quite shake the thought. The sight of him being hung and then his body exploding was a reminder to him how dangerous the profession could be. No, that wouldn't be him. He was too smart and too good to end up like his partner or like Ken. They couldn't see the danger right in front of them, but he would be better.

Rodrigo looked at his watch. It was five in the morning and he still hadn't gone to sleep. He went back to the mini bar and took the rest of the bottles out. He was going to drink away his negative thoughts and project that he was in full control of his thoughts and in control of his future, even though deep down inside he knew it was a lie.

*

The crime rate in Granada was usually of no concern to most tourists. Besides the occasional pickpocket, the city was generally a safe place to live. Diego Luna had been able to operate this long because there was no strong underground crime scene here. No one here really knew much about him. Even in the city of Trevélez, people knew about a kind man that lived in a big house above the city. No one knew about the true Diego because no one expected a criminal of his pedigree to be here.

Diego had two daughters, both students in Madrid. He had an ex-wife that he never talked to, and they had had a nasty divorce. He had been very close to Vega, the man the police shot down. Some in the police department thought they were lovers. Diego had sold guns to many Europeans that knew they were illegal to own, and even to foreigners from Africa, and as far away as South America. He was a well-connected man, but had few resources within the region to help him.

The only real connection the local police had with Diego was a woman named Clara that lived in the city. Clara was Vega's sister, and was a teacher at the nearby university. She was middle-aged, had curly hair, and wore glasses. She was a feminist and didn't like government intrusion on the daily lives of citizens. She lived in the Zaidin neighborhood of the city, where many residents were from North and West Africa, as well as South America and China. On Saturdays like today, gypsies would come out and sell fruits and vegetables, clothes, and other items. Also, on Saturdays mornings, Clara would teach a free class at the homeless shelter on getting job interviews and enhancing job skills. Clara loved the neighborhood because of its diversity, and she lived across from a corner café that was famous for its coffee.

Mauricio closed the folder with the information regarding Diego as he sat across from Rodrigo at the café across from Clara's residence. He handed the folder to Rodrigo. Mauricio wore all black clothing with a black Ascot cap on his head. Rodrigo wore a navy blue shirt and black slacks, and had shaved his goatee. The plan was to be inconspicuous, but there was only so much you could do. They had a direct view of Clara's place through the large window on the side of the café that also showed the heavy pedestrian and street traffic. A row of police cars made its way across the street with their sirens blaring. Mauricio sighed, and looked out the window to the building across the street. Clara would be coming home anytime now, after her class. Rodrigo finished reading the information in the folder and, looking up, saw the look of concern on Mauricio's face.

'You don't think she knows where he is?" Rodrigo asked.

"Don't know."

"You're afraid we might have to kill her?"

Mauricio turned to face Rodrigo. "Remember who you are talking to. If you try to down talk me one more time..."

"What are you going to do?"

The two men stared at each other before Rodrigo laughed. "I'm just messing with you."

"What's gotten into you? You think you're this invincible super hitman that isn't afraid of anything. Your day will come, Rodrigo. You're feeling yourself right now, and that's the last thing you want to be doing. You are human, you bleed, and you can get killed. Remember what happened to your partner."

"Don't talk about my partner," Rodrigo snapped back.

"And you want to call out cowards."

Rodrigo was about to say something else when he saw Clara walking toward her apartment. "There she is," he said instead. "Did you ever wonder why the police didn't make a move on her?"

"There are certain things the law needs that we don't," Mauricio replied, and stood up. "Like warrants."

Mauricio left money on the table, and they headed toward the door. They left the café and jaywalked across the street, causing a few cars to honk their horns. Clara entered through the front door of the building as they crossed the street.

"This one is mine, okay?" Rodrigo stated as they made their way to the door.

"She's not a target," Mauricio said, and they walked inside.

Inside, the building looked worn. The carpet was stained, a rusty chandelier was above the entryway, and the air smelled of cigarette smoke. Someone wasn't following policy. There was a faint sound of a television coming from one of the rooms on the first floor. Mauricio took a few steps on the staircase that was in front of him and looked upward. Clara was still climbing the stairs.

Mauricio made his way up the stairs with Rodrigo following behind. They walked up casually as to not draw attention. Clara stopped at her apartment and began to open the door. Mauricio and Rodrigo made their way onto the hallway of her floor. Clara opened the door, and turned her head to see the two men coming down the hallway. She flashed a friendly smile, but then remembered she had seen the two on the news. She quickly went inside and tried to close her apartment door, but Rodrigo put a foot forward to stop it from closing.

"Leave immediately! I'm calling the police!" she shouted in Spanish.

"Where is Diego?" Rodrigo shouted, pushing open the door. "Where is Diego?"

Rodrigo put a gun to her head, and Clara froze. He grabbed her by the neck and she struggled to breathe. Rodrigo could feel the life draining out of her. Mauricio went over to them and placed his hand on top of Rodrigo's gun. Rodrigo lowered the weapon.

"She's not the target," Mauricio said. "You need to get yourself together."

Clara was trembling in front of them. "Please. I'm just a teacher. I can't help you."

"You know exactly who we are looking for, lady," Rodrigo said, understanding her Spanish just enough to get the bulk of what she was saying. "Vega was his closest confidant, and you are his sister. You're the only person that knows him around here."

"Please..." she said again.

The sound of movement came from the back room. Mauricio quickly headed in that direction. Rodrigo placed a gun to Clara's head again, thinking about pulling the trigger because she lied. He was going to be the man now, the most feared hitman in the world.

"Rodrigo, this way!" Mauricio shouted.

Rodrigo lowered his gun again and followed Mauricio. Clara gave a sigh of relief and started crying. She went to the kitchen to call the police.

Diego was making his way down the fire escape of the only bedroom in the apartment. Mauricio and Rodrigo gave chase. Diego began to jump steps as he noticed the two men behind him. Diego dropped to the alley, the mercenaries not too far behind. Diego was never much of an athlete. Still, he ran down the alley as fast as he could. He made his way to the street and ran past a pair of cars coming in opposite directions. Mauricio and Rodrigo had to pause wait for an opening before crossing the street.

Pedestrians gave Diego confused looks as they saw him run. Mauricio and Rodrigo continued to follow as Diego turned the corner. Around the corner was the gypsy market where crowds were gathered near stands of items for sale, and clothing was hung on racks. Diego wound his way through them shoving past the crowd. Mauricio sprinted down the street, avoiding the sidewalk area. Rodrigo continued down the sidewalk and a rush of pedestrian traffic at the corner impeded his movement. He tried to shove his way through, but failed to do so. He thought about reaching for his gun, but figured that would draw too much attention. Instead, he waited until the crowd went through.

Diego turned down another alley, looking back to notice only Mauricio behind him. Diego began to try to open the doors alongside the alley. Most of them were locked except the last one to the right. He opened the door and entered the building. Mauricio was only seconds behind.

Diego rushed through the back of the apartment and ran up the steps. Mauricio took out his gun and followed. There was a little girl in the hallway and Mauricio held the gun from her view. He then proceeded up the steps.

He made his way to the second level, and pointed his weapon. The door closest to him was closed. He looked around and noticed the only one that was left open was toward the right and at the very end. He heard a woman shouting from there. Mauricio went to the door and saw it looked like it had been busted open. He went inside, his gun still pointed, ready to shoot.

Inside, there was a large fan blowing loudly in the corner and a woman breastfeeding her baby, standing near the kitchen. She saw that Mauricio had a gun and nodded her head toward the back. Mauricio rushed toward the bedroom, where Diego was waiting for him. Diego knocked the gun out of Mauricio's hand and shoved him to the wall.

Mauricio took hold of Diego's shirt and pushed him off of him. Diego tried to charge at him, ramming his shoulder into Mauricio's chest. Mauricio elbowed him in the back of the head. Diego swung wildly at his waist. Mauricio grabbed at his hands and pushed Diego off of him. Then he followed that with a jab to his cheek.

Diego fell backward to the side of the bedroom, knocking down a lamp in the process. Mauricio tried to kick him, but Diego grabbed hold of his foot and struck his kneecap with the side of his fist. Mauricio shouted in pain and kneed Diego's face against the wall, causing blood to pour out his nose. He repeated this action three times. Diego went limp. Mauricio picked up his gun and headed toward the living room.

"Sorry for the inconvenience, ma'am," he said to the woman standing there.

The woman of the apartment began screaming something that Mauricio didn't understand. Diego staggered out of the bedroom, and Mauricio put the gun down. Mauricio walked around the room and lifted his hands upward to signal for Diego to come get some. Diego noticed Mauricio was directly in front of the glass window that led to the balcony. Diego charged at him and shoved Mauricio out the glass window. The two of them were suspended in the air for a moment before crashing down on one of the clothing stands below, breaking it in half.

Pedestrians ran away from the scene. Rodrigo saw from down the street and began running toward them. Mauricio's back throbbed in pain as he held on to his back. Diego got up, with one of his legs badly bruised, and he tried to run with a limp. Rodrigo ran faster to catch up to him. Diego placed his palm toward Rodrigo, with the index and little fingers raised while the middle one was held by the thumb, the Spanish equivalent to the middle finger. Diego flashed a smile and ran across the street. Then he was hit by a speeding bus coming down the street that slammed on its brakes.

Diego went flying in the air. He landed against the windshield of an approaching silver coupe coming up the street. The window shattered and Diego lay still on the hood of the car. Traffic came to a halt. Rodrigo went to help Mauricio off the stand. Everyone's gaze turned to Diego on the car.

"You okay?" Rodrigo asked.

"I'll be fine," Mauricio said, holding on to his back. "Let's get out of here."

Mauricio placed his shoulder around Rodrigo as he helped him get down the street. Rodrigo hurried the pace and used all his strength to take Mauricio to the nearest alley. They took a few more steps before Mauricio leaned against the wall.

"We did it!" Rodrigo shouted.

"No, a car did it."

"Who cares? We got our man. We make a good team, don't you think?"

"I think I need something for my back and that you need to get your head checked."

"Only me?" Rodrigo questioned. The two of them laughed as pedestrians rushed by the alley, heading toward the scene.

30.

Red stared at herself in the dressing room mirror, took off her black pencil skirt, and sighed. She looked at herself wearing her white lingerie and wasn't pleased. She needed to work on her abdomen region. Luckily for her, she had no one to wear this for. For now, she was going to purchase the skirt as she liked the way it fitted her. As for her lingerie, she bought it because even without a man she liked to feel sexy in her clothing. Still, it would be nice to have someone to show it off to.

But where was she going to find a decent man in her profession? The men she met only wanted her for her body. Then again, one could argue that was the type of man she attracted with her clothing. She just wanted someone decent, serious when need be, and could make her smile. Someone she could trust, and then maybe, just maybe, she would start to show the real her to him.

Her cell phone on the counter inside the dressing room started vibrating. She pressed the button for speakerphone and started putting on her jeans. "What do you want, Rodrigo?" she asked.

"We're back at Mauricio's hotel room. Could you get something for Mauricio's back? He hurt it real bad in our chase for Diego."

"Only so much I can do without a prescription. So, did you get him?"

'He won't see another day," Rodrigo replied.

"Who did the hit, you or Mauricio?"

There was a pause on the other end. "We'll talk about it later."

"Um, okay. Anything else you need?" Red asked.

"I could use a backrub myself."

Red ended the call. She put on the rest of her clothes, and left the dressing room with the skirt in her hand. It wasn't practical for her line of work, but that's what made it so fun.

Ten minutes later, she was browsing the aisles of the pharmacy, looking for ointment, or even better, some painkillers. She decided to buy both. She made her way to the counter when a bearded, middle-aged man with thick hair stood in front of her.

"*Perdone, pero usted es muy hermosa,*" he said.

"Oh, I don't speak Spanish," Red replied.

"*Mis disculpas, señora,*" he replied, and he moved out the way.

Red looked back at him and forced a smile. He gave her a hard stare, and then walked away. Creepy, she thought, and went to buy her items.

After she left the store, she headed toward the hotel where Mauricio was staying. The day was warm and the streets were filled with pedestrians moving about. Her instincts told her something was wrong. She looked behind her and saw the man from the store walking up the street. However, his head was turned and facing the street. Red turned back around and continued to walk down the street at a steady pace. When she made her way to the corner, she crossed the street and went in the opposite direction of the hotel.

She crossed the street and began to walk in the direction she had come from. She turned around and saw the man cross the street as well. This time, he had no qualms about being noticed. Red turned back around and hurried her pace. She rushed toward the corner, and once she turned aside, she waited behind the building.

The man made a light jog down the street. As he passed the corner, Red stuck out her fist and swung it toward his face, landing hard against his forehead, and causing him to fall backward. Red put placed her foot against his neck. He looked up at her, struggling to breathe.

"Who are you and what do you want?" she asked as pedestrians passed by them on the street.

*

The hotel room door opened and Red came in with a bearded man in front of her with a gun to his back. Mauricio leaned up in bed as Rodrigo stood near the television. Red closed the door and shoved the man forward.

"This guy here works for the detectives. He was told to keep an eye out for me in case I try to leave."

"Why bring him back here for?" Rodrigo asked. "Kill him already."

"Not necessary," Mauricio said while grimacing. "He's just doing his job, and now that our job is done, he is too." Red handed Mauricio the bag of items she got from the pharmacy.

"We can't let him walk away," Rodrigo said. "What if his job was to kill us when the job was done? I don't trust this man. It's better to get rid of him as quickly as possible."

"Okay, handle it," Mauricio said, and turned his attention to the items in the bag.

Red handed Rodrigo her gun. Rodrigo looked at the gun for a moment, and then at Mauricio. He was busy putting pills in his mouth and wasn't paying him any attention. He looked at Red, who seemed to be waiting on him to follow through. The man in front of him looked nervous; his body shivered, and he closed his eyes.

"Red, can you get me a glass of water?" Mauricio asked.

"Sure." Red went to get one of the plastic cups near the vanity mirror and sink.

Rodrigo raised his gun. He placed it on the man's forehead. His finger touched the trigger and all he had to do was press down.

"Could you do it a little more to the right?" Mauricio said. "You're blocking my view of the television." Red walked past Rodrigo and the man to sit next to Mauricio.

Rodrigo looked back at the man in front of him. He couldn't help but think that this man could be someone's husband, a father, and a brother. The fact he was standing directly in front of him was just too up close and personal for his taste. Rodrigo put the gun down. "Go over there and sit," he said in Portuguese, and the man understood enough that he took a seat in the corner of the room.

"Good job," Red said with a smile.

"Now that we got that out the way," Mauricio said. "I'm going to call our friends and tell them that it's been done. I'm sure the news will travel soon enough."

"We're going home!" Rodrigo shouted.

"No, you're going home. I'm going back to settle a score. You guys want some room service while we wait?"

"I'm tapped out from shopping," Red said.

"I don't want to charge any more on my credit card until I find a bank," Rodrigo said.

"Well," Mauricio said, turning his head to face the man sitting down. "We could take his money." The man looked around the room at the many eyes looking at him and wondered what was being said.

*

The park was nestled away from the city and offered great views of the Sierra Nevada Mountains in the far distance. A few people were walking about, and some were bicycling through the path that carved around the park. Grass and trees were in abundance, and overall it was a peaceful place to be. Mauricio, Red, Rodrigo, and the man Red captured were all sitting at two different park benches waiting for the arrival of the detectives.

The painkillers and some whiskey made some of the discomfort with Mauricio's back go away. He leaned forward on the park bench, thinking that a few days' rest should have him feeling normal. He looked around and found it strange to be in a place so serene and quiet. The last few days had been filled with nonstop action and it was nice just to relax and enjoy nature. However, that feeling was short lived as the two detectives came walking along the grass with their cheap-made suits.

The detectives stood in front of the benches. "Technically, it wasn't all of you that killed him," Solis stated.

"Hello to you, too," Mauricio said. "Without us bringing him out, he wouldn't have been killed. I wouldn't suggest backing off our deal."

"Relax," Armas said, placing a hand out in front of him. Then he turned his attention to the captured man. "What's he doing here?"

"You don't remember the guy you hired to track us down?" Red asked.

"Of course I do. He was to make sure you didn't try to flee," Armas stated. "You can go now," he said in Spanish, and the man ran off.

"You should really hire better trackers," Red said.

"Thanks for the advice," Armas replied. "Well, a deal is a deal. Your flight leaves tomorrow morning at the same airport you came in through. A man named Carlos will be your pilot so you should ask for him. It's been a pleasure doing business with you all. I really do hope you get your man."

Mauricio nodded to him, and Armas and Solis walked off. "How do you know he's not playing us?" Rodrigo asked.

"You are skeptical about everybody, aren't you?" Mauricio asked. "Red, please give Rodrigo some assurance."

"Detective Armas, ex-military, unmarried, has family in the city, two brothers and one sister. The sister has two boys, aged ten and eight, that walk home from school. The two brothers are successful in business and work late hours. Sometimes they work late and are alone in the office. Detective Solis, married, spouse works as an office assistant downtown. She goes to the gym every Tuesday and Thursday. The parking lot at the gym has no security cameras."

"Now, that's how you track," Mauricio said.

"And I had time to go shopping," Red said.

"Showoff," Rodrigo replied.

"Just be glad we have a chance to go back," Mauricio said.

"Let's commemorate this moment with a drink," Rodrigo said, and reached into his pocket to take out a stack full of bills. "I got money now."

"So wrong," Mauricio said.

"You are the one that made him pay for our meals."

"A meal is a necessity to survive. There's a difference."

"Now, you are dangerously in the gray area," Rodrigo replied.

"Everything we do is in the gray area," Mauricio stated.

"This is true," Rodrigo said. "Oh well, I'm drinking."

Rodrigo stayed true to his word. Later that night, they found a quiet bar on the outskirts of town that incorporated matador themes with plenty of pictures on the wall depicting great bull dances. There was music playing inside, a rotation of love songs and upbeat ballads. The place was a hole in the wall but that's what they preferred at this moment. There were no cameras, no crowds, and a young staff that looked like it rebelled against watching the news. It was still taking a chance, but Rodrigo insisted they drink. Mauricio liked the idea because it would help him de-stress from the last few days. He wouldn't have dared eat the food here, but figured they couldn't mess up drinks.

A few drinks in, and Rodrigo was already discussing his first love. "She was a biter." Mauricio and Red laughed. They continued to drink and become intoxicated.

"Seriously, she was," Rodrigo said. "Every part of my body she just had to bite. It was uncomfortable at first, but then it just really start to hurt. I would have bruises all down my arms and legs as if I was getting beaten. Then came the worst of them all. She bit down on my best friend down below. That was the loudest I ever screamed."

Mauricio and Red laughed some more. "What about you, Red?" Rodrigo asked.

The laughter died, and Red's face became serious. "Sorry," Rodrigo said. "Okay, how about you, Mauricio?"

"Okay, but this can't leave the table and never be shared out your lips."

"Your secret is safe with me," Rodrigo replied.

"Cross my heart," Red said, crossing her heart with her fingers.

"There was this girl I had a crush on for the longest time. Her name was Lily. I could never forget her smell or the way she made me feel. She was just this addictive presence I found myself attracted to. I was no more than thirteen, fourteen, and she was in my first class, always sitting in the front row, always turning around to smile at me. She would just light up the room with her eyes. Man, I had it bad for her."

"Quit stalling and give us the details," Rodrigo said.

"I finally convinced her to go out with me. We went on a few dates, nothing special. We enjoyed each other's company. I took her to the park late at night and made sure to take her to a spot where no one would see us. And then she looked at me with those beautiful eyes, and said those three words that would make your heart melt. I love you. I kissed her, and made love to her under the stars."

"Wow, that's beautiful," Red said.

"Wait, did you tell her you loved her back?" Rodrigo asked. "You didn't! You dog!"

They shared another laugh. "That we all may have beautiful relationships going forward," Red said, offering a toast with the others. They placed their beer bottles together. Then they all took a long drink.

"It's not meant for everyone, you know," Mauricio said.

"What isn't?" Rodrigo asked.

"Love. It's like this mysterious feeling that everyone wants but no one wants to work to get it. And even those that work years and years to get to this feeling, lose it as quickly as they get it. It makes us live and kills us at the same time. Sometimes I wonder if it's even worth it."

"Okay, I'm cutting you off now."

"No, listen," Mauricio said, moving his shoulder in front of Rodrigo to block him from getting his bottle. "What I'm saying is the truth. I want you both to know that once you find love, it's not for you to keep. So when you have it, you cherish it with everything inside of you because you never know when you will have it again."

Red took a long drink of her beer. Mauricio looked off into the distance and Rodrigo stared at his beer bottle. Red looked at the somberness in her peers and placed her beer back on the table.

"This is supposed to be a joyous occasion," she said. She nodded to the music that was playing. "Mauricio, let's dance."

"No, I'm done, take Rodrigo."

"Oh no, you're not getting out of this one. Come on," she said, taking a hold of his arms.

"Okay, okay," Mauricio said, putting his beer on the table.

Red began to dance around him as Mauricio stood there. She turned around and rubbed her backside against his body. Mauricio laughed and Rodrigo cheered her on. She turned back around to face him.

"Life goes on," she said.

"What if I don't want it to?" Mauricio asked as she put her arms around his neck.

"Then you will never move on," she said. "You know, when I first heard about you, I thought you were a very good hitman."

"So you changed your mind?"

"Now I think you are the best ever." Red let go of her grip and went over to dance with Rodrigo.

31.

The men and women that sat in the conference room in downtown Salvador were ambitious, and didn't mind dealing with a bit of risk. The top businesspeople in the Corporation had been blown to pieces and the people in this room were willing to take their place. They had been waiting for an opportunity like this. They were tired of getting a lower cut since they were not in the board room making the important decisions. Now that they were here, they couldn't have been happier.

They all had one goal in mind—to make money again. The city was ripe with opportunity. The people of the city were beginning to put their trust back into law enforcement, and money was going back to small businesses and big banks. Money was pouring into the city again and they just needed someone to take it to them. Of course, certain businesses were off limits. Any member that was involved in a business they deemed too close to their own personal interest and that would garner attention would not be targeted. This would ensure that only the competitors would be targeted and that the members could go to work in peace. They also knew that money didn't necessarily need to be stolen from other businesses in order for them to profit. Even an explosion or a break-in was good enough. That brought the stock prices down, and the competitors would reap from the benefits.

The members of the new Corporation had a lively discussion earlier about how to avoid the pitfalls that Carlito had gone through. Carlito had wanted to put restraints on Malestar and was too hands-on about how the money would come back to them. The new Corporation wasn't going to ask questions. They would just gladly take their cut and go about their business. The only task left was to find the right person for the job.

There were many in the pool to choose from. The prisons were filled with criminals, but they needed someone smart, elusive, and crazy enough to place himself in dangerous situations. By default, this shrunk the pool significantly, as if a criminal was in prison, then he wasn't good enough to not get caught. But the Corporation took into consideration that everyone eventually does get caught, or has a high probability to be caught. Then someone suggested why not have someone that already has a relationship with the group and even though he was trying to take over the city, they could enjoy the profits of him doing so? A few phone calls and some bribery, and he would be released in their hands. After some debate, they agreed on Malestar, the mastermind criminal. They expected his arrival at any moment now.

The double doors to the conference room opened and Malestar came walking in. He used his right hand to touch the top of everyone's head on his side of the table. He wore a black suit with a bowtie and made his way to the empty seat at the head of the table. Malestar sat down and placed his feet on the table.

The business men and women looked at each other and wondered about their choice of a criminal. Malestar laughed and put his feet back down. "It's good to be back home!"

Malestar leaned forward. "I am grateful for your assistance on freeing me. Do not think for a second I am not. I know there are police out there looking for me and wish me dead. There is a price on my head, and you took me in. I am grateful for that. That said, I'm assuming you know what type of person I am and what I want. If you don't, let me remind you. I want blood on the streets. I want businesses to collapse, and I want more money than the entire state of Bahia.   You get me access, names, locations, and the men and women to do it, I will ensure you that you will receive your cut. However, I will be in charge. Let that soak in those greedy little membranes of yours. I hope you all are thinking of something worthy, invigorating, and very dangerous. So, what do we have in mind?"

"The Mansão Margarida Costa Pinto building," Jorge said. Jorge was one of the men that had rescued him from Spain. He now got off his chair to turn off the lights. He flipped another switch and the projector screen came down. Then he went to a laptop to turn on the presentation. Malestar moved his chair to get a better view. Moments later, footage of the building appeared.

Jorge began to speak. "The building was completed in 2001, and has forty-three floors, four elevators, and is close to one hundred fifty-five meters tall. The building has two entrances, the lower main entrance and the upper one. From the main entrance, the building has thirty-six floors, from the secondary entrance, it has forty-three floors. Here are the schematics."

A 3D design of the building appeared, broken down to individual rooms. Malestar turned his back at Jorge. "And what is the purpose of striking these businesses?"

"You are mistaken. The building is a residential condominium."

"How cruel and lovely! And the reason being?"

"It's simple. We want the land. We will cause ownership to collect their insurance, and residents would be so frightened, and their reputation so ruined, that they wouldn't dare build again at that location. We will send them a nice care package in form of a check that would get them out the door. Then everyone in this room would place their businesses in a newly made building that is to our liking, built by our own in-house construction company."

"Why don't you just buy them out?" Malestar asked.

"We tried. They won't budge. So we will force their hand."

The computer moved to another screen where there was simulated animation of the explosion that would take place. "The bombs need to be strategically placed inside the building, forcefully if need be. We will provide you enough manpower to ensure that the job is carried out. We might need you to recruit, if need be. Once all bombs are placed, head to the rooftop. By the time the shooting starts from the first floor, we suspect the police would be called and sent over. Don't worry about their presence in the air. You leave that to us. There is no secondary escape route."

"Yes, there is. I could jump." This response was met with laughter.

The computer turned off. "As you can see, this plan is very dangerous," Jorge said.

Malestar stood up. "It is striking to me how we are so close and yet so different. Greed fuels you to kill, or at least have someone else do it. But in the business world..." Malestar moved to touch the top of the heads sitting down around the conference table. "You are called mavericks, entrepreneurs, and geniuses even. You do whatever it takes to get what you want, and in that regard, you are just like me. I look around this room and see the biggest organized crime group there is, filled with day traders, hedge fund managers, and other businesspeople. It's your greed that hurts the average person on the street more so than me. And yet, you are free to do as you wish."

Malestar stood next to Jorge and placed his hands on his shoulders. "You have created a brilliant, sadistic plan."

"Thank you," Jorge said, trying to mask his fear.

"I need some time to think it over. In the meantime, could you show me where I will be staying?"

"I can do that."

"Do you speak English, Jorge?"

"A little bit," he replied in English.

"Good," Malestar replied in English. "You know, Jorge, this could be the start of a very beautiful friendship—you scheming, and me killing. Who's going to stop us?"

"Hopefully no one."

Malestar laughed. "I want to say something to you privately," he said. "And that is if you or anyone sitting down dares to cross me, I will personally remove their limbs and feed them to the stray dogs of the city. I'm sure you can relay that message a lot more cordially than I would. I wouldn't want to disturb this new friendship between us. Do you understand?"

"Yes," Jorge replied.

"Good," Malestar said, switching back to Portuguese. "Lead the way, and to everyone else, don't do anything I wouldn't do."

Malestar left to a room full of smiles. Jorge left the room and Malestar followed him. He could see this new Corporation as his puppets. He may not have gotten the weapons he wanted, but that's because the old Corporation hadn't given him what he wanted. Now the world would be his again, and this new Corporation would help him get whatever he wanted. They just didn't know it yet.

Malestar's residence was not what he expected. It was a modest two-bedroom apartment in the Caminho das Árvores neighborhood that was located in the southeast zone. The area was filled with skyscrapers and views of large trees and the streets below. Malestar's new residence offered the same views. Malestar figured he would be bored here and that he would need to bring some drugged women to keep himself entertained. Then again, the point was to stay away from attention of any kind until the Corporation could buy back some of the police officers that had left their budget.

"It's the best we could do right now," Jorge said as they walked through the place. "Once we have more funds, we will have better accommodations. I hope this place is to your liking."

"It will do," Malestar said, walking around with his hands behind his back.

"If you need any expenses for food, clothing, or anything else, you let us know. I left a cell phone for you in the kitchen. There will be armed guards around the hallway and down below in the lobby. Security shouldn't be an issue, and they will be tipped off in advance if the police are coming."

"And what about the crew I need?"

"We are gathering up young men from the slums as we speak. This will take some time. However, I think you will be very pleased with the progress we have been making. Dire circumstances make the most dangerous commitments seem worthwhile. Some are very eager to join our organization."

"Looks like you have everything planned out. What do you need me for? You just need a fall guy if things go wrong?"

Jorge didn't reply.

"That's it, isn't it?" Malestar asked, taking two steps closer to Jorge. "You'd have no problem sending me back to jail, would you? You don't think I would tell who told me how to bomb the place and provided me the firepower to do it because you think I have some obligation to some street code to not tell. Is that it?"

Jorge gave a hard swallow. "We don't plan on being caught."

Malestar moved away from him and made his way to the large window in the living room. He looked at the city below him and thought about how all of this could be his. One day it would be so. But his mind couldn't get past the vengeance that was running through his body. Mauricio Campos would have to pay, along with Vesco.

"Can you get me a small team to handle a personal matter?" Malestar asked with his back still turned.

"May I ask the reason?"

"No, you may not," Malestar replied.

"Very well. Just make sure you don't get caught. We still need your services."

"I'll take that as a compliment."

Malestar continued to look out the window. Was his counterpart out there somewhere? Had he returned to seek revenge? Malestar thought the odds were good. They needed each other in a strange way. They were attracted to the conflict like moths to the light. They were both from the same mother named Fear, and reacted in the way that best suited their survival. The both of them had experienced pain at some point, and were numb to taking life away when needed for their survival. However, Mauricio didn't know the pleasure involved with giving out pain like he did.

The last few years that Malestar had been chasing money and stealing from the rich, he forgot how satisfying it was to just kill for the sake of doing so. Before he became involved with the Corporation, he used to work freelance after being released from the psychiatric ward. He had mostly found prostitutes to perform his artwork, and buried them all in the same location. He also had killed a police officer. But then it became all too easy. Those women had already suffered enough. He wanted to make sure other people suffered, especially those that had lived a well-to-do life.

There was only one way to ensure this. He would hit them where it would hurt the most, and that meant their pockets. That was the only way they could suffer and their families as well. For them to go lose it all and ruin all of their success in life was more painful than physical pain.

They needed to be taught a lesson, and he was the professor that would give them the passing grade.

Taking money from them wasn't enough. Something else had to be done. Maybe it was time for them to feel physical pain as well. The few that were privileged were born into families and always had everything handed to them. They didn't know how it really felt to be all alone in this cold world. They didn't know how to survive and that you had to take out your friends and family to get ahead. When it came time to do this next job, he was going to have fun and make sure those people that could afford to live in that high-rise community suffered.

"I want to show you something," Malestar said, and turned around to face Jorge. "We're going on a trip."

32.

They had driven outside the city limits of Salvador for what seemed like forever, but in reality it was only a few hours. Jorge did the driving while Malestar waved his arm out into the air as they drove on the dirt track road. As they drove down the road with nothing but mountainous landscape around them, Jorge began to wonder the reason for coming here. He started to think that Malestar had brought him out here to get rid of him. Then again, that would be stupid. There would be nothing to gain but perhaps the pure satisfaction of doing so.

"Stop here," Malestar said.

Jorge pulled over to the side of the road. Malestar looked out the window. There was nothing but barren land that stretched on for miles. The sun beamed down and the heat was much higher here than in the city due to altitude.

"It's a beautiful day, isn't it?" he asked.

Malestar stepped out of the car and began walking. Jorge looked on for a moment, reached into his glove compartment to get his gun, placed it in his back hip, and then got out of the car to follow Malestar. Malestar began to whistle as he walked further.

Jorge kept his hand near his gun. He wasn't going to be killed out here in the middle of nowhere if that was the plan. He kept two paces behind Malestar. Then Malestar suddenly stopped.

"Put your gun away," he said with his back still turned. Then he looked off into the distance. "Life is made of memories. That's what gives life purpose. Without them, all of this is nothing more than a fleeting moment."

Malestar looked down at the square metal plate that was in front of his feet. He bent down and removed the metal plate and extended his arm inside. Jorge stood behind him, still not understanding what the purpose of this trip was. Malestar took his arm out and was holding a large, black bag, and judging by the grunting noise Malestar made, Jorge guessed the bag was quite heavy.

Malestar stood up and flipped the bag upside down. Body parts poured out of the bag. There were limbs, ears, heads, and other bodily extremities. Jorge could tell from the heads they were all young women and one male. A police badge was also on the ground. The eyes in severed heads were still opened wide, and their mouths open. The smell from the body parts was repulsive. There were insects on the outside of the body parts, and they had made a meal on the flesh.

Jorge ran off to vomit. Malestar stood over his work, admiring what he had done. The memories came to him and gave him an evocative feeling. He turned his head to see Jorge vomiting away. He smiled, made his way over to him, and patted his back.

"Since we are beginning the start of a friendship, I want to establish my position on betrayal. You can join what's over there if you ever decide to try to turn me in or take me out."

"I didn't plan to," Jorge said, wiping his mouth. "You are crazy."

"Yeah, that's what they say," Malestar replied. "This was a good trip. All the beautiful memories are coming back to me."

"How can you do this? And how can you kill your own sister?"

Malestar grabbed the back of Jorge's hair. "Because I do what I please! Now, I want you to gather everything on the ground and place it back in the bag. We're taking it with us."

"Please...I can't."

"You can do anything in the world that you want. That's what's wrong with people. They put limitations on themselves. Your actions are stronger than your negative thoughts. Find that inner strength in you to fight against what society tells you is right and wrong."

"I don't want to!" Jorge shouted.

Malestar let go of his hair. "You are weak, and that is good for the both of us. I had to make sure you wouldn't go try to increase your power. But you're like a helpless little dog. Isn't that right?"

"Yes," Jorge said with his knees on the ground.

"Give me your gun," Malestar said. Jorge looked at him and thought about reaching for his gun himself and shooting him. But he wouldn't have the time. He was afraid of Malestar in every possible way and thought it was better to do what he was told.

"Give me your gun!" Malestar shouted. Jorge nervously reached for his gun with his arm shaking, and handed it over to Malestar.

Malestar showed no emotion as he placed the gun against Jorge's temple. "You will put the body parts in the bag, yes?"

Jorge nodded that he would.

"And you will give me a crew to take out the mayor."

"Yes, yes."

Malestar removed the gun from his temple. "Hurry up and get to it."

Jorge got to his feet and headed toward the body parts spread out against the barren land. He worked diligently, trying not to look or smell. Both men had been sweating from the heat. Malestar extended his arms to his side and looked up into the sky.

"If you prick us, do we not bleed? If you tickle us, do we not laugh? If you poison us, do we not die? And if you wrong us, shall we not revenge?" Malestar looked around as the Shakespeare passage he just quoted in English was one of his favorites. "We shall revenge," he said. "And it will all be so splendid!"

*

There was no time to settle in. Mauricio had arrived in Salvador only hours ago and now he was late for the meeting with Vesco. The taxi dropped him off at the yacht club on the harbor that bordered the south coast of the city as palm trees swayed in the cool wind. Yachts were lined up in the turquoise water below as a flock of birds making noises hovered above. The local business district of the city and their high-rise buildings provided the perfect backdrop for this scenic location. Mauricio stepped out the taxi and walked toward the yachts.

Right away, Mauricio was approached by two off-duty police officers with guns in their jackets. They checked Mauricio for weapons, patting him along his white sports coat and powder blue slacks, and then pointed toward a yacht on the far left corner. As he got closer, Mauricio could see Vesco sitting down on the deck with an open pink shirt that showed his hairy chest, and a pair of sunglasses on top of his head. He had a red punch drink in his hand and Mauricio could only guess there was a fair amount of alcohol in it.

"Mauricio!" Vesco waved Mauricio over.

Mauricio stepped onto the yacht and took a seat across from him. He noticed there were two more bodyguards on the boat. "What's with all the protection?"

"One can never be too careful. You want something to drink?"

"No, I'm good."

"I take it you've heard the latest regarding Malestar?"

"He's out and about over here. Doesn't surprise me, really, with people like you setting the bar so low for law enforcement."

Vesco smiled. "It's not the police force that got him out. Well, not completely. The Corporation is still out there, and they brought him back here to do their will."

"Then it looks like you got a lot of work to do with you being mayor and all. By the way, is this here on the taxpayers' expense?"

"You've changed," Vesco said, taking another drink.

"How so?"

"A lot more frank than I remember."

"Don't pretend to know me. You should worry about yourself and your family. Where are they, by the way?"

"They are at a safe place. However, I don't want them to be in hiding for long. That is where you come into play. Keep in mind you still have a job to do."

"I just might decide otherwise," Mauricio said.

"I'll double the payment."

Mauricio looked away for a moment, and smiled. "Everything to you is about money."

"What can I say? I'm a man that came from nothing. I sacrificed to get to where I am, and to put food on the table. Now look at me. I have fancy boats, nice clothes, and plenty of money to spend."

"And you have to constantly look over your back to see if someone wants to kill you."

"With great fortune comes great danger. I still think it's better to have than to have not."

Mauricio nodded. "I need more money for expenses."

"Fine."

"And a car."

"Consider it done," Vesco replied.

"And access to some standard police-issued weapons."

"You got it," Vesco said, taking another drink. "You know, when I was chained up against the fence..."

"Just a precaution."

"No offense taken. When I was there, I was told more about what happened with your girlfriend. The news is very much regretful. I also found out you like boating. I can sell you this one for a discount. I have my eye on another beauty. But this one has been steady and you could use the vacation after all of this is over."

"Give me the full specs."

"Twin diesel engine, four years old, fiberglass hull, two thousand engine hours, Amtico flooring in the galley, a new amplifier in the flybridge, and fully furnished with a washer and dryer."

"Sounds nice. Took this from a big-shot drug dealer?" Mauricio asked.

Vesco laughed. "You think I'm the worst person in the world. Keep in mind, I don't pull the trigger."

"That makes you better?"

"Think what you want, but I've turned this city around," Vesco said.

The crime rate in Salvador had shown steady improvement recently, even with Malestar's attacks taken into account. The number of homicides had gone down even though it was still five times the rate of the United States. But compared to other large cities of Brazil like Rio de Janeiro and Sao Paolo, Salvador was generally safer, especially the downtown and central areas of the city. Still, there was a high poverty rate in the slums, and a disparity in income and employment between shades of skin. Prostitution was still rampant, and a third of the residents did not have basic amenities like sewage lines and septic tanks. There was still much work to be done.

"I'm not here to judge you, Mayor," Mauricio said. "I'm here for your cooperation in taking down Malestar, and having the resources to do so. There are not too many people willing to take him on, so I don't make enemies with alliances."

"A wise man. There are some people I want you to meet."

Vesco stood up and headed toward the back of the yacht where there were stairs that led below the deck. Mauricio followed behind. They made their way across the galley and upon a sitting area, where Vesco's wife and daughter were watching television. His daughter immediately stood up.

"Is there something you want to say?" Vesco asked.

"I want to thank you for protecting my father and the rest of the city," she said in Portuguese. "I find you very attractive, and would take you to bed with my father's permission."

"What did she say?" Mauricio asked.

Vesco cleared his throat. "She said she is very grateful for you returning to the city and the city needs you."

"*Obrigado*," Mauricio replied.

Vesco's daughter flashed a smile, and returned back to her seat. "You see, you may not realize you have an obligation, but you do, because it's more than just me depending on you. Now, if you excuse us, we have a dinner to plan for."

After his meeting with Vesco, Mauricio took the taxi to a rental car shop near the harbor to pick up his car. The car Vesco got him was a black sports car that was a few years old, German, and had a multicolored shield with a horse rising upward as an emblem above the bumper. The dealership was run by a man with dreadlocks who looked like he smoked marijuana all day. This was obviously an outfit run by the drug cartel judging by the amount of sports cars in inventory and no name needed to borrow and no receipt given. Mauricio shook his head as he took the keys from the owner, who then showed him the car.

Mauricio sat in the car for a moment, and turned on the engine. The song that was playing was "Estrelar" by Marcos Valle. Even now back in Salvador, he wasn't going to be able to enjoy its beauty and be able to relax for a long period of time. He would have to find his moments, this being one of them. Here he was in a nice car, with the weather perfect, and his health relatively well. He tried to concentrate on the positives around him and not the fact he wished Claudia was here with him, but it didn't take long for his mind to drift elsewhere.

Mauricio drove the car out of the lot and made his way adjacent to the harbor. Out of curiosity, he checked the glove compartment. Inside, there were two guns, a smoke grenade, and a police officer badge. Mauricio laughed out loud. There was something to be said about corruption. He figured the city would never be cleaned up the way most envisioned, but the corruption could at least be minimal with the right politicians.

Mauricio then realized this was the first time he wondered about outside circumstances that dealt with a target. Before, it was all about finding the target, killing him, and collecting payment. Now, he thought about the consequences of doing so and the actions of the person that was hiring him. He was changing. He used to be numb about doing a job, but now he was feeling anger. Maybe that was a sign that he needed to get out of the business. He always told himself that if he had any emotion then he would no longer be effective. He knew that having emotion about a target could lead to bad decisions and overaggressive behavior.

But there was no way he was going to subdue the anger he felt when it came to Malestar. Anger couldn't be that bad if it was fueling Malestar. He had read somewhere that the best fighters never fight with anger. Did cops feel the same way? Did judges make decisions that way? It was nearly impossible not to make decisions without emotions. He was fortunate to be able to do so for so long. But with the death of Claudia, he was becoming human like the rest of society. It was ironic, he thought. It took death to make him numb, and death to make him feel alive again.

Mauricio did not want to have thoughts of sorrow and tried to think of something else. He increased his speed on the road and changed lanes. He tried to live in the moment. He had to deal with the fact that he was living in the now and the past was there for a reason. Mauricio took a sigh, and tried to get lost in the song that was playing. Now he was finally getting his mind at ease.

By the time the chorus came around, a row of motorcycles was coming down the opposite lane, speeding in perfect formation. A closer look showed that many of the riders were wearing purple clothing. Mauricio instantly knew it was the Corporation. He made a U-turn in the middle of the road and sped up to follow them, revving the engine in the process.

33.

Mauricio sped through traffic to catch up to the motorcycles. He also kept a safe distance in case they decided to fire back at him. He followed them for a few minutes as they continued south down the harbor. Then Mauricio realized where they were going. They were going to kill Vesco.

When he was a safe distance, he began to slow down. He contemplated whether or not this was a good idea. He was only one man, and the group of motorcyclists looked like grown men as opposed to the teenagers that Malestar had employed. With this change, Mauricio figured the Corporation was new and improved, and far more dangerous. It didn't take Malestar long to make his presence felt again. The city would continue to be doomed by its internal corruption.

He thought about calling the other mercenaries to get some assistance in what he presumed would be a gunfight. However, they wouldn't be able to arrive in time. That and the fact they had no allegiance to Vesco other than the fact he was paying. This was his own personal decision and he hadn't decided the reason why he was doing it himself.

A small part of him wanted to turn around and let it be done. Vesco was a cockroach that fed on the scraps of what the people worked hard for, and would do anything for survival. He was just another crook in the political field and maybe he deserved what was coming to him. If the world and the people inside of it had a way of working itself out, who was he to interfere with fate? His father once told him that everything was written and destined before you had the chance to make a decision. Mauricio then asked what the point of making decisions was and he told him that the path always changes, but the conclusion is always the same. He told him fate always did what was best. Then again, fate had taken the only woman he truly loved. It was time to control his fortune and change Vesco's if he could. Besides, he still wanted the money even though it wasn't as important as before. With Vesco dead that would be rather difficult.

The motorcycles rumbled up to the yacht club. The riders parked their bikes out front and started to walk toward the yachts that were lined up side to side. Mauricio quickly parked his car and made a swift estimate of how many men they were. He counted eight from six bikes. They had guns in their hands. Mauricio knew the odds were against him to attack. He stood outside his car and looked for Vesco's yacht. There were lights on from the boat. Mauricio took out his prepaid cell phone and dialed Vesco's number.

The first few rings, no one picked up. "Come on," Mauricio said as he saw the riders get closer to the yacht. Finally, there was a response on the other end.

"Is there a problem, Mauricio?" Vesco asked.

"Get out now!"

"I'm afraid I can't do that."

"There's a crew of...."

The sound of gunfire rang into the afternoon air. Vesco's bodyguards that stood outside the yacht were firing at Malestar's crew as both sides ran for cover. Vesco had four armed men and they were being taken out quickly, but not before shooting down some of Malestar's crew. Mauricio figured a surprise attack from the back would help balance those odds.

He made his way toward the shootout with his gun drawn, staying behind a row of cars parked across the street from the yachts. Two of Malestar's men had their backs turned, wearing purple bandanas that covered most of their face. Mauricio shot them both down, one in the back of the head, and the other in the chest as he turned around. Mauricio continued to fire thirteen shots as he made his way closer to the boat using the parked cars along the street as cover. The other members at first began to shoot back at him and the boat, but then they began to scatter. Mauricio crept closer to the yacht as gunfire continued between Vesco's bodyguards and Malestar's crew. Vesco's bodyguards were more skilled with their guns but were also outnumbered. In the end, there was only one person standing besides Mauricio, and that was a man with a purple bandana around his neck who had jumped aboard the yacht.

The man quickly made his way to the deck and to the stairs. Mauricio got on board, cautious in his movement. He kept his gun pointed as he heard noise from down below. It would be any moment now where he would hear gunshots to signal the end to Vesco and his family.

The gunshots never came. Mauricio looked down the steps to see if the man was in view. There was no one there. He didn't like the open area at the end of the steps. He could hear the man still searching below. Mauricio took a deep breath and decided he was going to head down.

Mauricio turned quickly and headed down the stairs. At that moment, the man came back toward the stairs. He saw Mauricio and was about to raise his gun when

Mauricio jumped the remaining stairs and landed on top of him. The man fired, but the bullet ended up against the ceiling.

Mauricio tried to get possession of his gun while the man did the same with Mauricio's weapon. The man tried to hit him with his forehead. Mauricio dodged the blow, and pressed down the man's trigger hand. The remaining bullets filled up the galley area. With that done, Mauricio moved his arm to strike the man in the face with a succession of elbows to his nose. He started to bleed and shouted in pain. The man used his remaining strength to lift up Mauricio's gun to point it at Mauricio.

Mauricio made another elbow to the man's mouth and took out two of his teeth. Blood spurted out of his mouth. The man wrapped his legs around Mauricio's back and let go of his own gun to try to grab Mauricio's arm. Mauricio blocked the hold with his own arm and gouged the man's eyes with his finger. The man screamed in pain and let go of his grip on Mauricio's hand with the gun.

The man removed his legs from Mauricio's back and head-butted Mauricio in the face. Mauricio moved upward and to the side and tried to aim his weapon. The man got up and headed for the stairs. Mauricio shot him once in his foot and the flesh popped into the air. The man shouted in pain and held on to what remained of his foot.

Mauricio ran to him and threw him backward off the steps. The man landed on his back. Mauricio caught his breath and stood over him. He pressed a foot against the man's abdomen and pointed the gun to his head. He then pulled the trigger.

His magazine was empty. The man laughed and spat out more blood from his mouth. Mauricio stared at him calmly, dropped the empty magazine, and took out another magazine from his sports coat and placed the new magazine inside. The man's face suddenly changed to fear. Mauricio pointed the weapon once more at his face, and pulled down on the trigger.

He left the man on the ground to look around the boat. He searched everywhere but Vesco and his family were nowhere to be found. The cell phone in his pocket began to ring. Mauricio answered the call.

"Your call dropped. What happened?" Vesco asked on the other end.

"Where are you?"

"Having dinner with my family, of course. Why you ask?"

"Because Malestar just sent men to your yacht to kill you," Mauricio replied.

"Mauricio, the entire city knows I'm at the annual charity dinner for cancer research."

Mauricio ended the call, realizing he had been set up. A flurry of thoughts crossed his mind as to the reason. Before he had time to process an answer, Malestar came down the stairs while clapping his hands.

He stood in front of Mauricio, who pointed his gun to his head. Malestar laughed and opened his suit jacket, revealing a bomb strapped around his waist and his other hand attached to a trigger button. Mauricio lowered his weapon.

"Now, that's better," Malestar said and walked over to the mini bar that was near the seating area. "Do you want a drink?"

"Why are you here, and why did you set this up?" Mauricio asked with nervousness in his voice.

Malestar poured himself a glass of vodka. He finished the vodka in one drink. He then licked his lips.

"Ah, there is still much in life to enjoy. You know, lots of people have me all wrong. They think I don't enjoy life and don't feel happiness. Nothing could be further from the truth. I love my life right now. You can't replace the alcohol, the women, and the suffering in my victims' eyes. I bleed like anyone else, and I like to feel like everyone else. It just so happens that I like to feel in a way that others don't."

"Answer my question."

Malestar grinned. "I'm here because I understand the human need for revenge. I know you feel this. So do I.

The logic conclusion is that one of us will no longer be able to take advantage of our unique skill set. You caused me a great deal of pain, and I have done the same to you as well. Let's call it even. We could work together and own this city. I could make you richer than you would have ever gotten doing the petty jobs you're now doing. You have vast potential in killing. I can see that by the work you left here. Why not put it to use? I want you to tap into the darkness that you have inside. Together there is no stopping us."

Malestar again finished the vodka in his glass in one drink. "All of these bums I hire don't have the fire that you have. That ability to take life so efficiently and effortlessly. You're a true professional. I admire that. Now, I'm giving you a chance to live and make money. What do you say?"

"Was Vesco in on this?"

"Don't be ridiculous. He doesn't have the brainpower for this sort of operation. I will take him out when the time comes. You didn't answer my question."

"Can't do it," Mauricio replied.

"And why is that?"

"After I take you out, I'm done with this. All of the killing, the dead bodies, the gunfire. Done. I want to just go and fish somewhere."

Malestar smiled. "And you think you will be able to take me out? Let's look at the situation. I have you right where I want you. I could blow us both up, or I could signal for the rest of my men outside to come in and fill you up with bullets. I think you need to come to a better decision."

"I will never join you," Mauricio stated. "And if you want to be a coward and send in a bunch of people to do a real man's job, so be it."

"And I suppose you are a real man. Tell me, what kind of man puts the woman he loves in danger to be killed?"

Mauricio raised his gun and pointed at Malestar's head.

"Do it!" Malestar shouted. "Take us both out of this miserable world! We should go together. We deserve each other!"

Mauricio resisted the urge to shoot him. He valued his life more than Malestar did his own. Mauricio lowered his weapon once again.

"I'm a busy man, Mauricio. There will be a time and place for me and you to finish what we started. But as of now, I have a job to do. As you say, punch the clock? You're making a grave mistake by declining my offer."

"Somehow I think I'll get over it."

Malestar waved his arm toward the stairs. "After you."

Mauricio slowly made his way toward the steps. He didn't know if Malestar had something planned to kill him as he did so, such as a hidden weapon to attack him. Mauricio raised his gun and pointed at Malestar as he got upon the stairs. Malestar pressed the gun against his forehead, and then backed off and gave the gun a kiss.

Mauricio backed his way up the stairs until he got on deck, where a group of Malestar's men were lined up on each side of the deck. All of them had purple bandanas wrapped around the lower section of their faces and guns in their hands. Any one of them could take him out at any time. Mauricio walked past them as Malestar followed behind on deck.

Mauricio made his way off the boat without bothering to look back. He knew Malestar was right behind him and could shoot him in the back at any time. However, he knew there was a certain code between people that kill, and a strange mutual respect the man had for him. He was right. There would be a time and place when they would face again. Malestar knew there was a good chance Mauricio could finish him once and for all, so if there was a delay, that meant Malestar was planning something big.

"Mauricio!"

Mauricio turned around to face Malestar and his group of men. "I expect you to be ready when the time comes."

"You can bet on that," Mauricio replied.

"Until then, you should go out and live. Maybe have some dinner with your friend. He's going to need all the help he can get."

Instantly, Mauricio turned back around and ran toward his car. He took out his cell phone and dialed for Vesco. There was no response.

34.

Mauricio got inside his car and drove off. He sped down the street and tried again to call Vesco. Again, there was no answer. Then he dialed for Rodrigo.

After a couple of rings, Rodrigo picked up the phone. Rodrigo was at his mother's home and playing with the dogs in the backyard. "Yeah?" Rodrigo asked.

"Do you happen to know where the charity dinner with the mayor is for tonight?"

"Yeah, it's the same place every year."

"Give me the address." Rodrigo gave him the address and Mauricio put it in his phone.

"What's going on? Do you want me to come with?"

"No time for that," Mauricio replied. "See you later."

Mauricio ended the call. He increased his speed and changed lanes. Impatience was building up inside of him and he could only hope he would make it there in time.

*

There was much chatter amongst the tables spread out in the conference hall and the sound of fine dinnerware being used. The dinner attendees were all dressed in formal clothing and speaking to each other in casual tones. There was a mixture of power players in the city from politicians to businesspeople. Jokes were told as often as personal stories about how profits were increased. Drinks were refilled and more food was put on the plates. Everyone seemed to be having a good time and Vesco was no different as he sat with his wife and daughter.

He talked to the police chief about how to decrease crime in the city. The chief thought putting more money into the police department would help, and lower the corruption that was taking place. Vesco argued that more emphasis needed to be focused on building informants and an outreach program for the teenagers of the slums. The chief found it curious that Vesco had a change of opinion on this matter, and turned his head to talk to someone else. Vesco was about to say something else but his wife held his hand tight to signal for him to let it go.

Vesco looked at his watch and realized it was time to get on stage.

Vesco excused himself from the table and made his way onto the stage. He stood in front of the podium and cleared his throat against the microphone. After a few moments the attendees in the room grew quiet. Vesco looked around the room and appeared confident in front of everyone.

"If I could get your attention for a moment," Vesco said. "I know some of us could use a break, from what I can see."

There was laughter in the room. "But as you all know, we are here for a purpose. We are here to raise awareness of a cancer that plagues all of us in some way, and we are here to raise money to putting an end to this horrendous cancer once and for all. If we all stay determined and not stray off course of our mission, I think we can find a cure in the next decade. This challenge is very much like the one we face in rebuilding this city today. We all want the same thing, a safe place for our children, a fair shake at job employment, and a livelihood we can all enjoy. And just like our city, it's the people that make this possible. The people like you, who don't waver when it comes to a challenge and are resilient while making it a better and more fulfilling life for everyone. So let's give yourselves a round of applause."

There was clapping in the audience. Vesco soaked in the moment. He once again got command of the room and had everyone feeling warm inside. This was his skill as a politician and he felt like he was the king of his domain.

"I know all of you are anxious to return to your dinners. The food is quite excellent, I might add. Feel free to buy another dinner plate if you must. Also, you can donate as much as you like. We are not the type to turn down money."

Once again, there was laughter in the room. "Everyone, enjoy the evening!"

Vesco was about to get off stage when the doors to the conference hall opened up. A gang of men newly hired from the Corporation rushed in with their weapons drawn. There were four of them. The attendees froze in fear and shock.

"Everyone to the ground!" they shouted.

People screamed and dropped to the ground. A man from the gang went around with a black bag and started collecting jewelry from those on the floor. A few tried to resist, but after guns were placed to their heads they quickly obliged. Vesco stood on the stage, his body frozen, and couldn't believe what was happening in front of his eyes. Then he looked at his daughter and wife on the ground and made a step toward them.

"No one move," one of the gang said, and shoved a gun to Vesco's back. "Walk."

"Here they are," another member of the gang said with a gun pointed to Vesco's daughter and wife. "Just as pretty as in the pictures. I want to be the first to get inside and feel their warmth."

"We have strict orders," the one behind Vesco said. "We don't want to mess this up."

"And who is going to stop us?" the man asked.

"I am," Mauricio said, and glanced around the corner with his head through the conference hall doors. The gunmen looked at each other and began laughing. "Kill him!" the one behind Vesco shouted.

The bullets started to come in Mauricio's direction as he retreated to cover against the wall next to the doors. He then took out the smoke grenade from his sports coat, pulled the pin, and placed it in the room. Seconds later, an odorless gas filled the room, visibility was low, and people began coughing.

Mauricio made his way into the room with his gun pointed. He remembered the location of all four gang members that were inside. He headed for the first one near the door and shot him in the back of the head. The second one was opposite to him. He fired in Mauricio's general direction but was badly off. Mauricio fired at him twice in the chest. He fell backward, shooting his gun into the air.

The man who was next to Vesco's wife and daughter shouted in Portuguese, "I have them both and I will kill them!" The man tried to look through the smoke and coughed as he did so. Mauricio made his way around him as the man frantically looked around. Mauricio snuck behind him and placed an arm around his throat. Then he placed his hand around his mouth. Mauricio put him to sleep and dropped him to the ground.

"Go! Leave!" he shouted to Vesco's wife and daughter.

Mauricio turned his attention to the man behind Vesco as the smoke began to clear up. The man had a smile on his face and pointed to Vesco's head. "Put the gun down or I will shoot!" he shouted. "Your gun down! Now!"

Mauricio had no other choice. He thought about shooting at the man but he didn't have a clean shot. He could see the fear in Vesco's eyes. The man was counting on him. Still, he had no play here, and raised his hand to show that he was putting his weapon down. The man only wanted an escape route and would use Vesco as cover. Mauricio put the gun on the ground and kept his hands up.

"The city belongs to us!" the man shouted. He started to make his way off the stage with Vesco as cover when a bullet burst the side of his head open. Vesco froze in fear and his body was shaking. Mauricio turned his head in the direction of the firepower. The shot had come from the police chief lying on the ground. Mauricio nodded in the man's direction and the man nodded for Mauricio to leave. Mauricio picked up his gun and headed out the front doors.

"You okay?" the police chief asked Vesco, who was still unmoving on the stage.

Vesco turned to look at him. "I can't be mayor anymore."

"It's too late for that," the chief replied.

*

Dr. Cuevas could hear police sirens as he finished his late-night run and stopped in front of his home. He bent over and tried to regain his normal breathing. His home was in the Vitoria neighborhood of the city, a green and peaceful place that was immediately south of Pelourinho. All the homes in the neighborhood were large in size and had palm trees in the front yard. There was no traffic on the street and the night was quiet.

Cuevas made his way to his door and reached into his pocket for his keys. As he did so, he felt a chill come across his body. He turned his head and Malestar was standing behind him.

"After you, Doctor," Malestar said.

Cuevas opened the door and was shoved into his living room. Malestar closed the door behind him. Cuevas tried to remain calm and took a seat on his living room couch. He turned on the lamp nearby. Malestar stared at him. Cuevas waited a moment longer and then picked up the book that was on the couch with a bookmark showing that he had nearly a third left to go. He began reading as Malestar stood in front of him. Cuevas didn't bother to look up.

The room grew quiet. Finally, Malestar spoke. "I've changed."

Cuevas put the book down. "In what way?"

"I've grown weary of the chains that hold me."

"You've always been that way," Cuevas said.

"No, this is different," Malestar said, pacing around the room. "I yearn to grow. I want to show others the joy and pleasure of following what your mind tells you to do. I know people want to be like me. Take you, for example."

"What about me?"

"I remember distinctly the way you looked at the assistant that did all the recordkeeping in your building.

You wanted her. You craved her. And all she did was ignore you and go about her business. I know what was going on inside of your mind. Every time you saw her, you wanted to take her against your will..."

"Now, wait a minute."

"Don't interrupt me, Doctor," Malestar said and stopped his pacing. He stared at Cuevas and his eyes looked like he could kill at any moment. When the doctor sat still and didn't say a word, Malestar began to pace again.

"I know what you wanted. I could see it in your eyes. You shouldn't feel ashamed for what you were feeling inside. You should feel ashamed for not getting what you truly desired. That was your mistake. I want to show people like you that you don't have to be afraid."

"You have to understand that the masses think this type of thought process is madness."

"I would assume so," Malestar said, stopping once again. "But I will be heard. Did you know that tonight was a celebration? There was laughter, and there was wine, and everyone was dressed in their fancy clothes. I provided the entertainment. I provided death and pain. Without me, I'm afraid the party wouldn't have been the same."

"You need help, Malestar," Cuevas said.

"That's your problem, Doctor. You always think you can fix me. You already know you can't do that. I am what I am. There was a time when you believed in me. There is no fixing. There is only enhancing. I don't need people like you telling me that I can't be what I want. I need people telling me that I could be so much more."

"You know I won't tell you that. Why are you here?" Cuevas asked.

"Yes, that is the question," Malestar said, leaning down and touching Cuevas on the chin. "I've always appreciated you trying to help me when I was younger, but now I realize you are just like the rest of them. I can't have that image in my mind."

"It's not that..."

Malestar put his index finger to his lips. "Your words do not sway, and my pain does not go. `I must do what's necessary."

"You won't feel better," Cuevas said.

"That's not the point." Malestar took a hold of Cuevas' neck and began to choke him. Cuevas tried to fight back but Malestar's grip was too strong. The face of Cuevas turned white. He knocked over the lamp and book nearby. A look of joy came across Malestar's face. He thought of his sister and everyone else that he had killed.

Cuevas' eyes rolled to the back of his head and he drew his last breath. Malestar kept his grip for a moment longer, and then let his hands loose.

He got up and looked at his latest artwork. A fine piece of art it was. He would have to add him to the collection.

He thought about the many ways to keep the body fresh. He thought about cutting off the skin and separating it from the flesh as much as possible. He would carefully cut around the ears, eyes, and lips when removing the skin from the head. He would remove as much fat as he could. He would take measurements and take digital photos. Then he would recreate the body through wires and make Cuevas whole again using taxidermy procedures. He would comb the hair, sew the incisions, and allow the skin to dry. Malestar thought the process was too time consuming, and dismissed the thought.

Then he thought about putting the body in a steel tube and stripping the body of all personal items and clothing. Then he would freeze the body. It was unfortunate he didn't have liquid nitrogen because that would have worked best. Cuevas wasn't worth the hassle. Malestar wanted to see his face again and have the memories come back, but the upkeep of the body sometimes wasn't worth it.

Perhaps he would put him in the trunk with the rest of the bodies he had just collected. He thought about having all the heads posted on a wall somewhere. If he ever had some type of retirement, then he could see himself sitting in a rocking chair somewhere, swaying back and forth and admiring his works. He would miss the action but at least he would have the memories.

In order for him to even have the memories, he would have to do the bidding of the Corporation. There would be a day and time when he would break from them, but as of now, he needed their loyal men and their money. He knew there was a great risk that he would never succeed with the job they wanted him to do, but until then, he was going to live every day like it was his last.

"You don't deserve to live," Malestar said, kicking the doctor in the face and then laughing.

35.

Rodrigo wasn't getting much sleep. He leaned up in the bed in his childhood bedroom a few hours past midnight. He had come to his mother's house because he was tired of being in the inner city and wanted a retreat from it all. This was his haven to think and regroup. However, lately his mind was preoccupied with thoughts he couldn't control.

He hadn't been the same since he returned home. On the trip, he was really starting to believe in himself. He had almost convinced himself that he was fearless and he was going to be even better than his former partner and the legendary Mauricio, who made a name for himself in a short period of time. There was no reason he couldn't do the same. Rodrigo thought he could get past all of the bloodshed and guilt. But he was wrong. It turned out he was a mere mortal after all.

Rodrigo went to the kitchen to get a late-night snack. He opened the refrigerator door and looked through the meals that his mother had prepared days ago. He wasn't impressed by any of them. He closed the refrigerator door and found a man in the dark standing in front of him.

Rodrigo froze in surprise.

"That's not the appropriate reaction when someone breaks into your home," Mauricio said.

"What are you doing here?"

"Don't feel safe at the hotel."

"I don't feel safe with you around and breaking into my house at night," Rodrigo replied.

"It's been a crazy night," Mauricio said and headed toward the living room.

"Be quiet, you'll awake my mother," Rodrigo said. "She's known for calling the police. She found a rat in her house and called the police about it. Who does that?"

"Remind me not to get anything from the refrigerator," Mauricio said as he sat on the couch and leaned back on his head.

"You want to talk about it?"

Mauricio shot Rodrigo a look. "Guess not," Rodrigo said. "Have you talked to Red?"

"A while ago."

"Did she say anything about me?"

Mauricio smiled. "Women like Sophie are no good for you," he said, and closed his eyes.

Rodrigo took a seat next to him. "I know she's a little bit dangerous, but I think that's what attracts me. And you know me, I can handle some danger. She keeps putting me off, but maybe that's some type of game she's playing. Or maybe she's truly not interested. I'm not going to put any more time and energy into it. And maybe you're right, maybe it's best that I just drop the whole thing and concentrate on the common goal. There are too many women out there to be concerned about one. What do you think?"

Rodrigo turned his head to see and hear Mauricio snoring. Rodrigo sighed, got up, and walked back to his bedroom. Mauricio continued to dive deeper into his sleep and entered a dream state.

Traditional benga music was playing loudly as an adult Mauricio was standing in the living room of his childhood home. All the people that he had killed flashed around him. Bullets went around his body and disappeared into the walls. He stood there, confused at what was going on, and terrified at the dead bodies flashing in front of him. The music came to a crescendo, and then there was silence.

Darkness arrived. There were the sounds of whispers but Mauricio couldn't make out what they were saying. They were getting louder. Mauricio took a step in the direction of the whispers and then they stopped. Mauricio froze in the silent dark. Then a faint light came from the other side of the room.

Mauricio turned around to see a small fire in the corner. He started walking in that direction. As he came closer, he realized it was his parents huddled in the corner of the room. They seemed scared by his presence. Mauricio offered a hand in their direction.

"It's me," he said.

His father looked at him as if he was a complete stranger. "We don't know who you are anymore. You are not our son."

The words immersed into his flesh and pained him internally. "It's me, Mauricio."

"You are not the child we raised," his father replied. "You are lost."

"I know who I am," Mauricio said. "I'm still the same person. You are the ones that left me. You left me alone in a cruel world! What was I supposed to do? I'm not a perfect man, and I never pretended to be. You're just going to have to accept me for who I am. I know what I'm doing, and I know who I am!"

The light went out and his family disappeared. There was now darkness again. For some reason, Mauricio was terrified. Then Claudia appeared before him.

Light came back on and there he was standing in a boat with the ocean all around them. Claudia gently touched the side of his face. She seemed at peace and a smile was across her face. Mauricio cried at her touch.

"I have always loved you for who you were. No questions asked," she said. "But you can't go on like this. You can change. I know you can."

"Claudia..."

"It's the only way," Claudia replied. "I want you to live. Finish your job and live."

"I want to live for you," Mauricio said, and tried to touch her back, but her physical being had disappeared. His hand was left to the wind. He stood on the boat and looked off into the ocean. There was nothing but the sweet sound of the waves against the boat. Mauricio sighed, and longed to see Claudia again. He also understood he had a job to do. Mauricio walked around the deck until he found a seat, and sat down. He was going to enjoy the calm before the storm.

*

The sun was visible in the morning sky as there was unusual commotion amongst the streets of the slums. Normally, people were still sleeping in this early, from late-night shifts, long days of work, or working corners and other illegal activity. On this morning, the youth was already up, and so were a good majority of the adults. A guest speaker was outside the market that everyone knew was the place to shop for food during the day, and shop for drugs during the night. The smaller children that knew their way around the neighborhood were used as spies. One boy held his post until his relief came to watch the corner. Then the boy ran down the block and turned the corner to go to the market.

There was a crowd already there. The boy pushed through the crowd to make his way up front. There he was, the man that was telling the youth of the neighborhood to join him and trying to get the blessing of the adults. He was dressed in a white suit and one of his eyes was smaller than the other. He didn't look attractive, but his words were seducing.

"I know what the media has said about me. That I'm a monster, a predator of what's good out there. Do you know why they say that? Because they don't want you to have power. They know the power rests with you, the people of the city. They want to tell you what justice is, and have you believe that they have your best interests at heart. We all know that is not true. It's very simple what they want. They want your money, for you to fear them, and for you to depend on them. They want it all. But I want you to have a fighting chance in this world. I want you to take what's yours."

"It's too dangerous," someone shouted.

"Dangerous? That's a word for those that are afraid, afraid to stand up for what they believe in. If that's the case, you will never be free from their grip. But if you fight with me, I promise you I can make a dent in their plans to control you all."

"Why should we help you?" someone shouted. "You're on their side anyway."

Malestar closed his eyes for a moment and rubbed his forehead. He then looked back into the audience. He could tell by their faces that many were skeptical about his intentions. He wanted to kill the people that shouted out but that wasn't going to help him right now. Right now, he needed to show compassion, no matter how phony it was.

"I know you have your doubts, but believe me, I know how it feels to struggle, to yearn for things you cannot obtain. I know how it feels to be held back and be told what I cannot and can do. Here is your chance to make a statement. Here is your chance to show the world you are not afraid. If you fight with me, I will take it to the powers that be that have the money and the power. I am not a terrorist. I'm not trying to attack those in power for the sake of doing so. I'm doing this for you, so that we all can take back what rightfully belongs to us."

Malestar looked down upon the eyes of the teenagers that were watching. They were eating up his words. He raised his arms in the air and looked out into the distance.

"Come with me if you want to fight!"

The teenagers in the crowd began to lift their hands into fists and shout back that they were going to fight. Some of the adults and elderly in the crowd shook their heads in disgust. The boy that had come to see Malestar speak lifted his hand in the air as well and was willing to fight for his neighborhood. The mother of the boy, whose name was Luisa, shouted out for her child. It was no secret to anyone what Malestar was planning and she feared for the safety of her child.

Malestar made his way down the street with the group of teenagers surrounding him, some of them already wearing the signature purple color. Some of the adults of the slums watched from their shacks as Malestar flashed a smile. They knew he had a hold on their youth and that the young ones were willing to die for him. They also knew they were powerless against him. It was hard to have their youth stay the course and live in a poor economic situation when there was a quick opportunity right in front of them. There was a criminal once before during their youth that had done the same thing and most of them had been persuaded as well.

His name was Roberto Salgado, but he was better known as Robin as in the fable of Robin Hood. The slums were all but ignored by those that dwelled in the suburbs and they were desperate for food and jobs. Their pleas for change and assistance were ignored as well. They had to make money on their own, and a lot of ways led to illegal activity. However, Roberto had another plan in mind. He was going to force the city dwellers to help them whether they liked it or not.

It took months to build up the support he needed to fight back. Unlike Malestar, he didn't have the luxury of having weapons and financial backing. He took in donations from those who were already poor and from people in the city that wanted to give them a fighting chance. Roberto was a man that knew how to talk to people and persuade them to give him what he wanted. The youth was on his side as the generation ahead of them believed that wealth could be obtained through hard work and a bit of luck. The youth said the rules were not fair in the first place. They were going to take back the city the same way Malestar was suggesting now.

They planned an attack to strike in the next few weeks. They had their weapons in place and the target building to attack. They were confident the message would be sent and no longer would they be ignored as second-class citizens. The majority of the slums were filled with people from African heritage; those with lighter skin were in the city and had the majority of the money. The youth were tired of the discrimination and were going to demand an equal playing field, and if that meant through violence, so be it. The people were hungry for what they felt belong to them, and Robin was the man to make it happen.

However, he never had the chance to lead them to war. Intelligence on the attack was gathered by the police from a mother that was afraid her sons would be killed. That night, the police went to the slums in droves of trucks, vans, and police cars. The youth on the corners spotted them first. They ran to find Robin, who was asleep with his girlfriend.

The boys shook him awake, and Robin ran to put on some clothes as they heard the sound of gunshots outside. Robin grabbed his gun nearby and was about to make his way to the door when the door burst open, and a group of police officers came rushing in. Robin ran back into the bedroom and locked the door. Inside, the boys had hidden under the bed. The woman went inside the closet. There was no place for Robin to hide. He tried to get to the window but the bedroom door opened.

The police shouted for him to turn around. He did, and he was filled up with bullets and his blood sprayed all over the room. Robin fell to the ground, and the police took his body outside to drag down the streets of the slums. The message was clear. The adults retired to their homes and the teenagers were shot down on the street. Some had cried out for their young. It was then the inhabitants of the slums knew that the power structure would always exist, and they would always be at a disadvantage. It was too late to change course now.

The same feeling was shared today. The adults that were once the teenagers feared the same circumstance. But there was one main difference between Malestar and Robin besides the fact that Malestar was a psychopathic killing machine. The difference was the attitude of the police. When it came to the crimes of Malestar, they seemed to look the other way. Malestar had something that Robin neither had nor had the aptitude of discovering. Malestar knew the way to getting the people what they wanted was to have the lower-paid people of the city help, not with their heart but by their greed.

Malestar continued to walk down the street with teenagers surrounding him and little boys running down the street to catch a glimpse of him. The slums were still desperate for a hero and he was going to provide them a guiding light. He knew as long as the hunger was there that there would always be a group willing to fight.

36.

Mauricio woke up to an empty room and feeling well rested. Mauricio got off the couch and walked out of the room, heading to the kitchen. Rodrigo's mother was there cooking breakfast. She didn't seem to mind his presence at all. Mauricio figured Rodrigo had told her that he was here. She looked at him once, flashed a smile, and continued cooking. Mauricio went to the backyard, where he saw Rodrigo standing outside with a cup in his hand and the dogs moving about. Mauricio stood next to him.

"Another day in paradise," Mauricio said.

Rodrigo grinned. "For some, I suppose."

"You know, life is what you make it, Rodrigo."

"Meaning?"

"Meaning everyone in this city has a different view of what happiness is. If you think it's materialistic wealth and you strive to get it, then your happiness will be hard to get. It's a simple numbers game. Most people born into this life won't ever get to have it. There are just too many obstacles in place and the people in power won't relinquish what they have. They have no problem with having guilt either. That doesn't mean to say that you should never strive to be better, or always push for more. But you shouldn't rely on money as a source of happiness. Because you know what gets pushed on the wayside? Love. I've seen people with the biggest pockets without an ounce of it, and rotate wives like it's going out of style. Don't be like them. We tend to lose ourselves in what we do and what we're trying to become. This job is not the be-all."

"I was afraid of that," Rodrigo said.

Someone was knocking on the front door and there was movement from inside the house. They heard Rodrigo's mom answer the door. "Expecting company?" Mauricio asked.

Rodrigo went to check on his mom and Mauricio followed behind. He went to the living room, where Rodrigo's mom was hugging another woman. "That's my mom's friend Luisa," Rodrigo said. "They grew up together in the slums. I haven't seen her in a while myself."

Luisa came over to hug Rodrigo. Then she gave him a kiss on the cheek. Rodrigo switched to Portuguese. "It's been awhile, Luisa," he said.

"Actually, I came to see you," she said.

"What's going on?"

"Your mother told me what you do and I think my child is in trouble. He needs your help. I think he may be following that crazed man with their attack."

"Are you talking about Malestar?" Rodrigo asked.

"Yes, that's him. He's going to attack the Mansão Margarida Costa Pinto building tomorrow night. He's gathered up a lot of the boys from the slums. I don't want my son to die. You have to save him."

"I'll do what I can," Rodrigo said.

"What's going on?" Mauricio asked as Luisa went to Rodrigo's mom to explain the situation to her.

Rodrigo switched back to English. "Malestar is planning an attack tomorrow night and she fears her son might be involved. At least we know where to be when it goes down."

"Why doesn't she just tell him no?"

"It's not that simple," Rodrigo replied. "She's a single mother and boys that age are easily influenced. Some of us are not fortunate to have two parents that tell us what's right and what's wrong."

"Well, let me talk to the kid. Text me the address when you get it. As for the attack…"

"I should talk to the kid, seeing that you don't speak Portuguese."

"Good point," Mauricio replied.

"You think I should tell Vesco about Malestar's plans?" Rodrigo asked.

"We're going to need all of the help we can get. Let Red know as well. We can get the help of anyone clean left in the city, but we don't want to announce this to the world. Tell Vesco we only want people we can trust."

"Got it."

"Also, get me the best weapons you can get your hands on. We'll convene later to discuss a plan."

"Where are you going?" Rodrigo asked.

"I'm going to enjoy life while I can."

"You don't have to talk to the kid if you don't want to," Mauricio said as he headed toward the front door.

"I know," Rodrigo replied.

Mauricio drove back into the city with his rental car and made his way to the beach. Along the way, Rodrigo texted him to stay ready and that he would try to find the kid in the morning. As for Mauricio, he just wanted to be left alone. He got out of the car and walked down the pathway directly adjacent to the beach. There was a fair amount of people already around in bikinis and shorts, enjoying the warm weather. Mauricio stepped onto the sand and walked toward the water.

He stood there with his hands in his pockets looking out into the ocean water. He enjoyed this moment of tranquility and closed his eyes. The demons of his past came swiftly with the bodies of all the men and women he had killed flashing across his memory. He quickly opened his eyes. Claudia was right. At some point he had to quit. He just didn't know if it would be anytime soon.

Mauricio walked into the ocean until the water was waist level. The water swept over his clothing and he didn't flinch. A wave came toward him and splashed his chest. Mauricio placed his hands out in front of him and stood perfectly relaxed.

Mauricio closed his eyes once again. The images of his past came stronger than ever before, and he realized that he could not escape them. He had to embrace them. The traditional music of his past played in his head. He saw all the bodies once again, Claudia, and Ken. This time, Mauricio tried not to run away from the images.

"I'm sorry," Mauricio said softly. "I will avenge for all of you."

The images stopped in his mind. His mind was clear, at least for the moment. Now he was focused to do the job he did so well.

*

Red opened the hotel room and Rodrigo came in with a box in hand. She closed the door and Rodrigo placed the box on the bed. Rodrigo turned around to see Red in her white tank top and repressed his sexual thoughts.

"I come bearing gifts," he said.

Red went to the box and saw that it was filled with guns. "You know a woman loves her toys."

She picked up a few guns from the box and aimed them at the wall. "So where's Mauricio?"

"Who knows," Rodrigo replied. "You know how he's in his own world. Doesn't matter right now. What does is tomorrow night. Are you ready for it?"

"I'm ready for anything."

"I bet you are."

"What's that supposed to mean?" Red asked.

"Let me ask you a question," Rodrigo said, sitting on the bed. "We all know you're a sexual predator that uses her body to get what she wants. How come you never tried your charm on me?"

"Rodrigo, we talked about this."

"I'm not good enough for you?"

"I swear, you act like a child sometimes." Red took a seat next to Rodrigo. "You couldn't handle me even if you tried. Now, I'm going to tell you one last time. I'm a professional, and I never mix business with pleasure."

"What if you retired?"

Red laughed. "No man is worth retiring for. Besides, I can't be your woman and trying to protect you all the time." Rodrigo flashed a smile. Red stood back up.

"Your head should be on tomorrow," she said. "It's going to be hard for me to even sleep tonight."

"You afraid?"

"Don't act like you're not."

Rodrigo went to the box of guns and picked up a handgun. "This was supposed to be about the money."

"From what I know, we're still getting paid."

"You know, this could be our last night on this earth. I say we use this time wisely. I'm going to give Mauricio a call."

"That's the first good idea I ever heard you say," Red replied.

*

Mauricio decided to go to the hospital, as he had thought of Claudia's wish to have a child. He snuck into the maternity ward and looked at the newborn babies through the viewing window. Claudia's favorite song, "Come Away with Me," by Norah Jones, played in his mind. His phone vibrated in his pocket, and he went to take a look at it. Rodrigo had left him a text message. Mauricio put the phone back in his pocket and imagined the future he would have had with Claudia.

He could see himself with kids running around the house and him chasing them around in a playful manner. Claudia would be resting on the couch, watching her favorite television soap opera, and he would stop by her to gently kiss her on her cheek. He would look into her eyes and love her just as much as he did the moment he first saw her. They would have lived a joyous life together and been comforted by each other's company.

Then he saw in his mind what would have happened if he stayed in the business. He would be chasing down a criminal somewhere in South America with a gun in hand. He would follow the target down the crowded streets and try to get an open shot. The target would have a weapon as well. The target would grab a little girl from the street, stop, and turn around with a gun to the little girl's head. Mauricio would be forced to stop as well. The target would demand that Mauricio put his gun down or else he would shoot the girl. Mauricio would have to put his gun down.

The target would laugh and laugh. Then he would fire at Mauricio and a few bullets would land in his chest. He would fall to the ground in disbelief. He had once thought he was invincible. He would touch the blood on his chest and realize that this was the end and he was going to rest like a dog on the street. He would leave Claudia with a household full of children and without the husband she loved with all her heart.

Mauricio let go of those thoughts and concentrated on the innocent that were behind the glass window. He held out his hand against the glass as if he could touch them. What he saw in front of him was the perfect world. A world where everyone was innocent and there was no evil to fight, no struggle to go through. Then he wouldn't have to do what he was hired to do.

But the world didn't work that way. He viewed the inhabitants of the city very much like the babies in front of him. They needed to be protected. They needed to be saved from the forces of evil that were intent on destroying the fabric of society. The police could only do so much. This was his purpose on this earth, and there was no turning back now.

Mauricio thought about going with Rodrigo and Red to get a drink, but then thought otherwise. He had had enough alcohol and this was no time to celebrate a possible end of life. He planned on staying alive, at least long enough to finish the job.

*

The men sitting in the bar area were in a unison shout and slammed their fists against the bar. The bar itself was nothing fancy, with minimal décor and wooden tables and chairs. Red raised her shot glass in the air and then drank all the alcohol in at once. The men shouted in celebration. Rodrigo stood next to her, shaking his head. Red waved the shot glass at them and the men waved their own back.

"They're only buying you drinks so they can get you drunk," Rodrigo said.

"And then one of them could seduce me with his charm and whisk me away home. I wouldn't mind the guy at the far right doing that. He's kind of cute."

"I'm serious, Red."

"You're not my father," Red said with slurred speech. She collapsed on the bar seat and asked the bartender for another round.

"What's with you? You like flirting with danger? We're supposed to be here to have a good night out before tomorrow, and here you are getting drunk without knowing your surroundings."

"I can take care of myself. Always have, always will. What you need to do is to give me my space and let me drink."

"So afterwards those men can gang rape you?"

"Get lost!"

Rodrigo was about to say something else, but decided to walk away. He left the bar, slamming the door on his exit. Red didn't bother to look around. The bartender came around with another drink and she finished it down. The men on the opposite side of the bar watched her and one of them, a bulky man in his mid-twenties, began to make his move.

He made his way to her and turned around once to look at his friends. They encouraged him to talk to her. He turned back around and took a seat next to Red.

"Hey, lady, I got an exciting toy you can play with," the man said.

"Sorry, I don't speak Portuguese," Red replied in English without looking at him.

"Ah, a foreigner!" The man looked back at his three friends and gave them the thumbs-up. They laughed, and the man turned back around. "You are very beautiful. I don't know if you know this or not, but you are coming home with me. I have decided this, so it is done. You shouldn't worry because you're in the presence of good hands."

The man held out his hands. "These hands have never let any woman down. You're in for a surprise."

"I told you I don't speak your language. Step away before you get hurt."

"You really should look at me when I talk to you," the man said. "I find your attitude disrespectful."

The man placed a hand against Red's arm, and a rush of rage built up inside of her.

37.

Red grabbed the man's arm and twisted it the other way in one swift motion, making the bone come out of the arm. The man shouted in pain. He quickly grabbed his arm and walked toward his friends. At first, they didn't know what to do. A woman in the back of the bar began to call the police. The man couldn't wait. He ran out of the bar in search for help. The bartender rushed to the back, wanting no part of the scene that was taking place. The other customers in the bar left as well.

The three friends sought revenge. They rushed to attack her. The first that came at her, Red kicked in the groin. Another man rushed at her and Red grabbed the nearby glass cup and crushed it against his head. Blood gushed out of the wound. The third man sneaked up on her and punched her in her mouth. The hit drew blood, and Red held on to her lip. The man stepped back and smiled.

Red lifted up her hands to fight. The man charged at her and Red struck him in the face with a punch of her own, followed by a body blow to the stomach. The man held onto his stomach. Red wrapped her right arm around his neck and twisted his head to the left. The man fell to the ground.

The man with the kick to the groin and the one with the bloody face rushed at her and pinned her against the bar. Then one of them delivered a punch to her stomach. Red leaned toward the ground. The men continued to hold her up. The woman in the back of the bar shouted for them to stop. One of them took out a pocket knife from his pocket with his free hand. He waved the knife at her face.

"I'm going to cut your pretty face, and you will remember me. It's time to teach you a lesson."

The door to the bar opened again. This time it was Rodrigo with a gun in hand. He shot both men in the head with two shots. Their blood splattered across Red's body. She stood against the bar in shock. Rodrigo walked toward her.

"You okay?" he asked.

"My knight in shining armor."

"You're welcome," he said. "We better get out of here."

"You didn't have to kill them."

"I think I did," Rodrigo replied.

"You feel like a bigger man now?"

"We don't have time for this. Let's go!" Rodrigo made a move toward the door. Red grabbed a liquor bottle from the bar and then followed Rodrigo out.

Rodrigo had his car outside with the engine running. He got into the driver's side as Red got into the backseat. She lay across the seat on her back as she closed the door. Rodrigo quickly drove off.

"That's enough craziness for tonight. I have an obligation in the morning," Rodrigo said. "You fight pretty well for being drunk."

Red took a drink from the liquor bottle, and looked out into the night through the window with her head spinning, barely able to keep her eyes open. She was trying her best to feel happy, but her mind was filled with sadness.

"You know what I realized, Rodrigo?"

"What's that?"

"That you cannot run away from the past," Red said. "It just keeps finding a way to return."

"You're drunk."

"That may be the case, but what I'm saying is true. You can drink, you can run, you can pretend it doesn't exist, but you can't hide. I think you just have to invite it to the present."

Red took another drink from the bottle. "I want my innocence back, Rodrigo. As a little girl, all I wanted to do was collect butterflies. They were just so beautiful with their array of colors and how they came from being the ugliest creatures into beautiful specimens that would float into the sky. I used to run outside and try to catch them during the summer. There was so much beauty in the world back then. I thought my life was just going to be perfect and I would grow into this woman that everyone would love and cherish. I would have a few kids, a perfect husband, and a life full of nothing but happiness. But then I had to grow up, and boy, was I wrong."

Red turned her head to face the front, her eyes going in and out of focus. "The dream became a nightmare. And the funny thing is, I don't want to wake up."

Red dropped the bottle that was in her hands and closed her eyes. Alcohol spilled on the back seat floor.

Rodrigo cursed out loud as he looked through the rearview mirror.

"You need help, Red. You know that?"

There was no response. Rodrigo shook his head and kept his eyes on the road. He might as well let her spend the night at his place. These were not the circumstances that he had wished for. But Mauricio was right; Red was a head case and no good for him. When the lust for her wore off, there was nothing left but a scarred, abused woman.

But he needed to take his own advice. He needed help as well. Maybe not in the same way as her, but he also had struggled with demons from his past. Early tomorrow morning he would have to tell a boy to be somebody that he wasn't, and pretend he was someone he wasn't. Why should he pretend anymore? He was never going to be the cold killing assassin he had always dreamed of. Was that so bad? He would have to start loving himself if he was ever going to grow.

*

Jorge had been in this dark room for what seemed like days, but in reality, it was for a few hours. He remembered being taken into a factory building outside of the city and then Malestar shoving a gun to his back to get inside. The door to the room was locked. The room was hot and stuffy, and he was sweating through his clothes, even on this early morning. There were no windows in the room and the smell around him was repulsive. Malestar had kept the bodies he had killed in bags in the corner of the room. Jorge had vomited a couple of times, and wished he hadn't. Now he smelled his vomit as well.

He was now regretting making the move to revitalize the Corporation. Carlito had warned him in private meetings with the other members. He had heard of Malestar's reputation as someone who was random and could think of something intelligent one second, and put someone in a compromising position the very next. He was starting to see what Carlito was saying. But Carlito saw what he did, and that meant there was money to be made. Hopefully, his greed wouldn't do him in.

There was only so much a man could do in the city to become rich quickly and effectively. That was either to be a drug dealer on the streets, or a man behind a suit in business or politics. It had been that way ever since he had been born into this world, and before him, and it would be that right after him. This wasn't the only continent where this was true. It was just the way of the world—play or be played.

The downside to this was the dangerous consequences and situations one could sometimes face. Right now, he was in one of those situations. He was going to have to talk his way out of this one. He didn't know what Malestar planned to do with him, and he didn't want to stick around to find out. He had to remember that Malestar needed him to gain the support of the new Corporation. This must be a test of some sort. As long as he kept calm and didn't appear rattled, then Malestar would realize that he was in business with the right man.

The door opened up. Malestar walked in, wearing the same clothes he had worn earlier. He looked tired and his hair was all over the place. He stood for a moment to look at Jorge. Jorge tried to read his express but couldn't tell what emotion he was feeling. Malestar closed the door walked over to Jorge.

"Do you know why you are here?" Malestar asked.

"You are wondering if you can trust me," Jorge replied.

"Something like that," Malestar said, and touched the side of Jorge's face. "You have very soft skin."

"I'm not afraid," Jorge said.

Malestar laughed, and then ran his fingers through his hair. "I see a bit of innocence in you."

"That's a good thing, right?"

"No," Malestar emphatically said. "If you are to be trusted, I want to have someone that has experienced what pain is like."

"I have experienced pain."

"Tell me, what was the worst day of your life?" Malestar waited with his arms folded.

Jorge had to think for a moment. "Okay, got it. When I was ten, I was playing outside on the street with my brother. We were kicking a ball around, pretending to be the next superstar player for the Brazilian national team. Then, all of a sudden, a car came and we tried to run away. I ended up getting hit on the side of my hip. The pain was excruciating. I blacked out after that. When I woke up, I realized I was inside a hospital."

"And that was the most pain you ever felt?" Malestar asked.

"It was painful."

Malestar nodded, and then punched Jorge in the stomach, causing him to hunch over. "You haven't begun to know what pain is like," Malestar said. "But I'm going to do you a favor, and you should feel special because I only help people I like in some sort of way. You have a lot of potential, Jorge. I'm sure you can outlast Carlito. You just need to concentrate on what exists inside of you and all of mankind. Only then will you understand pain and use it to your advantage."

"What...what are you going to do to me?"

Malestar wrapped an arm around Jorge's shoulder and smiled. "I thought you weren't afraid."

"Well, I guess everyone gets afraid from time to time."

"Not everyone." Malestar grabbed the top of Jorge's hair and forced him to his knees. "Sit," he said, and headed back toward the door. Jorge dared not move. Malestar exited the room and closed the door. This time Jorge didn't hear the door lock. He stayed on his knees and tried to block out negative thoughts. He wanted to say a prayer, but figured it would go unanswered, especially coming from him. He had to remind himself that this was just a test. Hopefully, it was. Otherwise, he would never live to see the sun again. He thought of all the regrets he had in life, and what could have been if he would have made the right decision.

The door opened once again. Malestar stood in the doorway with a sackcloth in his hand that appeared to be moving from whatever was in it. Malestar had a sinister smile on his face. "Pain is knowing that danger will strike, and there is nothing you can do about it. If you want to be in my world, you have to understand how it feels."

Malestar turned the sackcloth upside down and two large rattlesnakes fell to the ground. "Welcome to my world!" Malestar shouted, and exited the room, closing the door behind him.

The rattlesnakes started to crawl in Jorge's direction. Jorge quickly stood up and retreated to a corner. They were approaching faster. He ran away from them and circled past them over to the door. It was locked. The rattlesnakes once again made their way toward him and Jorge let out a shout that he feared for his life.

*

The next morning, Rodrigo knocked on the door and waited. Outside the shack in the slums he stood on a clear day. Moments later, the door opened, and Rodrigo was escorted inside by the boy's mother. He asked for his name and she said it was Miguel. He was told Miguel was inside the only other bedroom in the shack. The home looked poorly constructed and there were cartons and trash everywhere. Rodrigo made his way to the back bedroom where Miguel was sitting on the bed and playing a video game with the television in front of him. Rodrigo decided to ask the obvious.

"How did you get this video game console?" he asked.

"My big brothers gave it to me," Miguel said, without looking at him. "I know what you are here to do. It's not going to work. Leave me alone."

Rodrigo sat on the bed and watched him play for a bit. Finally, he spoke. "Your mother only wants what's best for you."

"She only wants what's best for herself," Miguel replied.

"You have a lot of anger, and I understand that."

"You don't understand me at all."

"Can you pause the game?"

The boy sighed, and put the game on pause. "You're not going to change my mind. I'm a gangster. I'm going to be rich and get my mother anything she wants."

"What she wants is for you to stay alive."

"Well, I'm tired of being broke and wondering when I'm going to eat again. My mother comes home every day, hurting from a day's work. I can't stand to see her like that. I'm going to make her proud. I'm going to be the man and provide for this family."

"You're going to get yourself killed. You think that madman cares about you? You are just a pawn to him. You're just flesh and bone to protect him if a bullet goes his way. He doesn't care about you. That woman that's taking care of you does. When you die on the street, how do you think your mother would feel?"

"Who's going to take care of me? She can't! I want to get out of the slums!"

"Then do it the right way. Go to school, educate yourself. Stop trying to take the easy way out. If you and your mother work hard enough, you can move to a decent place."

"And what makes you think that's going to work?" Miguel asked.

"Because it worked for me and my mother," Rodrigo replied.

Miguel sighed.

"Now, where's your gun?" Rodrigo asked.

"What makes you think..."

"Where is it?"

"Under the bed."

Rodrigo got up and looked under the bed. He took out the pistol and placed it inside his waist. He then stood up in front of Miguel.

"You want to know what your most powerful weapon is?" Rodrigo asked, and then touched Miguel's forehead. Then Rodrigo turned to exit the room.

"What about you now? Is that what you use?" Miguel asked.

"Save yourself while you still have a chance," Rodrigo said, and left the room.

38.

Rodrigo returned home to find Red standing in the doorway to the backyard area. She stared at Mauricio, who was sitting with his legs crossed on the dirt. He had his eyes closed, with the palms of his hands facing upward. The dogs rested peacefully beside him. Rodrigo looked at Red and could see that she wanted to go over there, but she didn't know how to approach.

"How long has he been like that?" Rodrigo asked.

"About twenty minutes. It's some type of meditating."

"Never pictured him as the meditating type," Rodrigo replied.

"He never fails to surprise me."

Rodrigo took out a handgun from his hip and approached Mauricio. He stood next to him with the gun still in his hand. Mauricio didn't flinch.

"You're going to put that gun away?"

"How did you know?" Rodrigo asked.

"I've been in this business a long time. I can smell my instruments to kill."

Rodrigo grinned. "Actually, this is a gift for you."

Mauricio opened his eyes, stood up, and turned to face Rodrigo. He then took the gun from Rodrigo's hand. He held it for a moment, looked at Rodrigo, and then looked at the gun.

"Decent," he said.

"There's more where that came from," Rodrigo replied.

"That's how it always is."

"What's with you lately? It seems like you got your head in the clouds. You do know tonight is when we're going to track down Malestar."

"And you're doing this for the money?" Mauricio asked.

"Is there something wrong with that?"

"Only if you think there's something wrong with that."

Rodrigo gave him a confused look. Mauricio smiled and waved Red over. "Red!"

Red walked over to them. "So this is how it feels when assassins unite."

"We're not assassins," Mauricio said. "We're mercenaries. That's what I want to be remembered as."

"You're sounding like you're planning on not making it," Red said. "Didn't all that meditating get rid of destructive thinking?"

"Listen, you two," Mauricio said. "I really appreciate the help in all of this. The truth is, I'm doing this for Claudia. The both of you can split the money."

"Are you sure about this?" Rodrigo asked.

"That money is yours just as much as it is ours," Red said.

"You guys know why I'm doing this. I'm going to use the money I saved from all these years to walk away."

"For how long?" Rodrigo asked.

"That's a good question," Mauricio answered. "I don't think I can answer that right now. What I do know is that Malestar is going to be well prepared, and this isn't going to be some walk in the park. If you want to back out, let me know now."

"You know we're not going anywhere," Red said. "We're in this together."

"Agreed," Rodrigo stated.

"So be it," Mauricio said. "Do what you need to do to get your mind right for tonight."

"Like what you just did earlier?" Rodrigo asked.

"Yeah, like that," Mauricio said, leaving the backyard.

Rodrigo was right about one thing—Mauricio was feeling different. He was learning how to clear his mind, and the last thing on his mind was Malestar and the danger he was about to face. Right now, he was thinking about being at peace. He drove down the coastline of Salvador and an urge he couldn't resist came across his mind. There was one hobby he could do the rest of his life outside of the bounty business and that was boating. He felt it was time to get a new boat, and then maybe after he was done with it all, he could enjoy the ocean and nature, and live in his own paradise. He had been hesitant about doing this, but felt now was as good a time as ever. He had to think that he would survive this meeting with Malestar, and by making plans after the fact, it would help his determination when danger came around.

He didn't consider himself an expert in fishing, but he knew his way around a boat. He enjoyed the sport, and sometimes the good meal afterwards. He liked everything from common fish like Atlantic salmon and tilapia to more exotic fish in this region such as pompano and barramundi. But his favorite was grilled swordfish, with its enriched, dense texture and mild taste. He always had his with a side of wild mushroom risotto and a glass of chardonnay. Besides the tasting of the fish he caught, he would also enjoy the hobby.

He was one of those rare people that enjoyed the fishing shows on television and would tune in when he could. He remembered seeing one about some fishermen in northern Thailand who netted what scientists believed was the largest freshwater fish ever caught and recorded. The specimen was nine feet long and close to seven hundred pounds. The fish was endangered and the fishermen tried their best to keep it alive, but they were unsuccessful. Later, the fish was eaten by local villagers.

This was the type of legendary catch that Mauricio wanted for his own. In his mind, fishing was a lot like the line of work he was in. Patience was required to chase down a target, and there was an enjoyment in the hunt. The ocean, just like the world, was filled with the prey and predators. There was a society underwater and like the world of today, Mauricio decided not to be a part of it, but to watch from afar. He studied their movements and their habits. Right when you got them where you wanted them, then you struck and either threw them back in, or gutted them alive. Nature was no different wherever the location.

Mauricio stopped the car when he approached the harbor with boats lining the docking area of the marina. The afternoon had brought on a cool wind near the ocean. He walked amongst the marina and browsed the many boats that were around. The cityscape of Salvador was in view on the far end of the ocean. He pictured himself in one of those boats, and a smile swept over his face.

Then he heard the sound of police sirens. Mauricio turned his head to see a row of police cars coming up the street. He had been tracked, probably from Rodrigo's house. The police cars stopped behind his rental car and cut the sirens. No one came out of the cars. He waited. Still, there was no response. Mauricio was about to head back to his car when he saw a gray car coming down the street. It pulled up behind the police cars, and the passenger side door opened.

Vesco came out and buttoned up his suit. He nodded to the driver and walked over to Mauricio, who stood calmly. Vesco looked around for a moment, and then returned his gaze toward Mauricio.

"Another beautiful day. A good day to handle business," Vesco said.

"Some would say."

"Let's have a talk," Vesco said. "At the very least, I think I owe you a drink."

"You've got any whiskey?"

Vesco smiled. "Plenty of it."

Since the incident at the boat and at the charity dinner, Vesco had moved his family into a high-rise building downtown where there was around-the-clock protection from police officers, mostly those that had just finished the academy that were willing to do the job and too green behind the ears to be corrupted. They diligently went about their duty as Vesco led Mauricio into the living room.

Inside, the apartment was furnished with all the modern touches one would expect in the price range Vesco was paying. The walls were lime green and the floor was white and tiled. The kitchen was adjacent to the living room, and Vesco went behind the counter to pour two drinks. Mauricio went to the curtains in the far end of the room and took a peek behind them. There was a view of downtown and the immediate buildings in the area. There were many windows and rooftops for a sniper to make his mark. There was a reason Vesco kept the curtains covering the windows.

"All of my privacy is gone," Vesco said. "Well, the little that I had. I've learned a long time ago that politics would damper any expectation of having a normal life. I gave it some thought, you know, just to walk away from it all. But I figured it was worth it in the end. The money was just impossible to give up. I hope you can understand that."

"You don't have to justify anything to me," Mauricio said, standing in the middle of the living room.

Vesco prepared the drinks and handed one to Mauricio. He stood before him and said, "I want to thank you, if I haven't before, for saving my life."

"Don't mention it."

Vesco grinned. "I wish I was more like you, so nonchalant, so not afraid, so staying cool. If I was, I sure wouldn't be in politics. I would be doing something else altogether."

"Like killing people and getting paid for it," Mauricio replied.

"We all have to make a living somehow." Vesco went toward the hallway to go to the bedrooms and opened each door to check in on the women in his life. Both of them seemed to be napping peacefully. He gently closed the doors and returned to the living room.

"You haven't touched your drink," Vesco stated.

"I was thinking about putting this stuff down for a while," Mauricio said, studying his drink.

"I wish I could," Vesco said, taking another swallow, and then reaching underneath the couch to take out a manila envelope. He handed it to Mauricio.

"What's this?" Mauricio asked.

"The rest," Vesco said. "Thought I would give it to you in person. You can split it with the others as you see fit. You deserve it, whether you finish the job or not."

Mauricio took the envelope and placed it in the inside pocket of his suit jacket. "I'm sure there's a tip included."

Vesco smiled and finished his drink. He then went back to the kitchen to pour himself another glass. "I have a tip for you. If you somehow manage to live another lifetime, don't ever do this line of work."

Vesco poured the whiskey into the glass, and then shook the glass in his hand. "I read your profile before I hired you. I know you returned to Africa with your parents and then the tragedy that struck once you were there. But there isn't much known about your time in London and your stint with Her Majesty's armed forces. I have only the usual paperwork about how skilled you were as a shooter, but nothing of relevance to tell me who you were. What caused you to quit? What made you leave for Africa with your family?"

"I wanted get in touch with my roots."

"I know there was something more. Tell me," Vesco said.

Mauricio sighed. "My time in the armed forces was a lesson. I learned a lot and it was time to move on."

"And what did you learn?"

"That we were no different than the people were trying to kill. I suppose you can talk about the reason you are doing it, and say it's for the safety of the public as a whole, but I knew better. We had an agenda just like anybody else. You can tell the public anything as long as you give them a bit of fear. You can make a domestic attack, blame it on any country you like, and the public would gladly follow you. It was appalling. So I left. But then I began to run out of money fast. I was offered to do a hit, and I accepted it."

Mauricio looked at his drink for a moment, and then decided to drink it all at once. "After my first kill, a rush of guilt just built up inside of me to the point where I couldn't take it anymore. When you take human life, it changes you. I'm sure you've killed your fair share of people, but when you do with your action, your own hands, it completely changes who you are. I couldn't stand being in the city any longer when I returned from my trip. When my parents wanted to move back, I jumped at the opportunity."

"And what did a change of scenery do for you?" Vesco asked.

"It worked for a while. I got closer to my family and felt like I could breathe again. But then you know what happened soon after. I felt so much anger that I had to do something with it. There was only one thing I knew how to do well and so I reached out to my contact and he supplied me with jobs. I was efficient at what I did because I didn't want to think about anything else. I wanted to escape my past, and concentrated on my job. A reputation was made, but I didn't care at all about that. I only continued to hunt and kill, and every face from that point on was an empty one. I had become numb, a machine that was hired to do a job and not feel. Now, do you wish you were more like me?"

Vesco finished his second drink and moved to the living room. "When I decided to hire Rodrigo and his former partner, and be a part of the Corporation, I had no problems going to sleep at night. You want to know why? Because like you said, there is no difference between the good guys and the bad guys. I've come to accept that. There's a game being played, and you're either calling the shots or being played. I decided to be the one that called the shots; that is, until it got personal."

Vesco looked toward the hallway for a moment, and then back at Mauricio. "Family is everything to me, Mauricio. A man can become good or bad when it comes to protecting his family. Morals are not as important, and they never have been for me. I'm always going to do what's best for them."

Mauricio shook his head. "It's a shame people like you are in office."

"Think of it as job security," Vesco replied.

Mauricio smiled. "I guess you can call it that. You think there's a future for people like us after all of this is done?"

Vesco thought about the answer for a moment. "Only time will tell," he replied.

Mauricio nodded. "Thanks for the drink," he said as Vesco went back to the kitchen.

"And here I thought you were not drinking anymore."

"A man without urges is a man not living, and enemies are reflections of heroes," Mauricio said.

"Sounds like something Malestar would say."

Mauricio grinned. "The man sure knows how to leave an impression."

39.

The appearance of night always seemed to bring out the worst of mankind. Tonight was no different. Crimes were being made in discreet locations, and the city was alive with desire and fulfillment. On the surface, it seemed like another night in Salvador, but in reality it was anything but ordinary.

The residents of the Mansão Margarida Costa Pinto building had been going in and out of the building as normal with no expectation of danger. The neighborhood was a pocket of peacefulness in the robust lifestyle of the city. The people were aware of the crime around them but didn't experience any danger on a daily basis. The hallways were quiet except for the faint sounds of televisions and music being played. Outside, a group of motorcycles made their way to the building and parked in front.

Across the building and on the rooftop of a building across the street were the mercenaries, along with a group of young recruits and newly made police officers. Mauricio watched from a pair of night-vision binoculars. He watched as the drivers of the motorcycles got off their bikes with guns in their hands. He saw Malestar amongst them, wearing a black tuxedo and a white mask that resembled a skeleton with painted markings and teeth. Malestar waved his arms to his side as he entered the front entrance with his crew right behind him.

Malestar walked down the corridor of the lobby floor with a gun in hand, and made his way to the stairs. He began to sing the lyrics to the opera song "La Boheme" by Giacomo Puccini. Members of his crew scattered across the lobby to plant the bombs. Malestar made his way one floor up with four members of his crew behind him. They began knocking on the doors in the hallway and some of the doors opened. The people inside were immediately shot. Screams were heard. Doors were kicked down and more people were shot. Malestar danced in the hallway as killing was all around him.

"Go! Go! Go!" Mauricio shouted, and everyone began to leave the rooftop across the street.

Malestar made his way onto the next floor up. Again, his crew began to kick down the doors and shove people in the hallway to shoot them. Then they planted a select number of bombs in their rooms.

"Ladies and gentlemen, this is an exercise of our liberties as citizens. I'm only doing what we all should be doing, and that is enjoying my complete freedom as a creature on this earth. Now I know what you are thinking. That I have another agenda as to why I'm doing this, and I do, but I'm also here to give my hand to my fellow men, and awaken you all. You may shout, and you may scream, but this is what freedom feels like! This is how the world should live!"

A woman screamed from one of the rooms and Malestar lifted his gun and shot her in the head. Another couple tried to leave as well and Malestar shot them down too with bullets piercing their bodies and blood exploding into the air. The walls became painted with blood.

"We are making art today!" Malestar shouted. "On to the next floor!"

Malestar and his crew made his way to the stairway. A few of them went ahead of him and were shot down by Mauricio and his team coming up. Blood splattered across Malestar's mask as he made his way to the doorway. He immediately retreated back onto the floor. Mauricio led the way up, Rodrigo and Red not too far behind. They pointed their weapons upward and were met with more resistance. More of Malestar's crew came through the doorway as Mauricio headed their way. He tripped one of them and they fell down the stairway. The other man pointed his gun to shoot, but Mauricio shoved it away from him as the trigger was pulled. The bullet ended up against the wall.

Red and Rodrigo began to shoot down the man that fell and his body convulsed with the bullets being placed inside of him. The other man up the stairs shoved Mauricio against the wall. Mauricio turned him so his back was facing the stairs. Rodrigo shot him in the foot and the man shouted in pain. Mauricio punched him across his face and he fell backward down the stairs.

"Why did you do that for?" Mauricio asked. "I had him."

"Looked like you needed some help," Rodrigo said.

"Let's keep moving," Mauricio said, and they continued forward.

Outside the building, police cars parked in front of the building. Officers got out of the cars and were shot down by a group of teenagers dressed in purple in a nearby alley. There were more police reinforcements from the group that Vesco had arranged to come along with Mauricio. They stood near the entrance and began shooting at the teenagers in the alley. A bloodbath was taking place, and the body count was adding up. A helicopter approached the building.

Back inside, Malestar had made his way to the top floor using the opposite staircase. "Put them down!" he shouted as the men behind him gave him cover and placed the bombs on the bottom of the walls. Mauricio tried to make his way through the stairway door but the door was filled with bullets. Mauricio took cover behind the door.

"Mauricio?" Malestar shouted. "Is that you, my friend? I'm glad you can come to the party. Come, enjoy in this celebration!"

Malestar made his way toward the opposite stairway that was down the hall. A few police officers came out the door. Malestar shot them down, and one fell to his knees, pleading for his life. A gunshot wound had penetrated his chest and he held onto his wound. Malestar stood before him and laughed.

"You finally are starting to get it," he said, and then shot the man in the head.

"Malestar!" Mauricio shouted as he made his way to the hallway.

Malestar waved his hands up. "Sorry, I have plans." Malestar made his way to the stairway, and walked up to the door that led to the rooftop.

Mauricio felt like this was déjà vu all over again. He wasn't going to let Malestar escape this time. There was one more crew member left in the hallway and Mauricio was out of bullets. He threw his gun at the man's face and it landed against the man's nose, causing him to fall backward. Mauricio ran down the hallway and noticed the bombs that were lined up against the hallway.

"Get out of here!" he shouted to Red and Rodrigo.

Mauricio continued to sprint down the hallway, and he followed Malestar to the rooftop. Mauricio opened the door and found no one there. Malestar came from behind the door and shoved him to the ground. The gun went flying out of Mauricio's hand.

The helicopter closed in on the rooftop. Malestar kicked Mauricio in the face and he rolled against the roof. The helicopter came down and the ladder was let down. Malestar thought about attacking Mauricio some more, but he figured there was no time. He ran to the rope and waited as it came down to him. Then he turned around.

"Another lifetime, Mauricio!" Malestar shouted.

Mauricio got to his feet to see Malestar on the ladder and the helicopter ready to leave. Mauricio was determined not to let Malestar get away this time. He ran to him as the helicopter began to lift into the air. He landed against Malestar's back as the helicopter made its ascent into the air.

Mauricio held onto Malestar's back as Malestar tried to fight him off. The ladder began to lift toward the helicopter. The gunman inside tried to get a good shot at just Mauricio, but didn't have a clean shot. Malestar tried kicking him as well. Mauricio held on, and tried to climb upward. Malestar tried as well. Then, both of their momentum was taken away as the building exploded, and the impact caused both of them to lose their grip on the ladder.

On the ground level, Red and Rodrigo ran out of the building as the building exploded. The bombs went off in succession. The explosion lit up the sky. They jumped to the ground and fell hard on the concrete. Many of the police officers and Malestar's crew near the building were blown to pieces. Police cars were lifted into the air. Rodrigo looked back and shielded his eyes with his hands. Red leaned up as well.

"Where's Mauricio?" Red asked.

Mauricio and Malestar fell downward in the sky. Malestar continued to reach for the ladder while suspended in the air, and the moment felt like eternity. Both of them seemed like they were swimming in air. Mauricio, falling behind him, felt like this was the end. This was the last visual he was going to see, grasping for a man he had hunted for so long. He assumed the end was near.

Instead, he landed hard against the tarp of an unfinished rooftop of the next building over. Malestar did the same. Building supplies, paint cans, and other materials were knocked around as they landed. The two men laid still on their backs as the excruciating pain made them both unable to move.

Mauricio finally rolled to his side and saw he was close to the ledge. It was painful just to move, but he tried his best not to let the pain get to him. He noticed he had a large cut on his arm that he held over the ledge, and the blood fell down to the ground. Malestar started laughing. He was enjoying the pain. Mauricio looked at the smoke coming from the next building over, and Malestar did the same. Mauricio thought of all the innocent lives killed, and he thought of Ken and Claudia. He wanted nothing more than to get up and beat the brains out of this maniac, but he didn't have the strength.

Malestar was better at absorbing pain. He managed to get to his feet, and looked over Mauricio, who was still grimacing. Malestar was holding his back. Mauricio noticed he had a grin on his face. The helicopter in the sky had turned back around.

"Now you and me are closer than ever," he said. "Doesn't pain feel good?"

"Mauricio!" Rodrigo shouted as he ran with Red to the side of the building. Rubble covered the ground, along with apartment furnishings and dead bodies. The two of them walked through the damaged front entrance and tried to find Mauricio around what remained of the building. There was no sign of him.

"This can't be happening, this can't be happening," Red said as she continued to look. Then she saw the smoke still coming out the front entrance. "I'm going inside."

"Are you crazy?" Rodrigo asked.

Red didn't bother replying. She ran inside, covering her mouth with the inside of her elbow. Still, she couldn't help but to cough. She pointed her gun just in case there were any of Malestar's crew still alive and ready to kill. And she was right. There was a man reaching for his gun as his legs were covered with parts of the building. He stretched out his hand, reaching for it. Red went up to him and kicked the gun away. She raised her gun to shoot him, but thought otherwise. He was going to suffer on his own.

She headed up the stairs. Red couldn't help but to cough some more. She went to the next level up and there was a massive hole in the middle of the hallway. Next to her was an open room. Red decided to take a look inside.

What she found was the most horrific sight she had ever seen and an image she would never forget. On the ground and covered in blood were two children, one boy and one girl. The mother was in between them, holding on to her children and trying to protect them. Bullets had gone through all of their bodies and their flesh was torn apart.

Red felt like vomiting. She held it in. She looked once more and felt like the eyes were looking at her. She wanted to close their eyes, but she didn't want to touch them. Red felt like crying but the tears didn't arrive. Instead, she coughed some more.

She left the room and hurried out of the building. Once outside she gasped for air. This time she couldn't hold in her vomit. This entire massacre had disgusted her to her core. She had seen death plenty of times, but not like this. This was different, and something she hoped never to see again.

She cleaned her mouth and looked around for Rodrigo. "Rodrigo! Where are you?"

Police cars started coming down the street. It was time to leave. She ran to her car that was parked two blocks away. Her back was aching, her head was throbbing, and it felt like her chest was on fire. She arrived at Rodrigo's car and realized he had the keys. She cursed out loud.

Red did the only thing she could do and that was to run. She ran until her body gave in. She made her way to an alley and leaned against the wall to catch her breath. Police cars rushed by. It wouldn't be long before they reached the building.

Rodrigo walked around the other side of the building and looked around. That was when he noticed the blood on the ground that was next to the building adjacent to the one he was at. Rodrigo ran over, and then looked up. He couldn't see anything from this distance.

He could hear the police cars coming closer. Rodrigo sped up his pace and made his way to the front of the modern residential building and rushed inside. He quickly ascended the steps, breathing hard but keeping a steady pace. He made his way to the rooftop access; the door was locked. Rodrigo slammed his body against the door until it burst open.

He noticed right away that there had been a commotion here, and saw the damage to the roof area. He scrambled around the many items on the ground, and moved them in case Mauricio was underneath.

"Mauricio! Mauricio!"

He looked around frantically for him. The police had now arrived at the next building over. Rodrigo stopped at the center of the roof to catch his breath. He looked around and wiped his forehead. It was time to realize the obvious. Mauricio was nowhere to be found.

40.

The media was quick to arrive at the scene. Reporters stood near the damaged building and spoke into cameras about what was told to them by authorities. The story was the headlines of every news channel. Vesco got on camera and spoke in a composed manner to calm the inhabitants of the city. He did little to rid the somberness that was taking place in everyone's thoughts and feelings. The city was afraid, and the youth was rebelling to join a cause that didn't benefit them in the long run.

In the slums, news got around fast about Malestar and the bombing he did in the city. The pattern to participate in crime had returned. The middle-aged and older were afraid of the madman, and the youth took it as a sign of change. Malestar was gaining popularity once again. The gangsters that sold narcotics even praised the man for getting back at law enforcement. Now every lowlife criminal in the city was throwing their support for Malestar.

The crooked politicians had mixed feelings. On one hand, their urges for greed were fulfilled as they knew that Malestar meant more money into the government and for the protection of the public, since the public was easily influenced by fear. However, the loss of human life was hard to absorb when they had to go home to their families. There was guilt there they hoped would be replaced with buying new clothes for their spouse and buying their children a college education. They figured the sacrifice for their own children was more important than the guilt for the loss of the children from other families. All of them knew that if they really wanted to, they could turn in Malestar with a few phone calls. They knew who he worked for, and what the Corporation was doing. It was all a game they were playing, and the people that suffered the most were clueless about the rules.

More of the youth wanted to join Malestar's crew and were anxious to know when he would arrive in the slums again. The politicians knew this. Another thing they were afraid of was a citywide rebellion. They still had to control the people and at the same time make them believe that they were free. It was a tricky balance they had perfected for years. They knew Malestar would strike again, and before he did, they would figure out if it was worth another headline like this.

Members of the new Corporation didn't mind the violence at all. They would capitalize on the suffering of their fellow men no matter the costs. Most of them had psychopathic traits and didn't care about the children or their future. This was the way it was going to be, and they were enthusiastic about the future.

A citywide curfew was put into place for anyone under the age of sixteen. Parents marched down to city hall and attended the meetings with the city board to address the issue. Vesco did his best to side with the parents and enforce the law. He knew when there was outrage from the citizens that the best thing to do was to back them in their fight. Sides had been chosen, youth versus adult, and both struggled to gain control of the city.

*

"Jorge, my boy, I got a present for you!"

The doors to the warehouse opened and Malestar came in with two men and Mauricio in front of him with handcuffs on. Jorge had retreated to the corner and guarded himself with his hands over his head. He looked over once, and the sunlight burned his eyes. Mauricio was shoved into the room, and then handcuffed to a pipe on the other side of the room.

"No more snakes! No more pain!" Jorge shouted.

"That's no way to say thank you," Malestar said. "I come bearing a gift!"

Mauricio looked up as he sat on the ground. The man in the corner across from him looked like he had suffered a great deal lately. He must have been important as Malestar did not kill him just yet. As inconsistent as Malestar was in his need for terror, he was consistent in a twisted respect he had for certain people and determined to make them feel intense pain.

"Now," Malestar said to Jorge, taking out a gun from his hip. "We're going to play a little game. The rules are simple. You have one hour to put a bullet in that man's head that's sitting right across from you. If you fail to do so, I will have two men waiting outside to gun you down. I'm thinking I'm giving you more than enough time to finish the job, but I understand this is your first kill and it might take some time. They say it's hard to take a human life, but if you ask me, I'll say different."

Malestar walked over to Jorge and placed the gun in front of him. Jorge turned his head the other way not to look at Malestar, and still remained in a crouched position. Malestar leaned over and patted his head.

"Don't be afraid of what's already inside of you," Malestar softly said.

Malestar turned back around to face Mauricio. "As for you, you have nothing to be afraid of. I'm sure it's painless."

Malestar walked out of the room with his two men behind him. There was silence in the room. Mauricio looked at the gun next to Jorge, and then at Jorge. The man had clearly lost his mind. He was moving his head awkwardly and touching the wall.

"This is just a test. This is just a test," he quietly repeated to himself in Portuguese.

"Do you understand English?" Mauricio asked out loud. "I know a way we can both win in this situation. You give me that gun in front of you, and I will handle what is outside. Then you are free to go wherever you want. You shouldn't let another man control you."

"Can't run....can't hide," Jorge said still in Portuguese, now cradling himself and almost to the point of tears. "It's too late. I got greedy. I won't see my family again."

"Do you understand me?" Mauricio asked. "I can help you. It's never too late to change."

Jorge remained silent. Mauricio pulled on his handcuffs slightly and realized he wasn't going to get out of them, but he might be able to break the pipe behind him. He thought about doing that now, but that might provoke Jorge to reach for the gun. Mauricio thought the best course of action now was to remain calm.

"There's no shame in doing the right thing," Mauricio said. "We are all human, and we all make mistakes. Don't go down this road that Malestar is leading you. It only leads to pain and suffering. You can still be someone that makes a difference. Is this what you want to remembered for? You're not a killer. I can see that by looking at you. If you give me the gun, I promise I won't kill you. I have nothing against you, and I know how Malestar can manipulate people. You let me go, I'll get the both of us out of here alive. But you have to get yourself together. Don't let him ruin your mind."

Jorge turned his head to look at Mauricio. Then he looked at the gun and back at Mauricio again. Mauricio tried to read what his thoughts were, but had no idea what Jorge was thinking. Jorge got up and made his way to the gun in front of him. He picked it up and held it to his side. Mauricio noticed he was much calmer now.

Jorge continued to speak in Portuguese. "My grandfather was a businessman, and my father was a businessman, so naturally I became one too. You can say I was pushed into doing what I do now. I didn't like it at first, but with time, I learned to appreciate it. I began to realize that money is the key to life, the fruit one needs to eat to survive. What kind of life would I have if I didn't pursue it? I would be in the slums with everyone else, struggling to get by. I can't have that kind of life. But then again, I can't stand the one I have now. Something has got to change. I have to do what's best for me. That madman is going to kill me if I don't do what he says. I'm sorry, but if it's any consolation, this is not the life I wanted."

Jorge raised his gun toward Mauricio.

"Now wait!" Mauricio shouted, and now tried to break the pipe away from the wall. He aggressively rocked back and forth, trying to free himself. His face showed fear and pain as he struggled to break free.

"Don't do this! I can help you! Please, let me help you!"

"It's too late for that," Jorge replied, and lifted the gun higher.

"I will hunt you down in the afterlife! You hear me!" Mauricio shouted as he used all his strength to break free. The pipe was loosening from the wall. Jorge had tears in his eyes. Mauricio shouted from the pain in his wrists and knowing he could be killed at any moment. Finally, the pipe broke away from the wall, and Mauricio charged at Jorge, still handcuffed to the pipe. Jorge stood still, the gun aimed forward. Then suddenly he lifted the gun toward his chin, and pulled down on the trigger.

Jorge's head exploded, and his brain matter went on Mauricio as he charged his body and forced Jorge to the ground. Mauricio fell on top of him with a dismantled brain next to his own. Mauricio backed away immediately. He then reached for the gun that Jorge had dropped and headed for the door.

Mauricio banged twice against the door using the pipe behind his back. Then he moved to the side of the door. The door opened, and Mauricio struck the first with the pipe to his stomach. He fell backward as Mauricio turned all the way around and fired his gun twice. The second bullet landed in the other man's chest as he approached Mauricio.

The man that fell to the ground got up, and Mauricio ran back into the room. The man chased after him as Mauricio shouted in fear. He fired the remaining bullets inside the gun as he made his way toward the wall. The first few didn't connect on flesh, but the next few did. The bullets landed in the man's chest and esophagus, and he spurted out blood. The man fell next to Mauricio against the wall. Mauricio continued to press down the trigger even after just hearing the clicking sound.

Mauricio reached around on the ground for the man's pockets. His hand was drenched in his blood as he found the key to the handcuffs. After a few minutes, Mauricio managed to place the key upward into the lock, and unlocked himself from the handcuffs. He picked up the gun from the dead man's hip, the car keys from his pocket, and made his way outside.

A black car was parked out front. Mauricio looked around and realized he had been in this building before. Malestar was still using it as a torture station of some sort. Mauricio ran to the car, got inside, and closed the door. His thirst to kill Malestar was stronger than ever before.

*

Vesco was in his office reading the morning newspaper when Rodrigo walked inside and sat before him. Vesco didn't bother looking up and continued reading. He turned the page to follow a story on the front page. Rodrigo stared at him. Vesco looked at him for a moment, and then back at his paper.

"Is there something I can help you with?" Vesco asked.

"How can you come back to work at a time like this? There's a large amount of people out there upset about how you run the city and your life is danger. Yet, here you are, sitting down like everything is just perfect."

"I came into office to do a job, and that's what I intend to do. You just caught me on my down time."

Rodrigo shook his head and grinned. "You know Mauricio is missing."

"I'm aware he hasn't reported anything back. Not like him."

"So, what's the plan?"

Vesco put the paper down and turned to face Rodrigo. "The plan is for you to stop whining like an uncontrollable baby and go out and do something about it. That's what I hired you for. You always were the weak one."

"What's that supposed to mean?" Rodrigo asked.

"I think you know. When I first asked for your services, it was your partner who said you were too young, and too inexperienced for a job like this. We went back and forth on it. I actually was in support of you, but you have proven me wrong countless times over. You let the best thing to ever happen to you die right in front of you. You're a nobody still, until you prove otherwise."

"If that's the case, why did you put me on this job?"

"Distraction."

"What?" Rodrigo asked, leaning forward.

"Malestar was in hand in hand with the Corporation to terrorize the city and all the businesses that were not a part of them. Now that he has somebody chasing him around, it gives him something else to do besides running this city to the ground."

Rodrigo stood up. "Then you can count me out."

"You're going to turn your back on your new friends?"

"I'm turning my back on you," Rodrigo said, heading toward the door.

"Wait," Vesco said, and sighed. Rodrigo turned back around.

"Another reason I hired you is that I saw the same potential I saw when I first heard about you. You are unsure of yourself. Anyone can see that. But once you know who you are, I see a bright future for a man like yourself. You are eager to learn, desperate to please, and have a strong sense of loyalty to those on your side. You really believe you are doing something rewarding."

"Well, don't you feel the same way about your job?" Rodrigo asked.

"That's irrelevant. What's important is that you go out there and find Mauricio. You and I both know he's the key to stopping Malestar."

"I couldn't agree more," Rodrigo said, and left the office.

Vesco checked his watch, and then went back to reading his paper.

41.

"I don't think this is a good idea," Red said to Rodrigo as they walked down the street of the Alagados slums in the late morning. The residents were watching from their windows and the little boys that served as lookers ran down the street to see where they were going. Red was more nervous than Rodrigo, as he seemed confident in what he was doing.

"Too many ears to the street here," Rodrigo said. "Somebody has to know something."

"Where are we going?" Red asked.

"A place where deals are made. Drug dealers know the most about what's going on around them."

"Are you crazy?"

"Just enough to get the job done."

Rodrigo led the way to a corner store where there was a fruit stand outside, and canned goods, frozen foods, and snacks were stacked along the aisles. The bell went off as they entered. Rodrigo made his way to the cashier, an older man with white curly hair who showed no emotion. Rodrigo stood at the counter and stared him down. The cashier slowly reached for his gun.

"I need some uppers," he said.

The cashier studied him for a moment, and then nodded toward the side of the store. Rodrigo looked to his right, where a hallway was located that led to the back. Rodrigo and Red made their way toward that area as the cashier looked in their direction.

There was a rusted brown door which Rodrigo found unlocked. He opened the door to see three men playing cards at a corner table, all of them older men wearing tropical shirts, shorts, and flip-flops. The men had red eyes as they looked at their visitors. Beer bottles, money, and coke were also on the table. Samba music was playing in the background. Red stood uncomfortably as they could feel their eyes undress her. Rodrigo pulled up a nearby chair and sat at the table.

"I don't want to waste your time, and I only came here for one thing, and you're going to tell me what I want. If you don't, well, I can promise you two things. One, you will die a quick death, and two, your family won't be able to put your bodies in an open casket."

The men looked at each other and laughed. "The nerve of this guy," one of them said. "Who are you?" he asked, turning his head to face Rodrigo.

"It doesn't matter who I am. Now, I want to know where Malestar is."

"Malestar?" the man asked. "Now, what do you want with him?"

"That's my business," Rodrigo said. "Where is he?"

"Son, you don't want anything to do with him."

"Where is he?" Rodrigo sternly asked.

"Why?"

"I'm going to kill him," Rodrigo replied.

The man sighed. "I don't appreciate a man barging in and demanding answers from me. Do you know who I am? I could have you killed for less than nothing. You and your family. You are fortunate that we have similar interests. I don't agree with many of my peers. This man named Malestar has taken many of the youth from here and used them for his cause. We need this youth to work for us. We are the ones that have invested years in them, and now with a few bombings and a few speeches, they want to go work for him. He's bad for business. If I knew where he was, I would kill him myself."

"Well, sorry for wasting your time," Rodrigo said, standing up.

"That's what the other guy said."

"What other guy?"

"A man came in here earlier asking for Malestar. He said he was going to stay close until..."

"Do you know where he is?"

The man grinned, looked away, and started playing cards with the other men again. Rodrigo shook his head and headed out the door with Red. Back on the street, Rodrigo took a look around with his hands on his hips.

"Mauricio is around here," Rodrigo said.

A white truck drove down the street with an open trunk for cargo. The driver honked its horn as it arrived. Rodrigo and Red quickly got off the street. Teenagers with guns in their hands ran out their houses and over to the truck. The truck stopped and the teenagers got into the trunk area, closing the trunk behind them. The truck then drove off.

"We need to find Mauricio fast," Rodrigo said.

Red took out her cell phone from her pocket. "It's worth a shot."

She dialed his number and waited. There was no response. "Nothing," she said.

"Well, let's follow that truck," Rodrigo said, and they quickly ran to Rodrigo's car.

Rodrigo was a far enough distance back not to be seen as it was easy to follow such a large truck. He turned on the radio, but Red quickly turned it off. Rodrigo tried to turn it on again, but Red shot him a look.

"You ever think that we were just being set up?" Rodrigo asked.

"What do you mean?"

"Like we were just used to slow down Malestar so that Mauricio can have him all for himself."

"Well, Vesco underestimated us since we are still breathing. Besides, I don't think he would do that."

"He said the same thing," Rodrigo said. "But I don't believe a word that comes out of that snake's mouth."

"That's strange. You should believe politicians."

Rodrigo smiled. "I guess politics are the same everywhere."

"I really don't pay attention to what's going on back home. I've been to a lot of places and it all seems the same. Corruption is everywhere. You can't escape it."

"So tell me about America," Rodrigo said.

"Nothing really to say. You have a country divided and a country together at the same time. You have the Easterners with their liberal ideas and fast-paced life, brash attitudes, but at the same time more accepting; you have the Southerners who are proud of who they are, that fill their tummies with pork and grits, and give you southern hospitality as long as you go to where you're supposed to be at the end of the day; the Northern and Midwesterners have three months of sunshine where they spend the day tipping cows, running through cornfields and going shopping, and hibernate the rest of the year; and then you have the West, full of sunshine, crime, alternative lifestyles, and such, with a group of people full of themselves and adopting every kid they can get their hands on. All of these people don't want anything to do with each other, but if you put a pigskin football in front of them, then all of a sudden they are best friends. That's America."

Rodrigo laughed. "Sounds like a fun place."

"Now, you tell me about Brazil."

"It's about poor and rich, and a small middle class. Poverty is high, and race is never brought up, even though it's an issue. Corruption is a part of life. A better life is made through connections more so than education. We have an eclectic mix of people with all shades and backgrounds that enjoy a simple life and one that is visually stimulating. Our sports stars are our celebrities, and we enjoy family and beautiful weather."

"I'm jealous already."

"Then why don't you move out here?" Rodrigo asked.

"It's going to be hard for me to stay anywhere for too long. I'm not the settle down type. Can you picture me with a house with a white picket fence, and kids running around, and I'm in the kitchen, barefoot and pregnant? I refuse to be that way."

"That just tells me you haven't found the right guy."

"I hate when people say stuff like that. That guy doesn't exist. You either take someone for their faults or you don't. Believe me, the man that wants to be with me has a lot to deal with."

"Starting with the fact you're a skilled assassin," Rodrigo said.

"That is just the start of it."

"I blame the media. They're always telling you that this should be your dream, and to think like this. Not everyone is going to have a partner, and not everyone is going to be guaranteed a life of happiness. You're just going to have to live the way you want to live."

"I think I'm doing that pretty well," Red replied.

The truck started to slow down as other cars passed in front of them on the highway. The truck slowly began to make its move to the side of the road. Rodrigo had to slow down as well.

"What is this about?" Red asked.

"I don't know, but it can't be good."

The truck was at a complete stop. Rodrigo thought about driving forward, but couldn't afford to lose track of where the truck was going. He slowed down and pulled over on the side of the road behind the truck. He cursed out loud for having to do so.

"Tell them we can help them if they need roadside assistance," Rodrigo said to Red.

'Why don't you?"

"You're a pretty lady. They will trust you."

"I don't think so," Red replied.

They waited. Moments later, the teenagers came out of the truck with their guns in their hands. They aimed their guns at Rodrigo's car.

Rodrigo quickly put the car in reverse as the bullets started flying. The car reversed quickly as bullets penetrated the hood of his car. Rodrigo backed his way to the highway where he was almost struck by an oncoming car coming from behind. The driver of the car honked the horn loudly, and Rodrigo spun the car into the next lane over. He had only a few seconds before he would get into a crash from a car coming toward him. Rodrigo sped up, and tried to cross the divide. By then, the truck had already taken off. There were two cars going down the road at a speed which made merging impossible for the time being. Rodrigo could see the truck going further along the road.

"We're going to lose them," Red said.

"I know, I know!"

Rodrigo cursed out loud and slammed his hand against the dashboard.

*

The car sped down the highway trying to catch up to the white truck ahead. The car had been stolen only two hours before, and had been tracking the truck ever since it came to the slums. Within a few minutes, the stolen car was at a safe distance to follow, and the driver slowed down so that he wouldn't be noticed. He had seen what the car ahead of him was doing, and he could only conclude that the driver was an amateur.

Still somewhat bruised, Mauricio kept his eyes on the truck ahead. His wrists were still throbbing in pain, but he learned a long time ago how to suppress the feeling. He was in a zone now, a place where any outside emotion besides the anger he was feeling was not accepted.

He was being more spontaneous than usual. Usually he was a man that thought in a logical process to figure out the best option. Now, he went with his gut feeling. He didn't know if it was the right or wrong decision, but he didn't care. It felt right, and that's all that mattered. He had been taught that making decisions with an angry mind was not wise, but that was a thought he had longed blocked out.

Mauricio looked through the rearview mirror and he could see that the car that had been following the truck had now caught up behind him. He assumed it was Rodrigo or Red driving. If it wasn't them, it could have been the drug dealers he spoke with earlier or vigilante police officers that decided not to take bribes. He thought he had recognized the car from before, but didn't care to go back into his memory bank to think about it.

The truck began to exit off the highway, taking an exit that led north. Mauricio slowed down even more so than usual to not be noticed. The car behind him did the same. The truck made its way down the streets of a neighborhood that looked barren from human activity. There were warehouses and worn buildings covered in graffiti and trash covering the ground. The truck made a turn, and Mauricio waited before turning the corner. He looked through the rearview mirror, and he saw that it was Rodrigo driving behind him. He wondered if Rodrigo had figured out that it was him. Rodrigo didn't seem anxious to turn either.

A moment later, Mauricio turned the car to see the truck pull in to an empty building. Mauricio pulled over to the side of the street, and Rodrigo did as well. Everyone got out of the vehicles and met on the sidewalk.

"Don't stay too close when you are trying to follow," Mauricio said.

"Hi, Rodrigo. How are you doing? Did you get hurt when the building exploded?" Rodrigo said.

"You have plenty of firepower?" Mauricio asked, completely ignoring Rodrigo's sarcasm.

"Yeah, we got enough," Red replied.

"Good. It's probably a warehouse full of them. Our odds aren't great, but we will do the best we can."

"You really think this is a great idea?" Rodrigo asked. "I mean, I think we should really think about what we are doing."

"Now you want to be rational?" Red asked. "This coming from the same man that stormed his way through the slums."

"I know my slums," Rodrigo replied. "What we are about to do is suicide, and we don't even know if he's in there."

"Does it matter?" Mauricio asked. "My gun is filled with bullets, and those bullets need a home to go to. Now, who am I not to give them a place to rest their head? You two in?"

Rodrigo sighed and looked around. The logical part of him told him that this was nothing but trouble. He looked over at Red. She would follow Mauricio to the depths of Hades and back. There was a point when he would do the same, but he also wanted to live. He was starting to realize that to be as good as Mauricio, one had to be somewhat suicidal and brave at the same time. The man was special, but it was something to appreciate, not imitate. Still, he wasn't going to hang him to dry in a warehouse full of Malestar's young army.

"I'm here already," Rodrigo finally said.

"Let's go then," Mauricio said.

"Wait," Red said. "Shouldn't we have a plan?"

Mauricio nodded. "The plan is simple. Get in, shoot everybody in there, and get out. Good enough for you?"

"Works for me," Red said.

"What kind of weapons you have on you?" Mauricio asked.

"The usual," Rodrigo replied. "They're in the trunk. I have handguns, rifles, scopes, and grenades."

"Give me a grenade and scope, and let's get to work," Mauricio said.

42.

The perimeter of the building was surrounded by a fence that they were very easily able to get through. Dirt covered the grounds nearby, with more trash, including needles and beer cans. Mauricio had guessed that this was the location of a late-decision meeting. They made their way around the front entrance of the building as not to be seen. They had to climb a hill to reach the side of the building, where they could see two parked trucks on the side. A few of Malestar's crew walked nearby the truck with guns carried by a shoulder holster. They looked around aimlessly, more concerned about pretending to do their job than actually doing it.

"I don't like the numbers for this one," Red said.

"I didn't ask for your opinion," Mauricio replied. Mauricio took out his sniper rifle with scope and silencer, and held it out in front of him. He looked through the scope at the area below. Mauricio put the crosshair on the two young men and the boy that was walking around. He hesitated for the child. He would only fire in his direction if the kid fired at him first.

Rodrigo squinted his eyes to look below. "Wait a second, I know that kid. That's Miguel."

"Who?" Mauricio asked.

"Just leave him to me."

"If you insist." Rodrigo ran down the hill. Mauricio shot two heads off, both in the cranium within seconds of each other, and left Miguel to live. The boy stood there in shock. Rodrigo sprinted to him and grabbed him. Miguel tried to fight him off, but Rodrigo was too strong.

Rodrigo ran back up the hill with Miguel in his arms. "Let me go!" he kept screaming.

"This won't take long," Rodrigo said, and carried Miguel back to the car.

It was there he placed him in the trunk and closed the top. "It's for your own good," he said, and ran back to Mauricio and Red.

"You know, there's an adoption process," Mauricio said.

"Funny," Rodrigo replied.

Mauricio and Red headed down the hill with Rodrigo following behind. Red had the grenades in her hand. Mauricio made a sweep of the area near the trucks and found that no one was nearby. He could hear shouting coming from within the building. There was a side door to enter which Mauricio presumed was used just minutes before. Mauricio turned to Red.

"Are those smoke or real grenades?"

"One of each. One of them is a red M18."

"Do you know which one is which?"

Red looked at the grenades in her hands. "I'm pretty sure the one in my right is the real deal."

"How sure are you?" Mauricio asked.

"Seventy-two percent."

Mauricio looked at her for a moment longer, and then opened the door. There was a group of young men raising their guns in the air at a speaker who had a microphone in front of him and was one floor higher than his listeners. To the side of them was the elevator and a set of stairs. Mauricio couldn't make out the words but he could tell from their expressions that they were ready to die for their cause. He shook his head as he realized that this was another group of young people that had been brainwashed. The same way he was when he believed in what people in power had told him.

Mauricio kept his gun pointed and raised a fist to tell the other mercenaries to stop. He then put out one finger and waved Red over to him. The group of young men was still shouting in unison with the speaker in front of them.

"Light them up," Mauricio said.

Red threw the grenade into the room. It turned out to be the smoke grenade. Red smoke filled the room, and the crowd began to cough and disperse. The mercenaries began to shoot what they could in the dark. Mauricio headed toward the stairs. Red and Rodrigo stood on the ground level as gunshots started to go off.

There was a young man downstairs that was shooting blindly in the smoke, hoping his bullets would land in the intruders. He ended up shooting three members of his own crew, as bullets ripped through their chests, arms, and legs.

Rodrigo and Red retreated behind cover. They fired back at their assailants, who looked for them in the smoke. Red did most of the accurate firing and increased the body count. Rodrigo kept moving, and shooting anyone in his way.

"We've walked into a war zone!" Rodrigo shouted as he took cover behind a steel machine.

"Give me cover!" Red shouted back as a round of bullets landed in front of her cover. Rodrigo shot in the direction of the shooting as Red joined him behind his cover.

"We can't stay here and hide forever," Rodrigo said.

"So what do you suggest?"

"We go out firing," Rodrigo said, and stood up to shoot some more.

Upstairs, Mauricio looked around for Malestar. He made his way down the hallway where a restroom was located in the right corner. Mauricio swung it open and a man was waiting there with a gun in hand. Mauricio quickly got out of the way as the gun fired. The man ran out of the room and Mauricio fired once into his throat. Blood came out like water from a garden hose and the man fell to the ground.

Mauricio continued down the hallway where there was a series of rooms in front of him. As Mauricio went forward, a young man came out one of the rooms. He reached for the gun on his hip but didn't have time to reach for it. Mauricio filled his chest with bullets. Mauricio went into the room where two young men were waiting for him, holding their guns sideways as they fired at him. Mauricio slid across the floor to avoid being shot. He then raised his gun and shot both men down.

Mauricio stood up and saw one of them was still breathing. Mauricio reached into his jacket for another clip and reloaded. He shot the young man once more in the chest and then he was quiet.

Mauricio went to the corner of the room where there was a map of the city, money, guns, and a two-way handheld transceiver on the table. The sound of gunshots could be heard from downstairs. Mauricio went to the map and studied it for a brief moment. There were red markings across the map and then a connecting line to all the spots. The building the Corporation had just bombed was marked with an X. The next one following the line was the Oceania, a thirteen-floor building in the Barra neighborhood. The transceiver on the table made a sound of static and then there was the sound of Malestar's voice.

"Ze, are you there?" Malestar asked in Portuguese.

Mauricio picked up the transceiver. "He's kind of dead at the moment. Is there something I can help you with?"

For a moment, there was silence. Then Malestar spoke. "I assume you know my next move."

"It's not going to happen this time."

"You do know you were only hired to throw me off my game? Vesco didn't truly think you were going to stop me."

"Well, he guessed wrong. Every move you make, I'm going to be there to haunt you. You want me out of the picture, you're going to have to man up and take me out."

"How dare you challenge me! When I'm through with you—"

"Hold on," Mauricio said. A man dressed in all purple rushed into the room and Mauricio quickly shot him down with a bullet to the forehead. "You were saying?"

"You want to kill me, then you come and get me."

"Name the place," Mauricio said.

"Itaparica Island, southern shore, tomorrow night. No friends this time, just me and you. I'll be waiting on the beach near the Carioca Bar."

"And what about your immediate plans?"

"My guess is that you took away my manpower for that," Malestar replied.

"No games or running away."

"Mauricio, I have to admit, I've been holding out on my dessert. I'm going to enjoy killing you."

There was static on the other end, and then there was silence. Mauricio stood there for a moment and listened. A few more gunshots went off downstairs and then there was none. Mauricio left the room and went back downstairs.

The room was filled with dead bodies and those barely moving. Blood covered the ground. Mauricio walked amongst the bodies and looked for his fellow mercenaries. He found Red in the corner of the room behind a storage crate. When he approached her, she raised her gun at him and then lowered her weapon when she realized who it was. She was holding her right arm with her left hand, and Mauricio could see the blood flow down from her wound.

"Just a scratch," Red said while grimacing.

"Looks like more than that."

"These kids didn't have the most accurate aim, but they were fearless. It was a bloodbath. You need to check on Rodrigo."

"You need a hospital."

"I already called Vesco to handle it. Now go."

Mauricio left Red and walked further in the room. There were the sounds of whimpers coming from some of the fallen. A young man that was doing so was heavily breathing in the middle of the room as Mauricio approached. Mauricio saw the multiple gunshot wounds to his chest and figured he didn't have much time.

"The city...it belongs to us," the young man softly said.

Mauricio kneeled down beside him and took the gun away from his hands. He took the clip out and realized there were no bullets left. The young man in front of him was coughing up blood.

"I did this for my family," he said.

The life slowly left his eyes and then he grew limp. Mauricio got back up and shook his head. The loss of young life was not needed in his vengeance plot to kill Malestar. He preyed on weak minds, and the young man that died was no exception. He knew there was more to come, and if it wasn't Malestar, then it would be the drug dealers in the slums. As long as there was poverty, there would be soldiers willing to die for a vision that only benefited those at the top.

Mauricio made his way around the room and then circled back toward the front entrance. That was when he saw Rodrigo lying on the floor. Mauricio rushed over to him.

He leaned Rodrigo up toward him and felt for a pulse. Rodrigo was still alive. "Rodrigo, stay with me."

Mauricio lightly slapped his face to draw Rodrigo back to consciousness. Rodrigo was not reacting. Mauricio took a look at his multiple wounds. There was a gunshot wound to his abdomen, one to his leg, and one in his shoulder. He was bleeding furiously. Mauricio figured that Rodrigo was in shock.

"Stay with me. You can't go out like this. You're better than this. Help is on the way."

He heard a shout in the room. The fact that someone else was alive besides Red and Rodrigo made Mauricio angry. He gently placed Rodrigo down and made his way to the source of the shout. There was a young man resting against the wall with a gunshot wound in his stomach. He was breathing hard as his chest moved up and down. He was lucky the gunshot was not fatal. Mauricio stood before him and lifted him up by his collar, and then shoved him against the wall.

"Please, give me help," he said.

"Mercy will not come to those that seek to destroy."

"You're no better than me."

"I am getting sick and tired of people like you trying to convince me that we are the same. You want to know why I'm not like you? I don't have my mind clouded on trying to fix a system by destroying everyone in the process. You want to fix a system? You demand to be a part of it. You don't fight it head on. That is a fight you will never win. This is not your war. You are following a madman, but you are too dumb to realize your life is worth more."

Mauricio let go, and the man dropped to the ground, starting to go into shock. Mauricio hurried back to Rodrigo. He checked his pulse once again and found that he was still breathing. He then heard a car speed down the street. He rushed outside to see a white compact car pull up to the curb. A man got out the driver's side and waved Mauricio over. Mauricio went back inside and carried Rodrigo out the door and placed him in the backseat with the help of the driver. Then he went back in for Red.

By the time he did so, he could hear sirens coming closer to the building. Mauricio helped Red up from the ground, and she kept her arm around his neck as they left the building. Mauricio helped her into the backseat, and then he got into the passenger side. The driver, whom

Mauricio suspected was a recruit from the police academy, quickly drove away from the curb.

Mauricio looked at the young man and couldn't help but to think how different he was from the young men that were dead inside, and yet, he was so similar. Like them, he didn't understand how the real world worked. He thought he was going to make a difference once he was out there on the streets. Mauricio guessed him for a middle-class kid that saw the drug problem and poverty, and thought that he would keep the streets clean to make it a better place for all of the hard-working citizens. It was a noble cause. Mauricio wondered how long it would take for the young man driving next to him to become like the rest and for corruption to be acceptable. Maybe he would be different, and maybe he would succeed in being an officer of the law. The odds were against him, but just like everyone else, he had a chance to make his own future.

Mauricio turned his head to look back at the other mercenaries. They were badly injured but they were fortunate to get out of the building alive. Only time would tell if they would survive to see another day. He looked past them and through the window and saw the police cars pull up to the curb of the building they left behind. Mauricio could only see the situation as the wolves coming back to see their dead.

43.

The waiting room was a place Mauricio didn't want to be. The space was small, and he sat across from Red in the uncomfortable chairs the hospital had provided. There was silence in the room as they waited. Hospital staff occasionally walked by. There was a stack of magazines that Mauricio couldn't read. They looked like they were full of gossip anyway. Red already had her wound seen by a doctor, and bandaged up with the bullet taken out. They gave her something for the pain and her eyes were barely half open. Mauricio assumed she was in la-la land.

He didn't want to think of the possibility of Rodrigo not returning, but loss of life had always been continuous to him. His parents in Africa and Claudia hit home the most, but there was also loss in his brief stint in the

Middle East. The targets he took out were blocked out a long time ago.

Perhaps it was time to see a therapist. He needed someone to sort his thoughts out. Then again, he wasn't going to spend money just to have someone listen to him. The person in front of him would do just fine.

"How you feeling?" he asked Red.

Red didn't respond. She instead rested her head to the side and smiled. She was really enjoying her medication.

"I guess you will have to do since I have to tell somebody," Mauricio said. "I don't know where to start. All of my life, I've just been blocking all of these thoughts or burying the feelings I had deep down inside. It's just hard for me to talk about, you know?"

"Aren't the bluebirds so beautiful?" Red asked, and raised her hand out in front of her.

"Ever since the fire in Africa, I've been a different person. Or maybe it was before that. I had lost my ability to connect to another human being. Do you know how that feels? You start to feel like a robot, just a machine made to only have one purpose, whatever that purpose may be. There was no right, no wrong, just that I had a job to do and I knew I was good at it. The moment I felt like I was doing something wrong, I would quickly block the thought. There was a part of me just itching to get out, but I couldn't allow it. I had to be this tough guy, not feel anything, not allow myself to be human again. But Claudia changed me. She made me feel alive again. Now that she has been taken away from me, I'm resorting back to my old form. But that's not who I want to be. I want to feel what everyone else does. I'm going to see this mission on out for Claudia, but I want to able to just...be."

"It's so beautiful," Red said, and closed her eyes.

Mauricio grinned. And to think people paid money for this.

The doctor came down the hallway and stood before Mauricio. "You can see him now. He's stable," he said in Portuguese.

"I don't know a word you are saying," Mauricio said, standing up.

The doctor walked down the hall, and Mauricio followed him. The doctor led the way to Rodrigo's room, and walked off. Mauricio opened the door and walked into the room. Rodrigo was lying in bed with his eyes closed. His heart rate was a steady pace from what Mauricio could tell on the screen. Mauricio was filled with guilt and anger when he saw him. At first, he couldn't stand to look at him, but then he figured he had to face his guilt. He turned to face him.

"You shouldn't be here, kid," Mauricio said. "It should be me there instead of you. I know I told you a lot of things about what it takes to be a good mercenary, but

I want you to forget all of that. I want you to be a better man than me. When you wake up, I'm going to advise you to walk away from all of this, and in fact, I won't give you a choice. This is not for you. This isn't for anybody."

Mauricio looked at him and wondered if he should try contacting Rodrigo's mother. He wondered if someone here had already done so. He would want to know if this was his son. Seeing him like this was further proof that Mauricio would not be a good father in the career he was in. He had made the right decision when holding back having a family with Claudia. He couldn't imagine a child having a single father who was never home and was out killing people for cash.

There was knocking on the door. Mauricio looked through the window of the door and saw Vesco standing there. Mauricio headed out of the room as Vesco took a few steps away from the door and leaned against the wall in the hallway.

"You were close, but close doesn't get you paid."

"Did you really come here to ridicule me? Because I'm starting to think I want to add you to that list I need to kill."

"Relax," Vesco said. "We're making a move on the Corporation and I'm wondering if you want in on it."

"Who is we?"

"A group of young police officers willing to get their feet wet. We're going in tonight. I got a good lead of where they are holding their next meeting and I'll text you the address. I thought you would be interested in taking down some corruption."

"You thought wrong," Mauricio said and turned to walk away.

"You're still a killer," Vesco said, making Mauricio turn around. "It's what you are. You can't escape it no matter how hard you try. You have a gift. Don't walk away from something so special."

Mauricio rushed over to Vesco. "Let me tell you something that will penetrate through that thick skull of yours. The arrangement between you and me is over. I saved your life and this is what it gets me. What's between me and Malestar has nothing to do with you. Do you want to know why the city is the way it is? It's because of people like you who are behind the scenes. You don't want to make a difference. You just want to look like you are."

"I'll double your pay."

"Your money is no good to me," Mauricio replied.

"Then help me because it's the right thing to do."

"It's time to help myself." Mauricio walked away.

"You'll be there," Vesco said as he walked away.

*

It was intermission time at the opera house. The opera that was playing was a tale of deceit and fatal attraction. A woman was desperate to get the man of her dreams. The man was married and was a devoted husband. He was also her boss. The woman went to the man's home while he was at work, and killed his wife. She then buried her body in the backyard. After, she wrote a typed letter on behalf of the wife that she was going to leave for good.

The man was distraught. He couldn't work or leave the house. Of course, she was there to comfort him. Slowly he began to have feelings her. They would marry, and have children of their own. And then she would tell him the truth. That was when the real drama would begin and in the end, he ends up killing her. It was a modern twist on opera, full of dominating stage performances and well-rehearsed stage placement. The opera was intended to bring in a younger audience and those not familiar with classic opera. Malestar was here because it was the only opera available during the little free time that he had.

He had never thought about why he was intrigued by opera. Perhaps it was the melodramatic scenes and the common themes of revenge, murder, and lust. The characters always did something they deeply wanted, and thought about consequences later. These were the people that really lived. And what was life but a song and dance as well? There was much theatrical work being put in each human's eyes, but in reality, the joke was on those that didn't do what their heart desired.

He knew every play need a hero and a villain. The only thing he didn't like about some of these plays was their sense of a moral compass. Morals were only meant to benefit a group of people, and hurt the minority who thought otherwise. He decided he was going to write his own play, one where the villain was going to win. Of course, he needed a tough nemesis, one that was good enough to stop him against his goal. He had chosen one, a fierce competitor that would see it out to the end. It was a good show they were putting on for the people of Salvador, and Malestar felt this was his own intermission before the final act.

As he watched down below from his balcony seat, a beautiful young woman in a pink blouse sat next to Malestar. She ran her fingers through her hair, and looked down below with him. She smelled of rose petals and Malestar figured she wasn't much older than twenty-two. Malestar's mind started racing. He could seduce her, drug her, and use her as one of his pets. She would do what he said if she wanted to live. He loved taking beauty and making it raw and hungry to live. Their perceived strength would be their weakness. When he was done with her, he would toss her back into the wild, and she would be no good for anyone, used and scarred from what he had done to her. That would be the moment he realized he had done his job. Until then, he would have to gauge his chances of reeling her in.

A part of him wanted to prepare for tomorrow night, but that was all business and no fun. What was life if you couldn't indulge in the pleasantries of it all? He didn't want to put any pressure on himself. Right now was all that mattered and the young woman that he would make his own.

"Lovely play so far," Malestar said. "You've missed a lot."

"I was watching," the young woman said. "I just hoped I could get a better view."

"You've come to the right place," Malestar said with a grin. "I'm a man that knows how to live life and my company alone should improve yours."

"I know who you are," the young woman replied.

"You do?"

"My name is Bernadette," she said, and turned to look at him. "I can relate to you because like yourself, I came from the slums and made something of myself. I know struggle, pain, and all the things a hard life comes with. But unlike you, I chose to live in a way that benefits everyone."

Malestar leaned forward. "I'm intrigued. What brings you up here if you don't agree with the way I live my life?"

"A boy."

"Can you be more specific?"

"His name is Miguel. He is my cousin. His mother was very worried about what would happen to him, and she even had someone come talk to him to try to get him away from your influence. But you have a strong grip. You know the power you have over the youth. He was at a shootout earlier today when some mercenaries were looking for you."

"Let me guess, you're upset he's no longer alive."

"He's still alive," Bernadette said.

"Well, there you go. All is well," Malestar said, leaning back.

"Do you ever feel guilty?"

"Guilty? Guilt is a disease brought on by mankind. The feeling will only hold you back. I can teach you how to grow if you so wish. I can open you up to a new world with no limits. It's society and the people in your neighborhood that are holding you back. What you need is someone to lead you the right way. I can be that man for you."

"I figured you would say something like that. I'm not here to join your cause. I'm here to fight against it."

"And what exactly do you plan to do? Lecture me on morality until I come to my senses? You are out of your league. Go back downstairs with the other sheep and enjoy the play."

Bernadette took a knife from the pocket in her blouse and made a move toward Malestar. He had seen it coming. He grabbed her wrist before she had the chance to plunge the knife into his chest. He took the blade away from her hand and placed it in his own pocket. Then he grabbed her by both of her wrists and pulled her in close.

"You see, you could have been on your way to your pathetic life and I would have never thought about you again. But instead, you've chosen the path you are about to receive. You will belong to me now, and you will do what I say from here on out. Life will not be easy for you. Of course, you will be so high most of the time that you will forget how it feels to be happy or depressed. You will suffer greatly by my hands. Then one day, I'm going to take the drugs out of your system, cook you the finest meal, and you will be free to leave. But you won't be thrilled about it. No, it would be too late for that. By then, I will own you where it matters, and that's up here," Malestar said, pointing to his mind. "Then you'll realize you are a slave to me as much as you are to the system that generated your fears and morale."

"Let me go!"

"Not just yet, my pretty lady."

The opera was starting up again and the actors returned to the stage. Bernadette tried without success to loosen her grip from Malestar. Malestar carried her toward the back of the balcony while those seated around him pretended not to look. They knew who the man was and what he could do. One of them had thought about calling the police but they knew that it would be a joke to do so. He owned the police from what they could tell. It was best just to pretend everything was normal, even after they heard the woman scream for her life as she got dragged away.

44.

The night was cool as the ocean waves came roaring in. There was a nice view outside the new hotel that Mauricio and Red were staying at in the Barra neighborhood of the city. Mauricio stood in the sand and tried to subdue the anger that was inside of him. The world had felt like such a lonely place lately. He felt like a failure and that he couldn't protect the people that were close to him. He was losing his edge, and his ability to stay on top of his game. His life was falling apart, and the numbness he had for so long was crumbling away.

It was only fitting he had his back turned against the skyscrapers of the city. He was an outcast from society, a drifter with no real place to call home. He was a man that was afraid he was merely a killing machine, but also afraid to be anything more than that. Some would even say he was doing the world a favor. But did they even care that he existed? He knew the answer was no, and the selfishness of mankind would never fully appreciate him.

He wasn't asking for a celebration in his honor, or any type of medal. He just wanted their approval in some sort of way so that his life would have some meaning. There had to be more to life than just doing a job. Unfortunately, that's all he knew.

Mauricio dug his feet into the sand and lowered his head. The sadness he had long resisted to take over him was slowly overtaking him. This time he embraced the feeling. All of the painful incidents of the past came back, along with suicidal thoughts. A part of his mind wanted him to go out with a bang, and shoot everything that was considered an enemy until his inevitable end. But the more rational side told him to wait until tomorrow night to have his revenge, and then sail away in the beautiful waters that were before him.

A text message from Vesco came in on his phone. Mauricio took his phone out of his pocket to read the message. It was the address to the raid they were going to do tonight with a time as well. He was conflicted about what to do. He had told Vesco he didn't want to help at all, but this new sadness wanted to keep fighting and see to it that he would face a death that he deserved. He had killed so many people that he deserved the opportunity to be killed any chance he got. Wasn't that how nature worked? He was an oddity just to be standing right now. He needed to balance the scales of good and evil. He didn't know exactly what he would consider himself but maybe that was the problem with him. He had to choose a cause. Or did he? Life had to be about the relationships you made and how you lived your life. Everything else could very well be just a distraction.

He heard someone behind him and turned around to see Red walking toward him with her arm in a sling and cast. Even though injured, Red was still seductive. She wore a V-neck tee and jean shorts and had a beer bottle in her free hand. She stood next to Mauricio and handed over the beer.

"Thought you might need this," she said.

"Looks like you need it more than I do."

"You should learn to take presents," Red replied.

"Is that right?" Mauricio said, taking a sip.

"Take your life, for instance. The fact you're still alive is a gift. You should use it wisely. You have a skill that most people don't have, and you can make a difference."

Mauricio grinned. "It sure doesn't feel that way."

"Sounds like you want to quit."

"It does, doesn't it?"

"Well, that's not going to be me. As soon as I get healed, I'm going to go back to what I do best. I don't know any other way to live."

"I have to give it to you, Red," Mauricio said. "You're fearless."

"I have to be. I can't afford to look back." Red stared at the ocean for a bit and then returned her gaze to Mauricio, who had another sip of beer.

"There's people out there, mostly men with a long line of money, that think they can get whatever they want their hands on, and could care less how it destroys everyone else involved. I've seen it countless times in my own country, and I've seen it here. They see life as a buffet, and we're just supposed to be placed on their plate. It's like we don't have a choice. They are only a small group, but they make decisions that affect us all. Do you think that's fair? They have power because we gave them power, whether it's some ridiculous claim to a royal bloodline, or money stolen legally through business transactions. The hardworking people suffer. I refuse to be used like everyone else. I want them to fear me as much as we fear them. I want them to be looking over their shoulder, wondering if I'm coming for them. I will never stop because my job will never be fulfilled. It takes a somewhat suicidal person to do what we do and knowing the risks involved. That's why Rodrigo should give this up. He's not cut out for this."

"It's a numbers game, Red. In the end, they will always win. You may be able to make a dent, but they have the power, money, and influence. If you want to have a successful run in this business, you're going to have to pick your battles. You have to know when to fight, and when to run. You can't make it personal. That's how you get yourself killed."

"And what exactly are you doing?" Red asked.

Mauricio grinned, took another sip of beer, and looked off into the ocean. "I'm trying not to think things out too much. I'm trying to...I don't know."

"Be like the rest of us?"

"Something like that."

"You know that's not the smartest idea you've had."

"I know," Mauricio replied. "But sometimes you have to just make decisions just because it feels right. Whatever emotion I'm having at the moment, I'm going to follow through on it."

"Wait a second, you're not a robot?"

Mauricio laughed. "I'm afraid not. I think I may have been short circuited sometime in the last few weeks."

"But you can't deny the reason you do this. Deep down inside you enjoy the hunt and the killing, just like me. Why shy away from it or pretend you are better than that? It's who we are. But every now and then, we are going to step away and appreciate life. Malestar is right about one thing; we should enjoy moments in life where we can do what we want. I think I'm going to do that now."

Red took off the sling from her shoulder and ran toward the rushing waves. The water slapped against her body, and she shouted in joy and surprise. She turned around to face Mauricio, who flashed a smile.

"Do what feels right!" she shouted.

Mauricio watched Red play in the water, splashing her freckled face and walking into the ocean until the water was waist high. The water against her body had accentuated her curves and for a brief moment, Mauricio felt an urge to pursue her. But he remembered Claudia, and the type of woman Red could be. No wonder she was so good at her job. He had to think of a different urge he wanted to fulfill.

There was an itch he wanted to scratch. That involved getting back at the members of the new Corporation, the people that were intent on destroying the fabric of the city. To Mauricio, these were the worst kind of humans— scumbags that pretended to want to help, and all they did was profit from the suffering and hard work of the lower class. Like Malestar, they had no compassion for their fellow humans. They needed to be stopped. He knew another crop would return, but if he did his job well, that wouldn't happen for years.

Mauricio looked at Red once more. As much as he disliked her use of physical appearance and her skill of manipulation, he had to admire the woman. She came from a harsh upbringing and dealt with it in the only way she knew how. He didn't agree with it, but who was he to tell people how to live? Red was going to be Red, not for him, but maybe there was someone out there willing to participate in her game.

"Do me a favor!" Mauricio shouted at Red.

"What's that?" Red asked back.

"Don't change," Mauricio said, and walked away.

*

There was much chatter in the room and talk of how the Corporation should move forward with the death of Jorge. There was a plethora of ideas of how to proceed, ranging from Malestar making a strike against the police department to going to other cities down south to strike against the competitors in the region. Tonight after dinner, the members would fill out their choice for a new leader on ballot cards, and the voting would be done anonymously with no names of voters. The count would be collected and the winner would be announced. Then they would have a sense of what kind of direction the new Corporation was going.

The gathering had taken place in the conference hall of a skyscraper downtown on one of the top floors. All of the members were dressed in suits as they walked around with silver plates in their hands. They had picked up their dishes from the two naked women lying down in the center of the hall, covered in sushi and other type of seafood. There were other tables of food nearby, mainly of barbecue pork that was finely cut up in small portions, then another table of utensils, plates, and napkins, and another table of alcoholic tropical drinks. There were no servers in the room as the new Corporation did not like anyone not involved with the organization to have the chance to listen in on their conversations. This time around they were going to be focused, determined, and reticent.

Outside the building, police officers exited an unmarked van and made their way toward the building. There were a few other cars parked out front, and Vesco got out of one of them. The police officers paused at the front entrance, waiting for his go signal. Another group of officers went to the opposite side of the front entrance and stood behind Vesco with their guns pointed. Vesco placed his hands on his hips and looked up. He knew there couldn't be failure for this mission. There was plenty of favorable press to be placed his way if he did this correctly.

"Secure the street," Vesco said, and the officers behind Vesco began to place police tape and signs around the perimeter. They checked the cars parked along the street and found one man calmly sitting in his car. They shouted for him to get out. The man reluctantly did, and they searched him for weapons as they patted him down against his car.

"We have a citizen," one of the police officers shouted.

"Bring him to me," Vesco said with his back turned. He looked at the building once more and realized that this was his signature moment. This would be the attack that would give the key to the city back to him, and the people would be confident in his abilities. He could imagine the many articles that would be written about him and the praise he would get from other government agencies. He would then fire the corrupt police captain and run this city with all the adoration from its citizens.

"Do you have a warrant for this?" the man behind Vesco asked.

Vesco turned around to see Mauricio standing in front of him. "Had a change of mind?"

"Not for you, but for the people of the city."

"Very well," Vesco said, turning back around. "My sources tell me they're on one of the top floors. We're going to sweep every floor until we get to them, if necessary. There's a security guard at the front desk that's loyal to their cause, but he shouldn't be a problem. Everyone else should be gone. The cleaning crew has already left."

"Then what are we waiting for?" Mauricio asked. "Get me a gun."

Vesco turned back around, and nodded to the officer next to Mauricio. The officer handed Mauricio his gun. "I knew you would come here. This killing business is in your blood. Plus, I think you want to make this a safer city for all parties involved."

"A safer city would be to take yourself out of the equation. I would be lying if I said it hadn't crossed my mind to take you out."

"Then why go to the trouble of saving my life?"

"Strangely enough, in some ways I think the city needs you. You are the face of what's good here, as misconstrued as that is. You have an obligation to give the people confidence, and to take back the streets that belong to them. The people need you alive."

Vesco nodded. "My men will be going in first. I want you to be their shadow."

"I'm willing to bat clean-up," Mauricio said.

"I need someone to make sure the job is done."

"It must be nice to stay down here with a bunch of police officers to protect you."

"I never get my hands dirty," Vesco replied.

"You just profit when other people do," Mauricio stated, and made his way to the other officers standing near the front entrance. They curiously looked at him as he gave a wink. Then he turned to face Vesco.

"Give us the go," he said.

Vesco gave a sigh. Mauricio was right, he did profit from all of this. But guilt was for suckers. He needed to make a name for himself and this was the only way he thought would work in the short term. He thought of his wife and his daughter, and the vow he made to protect them. He had meant what he said. Vesco couldn't afford to let Malestar and the Corporation destroy his city from the inside and corrupt the minds of the youth. This was his city, and he was taking it back for good.

"Do it!" Vesco shouted, and the police officers rushed inside the building with Mauricio right behind them.

45.

The security guard didn't even have time to reach for his weapon. He looked up from his magazine to see an assemblage of guns pointed toward his face. He froze in fear. This definitely wasn't worth the minimum wage they were paying him. One of the officers made their way around him and tied him up against the chair and placed duct tape around his mouth. Then the officer leaned in front of him.

"What floor are they on? Show me with your hands."

The guard showed ten fingers twice, and then showed two. Some of the officers headed toward the elevators. Others headed toward the stairs. Mauricio went with the group that went to the elevators.

Back inside the conference hall, the members of the Corporation stood and everyone faced toward the center of the room. A projector screen was placed in front where footage of the bombing of the residential building was shown. Retro music played in the background of the footage. There was a round of applause in the room. Then the movie showed the next project, another building that was owned by a competing company. A chorus of boos came from the members. The screen showed a demonstration of what the explosion what look like if completed. The chorus of applause returned.

But not for long. The police officers stormed into the room with their guns pointed. The members of the Corporation froze. Many placed their hands in the air. Mauricio watched from behind the officers. One of the officers began to shout demands.

"Turn the movie off and shut up!" he shouted.

The movie was stopped and the room grew silent. The officer took out a cell phone from his pocket, dialed a number, and placed the current call on speakerphone. He held the cell phone up for all to hear.

"Hello, ladies and gentlemen, this is your mayor," Vesco said from the other end. "Let me be the first to say that I was once a part of your family, a family that sought to destroy the city and become rich in the process. We all acted like spoiled children. Many of you were not around when we first started, but our intent was not to take lives of the ordinary citizens, but to take out criminals and other shady business people. Somewhere along the way that had changed, and now with you new members, anyone is a target. This cannot be. Now you will suffer the consequences. I'm sure many are wondering why I would admit to being a part of your group and will use this as testimony when you are court. But you see, you will never see a courtroom. You will pay for your crimes in the way you deserve. You will be put down like rabid dogs. I wish you well in your journey in the afterlife."

The members of the Corporation realized what was going on. This was an execution. Panic started to set in and some began to make a run for it. Even Mauricio was surprised by the news. The police officers began to fire and the members began to scatter.

Mauricio did not participate in the shooting. He watched as men and women ran for cover only to be filled with bullets. As he watched, everything seemed to be moving in slow motion. He watched as a woman got bullets to the chest and arms and then collapsed to the ground. Then he saw a man running toward an office door only to be met with bullets to the back, and then one to the back of his head. He fell as well. There was blood everywhere. Mauricio looked at the officers, and in their eyes he could tell that they were enjoying themselves. When the room was cleared of life, they moved in on the few that had escaped into the office room. For a brief moment, the massacre had stopped.

Mauricio ran in front of the officers heading to the office. "Wait!"

The officers stopped in their march and looked at him. "You don't want to do this. Take it from me, because I know what all of this killing does to you mentally. These people deserve a trial just like anyone else. You're not assassins, you're police officers. You're supposed to uphold the law."

The officers looked at each other, and Mauricio realized what he said was pointless. They didn't understand him anyway. Mauricio turned around and looked through the glass windows of the large office room. The people inside were terrified. One stood near the door like they had a fighting chance of stopping them from coming in. He saw the fear in their faces and tried to remind himself that these people deserved their fate for what they had done and they were planning to do. All of this time, individual targets didn't seem so bad, but as a whole, this didn't seem right. Then he thought about what he did in totality. It wasn't any different.

Mauricio moved out of the way. There was no way he was going to stop them. The police officers knocked down the door and he could hear the pleas and cries for mercy. There was none. The police officers stood in the room and began shooting at anyone in a suit. Mauricio stood outside the room and shook his head. He then made his way to the door where the second set of officers stood inside the conference hall. Mauricio walked past them and headed toward the elevator.

As he pressed the elevator button he thought he heard movement behind him. He looked down the hallway and caught a glimpse of a woman's face that glanced around the corner. Mauricio ran down the hallway and found the woman running to the restroom. Mauricio followed her inside.

She retreated to the last stall next to the wall. Mauricio kicked down the door. She retreated to the corner in fear and placed her hands out in front of her. "Please, don't kill me," she said in Portuguese. "I'm sorry. I'm sorry."

Mauricio placed his gun to her head. She couldn't bear to look and closed her eyes. Mauricio hesitated before pulling the trigger. This was what he came to do, right? This time there was no money involved, but a target was a target. He thought of his first target and how he had let the woman go that was involved. There was a part of him that always had morality, as little as it might be.

He removed the gun from her head. "You're going to testify against them."

Mauricio picked her up by her arm and took her out of the restroom. As he made his way to the hallway, there was a group of police officers standing there. They immediately pointed their guns at Mauricio and the woman, who both stopped. Then Mauricio and the woman started walking again. The police officers kept their guns pointed as Mauricio led her past them and toward the elevators. He pressed the button and calmly waited. The officers placed their guns down and headed back into the conference hall. The elevator doors opened, and Mauricio and the woman went inside. The doors closed as Mauricio stood behind her.

"Who are you?" the woman asked in English.

"It doesn't matter."

Mauricio led the way back outside where Vesco and other officers were waiting. Mauricio walked over to Vesco. He seemed surprised that there was a Corporation member still standing.

"Why is she alive?" Vesco asked.

"You didn't tell me you were planning a massacre," Mauricio replied.

"You think I'm just going to let them walk? The court system is a joke right now. I'm making sure they get what they deserve."

"Well, now you got a star witness to testify against all of their actions and all the people involved. You need a face for the crimes for authenticity reasons."

Vesco nodded. "You have a point there." Vesco turned to face the police officer next to him. "Put her in a police car and play nice," he said in Portuguese.

Vesco turned his head back to Mauricio. "How many did you kill?"

"None."

"That seems rather disappointing," Vesco replied. "You know, if you change your mind about the woman, I will look the other way if you want to kill her. She deserves the same fate as her peers."

"No, thank you, and you better not lay a hand on her. If I hear something happened to her, I'm coming after you."

"Will you take it easy? You have my word that she will be fine. You need to learn how to relax sometimes. I thought you wanted to have some fun. This trip must have been useless to you."

"No, I've learned something about myself tonight."

"What's that?"

"That I'm better than you."

Mauricio walked down the street, past the police barricades, and into the darkness of the night.

*

Everything around her was a blur. Her body felt like she was floating and glimpses of light seemed to come and go. She could feel sunshine against her face. She was sweating. Her eyes adjusted to the mixture of darkness and light and she realized she was in a trunk. The car was not moving. She panicked and could feel shortness of breath. She started to beat against the top of the trunk and screamed for someone to help her. But in the end, she knew it was hopeless. Bernadette began to cry, and started to think about her family and her cousin Miguel. She had failed him when she only wanted to help him.

The memory of being at the opera house and trying to convince Malestar to think otherwise came to her mind. Bernadette cursed out loud for having such an imprudent plan and thought about how unfair life had been to many of the people she had grown up with. As lucky as she was to move away, her bad luck ended up placing her in a situation like this. There was no running away from someone's bad fortune. The older generation had told her so but she had refused to believe it. Now she was starting to think they were right.

Then she realized she had so much to live for. She had a bright future and deserved a better fate. She had worked too hard to go out like this. A feeling of anger built up inside of her. She repetitively slammed her hand against the top of the trunk.

"Let me out! You let me out of here, you coward! Show me your face!"

There was silence. Then the trunk popped open. Bernadette looked up to see Malestar staring down at her in the early-morning sky. The man looked more sinister than ever before, and he seemed amused by her predicament. As he dragged her out of the trunk Bernadette tried to resist, but it was useless. She looked around to see that she was in the middle of nowhere, on an isolated road with no sign of civilization around her.

Malestar shoved her to the ground. He then took out a knife from his pocket. Bernadette began to crawl away from him but she didn't get too far.

"Do you know where you are? You're in a place where I've killed many of my victims. You should consider this an honor. Now have some dignity and give yourself to me."

"I thought you were going to make me your slave," Bernadette said.

"I've changed my mind with your attitude."

"Please, I can still be of good use to you. I can please you. I can do whatever you want."

"Yes, beg for your life," Malestar said as he stood above her.

"Please, spare my life. I can be of good use to you."

"And how's that?"

"I work as an assistant for the city council. I can put you in contact with all the important people that make decisions about Salvador. You can do what you want with them."

Malestar thought about the proposal for a moment. "I want names, addresses, and the businesspeople they talk to."

"You got it, just please let me go."

"Afraid I can't do that. But I will keep you alive."

Malestar picked her up and carried her back to the car. He then shoved her against the door. He held her wrists and pinned her down.

"I'm going to do you a favor. I'm going to make you experience pain, real pain. You're going to wish you've chosen death. If I feel that you've learn your lesson then I will let you live."

"You got it all wrong," Bernadette said.

"Is that right?"

"You want everyone to be like you. Is that it? You want everyone to be just as messed up as you are? Why do you think you're the only one that knows the right way to live? The truth is in numbers. You're the one that needs help, to be shown the right way to live. You're crazy. Why can't you see that?"

Malestar grinned. "I had a doctor once that sounded like you."

"You should have listened to him."

"That's what he said before I killed him. You will learn the right way to see the world. I will teach you to your dying breath. Now it's time to get back into the trunk."

"Where are we going?"

"To your new home," Malestar said, and took a grip of Bernadette's arm and headed toward the trunk.

As Malestar drove off, he couldn't help but to think about what Bernadette had said. Maybe he had convinced himself all these years that everyone else was wrong in how they thought, and he was one of the few people that knew the right way to live. No, it couldn't be possible. He was letting the woman get to his head. He slammed the top of his forehead multiple times with the palm of his hand. He didn't want to hear her voice again.

Bernadette reminded him of all the doctors that he had when he spent time in juvenile centers. He would try to tell them the way he felt and the reasons he did his actions. They wouldn't listen to him. They would just repeat their tales of morality and how society was better off with rules and everyone working together. He couldn't bear to hear these lies again. Malestar slammed the brakes and got out of the car.

He went back to the trunk and pulled Bernadette out. "What are you doing?" she asked.

"Deal's off," he said, and stabbed her in the stomach. The shock showed on Bernadette's face and the pain was so intense that she couldn't scream. Malestar then placed her back inside the trunk. He wiped his knife off with the inside of his shirt and got inside the driver's side of the car.

46.

Mauricio, with a wooden box and ice cooler in one hand, paid the large, bald man on the docks and went to the speedboat he had purchased. She was a good-looking boat and fairly new. It was painted cobalt blue and pearl white and was one of the fastest boats in the city. Mauricio undocked, put his items away, and started the engine. He put on his sunglasses and with the early-morning humidity, he had figured today was going to be a scorcher. The boat sped off into the ocean and the cool breeze made his tan shirt dangle in the wind. When he thought he was a good enough distance from the mainland, he cut the engine and stood on the edge of the boat.

He watched the slowly moving waters for a moment, and then picked up the box he had placed nearby. It was an oak box that Mauricio had had in his possession for quite some time. Mauricio opened the box and spread the ashes into the ocean. The ashes were from Mauricio's first kill and he had always kept it with him when he traveled. He had kept it in a storage facility and early this morning he felt it was the perfect time to take it out. Mauricio watched the ashes disperse in the ocean and stood with his hands in his pockets. If he could somehow bottle this moment and keep it forever, he would. This was the beginning of a new phase, one where he would embrace his inherited morality from his parents.

A plane came over the horizon with landing gear used for water-based landings, and suddenly it was in Mauricio's view. Mauricio watched the plane descend toward him and glide through the water until the plane was parallel to his boat. The engine was cut off and the hatch to the pilot door opened. Two people came out of the plane with gun holsters around their shoulders. Mauricio put the box away and waited for the two men to dock his boat.

"How could I refuse a free trip to Brazil?" Armas asked as he got out with a black bag in hand, and with his partner Solis, boarded Mauricio's boat.

"At first, I wasn't going to come but Armas brags about his military days and how he was the best pilot they ever had."

"Who needs you?" Mauricio asked. "I wanted help that could actually kill something."

"Then you only need me," Solis said. "You got something to drink?"

"Check the ice cooler on the other side," Mauricio said.

Solis went over to get a drink. Armas took a seat on the side of the boat and placed his black bag next to him. Mauricio looked at the bag.

"Anxious for your toys already?" Armas asked, noticing his glance. "I went through a lot of trouble to get them."

"I'm grateful," Mauricio said, turning his gaze back to Armas. "I have all the tools I need to kill the monster."

"I've dealt with worse," Armas said as Solis came over with a beer in hand.

"I don't think that's possible."

"You don't think we have criminals in Spain? I remember when I first joined the police force there was this man who many admired in his profession. He was a surgeon, but he lost his medical license. They called him Hombre de Cinta, meaning the Ribbon Man, as he always tied up the intestines of his victims in a neat ribbon. We first found the victims as prostitutes working the streets and left in alleyways. Then they graduated to working professionals. The entire city was afraid, including many in the force. Then I had the opportunity to meet him for the first time."

"What happened then?" Mauricio asked.

"We got a lead and I was the first one to act. I made the mistake of going without backup. The killer was holed up in an underground sewer system, and he was hiding there for days. I got inside, and the stench was almost unbearable. I covered my mouth, kept my gun pointed, and moved forward. Immediately, I realized that this sewer had been transformed to his liking. He had maps on the walls, pictures of his victims, and doors that shouldn't have been there. I should have backed out then, but my curiosity was getting the best of me."

"It still does," Solis said.

"I went further in and looked for him. I could hear movement up ahead. I started to move quicker. There was a door to the side of me. I found it unlocked. I opened it up and there he was, with a head in his hand that had been freshly cut off the body. The man was smiling and the blood was still dripping from the head. The very sight disgusted me so much that I couldn't gather myself, and I started to vomit. He laughed and laughed. He ran away. By the time I was done, he was long gone."

Armas continued. "It would be months before we would find him again. He was a very crafty man and a part of me wondered if he wanted to be found. He considered himself an artist and wanted his work to be acknowledged. By the time we captured him, he gave intimate details of every crime he ever committed. He bragged about them, and would only tell of them one by one, and he relived the moments of the kill. Now that was a sick man. He was motivated by his sickness, and what he did was more than a hobby. It turned him on."

"Disgusting," Solis said.

"I would put Malestar up there with him," Mauricio said.

"Do you know what his motivation is?" Armas asked.

"At this point, I don't think it matters."

"In my opinion, he wants power and control. He wants to be recognized as the genius he thinks he is. Most humans have compassion for one another. He's missing that part in his makeup. Now some people would say that he needs help, but he can't be helped, he is what he is."

"And it's my job to make sure he doesn't kill again," Mauricio said.

"Don't let revenge prevent you from doing a good job."

"Don't you know you're talking to an expert?" Mauricio asked.

Armas grinned. "I suppose I am."

"I have to ask. I was skeptical that you two outstanding police officers would help a hired assassin like me. But the question is, why did you two decide to help me?"

"I told you, a free trip to Brazil," Armas said.

Solis took a long sip of his beer. "We're not naïve enough to not know how the world works and how the law has flaws. We have to take advantage of our opportunities when we see them. When you came to Spain, we found ourselves the perfect opportunity to work outside the law and still get our man. You have something special that most lawmen wish they could do. We want to help because we know this opportunity is rare."

"Is that a compliment?" Mauricio asked.

"I suppose it is," Solis replied. "I'm getting another beer."

Solis went to the back of the boat. "Get me one," Armas said, and turned to face Mauricio. "He's still got a lot to learn but he means well."

"So let's talk about what happens tonight. I was thinking you two could be a second set of eyes for me. He's supposed to be alone but I'm not going to take his word for it. Take out everyone but Malestar. I can pay you with..."

"Your money is no good. You paid for the vacation and that is good enough for us," Armas said.

Solis came back with another beer and twisted the top off. He then handed one to Armas. "So how does someone score some action here in Brazil? I think my partner nceds to find the lady of his dreams for just one night if need be."

"What are you talking about?" Armas asked.

"I'll pay for it," Solis said.

"I don't need your help!"

"From the looks of you, it looks like you do," Solis said.

Mauricio laughed. "I'll tell you what, you do your job, and I take you to any place you want."

"So it's a job now?" Solis asked. "Can you believe this, Armas? We're hired hitmen."

"Settle down, my friend. Killing people is not as fun as you think it is. The moment you take a life away, it changes you," Armas said. "The man that stands before you is like a machine, and able to cast all personal morality aside to finish the job. You have to ask yourself, can you do the same thing?"

"I think I can," Solis replied.

"If you do," Mauricio said, "you're going to need a lot more alcohol than that."

*

The phone continued to ring. There was no need to answer the call because Malestar figured it was the Corporation, or what remained of them. The story was on every morning news program in the city. Apparently, the police had invited themselves in on a secret meeting, and killed everyone involved. Then there was news that there was one remaining member alive. The police report stated that the members of the Corporation had guns as well. Malestar knew that wasn't true, as did most knowledgeable people. Still, the adult population of the city would look the other way since this meant less crime in the city. Malestar knew he still had the youth, and with that, he still had a cause.

Malestar pulled the phone card to disconnect the phone in his hotel suite that overlooked the city. This could very well be the very last morning he would see the city that he had called home, the beautiful nightmare that gave him everything he wanted, and had taken everything away from him at the same time. He was angry his life had come to this moment. He needed to calm himself with some music.

Malestar went to the radio on the bedside table in the room and turned the dial until he came to a classical music radio station. There was only one in this area as many of his fellow city dwellers did not appreciate the sounds of opera and symphony. They were deaf to it all— the complexity, the truth about who they were, and music that spoke to the core of a human. Malestar was more than just a casual listener of the genre; he understood its rich history.

The tones and scales were introduced by the Ancient Greeks. Instruments such as the aulos and the lyre were the stepping stones for modern-day instruments. Then the monophonic chants, followed by the polyphonic chants that carried from the Middle Ages to the Renaissance. More instruments were used with more use of interweaving melodic lines, and then began the use of bass instruments. Musical notation began to take shape. Then came the eras—the Baroque Era, the Classical Era, the Romantic Era, and the modern-day era. Malestar preferred the Classical Era, as he appreciated the rawness and the underdeveloped sound. He followed the music of Joseph Haydn, the current song that was playing, and was quite familiar with his work.

Isolated from other composers for most of his adult life, Haydn was forced to become original. Before he became famous he was just a music teacher and performed street serenades. He worked his way up into becoming a court musician for a wealthy family. Then was his rise to prominence. He was well respected amongst his peers and the constant praise started appear. Beethoven had been his pupil and had learned from him.

Haydn was a man of many good traits but his major character flaw was greed when it came to business dealings. He always tried to get the most from his work. In terms of physical appearance, Haydn was not a handsome man, a survivor of smallpox whose face was pitted with scars. His nose was large and disfigured from polypus, but despite this, he was widely considered a genius. Malestar correlated himself with Haydn, although his genius was not yet discovered. Sooner or later, the city and the rest of the world would understand what he was doing.

The song that was playing was "Farewell Symphony No.45." Malestar closed his eyes and tried to get lost in the music. From the first movement in the F sharp minor, Malestar could only think about his nemesis in his mind. He had a thirst to kill him that wouldn't go away. At first, he enjoyed toying with his prey and waiting for the right moment to pounce and make the kill. But now Mauricio was becoming a nuisance in his plans, and was getting all of his undivided attention. His adversary was going to pay for that.

Still, Malestar was proud of himself for expanding the mind of Mauricio. He knew deep down inside Mauricio was a changed man, and he had made him experience pain in a way that would haunt him the rest of his life. Not only did he give him physical pain, he provided the most damaging pain one could inflict. He showed him that emotional pain was never ending, and every time he thought of Claudia, he would think of him.

Ah, the pleasure of being thought about in a hateful way made Malestar a bit calmer. Slowly, he was beginning to remember the pleasures of life. He remembered how it felt when he killed his sister, how it felt to see all those victims beg for their lives in the moment they knew their lives were all but over. He could relive those moments as long as he lived, and this gave him great joy. He thought about the dead woman in the trunk of his car and how much he wanted to ejaculate on her dead body. Yes, he was going to enjoy every pleasure he could get out of life as long as he lived.

At last, the music had taken over his mind and he was free from thoughts. The last movement was fast tempo and returned to the home key. Malestar began to dance to the music. He started to talk to himself while he danced with his arms swinging in the air. "When the wages of war tear apart and pit brother against brother, son against father, and husband against wife, what side is there left? This is the failure of the human mind. I am beyond human! I am the future of the human mind! I will eat heartily, and I will conquer!"

Malestar stopped dancing as the music was reaching its crescendo, and went to the skeleton mask that was on his bed. He gently touched the mask that symbolized who he was and every other human on this earth. He was flesh and bone, and without human compassion, that's all he could ever be.

47.

Rodrigo sat up in his hospital bed to see Red sitting next to him. He seemed confused at first, but then realized what was going on. Red flashed a smile, stood up, and pressed a hand on his chest for him to relax.

"Good morning," she said. "Your mother was in here earlier but she went to make breakfast. She said no one should eat the hospital food unless it was a punishment and that you needed a home-cooked meal."

Rodrigo grinned. "That sounds like her."

"How are you doing?"

"I've been better. I want to get back on my feet and do my job. How's Mauricio doing?"

"He's fine for now. You shouldn't worry about him. You should be worrying about your own health. Rodrigo, I think you should really consider doing something else with your life. There are so many other things you could be doing right now. This line of work is just far too dangerous."

"That's funny, since you are doing the exact same thing."

"That's different," Red replied.

"Please tell me why."

Red sighed. "With me and Mauricio, we have scars from the past that won't go away. Taking life away is easier when your own life is taken away. You, on the other hand, have people that care about you, and want to see you live a long and healthy life. Why don't you do something productive for society?"

"What I do is productive. And tell me, what else am I going to do? Don't think I haven't seen or felt my share of pain. The slums out there need people like me. Who else is going to take out the bad guy before they do more damage? And please don't tell me it's the law that will clean up the streets. They need me."

"Your family needs you more," Red said.

"So this is some sort of guilt trip?"

Red took hold of Rodrigo's hand. "I'm trying to tell you what's best for you."

"What's best for me is to make my own decisions about my life. I can take care of myself."

"Is that why you're in a hospital?"

Rodrigo moved his hand away from Red. "You don't understand because you're a foreigner. This city has a heartbeat, a pulse that keeps it thriving. There are enemies out there wanting to flat-line us, and make us completely different. But we're not going to let it happen. We're going to fight back at all costs, and I'm going to be there with them."

"You know, you're right. I am a foreigner, and I don't understand your thought process. But I do know that there's a lot of world out there, and if you want to be stupid enough to kill yourself, then you're going to be on your own. Take care, Rodrigo."

"Likewise."

Red headed for the door as Rodrigo's mother was coming in. Red forced a smile and then went out to the hallway. She ran her fingers through her hair for a moment, and then took out her cell phone.

She dialed for Mauricio and the call went straight to voicemail. For a moment, Red thought about hanging up, but then decided to leave a message.

"Hey, it's me. I've been doing some thinking and I think I may go home for a while. I'm a little bit lost right now, and although home isn't exactly the place I want to go, it's the only place that gave me a sense of where I should go next. Just give me a call back, if...I mean when you can."

Red ended the call. She wanted to hear his voice one last time before she left, but now she could only hope he would call her back. This job had taught her a lot about herself and she wanted to thank him for all that he had done. Red was walking toward the elevator when the doctor that had taken the bullet out of her wound insisted that he take another look and see the progress. Red didn't fully understand him but repeated that she would be fine.

Red entered the elevator and a smile appeared on her face. She had no idea how the reception would be when she returned home, and the very thought of this excited her. It didn't matter what they thought about her now. She was more comfortable with who she was more than ever before. Yes, she had baggage and a tumultuous past, but it only made her stronger. This time she would return unafraid and face the demons of her past head on.

All of these years she had been hiding behind the character of Red when in fact, somewhere deep down inside of her was that small, innocent Sophie girl that had big dreams and trust for others. She desperately wanted to be seen again. It was time to let her see the world once more. She had been protected for years but now she was ready. Red had taken all the immediate bad guys around her out of the picture and then some. It was okay now, and Red could finally sigh and take a break.

She felt a happiness she hadn't felt in a long time. It was the feeling of being able to be free, to not hide behind her emotions. A new journey began now, and part of the fun was not knowing how it was going to end.

The elevator doors opened, and Red made her way to the taxi that was waiting for her on the street. The driver started the engine, and Red entered the back seat. The driver looked through the rearview mirror as Red leaned back in her chair.

"Where to, miss?" the driver asked.

"The airport. And you can call me Sophie."

*

Vesco rubbed the temple of his head as he sat in his office. As much as he had looked forward to returning to work, there were some things he did not enjoy, like the massive amount of paperwork that was sitting on his desk. However, he felt like this was the safe thing to do right now. Any public appearance could be met with aggression by the youth and by Malestar. He had already done his interviews for the morning and he was getting positive feedback for his involvement with the Corporation. It was only a matter of time before he would regain control, and the trust in his office and his actions would be restored.

His assistant came into his office and placed a manila envelope on his desk. "What is this?" he asked. She replied with a shrug, and left.

Vesco sighed and opened the envelope. Inside were photos of a dead Bernadette with her head chopped off, and nude pictures of her body. Vesco leaned back in disgust.

"Is this some type of joke?" he asked.

He pushed the letters aside and found a note that was made on printed paper. Vesco immediately figured this was the work of Malestar. A rush of nervousness built up inside of him, and he quickly got up to close the door. He then returned to his desk to read the note.

"To the mayor of the city –

Your words are poison to the minds of the youth. You think you have won but the war has just begun. I would watch my back if I were you. I will return for you, and when I do, I'm going to cut out the heart of your wife, and take out the intestines of your daughter, and throw them in front of you. Don't forget it wasn't long ago you sold out your beloved city for monetary gain. Your end will not be pleasurable."

Vesco looked at the letter for a moment and thought about what he should take from it. Malestar clearly wanted him to be afraid, but he was tired of being scared of the psychopath pushing him around. His job was to do the will of the people and nothing more. Vesco tore the note into small pieces and tossed the remains in the trashcan near his desk. He was not going to be bullied or intimidated.

Vesco turned to the picture of his family on his desk. A smile went on his face as he touched the picture. He decided to give them a call at the hotel they were staying at with around-the-clock protection. Moments later, there was a young police officer on the other end.

"How are they doing?" Vesco asked.

The police officer responded that they were doing fine. Vesco told him to keep the watch and that he wanted updates. Then he ended the call.

Vesco looked at the photo once more and another thought crossed his mind. What if the mercenaries talked? Sure, it was not in their nature to do so, but he didn't trust them. There was a degree of trust when it came to them as well. Red had nothing to gain by telling the truth to the public. This was just a job to her and then she would be off to the next one. As for Mauricio, the only thing he could gain from telling the world would be to get revenge. Sure, it was a possibility, but not a likely one. Mauricio was not one to make himself public, and avoided attention at all costs. It would take something drastic for him to act in that way, Vesco concluded.

That left him with Rodrigo. Rodrigo was a young man desperate to prove himself, but if he didn't get his way, maybe he would try to gain some respect in another way. That meant he could go to the media. Vesco was up for re-election and he couldn't afford a blow like that. In fact, he had tons of paperwork on his desk and a speech to prepare for. Rodrigo might need to be silenced before the possibility of him talking could happen. He was out of the running of getting Malestar anyway. Even though Rodrigo had worked for him in the past, there was no loyalty when it came to politics. This was a cutthroat business, and it was nothing personal.

Vesco picked up the phone once again. He called back his house to talk to one of the police officers. The police officer seemed annoyed that Vesco had called back. Vesco didn't care. He was paying good money for their services outside of work.

"I want you to go down to the hospital where Rodrigo Costa is staying. There should be two officers already there. I want you to relieve them of their shift. You got that?"

"And then what?" the young officer asked.

Vesco rubbed his forehead. He didn't want to say it. But Rodrigo was useless in his current condition and the risks were too high. This re-election campaign meant everything to him and it was security for his family. If he was in office again, he could once again use his control to benefit himself and those around him. As much as he tried to run away from the truth, power was everything in this world. He needed to continue having it.

"Take him out," Vesco said, and ended the call.

*

The sun was beginning to set. Armas and Solis had boarded their plane and Mauricio watched it glide over the ocean and take flight. He opened the cooler and realized that most of the alcohol was gone. He was tempted to drink a bottle himself, but knew he needed a clear mind for tonight. Mauricio hadn't expected them to stay that long but Armas was a man that liked to talk about his past and how the military had affected him. Mauricio could relate to that.

Armas had seen how the military had changed young men into killing machines and then spit them out when they were done with them. There was no turn-off button. When the military was long gone, they were still wired to kill, to hunt, and to be aware of their surroundings. They were taught not to feel, but to only react. Mauricio already had this mindset going into the military, and his actions became more pronounced afterward. For Armas, it made him appreciate the little things in life that much more. Armas wasn't fortunate to have a family of his own, but he began to appreciate the things around him that he did have. He was grateful for his home, his job, and indulged in eats and alcohol. He told Mauricio not to be focused on criminals so much that he would forget to live. Mauricio thought that was good advice.

Solis, on the other hand, provided nothing in the vicinity of giving good advice. He bragged about the good old days when he was a bachelor, and how he could easily get Armas a woman here in Brazil. He also talked about personal details of his love life with his wife. Mauricio didn't care for any of that, but in Solis' defense, he had been drinking heavily. Solis bragged about how he could keep everything together, but Mauricio knew better. Behind the false sense of immortality and toughness was a scared man. Mauricio ignored him for the most part and thought he had a lot of room to grow.

Then the sun had appeared to drift from above. The two Spanish detectives had said that they would fly to the island immediately and be there ahead of Mauricio's arrival. Mauricio didn't know if he could trust them to be there, but he had no other choice. He thought of the detectives as fairly good men that knew they had to work outside the law to be more effective. Vesco was similar, but he was also a selfish man that wanted to profit from death, and to reap the benefits of the fame afterward. Mauricio knew there was no clear line between right and wrong, but what benefited the masses was more important. There was too much politics in the legal system and he wished people would just do what was in the best interest of the general public. He had enough of the game that was being played, and just wanted to live in a way that was best for him.

Mauricio started the engine of his boat and headed in the direction of Itaparica Island. The boat cruised through the waters at top speed and the wind rushed at him in the humid afternoon. The hull of the boat briefly was pushed up in the water and then was quickly brought back down. Mauricio knew the imminent danger he was about to face and he struggled to keep calm as he felt the anxiety building. There was no turning back now as the night began to approach.

48.

The sky had darkened by the time Mauricio reached the beach. He turned off the engine and dragged the boat into the sand as the ocean waves came rolling in. Immediately in front of him was the forest, with palm trees decorating the entrance. The only light came from his boat, the bar further down the shore, and the moon that was becoming more visible in the sky. The night was quiet except for the whispers of the ocean. The atmosphere was serene all around him, but inside Mauricio's body his heart was racing and his eyes searched frantically for anything that could be a threat. He seemed to be alone at the moment.

He looked off toward the bar down the shore and saw two flashes of light come from the rooftop. That was the signal of Armas and Solis. Mauricio gave a nod in their direction as he was sure they were looking through a scope to see him. Mauricio picked up his guns from the boat and placed two in his hip, one in his hand, and one small pistol in the holster above his ankle. He got out of his boat, stood, and waited.

He waited for what seemed like an eternity. He recalled that the last time he was on an island he was still trying to cope with the death of Claudia. The fact was he never got over her. The pain was still buried deep down inside of him, but he knew how to manage it better, just like all of the other pain he had experienced in life. There was only one other way to get over the pain and that was not to bury it, but to own it, and embrace it. This was what Malestar preached but he took it one step further. He wanted to inflict the same pain on others.

The psychopath had been Mauricio's toughest target yet. He had some elusive targets in the past, and some even knew he was coming, but none had given him a challenge of this magnitude. Not one of them wanted to be found, and to return a target at Mauricio. Malestar was rare, a man that wanted to dangle his life in the face of danger and enjoyed doing so.

Mauricio kept his focus ahead and could see figures looming from the forest. As expected, Malestar had not come alone. Mauricio wouldn't bother raising his gun to shoot unless he could see them and get a clean shot. They started to emerge from the forest, a group of men covered in purple bandanas. Mauricio was about to raise his arm to shoot, but gunshots from a distance began to blow their brains out and they collapsed against the ground before reaching the beach. Some of them started to run but got a bullet in their head before they had a chance to get cover. Mauricio could tell the bullets were coming from the bar area, and smiled. A part of his plan had worked.

There was silence once again. Mauricio looked around and saw the light flash again from the bar. Armas and Solis had done their job. Mauricio turned to face the forest and waited for the appearance of Malestar. It was just going to be him and the monster, flesh against flesh, and bullet against bullet. Mauricio placed his arms to his sides.

"Here I am, Malestar!" he shouted. "Show me some pain!"

Then a figure started to emerge from the forest. Mauricio saw the white shoes, white suit, and skeleton mask and placed his arms down. Malestar calmly made his way toward him and didn't appear to have any weapons. Mauricio found it interesting the man would decide to wear white. It was the color of innocence and Malestar was anything but that.

Malestar stopped a few feet away from him. Mauricio slightly flinched at the sight of his mask. It was the face of evil, and he could see faint blots of blood on it.

"I am the creator of death, the alpha and omega of pain. I've come to relieve you of all pain, and problems of this world. The pain will only be for a moment."

"You lied. I thought you said you were going to be alone," Mauricio said.

"The same can be said for you."

Mauricio smiled. "You know, on the way over here, I kept thinking how great a feeling it would be to put a bullet in your head. Now, there's nothing more that I want to do than to make you feel intense physical pain." Mauricio dropped the gun.

"You sound like me," Malestar said, and stared off into the ocean. "It's a great night to die." Malestar turned his attention back to Mauricio. "Your move."

Mauricio charged at Malestar. He knocked him to the ground and Malestar began dropping elbow strikes against Mauricio's back. He also tried to lock up his legs. Mauricio got out of the hold and started to knee Malestar in the stomach. Malestar head-butted Mauricio in the face with his hard-cast mask, and it drew blood on Mauricio's forehead. Malestar then reached for one of Mauricio's guns on his hips and Mauricio did the same. Almost simultaneously they had a gun in each other's temple with Mauricio on top of Malestar on the ground.

Malestar gave a deep, sinister laugh. He dropped his gun and Mauricio could see through the sockets of his mask and into Malestar's eyes that Malestar was daring him to shoot him. It was too easy of a kill. He needed to suffer. Mauricio tossed his gun aside as well.

Malestar quickly wrapped his legs around Mauricio's throat and began to choke him. Mauricio struggled to breathe. Mauricio began to rise to his feet to relieve himself of Malestar's grip. He grabbed Malestar's legs and forced him upward. Then he slammed him against the sand. Malestar shouted in pain as Mauricio was breathing hard for air.

Malestar got to his feet and took a knife from his back hip. He then stabbed Mauricio in the abdomen. "You want to play, let's play," he said, and ran toward the forest.

Mauricio gave a loud shout and then controlled his breathing to absorb the pain. It wasn't a fatal blow but it would definitely inhibit his movement and strength. Mauricio held onto his wound and made his way into the forest.

The visibility was poor. He could hear movement in the distance and without sight, he was going to have to rely on his other instincts. His military experience would be put to use. Mauricio moved around the brush, trees, and dirt and revisited what he was taught. He made his steps as silent as possible. He knew what gave away his location was the blood that was coming from his wound. He placed his hand tighter against it. He walked, and then he stopped to listen. He heard movement coming from the south. He started to move in that direction.

The moonlight provided some visibility as he did so. He was once again the predator in search for his prey. Even in his days in the military, he had enjoyed this part of the game. The thrill of the chase was something you learned to love if you wished to stay sane. He had spent nights training in environments like this one and tracking became more than just a sport. It became a means to survive.

Mauricio caught a glimpse of Malestar running ahead of him. Mauricio picked up his speed to catch up. Malestar was circling back toward the ocean. Malestar looked back to see how much ground he was losing and tripped over a branch in front of him. He fell to the ground as Mauricio made his way over to him. Mauricio shoved a knee in his back and Malestar shouted in pain. Then Mauricio removed the mask that he was wearing.

Malestar turned over. "You're merely a man, just like anyone else!" Mauricio shouted. "You like to hide behind a mask because you think you are something special, huh? I promise you this. Your death will be extraordinary!"

Mauricio held up Malestar's face, and then gave repeated blows to the face with his fists. The punches drew blood that poured out of Malestar's mouth and he spat out the few teeth that were made loose. Mauricio continued to strike. He thought about Claudia, Ken, and all the people that were killed at the hands of Malestar and let the anger out with each punch. He continued to do so until his arm grew tired. When he finished, he looked at Malestar's face, beaten up and bloodied, and almost unrecognizable.

Still, he saw Malestar with a smile on his face. Then he coughed up some blood. "I told you," Malestar softly said. "You are no different than me. You see, pain is in all of us, and we all want to pretend it's not there. You can't run away from it. You want those that harm you to suffer. So do I. The world won't let me have complete freedom, and holds me back. They hold us all back. So I want them to suffer. What's the difference?"

At that moment, Mauricio realized he was closer to Malestar's line of thinking than he thought. Still, Malestar was reaching. What he felt was right for him to do was madness, plain and simple. Then he realized that giving pain to Malestar was pointless.

"You will never learn," Mauricio said, and took out the pistol from his leg. "Good riddance."

Mauricio was about to pull the trigger when he felt another sharp pain on the opposite side of his abdomen. He saw that Malestar had a knife in his hand and a smile on his face. He had the knife well hidden somewhere. The intense pain caused Mauricio to shout, and he pressed the pistol against Malestar's forehead. Malestar lodged the knife further until Mauricio grabbed hold of his arm with his free arm and pulled the trigger. The brain matter of Malestar flew into the air and across Mauricio's face. It was done.

Mauricio took hold of Malestar's arm with the knife still lodged inside of him and pulled it out. He tried to absorb the pain, but he couldn't this time. He let out a scream and realized that he was quickly losing strength. He could feel the life draining out of him and his mind was racing through random thoughts. He rested on his knees and looked at his wound. He was losing an extensive amount of blood from this one. He knew if he didn't get help soon that he was dead.

He shouted once again, this time in fear. He fell to his side and thought about shooting himself to get the pain over with. He tried to move his arm toward his head but he didn't have the strength. He let go of the gun and looked up into the night sky. Malestar was right about something. It sure was a beautiful night to leave this earth.

Mauricio could picture being with Claudia again. He could smell her, feel her, and remember the feeling he had when he was with her. He ran his fingers through the dirt and remembered how it was to touch her, and have her next to him. He was free around her. He was the person he once was before all the tragedies in his life. She was smiling at him with that smile that used to make him melt. There was no need to hold onto the pain anymore. His hand stopped moving.

Mauricio felt like he was somewhere else, a place where there was no pain or pressure to be something he wasn't. His parents were there as well and they greeted him with open arms. He was in complete happiness and at a place he wanted to stay. He was in complete peace and all the pain he had ever felt had gone away.

But then he felt other hands besides his loved ones' touch his body. He didn't know where the feeling was coming from. The pain started to return. He was being dragged away from his family.

"No!" he shouted.

Their grip was relentless. Then disturbing images flashed in front of him. He saw all of the targets he had ever killed with blood covering their faces and body. They all said the same thing.

"You don't deserve love. You don't deserve love."

The targets were carrying him. They placed him on a table and continued to touch him. Their eyes looked down on him with disappointment. They were saying something else but there was a loud buzzing sound. The hands were reaching for him again and now they were shaking him.

"Leave me alone!" Mauricio shouted.

"Easy, easy," Armas said as Mauricio lay on the moving bed inside the hospital and was being taken to surgery. Mauricio's body was convulsing. Armas and Solis had found him unconscious in the forest when they left the bar to make sure everyone was taken care of in the forest. They immediately transported him to the hospital, where he had officially been diagnosed as dead. He was jolted back to life and had been in an unstable condition ever since. Armas was told to leave and sit in the waiting area as they whisked him away. The double doors closed and Armas had no choice but to follow instruction.

Mauricio suddenly sat upward with his eyes wide open and let out a shout. He had to be restrained back down. His heart rate was alarmingly high. The doctors above him quickly began preparation for a sedative.

"I was just doing my job! Don't bring me back here!"

A needle was stuck into his arm, and soon after, Mauricio was returning to his state of tranquility and his escape from calamity. The ghosts of his past had gone away. However, his family was gone too. There was no one here he recognized. Instead, he was in a space full of nothing with no sights or sound. He walked around aimlessly, not knowing what direction to go. Then he stopped walking. Perhaps the action would come to him.

He waited, and waited. He was starting to grow more uncomfortable by the second. He was somewhere between ultimate happiness and the real world. There were images of his past that flashed before him. The speed was too quick for Mauricio to dive into each image and enjoy the moment. Then the images were gone.

Then he saw an image of himself. His other being started to walk toward him. He stopped in front of him, and told Mauricio to open up his hand. He did as he was told. Then a gun was placed in his hand.

"Your job is not done," his other self said. "You can't change the past. This is who you are. You take bad people off the streets for the greater good. So what if you get paid for it? Now go out there and do what you do best."

The image of him was gone. The nothingness had returned. However, this time Mauricio was comfortable in the darkness. As the doctors checked Mauricio's pulse, they could see it was rising again.

49.

The re-election campaign was having a party at their headquarters downtown, after a planned speech. It had been two months since Mauricio had killed Malestar and the news of Malestar's death brought back stability in the city that hadn't been there in a long time. The youth had been debilitated by the loss of Malestar, and the cause to take over the city had all but disappeared. The spotlight had returned to Vesco and he was enjoying every moment of it.

Vesco felt like he was sitting on top of the world. The city was starting to believe in him again, his dirty secret couldn't be exposed since Rodrigo was out of the picture, and the city was returning their confidence in him. He sat next to his wife as he wore his best tuxedo, and everyone else was well dressed as well. They sat around large tables with dignified guests from all over the city. Vesco's daughter sat across from him, and couldn't be more proud of her father. He had single-handedly saved the city from being taken over by the crazed Malestar. She clapped the loudest when his name was called and he made his way to the stage.

Vesco put his hand out as if to simmer the applause but everyone knew he wanted the attention desperately. Servers came across the front to serve food in the front tables and Vesco waited for them to finish. He didn't want anything to block the view of his speech. Vesco smiled as he looked around the room. He could feel the power being bequeathed to him. Yes, there was a brief time when he thought he should do whatever was right for the city, but now he figured he could make more money than ever before. He could pull a few of the officers from the force to work for him and clean up the city in ways that were not in line with the law. Yes, life was good, and soon he was back in business of making this job as profitable as it could be.

The applause began to simmer, and Vesco placed his arms out in front of him to silence the room. All eyes were now on him. Before he spoke, Vesco took in the moment. The flock was waiting for their leader to speak and to guide them through their pathetic lives. They needed him. Vesco made sure his gaze was toward the television cameras in the back of the room. The live feed meant the people of the city were watching. Every single one of them belonged to him.

"Our city has faced many challenges," Vesco said to begin his speech. "We all know we have faced some dire times. But when we believe in something greater than us, that we are a community that believes in the law and its protection of its people, then we can be safe and prosper in the most difficult times. A lot of people were afraid of this domestic terrorist named Malestar. Well, I'm pleased to say with the help of law enforcement that he is now off the streets and rotting beneath the dirt."

There was applause in the room. Vesco placed his hands out in front of him to calm the crowd down. "Malestar was working in conjunction with a few corrupt businessmen and women from this town, and we took care of that situation."

There was more applause. Vesco smiled for the cameras. This time he waited for the applause to die down. "The humble and loyal people of Salvador, I implore you to let all of your fears go. There's nothing out there to harm you because we will be here to protect you. You can trust the fact that the good people running this city have your best intentions at heart. You can depend on our protection."

"Liar!"

People turned their heads to the back of the room. Rodrigo stood there, and shock was displayed all over

Vesco's face. He froze in his bewilderment. There was chatter in the room and some people demanded for Rodrigo to leave. However, plenty of the news media in the room toward the back wanted him to speak. The room became quiet again.

"The world should know that you are fraud. Why don't you tell the world how you hired me for multiple occasions to kill any enemy that was in your way? Also, tell them how you were once part of the Corporation and hired three mercenaries to do your dirty work. Tell the people the truth."

The eyes in the room returned to Vesco. He didn't know what to say but he had to think of something. "The people of this city are not just going to believe some lunatic that came barging in. You should be arrested at once."

"And the truth is your beloved mayor hired someone to come and kill me. He wanted me to be silenced," Rodrigo said.

"Unfortunately, accusations without proof are worthless," Vesco said.

"I figured you would say something like that," Rodrigo said. He walked over to another man in the back that had just emerged from the news media crowd. Vesco recognized the face. It was all over.

"This is the man you hired to kill me," Rodrigo said. "He's been hiding me for the last two months. He's going to testify in court against you."

Vesco looked around the room and could see the disappointment and surprise in all of their faces. His wife had suspected he was crooked but not to this extent. Then he turned his gaze to his daughter, who looked ashamed and hurt by her father's actions. She had believed that he strictly followed the law and was an honest man. Vesco couldn't stand being here any longer.

He ran off stage and headed for the back door. The police officers toward the back of the room hesitated to move. Rodrigo did not. He left out the front entrance to follow Vesco on the side of the building. Vesco made his way to the street where traffic was heavy in the downtown area. He ran across the street and cars begin to honk their horns. They had recognized his face. Vesco stopped a black car moving in traffic and pounded the driver's side door with his fists. Vesco turned his head to see that Rodrigo was approaching.

"I need your car! I'm your mayor and I could be in danger. The city will reimburse you."

The driver saw Rodrigo give chase and stepped out of the car. He gave one last look at Vesco and moved out of the way. Vesco got into the seat and placed the car into reverse, crashing into the car behind him. Then he placed the car in drive. Rodrigo ran faster toward the car as

Vesco was approaching. Rodrigo waited until he had the perfect opportunity to jump, and did so, landing on the trunk of the car.

Vesco swerved through traffic to try to get Rodrigo off the car. Rodrigo held on with his legs dangling in the air. Vesco turned the corner at full speed and almost knocked Rodrigo off the car. Vesco desperately honked his horn to get other cars out of the way.

Rodrigo made his way to the top of the car. He looked ahead and saw a bus was in front of them. Vesco refused to slow down. The speed was making Rodrigo lose his grip. Vesco searched for other ways around the bus but there was no alternative. He drove forward and slammed against the back of the bus.

Rodrigo went flying into the air and through the back window of the bus, shattering the glass and landing between a middle-aged couple that was seated. People inside the bus began to shout. The bus driver slammed on the brakes. Rodrigo was helped to his feet by the passengers and shook off the glass that was on him.

"I'm okay. I'm all right," Rodrigo said as he made his way to the front of the bus and down the stairs. The bus driver quickly opened the door for him. The passengers looked at him in awe.

Vesco had already put the car in reverse and made a U-turn to merge with opposing traffic. Rodrigo limped and held his back as he watched Vesco leave. A crowd of people started to gather around. A doctor amongst the crowd went up to Rodrigo and wanted to examine his back. Rodrigo denied his help and took out his cell phone to make a call.

Back inside the campaign headquarters, everyone was still quite shocked. There was chatter amongst the room and the police weren't sure if they should do something about Vesco leaving. One of the officers decided to contact their superiors back at the precinct to reach the chief. A lot of the eyes in the room had their gaze on Vesco's wife, who nervously smiled at everyone. She was embarrassed and her body was slightly trembling. People began shaking their heads at her in disgust, and then came a few derogatory comments from the crowd. Vesco's wife ran away from the table to head out the back door. Her daughter ran out after her.

The crowd started to disperse. Many went to the officer Vesco had hired to kill Rodrigo. He was already in front of the news cameras in the back of the room, telling his side of what happened. As the news spread throughout the city, the positive reputation of Vesco was disintegrating. Needless to say, there was basically no chance of re-election.

*

Vesco returned to the hotel room where he had been hiding with his family to get some of his belongings. He quickly took out his suitcase and began to pack his clothes. He went into the closet to get the box on the top shelf that had all of the passports. He thought for a moment to take all of them but then he only grabbed his own. He would have to leave the country quickly before there was an investigation. Even then, they might consider him a risk.

On the way over here, he had thought about his options to avoid some serious jail time. He could hire a crooked police officer to drive him out of the country and maybe go somewhere like Argentina where he would have to change his identity and start a new life. Another option was to go to Manaus, where his cousin lived, and hide out there until he planned his next move. He could hide out in the outskirts of the city until his cousin came to pick him up. One option that was off the table was bringing his family with him. He was much too ashamed to even look at them. He would contact them when enough time had passed and he was safe enough to make a short call. They didn't need to associate themselves any longer with a criminal.

He was sweating heavily as he continued to pack and his nerves were making his hands tremble. He felt like his heart was going to come out of his chest. He decided to go the bathroom to wash his face and try to relax for just one moment.

He went inside, let the cold water run for a moment, and then looked at himself in the mirror. What had happened to the man that had everything together? How did it fall apart? It was bound to happen. How long did he think he could get away it? The truth almost always came out. He had just been hoping he wasn't around when it did.

Vesco splashed his face with water and ran his fingers through his air. He took a few deep breaths and felt more relaxed. He then grabbed a towel and headed out the door.

Someone blocked his view. Vesco was almost afraid to look up. When he did, he saw Mauricio staring back at him.

Vesco dropped the towel and trembled in front of him. He tried his best not to show his nerves, but he failed miserably. Mauricio took a step toward him. Vesco jolted back, and then fell backward on the floor.

"It looks like the ghosts of your past are coming back to haunt you," Mauricio stated.

"What are you doing here?" Vesco asked, getting back to his feet.

"Take a guess," Mauricio said, and took out a silencer from his back hip.

"Now, wait a minute!" Vesco pleaded. "Just give me a chance!"

Mauricio stood with one arm over the other. "State your case."

"When I hired you, I tried to do something good for this city. I was ridding it of an evil man. Doesn't that account for something? And you, thinking you're all high and mighty, you had no qualms about taking the job. You even saved my life! What does that say about you?"

"You were a means to get Malestar," Mauricio said. "I take one job at a time."

"Who's paying you for this? I'll double what they are offering. I can make you a very rich man. I know that's what you want. You want the big house, big boat, and go anywhere in the world you want? I can make that happen. I know players across the globe that would use your services. I can be your agent, and charge a small fee, of course."

Mauricio grinned. "You know, I have to hand it to you. You stayed a greedy snake until the end."

Mauricio raised the gun toward Vesco's forehead. "Any last words?" Mauricio asked.

"Let's make a deal."

Mauricio kept the gun pressed against his forehead. Vesco closed his eyes. He felt like the moment lasted forever. Then Mauricio removed the gun from his head.

"I'm not here to play judge. I only accept pay for my work."

Vesco opened his eyes and gave a huge sigh of relief. "First sensible thing you've said the entire conversation."

Vesco headed for the door and back toward the bed to continue packing.

"You made a lot of people mad now," Mauricio said.

"They'll get over it," Vesco said, and zipped up his suitcase. "Just give me a call sometime, and I'll see what I can do. In the meantime, I have to leave town as soon as possible."

"Of course," Mauricio replied.

Vesco rushed toward the door with suitcase in hand, and made his way to the elevators. Mauricio stood for a moment in the hotel room. Then he put his gun away. Sometimes it was better to let fate deal with other people.

Vesco ran through the lobby and out the front door. He was hurrying back to his stolen parked car when he noticed a crowd of people waiting nearby. He could tell they were from the slums from the way they were dressed. All of them had makeshift weapons in their hands, from bottles to tree branches. A few of them had knives. Vesco froze where he was.

Vesco looked to the side of the crowd and noticed a group of police officers standing next to them. Vesco had hired them to protect him, and they were supposed to be watching who went inside the hotel. Now they were looking the other way. They probably gave Mauricio his location and told the angry youths where he was staying.

"You traitors! All of you!" Vesco shouted at them. "You're no different than me!"

The crowd of people from the slums began to walk toward him. Vesco turned to look the other way. Mauricio was coming out of the hotel. Vesco took a few steps toward him.

"You have to help me out here," Vesco said. "They're going to kill me!"

Mauricio went up to Vesco, looked at him for a moment, and then walked past him and past the crowd. The crowd came rushing through and began to attack Vesco, pinning him to the ground. Mauricio didn't bother to look back. At first, his face was kicked in, which drew blood, and then he was attacked with bottles and stabbed all over his body. Vesco began to shout, but all Mauricio heard were the sounds of justice.

.

50.

The rain was coming down hard on this weekend night. The city of Salvador became drenched and the inhabitants of downtown and the coastal area stayed inside and watched television or used their wireless Internet to scourge the web for information and gossip. However, in the slums and the shacks where poverty abided, water had penetrated inside through the cracks of the makeshift homes. Children scrambled to get buckets to contain the water. The rules of the game were the same. The rich continued to get rich, and the poor remained poor. Since Vesco had left office, not much had changed.

The newly elected mayor vowed to make the city safe, and more equal pay for all of its citizens. The public ate it up. He was welcomed into his new position with open arms. He vowed to make his office more open to the public and that corruption would be found and taken out of the system. The majority of the people put their faith him, as he had won in a landslide. There was even a parade for him. He was a robust, middle-aged man with just enough charm to speak to the common people. He shook their hands and kissed their babies. Even though he made lots of promises, the truth was the economic system was not going to change.

Rodrigo listened to the radio in his mother's kitchen as the rain continued to pour outside, and the sound of the rain slamming against the house was heard. He was wearing a suit, and loosened up his tie. He had gone to an interview earlier for a security position at one of the law firms downtown, and the thought of sitting behind a desk all day made him panic. Still, he went on with the interview, gave generic answers, and left. Now that he was home, he was hoping he didn't get the job.

He opened the cabinet above the stove to get his painkillers, took two pills out, and drank from the kitchen faucet. His mother was in the living room watching television, probably one of those overdramatic soap operas she liked to watch. Rodrigo watched her for a moment from the kitchen doorway, and then returned to listen to the radio. The newly elected mayor was being interviewed.

"What are your thoughts on the widespread corruption that has plagued this city for years? Will it ever go away? How will it affect your job going forward?"

"That's a good question, and one I take very seriously," the mayor said. "Corruption is like a powerful drug. Once you take it, there's no turning back because it holds on to you and pulls at you to take more. Unfortunately, this drug has been taken by many in the city. How do you stop the drug from becoming so effective? You cut out the supplier. The greedy businesspeople that look to profit at every turn. When business and politics get together, corruption is sold. We just have to make politics stand on its own merit, and govern without big business trying to fill our pockets with their agenda."

"Is that possible?" the interviewer asked.

There was a pause. "In this line of work, you have to strive for perfection. Anything less should not be accepted. I came to office to try to clean up the back deals and the profit off of crime that was being made. You have my word that I will do my best to make sure this never happens again."

"There has been talk of building..."

Rodrigo cut off the radio. He shook his head and smiled. You got to love these politicians, he thought. It was the same talk every term. There were promises made and only a few of them kept. Still, someone had to run the city and it was always a matter of choice between the evils, lesser or more. He thought he would give this new mayor a chance to prove himself on the lesser side.

Rodrigo went to the refrigerator to get a beer. He popped off the cap and took a long drink. What was he supposed to do with his life? As much as he hated to admit it, Red had given him good advice. He had no place in becoming a hitman. He had thought of his mother and he didn't want her to see him in a closed casket. He had a responsibility to take a safe job for her sake. At first, this made him miserable, but he was starting to warm up to the idea of being around and not worrying about bullets coming in his direction.

He looked over the paperwork that he had received from the interview. It was a bunch of nonsense about what the company did, who the important people were, and how many cases they won over the years. Was this the type of literature that was supposed to excite him? Rodrigo balled up the piece of paper and threw it in the trash. If they called back, fine; if they didn't, he wasn't going to lose sleep over it.

Rodrigo went to the doorway once more to look at his mother. She was still tuned in to the television. He went back to the kitchen table and reached underneath it. His gun was still there. He took it out and felt it like it was a long-lost child. He was sad to see their relationship coming to an end. These security jobs only gave him a flashlight and a Taser. They might as well give him a whistle. So he and his gun were going to part. Or did they have to? He could still take it out on weekends with trips to the range. Rodrigo looked at the gun and wondered if he could still do something else.

There was a brief moment where he thought he could become a police officer, but he quickly thought twice about it. There was a brotherhood in the force, and he didn't want to get close to anyone. He worked better alone. Besides, there was too much corruption involved and he despised what was going on. If he joined the force, he could easily be persuaded to have a change of heart. He didn't want to change who he was or the way he thought about the world. He liked himself just fine right now, and he didn't want to take orders from some guy sitting in his office all day and then taking golf trips with the mayor. No thanks, he was fine with little or no management in his face.

Rodrigo held the gun out in front of him and remembered all the dangerous situations he was in before. It almost seemed like yesterday he was hanging out with Mauricio and Red, taking out bad guys while trying to take down a criminal mastermind. He couldn't afford to be in a situation like that ever again. He didn't know what he was thinking by even putting himself in danger like that. Those types of days would never be repeated.

But man, it was fun while it lasted.

*

The boat rocked in the rain as it stayed on the docks in the ocean. Mauricio had been listening to the radio as well. He needed something comedic for the evening and this was the perfect source for entertainment. He had been preparing dinner for tonight, leftovers from lunch, and rested on his small bed that was inside the bedroom compartment. He took a bite of his dinner and it was just as good the second time around. He looked around at his newly purchased boat and admired the framework that was involved. There was a lot of love given when this boat was made. He had always wanted to do something like that, something like building his dream boat from scratch. It would take a lot of work, but it was something he would enjoy. Then he could fish in his off time, and enjoy the nature that was around him.

With his new chance at life, the question of retirement frequently came to his mind. He wasn't a man of many trades, he was a man of many kills. The tricky part was finding something he would enjoy doing every day, yet be safe enough to not put him in harm's way.

That was going to be a hard feat considering he was used to the danger, and in a strange way, it made him feel normal. He didn't know how he would cope with a normal life. He didn't know how people could sit in an office all day, in the same routine, only spend a few hours with their families, sleep, and repeat. They were like caged animals. He needed to be out there where the action was, or at least away from it while doing hobbies he enjoyed.

At this moment, that mostly entailed fishing, shooting, working out, and boating. He could do any of those activities all day and be satisfied with what he was doing. He had had different hobbies as a youth, such as sparring and any type of fighting, but as he got older, he tried to avoid fights as much as possible. Of course he loved to track down humans and take them out, but that was out of the equation right now.

He thought about the possibility of becoming a bounty hunter. Not like the rip-offs that were on television, but a legit one that was only known around well-known circles. Every country could use more of those. He knew it was a tough business to break into as relationships had been formed for over decades, and his reputation was one of a killer. Could he stop and not pull the trigger? He thought he could. He could go anywhere in the world and set up shop. It didn't matter if the money didn't roll in right away. There was enough in his savings to give him a cushion for quite some time. That's because he hardly spent his money on anything lavish. Some hitmen spent all their money on nice clothes and big houses. All Mauricio needed was a place to rest his head, some food to eat, and some weapons he could use to carry him through the next job.

He also thought about pursuing relationships again. He wasn't thinking about falling in love or having a longtime, committed partner, but more in the realm of building friendships and contacts. That was his one regret with all the work he had done around the globe. He'd never made personal relationships with anyone, and he had no one to depend on, and no one to depend on him. Perhaps that was a good thing; at least it was at the time. The truth was that having loved ones made himself and everyone else a liability. He couldn't afford to lose someone close to him again. With a new line of work, maybe he didn't have to.

He continued to listen to the comedy show on the radio that was passing off as a legit interview. The mayor kept telling the public that he was the best man for the job and they had no reason for concern. Mauricio gave him a year tops. Then he would be just like Vesco, using his power for his own gain. The problem wasn't the businesspeople that wanted to make profits; the problem was the human nature of a politician. You can't put a snake in a cage with a rat and not expect it to feed.

Mauricio shook his head and took another bite of his dinner.

His cell phone vibrated on top of the microwave. Mauricio got out of bed, turned off the radio, and went to answer his phone. He looked at the number and smiled. Then he placed the phone against his ear and pressed the button to talk.

"It's me," the voice on the other end said.

"Hey, me."

"Interested in a job?" Red asked.

"What's the pay?"

"Does it matter? It's good money, and I'm willing to split. I could use the help on this one."

"I don't think I can, Red."

"Its Sophie now," Sophie said from the other end while lying in a bathtub covered with soapy bubbles. She held the cell phone against her ear and rested her head back while her body soaked in warm water.

Mauricio grinned. "I don't think I can. You see, I'm trying to relax. I don't need to see bullets, bad guys, crazy people, and corrupt politicians. I just want to go somewhere and fish, and be left to myself."

"Who are you trying to convince, you or me?"

He hesitated before answering the question. She could call herself Sophie all she wanted, but she was still Red, and still a dangerous vixen that knew how to get what she wanted. Being in business with her could be a dangerous situation. However, Mauricio had to admit that she had a point. He thought about it for a moment and then replied with an answer.*

Made in the USA
Lexington, KY
29 December 2013